Job Card

Maurice White

RUSTIK HAWS LLC

Job Card Maurice White

This book is written to provide information and motivation to readers. Its purpose is not to render any type of psychological, legal, or professional advice of any kind. The content is the sole opinion and expression of the author, and not necessarily that of the publisher.

ISBN: 978-1-64934-177-8 (Paperback)
Printed in the United States of America.

Rustik Haws LLC
100 S. Ashley Drive, Suite 600
Tampa, FL 33602
https://www.rustikhaws.com/

Job Card

(Written by Maurice Hutch Maddness White)

This is the story about a man named Hutch a driver who worked for an Interior Demolition Company doing jobs in various parts in New York City which called for its building to be remodeled from the inside. Hutch one of its drivers worked for this demo company as a young man, helping building its reputation up for years before Meepbo half owner/boss of the company took it over the whole thing from the other owner/boss Michael Giatanino so under handily.

Hutch a big strong kind hearted man with a very good sense of humor, but has the strangest luck in his life. Things are about to get even crazier meeting a greedy derange woman. 3 beautiful ladies to be his and 1 of them gets kidnapped by want to be mobsters Markola and his crazy cousin Mario who want the Credit card he carries aware he doesn't know what he's got in possession. In this first of three stories with car chases and fights, getting shot for something he doesn't know about yet. Having to put up with an on the job brown ass kisser who'd tell on his mother to get an edge on her to secure his supervisor position so he tells the boss everything on anyone there. The story on Hutch's life is how 3 Unlimited Funded Credit Cards that can't be traced when used but has access to Unlimited Trillions of Funds that come from somewhere, plus little bottles of experimental men's cologne which have women reacting to its scent as the man's body heats up and sweats activating its aroma. The gold capped cologne designed to have women getting mad at a man when he heats up and sweats, same thing for the blacked capped little bottle of cologne but this one makes women very afraid of the man. The Silver capped cologne also designed to make women very horn for a man that wares it and the more he heats up sweating the hornier women gets for that man wearing the scent making women aggressive for him. Working at this strange building in Manhattan a borough in the City of New York where the company he works for got a call to do a big job for interior demo on it. Hutch being a curious man always looking around the building he works at but in this case not understanding the things he took from this particular building would have his life changed forever winding up with 3 beautiful women in love him for life. Meeting all three Donna and Erikaa with Janet as they shopped at this supermarket for dinner, the four of them would never guess they would be together for life after meeting Hutch there. From going to a strip club to the regular clubs and party antics at his home, to the crazy chases plus his frat brothers the Grand Drunken Masters 4 Life. Having to help Hutch keep one of them from being kidnapped by a very impulsive entrepreneur he/she wanting to be a full woman and best hair stylist in NY named Marveece and her crew that doesn't take no for answer on anything, needing men in their lives willing to resorting to doing wild things to get one. With crazy antics at work and weekend parties with the Grand Drunken Masters 4 Life things would happen a little strange and now about to get even weirder and strange but so comical no one would ever believe it would happen. Which has this book asking you the reader a Question: What would you do with 3 unlimited funded Credit Cards that were untraceable plus cologne that makes women react in such a manner? Find out what happens and see how he learns about one card its unlimited value and the colognes in this first of 3 part comedy stories. This first story tells about how one big strong kind hearted man with such wild friends and family plus crazy antics on and off the job copes with everything, till he's shown why most things are happening because of the credit cards he's got shown to him by 3 women who found the love of their lives in him.

This story is dedicated to those people that came to me in a time of my life that everything was really going crazy and no one still couldn't believe there are things out there we can't explain and why they happen so funny to certain people but always show them never give up just learn to laugh at life. Advised by close friends I needed to put things down on paper and then asked by those I dedicated this book to, why not write about them in a book so some people would share my comical adventures that really happens and why this book is so out of the norm like the things that went on, so I dedicate this book to those whom encouraged me to do this book. (The events are greatly exaggerated but close too)

My Mother: Bettie White who put up with me continuing this whole thing at her house feeding me. Brothers: Derrick, Keith and Cordell and Sisters Connie, (twins of love) Sherri. Hornezes (we miss you so much, know you smiling down on us) and her twin Terri. Enid Moir & daughters Tamika and Attorney Zoey Moir (She doesn't have to worry about me but know I love and thank her so much)

My sons: Reese RJ #55 C/RSLB, Salute Victorian of Westing House high and Steve LT- A student, (one in kindred) Angel Rivera. Nephews: Tony and Derrick. Nieces: Cheryl, Alice, Dionne, Sherrie and Lynette. My Daughters always: Evelynn (squirt) and Evelaine (stuff). My Aunt like mother: Mable Bey, her Husband Uncle Ernie, Cousins: Robbie, lil Ernie, Donna, Tina, Dewight, Raphard, Nate, Dolly Leedorse (Donnie and aunt Dorse Moore. Grand Parents/ Eva and Allen Walker R.I.P)

LARRY SIMON: Attorney at Law Taken from us, Loved by all those who knew of his heart and kindness, type of man that went out his way to check on a brother or do a favor for a friend even acquaintance he just met, shared his kindness but love for his Daughter ALEX, family cousins Ronnie and Dolwin as he shared his love for his sisters Lisa, and Sue, especially for his mother Ms. Teresa Franklin and Aunts. We miss you and you will never be forgotten by all of us GRAND DRUNKEN MASTERS 4 Life (G.D.M.4.L) LARRY SIMON always a member of G.D.M.4.L and members Derrick /Dee White, Dave /D-Nice Dixon, Jazz/Rob Williams, 2Soon/Frank Cox, C-man/Carl McCombs, TYS/LIL-Rob Nevins, Mack/Allan James, Dougie/Allen James, Doug, Detrain, La-machine, Troy Henry, Herb, Tyrone, Steel/Darron Newkirk, Drea, Rob-Goodie, Eldest/ Maddness/Maurice. Friends of the GDM4L Nappy Red, Me2-, Ja, Dakim, Jeff Kinslow, Jeffery finely /LoveGOD, J Hope, Kevin Finley, Sheldon Henry and Unique for TV exposure and others whom loved our fallen very much, Larry your sayings will live on FAMILY&

FRIENDS COME FIRST.

My old brothers of Bedford block: Steven Battle- Gerard McGriff-Celwin- Norland and Chris Fungoland, to my cousins- Donnie and Jeffery (we miss you both) and Michael their sister Lisa Clemons. The Saint john St and Rogers ave crew Gary, Paul, Mike nose, Junior, Larry, Cookie, Peanut, Trina Etc. Plus new old friends Evelyn Youngblood and Dread James (Tunkey) Duke, Sandra James, Kysha Martin Sonia Spears, Ginean White, kindred family sisters I had somewhere. (Merlin and Lipp with John - R.I.P) If not for those people and others I can't name but know who they are this book wouldn't here so I like to Say Thank you for all your thought and encouragement to continue my strive for completing of this.

The Question is what would to do with 3 Unlimited Funded Credit Cards which are Untraceable and it comes with one small catch, you didn't know you had them but used it until someone close to you shows you what you have on your hands or in your pockets, this is what happened to a honest big man.

4:30 am Hutch gets up after knocking over the alarm clock to cut it off then shower and get dressed to take that long drive to another borough to get dirty looks from his co-workers as they clock in to work because he's already there getting his truck cleaned to start the day. He's only black driver working for this Interior demolition garbage company own and worked by Italians. Hutch was given the position of driver because the boss Michael needed a driver and he was not giving that position to another family member that has cost his company money instead of making money for the company. Working for the company since he was 19 years old and over the years he's become an expert at rigging up pranks quickly in order to get even with his co-workers at the company which didn't like him there. They would speak their native tongue in Italian to conspire to hurt him or make him quit, not liking a black man who out works them at the company. Listening to them talk knowing it's about him but not knowing which one done something to his truck to cause him harm and damage or making him take the hard dirty jobs because they didn't want it. Cleverly he started learning to speak Italian not letting them know he slowly could start understanding them as time went on. Whenever they would speak in front of him thinking he didn't understand anything they said or what they did to his truck cutting the air breaks or oiling them up. Hutch would know now what they were talking about as they walk pass him laughing about what they've done to his truck. Hutch would fix what they've done to his truck and would rig his own prank on them turning the tables on them so when they asked him about it, he didn't understand their bad English accents leaving them wonder which one of them decided to turn on the others. Hutch is a man 6'3" 278 lbs. and would lift bulky things over his head to throw in the back of the garbage truck from heavy office desks and refrigerators all by himself. Looking at the sizes of his arms and how really big he's gotten, they wouldn't want to fight with him because he could beat up the whole company. They had to try and find other ways to get the big man even though he was way ahead of them, Hutch would rigged up pranks faster and faster over the years at the company. They knew it was him by now and as he kept the whole company of drivers on edge of what he might do to them next. They still were Jealous how he invested his time and own money fixing up the truck assigned to him adding tinted windows, neon lights, little running lights along the sides and plates. A loud booming stereo system, chrome to the rims, bumpers and lighted chrome Mirrors, plus little flags American & Caribbean Islands with GIANTS flags on glow antennas. The boss would now has him to do all jobs dirty in very populated arrears of New York City seeing his truck was representing the company and tourist would love to take pictures of the truck and him. The boss's family member would complain about how Hutch was doing a lot of the work they didn't want to do anyways but wanted to be there in the most populated arrear to watch the women and get the credit for the work Hutch would do anyway. The boss would send them along to keep his peace in his family and his own sanity from all the complaining they were doing to him.

The day starts with a phone call to the company and it's for very big job of Interior demolition on this big building in lower Manhattan this part of the City of New York located near the Mayor office not far from the Brooklyn Bridge one block west off Broadway down on Chambers street. Not knowing this building was well kept secret in that part of the city being a (S.E.M.O.F) Science Experimental Military Operations Federal Building located in the borough of Manhattan, which somewhere in the personal department because they never knew the State had its own demolition crew. Someone ordered by an impatient superior officer told to call a demolition company and give them clearance for the building to be remodeled interiorly on a majority of the floors to make room for more experiments they for tests.

The call went out to City/State Interior Demolition Company where Hutch works for and not the States own Demolition Company which somehow got mixed up with the two names. Meepbo the newly owner of the whole Company got the call and wanted his best men to do the interior demolition and he had to have four drivers accompany the interior crew on this big important job. He had Hutch and three other drivers go, two were family members of the old boss since they stayed with the company. Still they would complain about Hutch getting the work and still jealous how he would enjoy working hard and bring home something from the job as a perk. How Meepbo knew this and other things about the whole company is because of his tell all company brown nose man named Monirem, this little sneaky man somehow always seems to be in the right place at the right time to watch whatever goes on then extorts his victim and still reports it back to the boss. After setting up schedules to begin the job and where to be, he assigns the company of drivers their schedule to work the day when they had come in for work. Like always Hutch gets to the garage first and pulls out his truck and wipes it down while listening to the Doug Banks morning show as the other driver and workers come to the garage to get their vehicles. Meepbo assigns Hutch and with the other drivers and Monirem-(kiss ass foreman) and his work crew to the building to starts their work and like usual Hutch is the first one at the work site after getting his breakfast at the sandwich shop he and lots of other drivers from the arrears would get their food from. Pulling in front of the address he was given by Meepbo, looking at the building while eating his food waiting for the rest of the work force to get there watching the people walking by listening as they too listen to the morning show. Hutch finished eating his sandwich then gets out of the truck to put on his coveralls with the sleeves cut out so he doesn't get them snagged on anything then puts on his bandana and shades while grooving to the music coming from the trucks stereo, finally Moni and the rest of the crew shows up which he goes to get his I-pod from the truck cutting off the stereo. Monirem gives Him a look shaking his head at Hutch and takes the work crew in the building to talk to the security guard that was expecting them, getting badges for the work whole crew they went to work bringing stuff out of the building to be crushed by the trucks. Hutch and the other drivers inspected some of the things to see what they could bring home like always. The things they bring out are heavy and big but people watch as Hutch lifts the stuff up throwing the things into the truck with a boom then crush it with the trucks blade. The more stuff came out of the building the more Hutch made his job look easy as he lifts up those heavy desk and other things from the offices throwing them in the truck while grooving to his music as people watched the big man work. A lot of women's heads turned looking at him lifting some heavy things that made most of the men walking by shake their head at how he got the thing up and over his head to throw in the truck. When a break in the stuff coming down to the truck happen it gave Hutch time to look up at the building they were working at, this building had no windows but an big air vent in the middle of the building on all four sides of it. That got him curious as to what kind of building doesn't have windows. He decides to investigate the building from the inside since there was a break going on and talking to one of the workers he knows on the work crew bring the stuff out and gets him to lend Hutch his badge for a while. He goes into the 68 story building passing the security guard as he showed that badge pushing the container to the elevator. Getting to the floor where they crew is working and pushing the container off the elevator but not getting off himself but going up to a higher floor to see what kind of building it was, his stomach lets him know he better go to find the bathroom real soon from the grumbling it's doing and he start looking for one.

The personal was getting their belongings to take home and not noticing Hutch walking around looking for the bathroom, seeing these men go in and come out of this room with the letters H.A.C Men room. Going towards the room as the last man came out and the door was closing slowly behind him but Hutch manages to stop the door from closing all the way going in the room thinking it's the bathroom. Once inside he sees it looks like a bathroom with mirrors, sinks, urinals and stalls with toilet bowls so he looks at himself in the mirror and says "This is one nice clean bathroom and those guys didn't funk it up!" Washing his hands first and drying them off leaning up against the tile wall pressing in one of the tiles by mistake. Watching the last stall door open up in its row after that tile was pressed he looks and walks to the stall, hearing someone coming in he goes in the stall not to be caught in there. Closing the door behind him it locks and this part of the wall opens up and three black Credit cards come out on this small display tray. Hearing the men leave out of the bathroom Hutch opens the stall door to see if they've really gone but the cards goes back into the wall so he turns back to look at the cards again seeing their not there and wondering what happened to them. Thinking quick how they came out he goes back to the wall opposite the mirror and pushing on the wall in spots till he hits the same tile again making the last stall door open up again. This time he takes the cards after closing the door behind him and puts them in his wallet then his stomach growls saying "Well since I'm here" A zippers echoes in the room with a loud "FARRRRT! & AAhh!" followed by Ba-Whoosh flushing. Walking out of the bathroom and going back to the elevator and right before the door closes he heard voices saying aloud "OH MY GOD WHO IN THE HELL LEFT THAT SMELL! And another one is heard "HOT DAMN LOOK AT THE SIZES OF THAT THING IN THE BOWEL WOULD SOMEONE CALL MATAINCE, WE NEED SPRAY ASAP!"(toilet bubbles) The man says "Did that thing just move?" Hutch just whistles pressing the elevator door close button and the elevator goes down. Ground floor getting off the elevator he bumps into hazmat of crew of four suited up and D.E.P agents carrying a case each of spray talking how they hope this is enough and where is Jason with that snake. The log left could back up plumbing for days or do they have to call in Rotor Rooter specialist for this one. Going back outside and found Moni by his truck as he starts to yelling at Hutch like he was his child asking him "where have you been and how come you wasn't there for all that time" he sees all those containers with stuff in them that has to be dumped because the worker couldn't lift most of that stuff. Hutch looks at him and laughs handing back the badge to the worker and gets to work throwing in the heavy stuff as Moni still continues to yell at Hutch but each time he was yelling at Hutch, he would drown him out with the truck crushing up the stuff in the hopper. Moni kept trying to make a big deal out of it but the truck would crush something big as Hutch controlled it looking at Moni making like he couldn't hear him from all the noise. In a short time after the truck was loaded and Hutch took it to be dumped while the other trucks was getting filled by some of the smaller things he couldn't get in his truck. Almost to the place where they dump the debris he stops off at the lunch truck where a lot of trucks stop to have a quick snack and talk with other drivers they know. Seeing his friend Gerard there and hearing him talk about this big booty woman with the face of a super model he met the other night get away from him. Hutch orders two dirty water dogs with the works hearing Gerard tell him she had this friend and they could have doubled or he could have took them both. Hutch laughed and told him that's every man's fantasy to have two hot or beautiful women at one time. (Hey you, reading this book right now! Let this be a lesson, if the women are not hot or beautiful looking they still sell tickets to Shanghai or Tibet because you got drunk and horny looking through beer goggles speaking to MATILDA Gorilla saying, she so fine looking and next day sober you can't claim you got BABOON-NIESHA!)

Chowing down the dogs as Gerard talks about one day he'll get to be with two and keep one for himself amazed how Hutch kills those dogs so fast then listen to him say careful what he wishes for as he gets some other things from the lunch truck and gets in his truck to head for the dump. At the dump site Hutch is let in front of a lot of trucks waiting in line there because they like him and he brings them things like juice or cold water even ice cream on hot days. He treats them very nice unlike the drivers they have waiting to dump their trucks and inside the scale office he always makes the woman there laugh when she's have a bad day and feels down, joking with her picking her spirits up. With her Foo Manchu mustache and Uni-brow above those chubby cheeks and crooked lazy eye stare she gives, he jokes on the other men that don't see her beauty like him. (What's in those hot dogs!) Suggesting all she's got to do is lose a few pound get to beauty shop have a lot of things waxed in between and weave it up, couple facials and order lots of strong Spanks before she knows it those transitional shade she'll be wearing will hide that eye in the day time for all those baby daddy's she could have. After dumping his truck knowing he's got to go down this one way street where these Lincoln Continental diver parks their vehicles on either side of the street making it tight for trucks to go down. Knowing if they were to scratch the car the insurance claimer would pay the driver for any and everything that's wrong with their cars claiming the truck did the damage and they know it, so refusing to move while having their conversation about nothing these drivers would get their way taking over that long block. Garbage truck drivers have a choice to either take a chance going down the tight street or go around which would take them an extra half hour to get back to the express way because of all the lights they had to go through. Hutch looked at the drivers as they stood at the front of their cars waiting for the trucks to come down the street, knowing they couldn't block the entire way but made it so tight that an inexperienced truck driver would get nervous trying not to hit every car there. Hutch had a surprise he's been working on with Galio the company's mechanic as he starts down the street. Stopping right before he gets to the first corner looking at the gauntlet of black and dark blue vehicles and their driver outside them with their arms folded hiding the cameras under their arms waiting for a truck to damage any of the cars parked. Hutch looks at all the men and they look at him as he revs his engine then checks his mirrors to see the things he and Galio had put on the truck is in place. Presses a button on his stereo cranking up DMX rap song (Up in here!) playing it loud! Shifts his gears moving forward faster and faster while holding his finger on a button just before passing the first car, pressing that button as black oil sprays a fine mist out of the pipes installed on the back of the truck along with the wire brushes scratching the sides of the cars not seen because of the oil mist of used black oil being sprayed coating what's being done. Even if the men tried to take pictures of the truck going by the mist would cover them and their camera lenses, other drivers wanting to know why the men before them are backing away and cursing loud at the truck going by till it reaches them and does the same to them. With cars covered in used blacken oil front and back Hutch stops after going through the whole gauntlet and cranks up Kool Moe Dee's rap (How you like me now!) and laughs at what he's done to all of them. Pulling away seeing the men trying to get in their cars dropping their keys and other trying to get the name of the truck after Hutch drove by but couldn't get into their cars or them cleaned fast enough to get after him. Other men were slipping and falling while cussing loudly very mad at what he did to them, trying to run after Hutch with the ground so oily.

Driving the truck as if it was his own personal sports car he makes it back to the building in Manhattan in a shorter time it took to get to the dump site. Parking his truck in the line behind the others just as lunch time starts and the way he saw the streets getting crowded with people looking for somewhere to eat. He goes into this sandwich shop and gets a turkey sub and juice then goes to his truck to roll down the windows so his stereo could be heard cranking out Red Alert mix at Noon on the radio as people walked by grooving to what they was listening as Hutch and the work crew were judging the women and how tight their outfits were clinging to their bodies as their boobs bounced up and down as they walked by. The rest of the day went by fast and before he knew it Hutch was home emptying his pockets on the dresser draw in the bedroom then taken a shower, just as he got out of the water his phone rang and he heard the answering machine play the message from his frat brothers are coming over to plan their weekend. Not long after he dried off and got dressed his brothers are at his door first to come in is Jazz followed by C-man then Mack, Dougie, Dave, Derrick, 2Soon, Goodie, LIL-Rob, Herb, La-Machine, a couple minutes later Tyrone and Steel, D-train, and Doug, Byron, Ron and Troy with Drea walk in even though it's Thursday they want to hang out but Hutch convinces them to make their plans to be ready for the weekend. They have a meeting on what to do over this weekend coming and before closing their meeting agreeing it's Hutch's turn to put everything on his Credit card because it's a bi week for some of them to collect their checks. He knows the following week they will settle up with him for whatever they spent over the weekend and the rest of the night they watch sports and Def Jam comedy cracking jokes before heading home to get ready for work tomorrow.

The next day Hutch is early like usual to the garage to get his truck and leaves to get his breakfast first before heading to the building back in Manhattan, parking his truck in front of the building and eating his food then changes into his work gear and waits for the crew to show up. While listening to the Doug Banks Morning show and seeing the people who could hear the radio playing so loud as they walk by look up into the truck at him as he laughs at Ms. Lenard and Bay-bay do their bit in the morning show. Half hour goes by and the work crew shows up with the other trucks as Moni gets out of the van he rides in and starts giving orders of what he wants done and what floors some of them are working on today. Short time later Hutch is talking with his friend on the crew and getting the badge to go in the building again but this time he gets off on the lower floor where he sees this lab coat laying on a chair with a badge of a different color than the one he's got on. Looking around before he takes the badge off the lab coat and gets back on the elevator and goes up to the floor where the work crew is to see how things are going up there. Moni see Hutch get off the elevator and storms over to him asking him "What is he doing up there when he needs to be down by the truck" making a big scene in front of all the works there but Hutch just tells him there is nothing to throw in the truck and he thought something was wrong because all the containers are up here if he just looks around. The floor has all the containers they use to dump stuff in up there and Hutch knows he's right, Moni gets very embarrassed that he made such a scene being wrong for what he said but Hutch just shrugs his shoulders and gets back on the elevator saying "I'll be down stairs when you are ready for me".

Two of the workers that know Hutch wonder why Moni yells and screams at him like that when he knows Hutch could kill him for it, the other worker comments "If he as big and strong looking as Hutch he would laugh at a little piece of shit getting up in his face too. When all he's got to do is step on his ass squashing Moni, but how could he get the shit and smell off his boot that complains each time he walks on it" They laughed about the thought.

When the door closed to the elevator Hutch was thinking he's going to have to get that kiss ass for trying to make him look foolish, putting his hands on his pockets and feeling the badge he took from that coat pressing the button to the ground floor but pushes the sub level 6 buttons by mistake instead. The elevator stops on the sub level 6 and asked him to swipe his badge for the doors to open so he swipes the badge he's got from the workers and the doors buzz then he takes the badge in his pocket and swipes watching the doors opens with a hiss coming from somewhere on the level. He pokes his head out from the elevator to see if anyone was going to approach him for being there but no one seems to be in sight and down the hallway are a lot of doors with Initials on them. Continuing further into the sub level floor he tries one of the initial that has C.E.P (Chemical Enhancement Project) on it and goes in the room where he sees all these tubes and beakers other lad stuff on the tables. Walking around the room then seeing these little spray bottles looking like colognes with different color tops to them that are Gold and Black the last one was Silver. He walks over to them and tries the silver color one first and likes the smell of it, looking at the bottle with initials F.H.S. on it, not knowing what the letters meant but likes the smell. Putting a few in his pocket then picking up the Black cap little bottle and instead he sniff it trying not to mix the two scents together on his body and looks at the letter F.F.S. He thinks it's Ok but not as good as the silver one he likes so he takes only one then picking up the Gold capped one that have on it F.M.S and sniffs that one as well. He feels the same as he does about the black capped one and takes just one of those bottles too then going back taking just a few more of the silver capped ones because those are the ones he really likes for some reason. Thinking this building has to be another one of those development places where they make the fragrance and perfume scents for a lot of colognes that's why the high security but not high enough to keep him from getting the news stuff before it hits the streets. All his pockets full he hears voices and knows he doesn't want to get caught with this stuff so he ducks down behind the table as the security guard opens the door to the lab and looks around then closes the door and continues to the next room. About to leave the room he runs back over to the tables and grabs two more of each color and opens the door slightly to see if the guard is still out there but there is no sign of him, Hutch bolts to the elevator trying not to make a lot of cling noise as the bottle hit together in his pockets. Presses the elevator button he hears footsteps coming but don't know from which way because there are four corridors that met at the elevator and he knows it has to be those security guards as they walk and talk getting closer. Pushing the elevator saying "Come on, come on" as they get closer and closer and sound like they're about to turn the corner, looking in the top of the elevators doors to see if he could see the light coming down he hears "Excuse me sir but why are you still here?" Busted and thinking how's he going to explain this to them as he turns and sees no one there. The guards are talking to another lab tech still in a room just around the corner from where the elevator, the doors opens up and he backs into it pushing the doors close button taking a big sigh right as the security guard looks around the corner to see no one there. Hutch is breathing a sigh of relieve with a chuckle he didn't get caught till the doors opens up and there is Moni standing in front of him "What the hell are you chuckling about" Moni starts up again about where he's been and what he's doing in the building instead of putting stuff in the truck. All Hutch did was look at him as he yells and yells about how this stuff not going to get out of there when he keep disappearing like that, Moni got up in his face because Hutch was smiling paying no mind to him and he didn't like what Hutch was doing.

Moni poked Hutch once and saw him stop laughing and said to him "So this isn't funny anymore, now I got your attention" about to do it again but gets his hand grabbed by Hutch. Looking at Moni while he tries to pull his hand back but can't and all the workers there stop working to see if Hutch was going to knock down Moni or throw him, they quickly starts to bet which one was going to happen. All Hutch did was squeeze his hand and tell Moni "You could yell at me all you want those are nothing to me but words. When it comes to putting your fingers or hands on me you better make sure you can get it back. I might just decide to keep what touches me" and all Moni could do was yell "let me go". Holding Moni's hand in a tight fist then hoisting Moni up in the air, Hutch stand 6'3" much stronger than Moni could ever be who stands only 5'2". Growling him "Did you hear what I said" and Moni meekly says "Yeah! Yeah! I heard you now let go of my hand!" All the workers watch and laugh as Hutch drops Moni on his butt and walks to the front of his truck to gets in. Embarrassed Moni couldn't leave well enough alone and runs to the other side of the front of Hutch truck and gets up on it as Hutch was pulling the little bottle he got from the lab out of his pockets and putting them in his bag. Moni saw what he was doing and starts knocking hard on the window loudly saying "What is that you are putting in your bag!" Hutch startled with some of the cologne bottles in his hands cracked one of the sliver capped one spilling some on himself, mad about it he rolls down the window and telling him "keep it down before someone hears you". Moni Answers "let him in the truck to see what it is that he's got there" Hutch pushes the door unlock button and lets Moni in his truck to keep him from yelling. He saw Hutch with those bottles of what looks like cologne to him, now inside the truck Moni got more nosey and wants to know where he got those bottles from. Knowing he couldn't tell Moni exactly where he got them from so to keep him quiet and figure if he gives him one then he's just as guilty as him, if he ever decides to tell the boss like he always does and knows the boss will get after them both. Moni would get it worse being the one in charge here at the work site, so he hands him one of the gold capped bottles and told him not to say anything about it. Moni takes the bottle smelling it, liking what he smells asking Hutch for another one but gets told "I only got those few so don't push it, be thankful you got one and not stuff in the back of my truck for poking me". Moni thought about that and shook his head getting out of the truck fast. Taking what he got from Hutch and going into the building to the bathroom and spraying some of it on himself so everyone could smell him and as he was walking out passing a couple of ladies as they smile at him first then as the scent hits their nose they frown up and look at Moni angry. They got mad he spoke to them making comments about how that shit colored man has the nerve to speak and wave to them. It was still early before lunch the day bright and sunny making the day hotter with winds blowing at time to cool things off as the containers starts to coming down to be dumped in the trucks, Hutch was working up a good sweat throwing all those heavy things in the truck but kept noticing all the women looking at him smiling waving blowing kisses at him while he worked. Moni directed some of the workers to keep things flowing fast and he too was working up a sweat as lunch time came around and everyone had worked up an appetite. At the sandwich shop Hutch was in line as more and more women starts to come in there and because he was heated from all that work not knowing the scent of that cologne was airing through the place. When these two women came in the place it hit their nose like the other women in there but this woman lets out "Hot Damn! Someone in here smells good and I aint talking about the food either!" All the women shook their heads agreed with her and starts looking at Hutch as he was wondering why they was looking at him with some of them licking their lips giving him seductive looks and others had that seductive sexy sneer look nodding their heads staring at him.

It was hard to see what they were thinking about doing to him if there was no one around at the moment and they got their hand a hold of him. Making it up to the counter and ordering his turkey sub with juice this woman walks over to him looking at how string he looks feeling his arms saying "I'll pay for that!" Being the gentlemen he is saying "That's Ok a man always pay his own way" but she said "It would insult me if I didn't get to do this" He just looks at her as she smiles at him in a very seductive was biting her lip at him, then say "I like a man that knows what to eat to keep in shape so he know what to eat later!" Every man in the place had their eyebrows raised up hearing what she as he still paid for his lunch but thanked her for the thought, so she gave him her card with her personal on the back of it motioning for him to call her feeling his arm again. Rolling her eyes up in her head grabbing his hand seeing how big they are then looking at his feet going "their big too!" Every woman in the place started looking down at his feet and back up at him smiling licking and biting their lips shaking their heads. Sitting down at the table to eat his food he's notices cards being dropped on his tray and as he looks at the women that did it motion for him to call her, he looks around as if this was some kind of prank but seeing it wasn't. Wrapping up his sandwich putting his juice in his pocket he starts to leave but at the door goes back and grabs up all those cards as all the men look at him and he says "What! I'm not stupid! Crazy! Not stupid!" As he leaves out the shop and tries to figure out what's going on with all those women in there. He went back to his truck to finish eating his food and looked at all the women now coming to the sandwich shop, so he looks at sandwich thinking they must make one hell of a sandwich to have such a rush of women to be going in there like that. He didn't know that it was his scent of the cologne lingering in the air in the place. It had women still in there feeling very horny and hungry for the man who left the scent. Talking about what he looked like calling their friends to get down there too. Lunch almost over and Hutch gets out of truck and starts working on the containers to keep ahead of the work crew, again he works up a good sweat but faintly he heard a lot of whistle calls and cat calls as he controlled the truck crushing the material. When he stops for a second the noise dies down he could hear the men talking about what they would do to her if they had one night with that, so he turns to see what they was talking about. He saw this woman thick in the right places that jiggled and lean in the waist and other places. She had every man looking at how in shape her body was and even had some women admiring her shape. The wind carries the scent of what Hutch had on, it caught her nose and since she was walking that way she follows the scent right to him. He stood there looking at her caught in her beauty and trying not to show a part of him that he could use as a kick stand if he leaned forward. The suit outfit she had on very classy looking, but sexy form fitting had everyone gazing at her as it clung to her body just right. Showing her thick thighs and wrapped her ass like a second skin. She walks up to him real close asking him "Working hard?" The big man with his back to the truck just looks at her as she leans into his body pressing her body on him getting a good whiff of what he's got on, she says something in his ear that made his jaw drop as his eyes brows raise high. Then she took out her business card writing on the back of it putting it in his chest pocket of his coveralls pressing her hand on his chest going "Umm that's solid too". Looking at him sweating she says "Don't forget to use that number because" cutting her word short again leaning into him standing on her toes in those high heels. She goes to kiss his cheek but instead went for his neck kissing it first then take a long lick that made the man buckle from her touch. She pulls away from him going "Umm salty! but I'll have you sweating all over and in buckets!"

She turns to walk away but stops suddenly after her mouth tingled from licking the spot where he spray the cologne on his neck and it reacted in her mouth which made her eyes get wide. She backs up into him reaching behind her feeling what she knows is pulsating right now and goes "Don't forget to bring this with you when you come over, after you call or call after you come all over" Walking away from the big man as he crumple and all the workers there just watch her jiggle walk down two blocks and turn the corner. They all turn back and look at Hutch as he shrugs his shoulder holding up his hand then say "Yall can take your hard hats from in front of your bodies now and go back to work". Thinking it's a good thing he's got on those loose coveralls or they would know he's just as excited as them even more as he walks with one leg stiff to the front of his truck to get something ice to use on it.

At the same time Moni was getting rude looks and bad attitudes from the lunch counter women at another place and wonders what he's doing wrong for them to be in such a way with him so going back to the van and having his lunch alone reading the magazine he found in the buildings bathroom. On the page he reads "Women want the man, the right scent" He liked what it showed the confidence looking model men tight lipped looking as if they was constipated grabbing a woman and knew he just had sprayed more cologne on showing his new attitude look. Thinking women would notice him and be drawn to him like in the magazine. Getting his mind all worked up and using a lot more of the cologne on himself not even finishing his food he steps out from the van and stands there for a moment as if he was king Leonidas in 300 returning home hearing the opera music playing for him as he stand there with his hands on his hips looking around thinking everyone should be bowing to him. People look at him wondering what's wrong with this clown and walk right pass him standing there like a store mannequin. Work started back up and Hutch was walking to the back of the truck when he hears Moni yelling how come he's not back there working on dumping the containers to fill the truck and Hutch looked at him saying "You're the one who needs to take a dump with that look on your face should eat more fiber" Moni looks at him and walks over to the containers and yells for him to come on and get them dumped because he's got plans for later, Hutch laughed going "Like taking a serious shit from the way your lips are clinched and jaws tight, it might come back up through your mouth so you better have plans!" They get to working hard and sweating more from the heat of the hot day and hot winds didn't help but make it worse but as Moni stood on the sidewalk by empty the containers when the wind blew up the street. The women coming towards him smelled the cologne and got very angry he was even standing there on the same sidewalk cussing and bumping into him even a couple took a swing at him to move out their way mad at him. This group of young girls starts coming down their way when the wind blew up the street they got a good whiff of Moni's cologne as they approached with each one having such a reaction in their faces. He was trying to be friendly by saying "Aw look at the little pretty princess" one of the girls asked him in such a way "What the F$@k did you say to me?!" The others girls start to kick and hit him calling him pervert and ugly shit color moron and one girl cussed him out like a sailor and threaten to cut him. The wind blew his scent again up to this group of old women touring the city was walking down that way towards them. They got a good whiff of his scent after the little girl walks away from him, their reaction to it was immediate as they told him to leave those little girls alone and starts to him with their purses and cane plus fist the ones that could get close to him. Waiting till they got down the street from him he shouts "You old bitches if he had any sense I should have knocked your old dry up ho bitches to the ground like a man should, if any one of you was there right now!"

Hutch and the other workers were laughing at what happened to him but stopped laughing when they saw her standing behind Moni as he was shouting down the block at the group of old women. Moni looked over to Hutch and the workers saying "I should just go down there and really beat their old asses!" Hutch looked at Moni trying in a very subtle way motioning to him to turn around but he was too busy calling them all kinds of names, till he caught on as to what Hutch was motioning for him to do and he shuts up and turns around to see who's in back of him. Moni puts his hands on his hips and starts to turn around quick but is met with this big hand (POW!). Slapping him hard enough for his head to spin back around for a few seconds he could see the old women still walking down the block. Blinking twice at the sight them there his head spins back to show who hit him. This gray haired woman was 6' 7" and had to weigh 357lbs as she told him that's her family he's cussing at, moving like a wrestle so quick to scope him up and body slam him to the ground. Grabbing him up again giving him stone cold Steve Austin stunner moving quickly she grabs him up for a pile driver followed a choke slam, finishing up with the rock bottom and peoples elbow, plus leg drop like Hulk Hogan saying "Your ass is lucky I didn't get Cali- Chi Town- Kak-a-lacky-Crunk- Dirty South- Med evil- Bed STY Do or Die- Rude Boy B-X style on ya shit colored ass heard meh!" Fixing her wig and brushing the dust off her dress and walking to catch up with her family leaving Moni laid on the sidewalk in pain. While that woman was making all those moves on Moni Hutch and the workers plus people on the street was going ooh and ah, woo damn and when she was finished they applauded her moves. Hutch and the workers was laughing so hard they couldn't help Moni get to his feet and when he did they could hear his bone crunch and crack making them all fall out laughing. Moni yells "How come no one helped me!" Hutch answers "What and get beat by Gran Mama Mon-soon!" That made all the workers fall out again laughing at Moni. He just got even madder and starts yelling at everyone "They need to get back to work before he has them all fired" holding his back and neck from being beat. Hutch went "Look just because you did Linda Blair proud and before you spit that green stuff at anyone, you need to cool down because there's a church not far from them and I can get some Holy water and burn your ass!" Moni in pain wanted to know who's Linda Blair and what Holy water going to do for him, so Hutch told him if he spins around four time and says these words his pain will go away. Agreeing to what Hutch suggested he asked "What words he's got to say?" Hutch told him spins saying the words "The power of Christ compels you!" making sure when he spins to say it! Moni does what Hutch told him and while he was doing that the workers was falling out with laughter but Moni stops after the fourth time saying he's still in pain, Hutch went "I forgot the water but keep saying it louder each time till I get the water". Hutch went to his truck an got a bottle of water as Moni was doing what he was told to do, then Hutch stood by him sprinkling water on Moni as he turned and said it louder and louder! Moni cousin Charlie pulls up and saw what Hutch and Moni was doing asking "What the hell's going on?" Hutch told Charlie "Showing him how stupid he looks yelling at people and lucky he got his ass kicked by a grayed haired woman and not me!" Moni stops turning around after hearing what Hutch said to Charlie and was mad he made a fool out of him that way, sending everyone back to work so they can get done for the day. Hutch is helping the work crew clean up when eye candy comes back up the block as all the workers stop and look at her, she walks up to him with her hair flowing in the wind looking so hot as he stands there froze like a deer caught in the lights. She looks at how they were cleaning up and says to him "Getting ready to get off huh, well not better than I can have you getting off with help!"

Pushing her chest up to him to give him a good look at how she has a couple of button of her suit open so he could see her cleavage and how good her chest looks. He looks her in the eye saying "Hi my name is" Putting her fingers to his lips stopping him from speaking. Telling him the way he's got bass in his voice she knows he's got an H sound name man and not some mousey sounding man with a M or C even T she likes mystery so let her figure out what it is after you're calling out my name "KIAMESHA" over and over. Licking his lips and grabbing his crotch her eyes got wide surprised her hand got more than what she was expecting. Telling him she has to work later but will keep her cell on vibrate where it need to be so call her twice and she'll know it's him then walks back down the block as all the workers including Hutch watches her jiggle till she turns the corner. They finish cleaning up leaving Manhattan to back to Queens where the company garage is and park their vehicles, Hutch gets there after the van unloads all the workers and they left for the day. He starts cleaning his truck for the next day when Meepbo comes out and stand there looking at him asking "How come you don't go straight home after you get back here" Hutch explains "For what to an empty home" he starts to wash his truck and this SUV pulls up with four women in and they get out to greet Meepbo. He shout to Hutch come meet his wife Toni and daughters Lorie, Carmella and Sheila since you never met them yet after all these year working from me boy. They wave "Hi" Hutch excuses his not shaking their hands or getting close because of the dirt on him and says "Next time" as a mild wind blew and they got a light whiff of that cologne still on him mixed with his sweating too they starts looking at each other making comment about how big his arms and hands look standing there watching him by their vehicle. Meepbo forgot something and told them they could get back in the vehicle and wait for him, remembering it's his wallet he left back in the office. Toni goes in the building with him saying "You always forgets your wallet somewhere" as his daughter watch Hutch washing the truck fantasizing about being with the big man. When Meepbo came back out and got in to leave Sheila was waving bye to Hutch and winking at him, he smiled and waved back not giving it a second thought as he went in his truck and cranked up the music and starts dancing while spraying the truck with water. All three women Sheila and Carmella were looking out of the back window as the vehicle pulls away from the garage.

Shortly after he's on his way home taken up no time at all to clean his truck, stopping at the grocery store to pick up a few things before his brothers came over because it Friday and they should be ready to act out for the weekend like always. Arriving at his six bedroom house he's still has a few more payments to make on it before it's finally his, taken out the grocery bags and beer heading inside to put them away. Then out in the back to clean out the pool with all the floating toys from the last big party they had with the Grand Drunken Masters 4 Life and lady friends. Going up to his bedroom emptying out his pockets on the dresser draw and going to get in the shower taken the sliver capped little bottle F.H.S trying to figure out what those letter means, knowing his brothers should be there in a little while he gets in the shower. A short time later he's out of the water and drying off getting dressed as the door bell is ringing. It's Dougie one of his brothers a Grand Drunken Master 4 Life followed by Mack, Steel, Jazz, C-man, Goodie, Herb, Tyrone, Byron, Ron, Troy, LiL-Rob, Drea, Derrick and Dave with 2Soon, last through the door is La-Machine and D-train they came in and grabbed a beer and a drink as well to discuss which place they was going to first. Agreeing the club first to see what females they can pick up and get a number from then breakfast if they get hungry before going any other place, but first they had to also discuss how much they were going to spend knowing they had to give it to Hutch so he could put everything on his credit card. Having a couple more drinks and given themselves a once over going to take a leak everyone noticed the little bottle of silver capped cologne on the bathroom sink Hutch left there and liked the way it smells so they all would use a spritz or two before leaving out. They get to the club in Manhattan the place is packed with lots of pretty women so they head to the bar to get another drink to really loosen up because they all are no wall flowers, they get their drinks and then head to the dance floor where a lot of women are dancing with each other because the men there are trying to look really cool and don't have time to dance. Every Grand Drunken Master seems to have a lot of women coming up wanting to dance with them, even ones with their own men was going over to the GDM4L pairing off to their favorite one dancing with him and other women they didn't seem to mind. The night went on like that for as long as they was in the club dancing with most all the women in there, nearing the closing of the club each Grand Drunken Master had one or two women except Hutch. The women wanted to go and get something to eat with guys agreeing. They get to this diner and go in filling one side of the diner ordering food and more drinks and after everyone had their fill the bill came to Steel who passed it down to Dave who passed it down to 2Soon and the rest till it stopped at Hutch who looked at the bill and wanted one more drink for everyone and told all 4 waitresses to put a nice tip on for them. One of the waitresses was talking to the other one. She still has to buy her sons sneakers and clothes. Hutch heard that and told her to put an extra two hundred on for all of them because they worked hard for it, everyone at the table looked at Hutch and Dave says "See that's what happens when he gets too tipsy, he gets generous with his money and other things" Hutch heard him answering "She and the others worked hard for it" mad he told the waitress to make it three hundred for each of them. The waitress said to him "Your wife is going to kill you for spending money like that" Hutch goes "I'm not married" Like E.F Hutton dropped a good stock tip all the women at the tables and stopped what they was doing and turned to look at him. He turns and sees them all looking at him and explains he and his brothers was raised right and know how to say thank you to a hard working woman. That comment made every woman in there look at all the Grand Drunken Masters 4 Life they were with as one woman asked "Wow! You all are blood brothers?" Dave answers her explaining since they were small they've all known each other and yes some of them do have the same mother just look at us! The waitress waited as Hutch pulls out his the Credit Card and hands it to her going "I mean what I said, there shouldn't be a problem. I just put a little bit more money from my account on that credit card" She and the other three waitresses walk to the cashier and swipe the card as Hutch and everyone were getting ready to leave. This loud cheering was heard on the other side of the diner where the waitresses went before they all came back with big smiles on their faces. Kissing Hutch thanking him for what he done letting him know they will remember him when they come back there. Outside the diner they didn't want the partying to end and suggest they all go to Hutch's place if that was alright with the ladies, each woman looked at the guys and answered they're grown but how are they going to fit everyone in that many cabs. Nine vehicles follow each other on the expressway to Staten Island where Hutch lives and shortly they pull up to his 6 bedroom house. Thirty seven people stagger in as he opens the door to his house "Make yourself at home but if you break it you bought it!" The ladies make a comment about how nice his place is and wonders what he does for a living to have such a big place with a pool. He answers "I drive a demolition garbage truck" The women look at him as he explains he bought this house when it was foreclosed on and got it for a steal as a fixer upper.

With a quick tour and showing where all the bathrooms are everyone starts to pair up and head to either one of the empty bedrooms or down to the basement game room. He's got a big pool table and big TV and stereo system there with some pull out beds down there with these two big sofas' and love seats everyone slept comfortably in his house.

Saturday afternoon Hutch walks through his house and sees bodies everywhere covered with sheets or a comforter he gave them the night before, going back to the kitchen and starts breakfast and makes coffee which has everyone moving to the smell of it. After everyone had taken a shower and then had breakfast and coffee to get them going, they exchanged numbers for later and left Hutch's house. Everyone one left except Dougie who stayed to help him clean up. Hutch and Dougie talk about what they're going to do that night, Hutch said he needed a new pair of pants and wanted to go to the mall to see what he could find so Dougie went with him. At the mall they were walking around to see which store Hutch wanted to go in and find his pair of pants. They went into this one store and start to pick out some as Dougie made a few suggestions. Then Dougie decides he wanted to get something too but didn't have enough for everything so Hutch covered whatever he wanted knowing he was going to pay him back for it anyways. At the cashier Hutch laid his stuff on the counter ready to pay for it when in back of them a man says "This isn't my type of store but I guess this outfit will have to do, I normally have my stuff custom Taylor made to go to parties!" The man talking to his lady friend who answer him "I told you we were going to this party weeks ago in advance" as they stood there behind Dougie and Hutch at the counter. The women at the counter was about to say something to the man insulting their store but Dougie at the counter annoyed "Custom Taylor made but he came in here how come he didn't have it order back then" The man heard what Dougie said and got angry telling him he doesn't know style and could buy his whole wardrobe twice with the money he's got in his pocket. Calmly Dougie turns looking at the man answering what he just said "Look man how you going to come in here and insult these women and what their selling the things in here and very nice, that's why I'm here" The man angry now says to Dougie "You look like a man that works and couldn't understand the finer thing in life, definitely don't carrying big money like me" Then trying to belittle Dougie by saying "How much you carries on your Credit card laborer" flashing a wallet of ten Credit cards bragging about them. Speaking to him in a Snobbish tone "Hey you there working man! If you have more cash then me on any of your labor Credit cards. I'll buy you and entire wardrobe here and give you my chain and rings to boot!" Hutch had sized this guy up and knew he couldn't let Dougie get played like that, slipping his own Credit card into Dougies pockets going take that challenge. Hutch knew he would have the same if not more on his Credit card than this fake flashy loud mouth and told Dougie to let the women behind the counter be the judge knowing he couldn't lose because he gave Dougie his black Credit card. The arrogant man says "If I lose, I would gladly give my Rolex all my chains and rings and even my girl as a show piece for your arm too" She got very mad at what he said and got on him, but he didn't want to hear what she was saying being so arrogant about not losing. Mad he even said that about her, she said "I'll go with" asking "What is your name again, Dougie!" She turns and looks at her boyfriend and told him since he feels he need to bet her she'll go with Dougie, the man then adds if (saying his name so snooty) "Dougie! Loses he got to buy me an entire wardrobe there at the store!". Dougie looks at Hutch after he'd slipped him his Credit card as Hutch nods and Dougie agrees to what the man said going in his pocket pulling out the Credit card.

Now handing it to the woman behind the counter, the man smirks walking around the store looking at what he's going to get knowing he's going to win this bet. The woman behind the counter swipes the man's card first because he insisted knowing no black man would have what he's go on his card, the woman saw it read 70,000$ dollars available Balance and he walks away from the counter sighing like he's got a hard choice to make with the stuff in there making the women behind the counter wish he loses the bet. The woman swipes the Credit card Dougie gave her and her eyes got very wide as she smiles and calls his girlfriend over to see what she was looking at, both their jaws dropped at what they was looking at. The man arrogantly said "What! He couldn't cover even this!" holding up a sweat from a rack standing by it. Mad they aren't answering him yet he demand to know why they are smiling as his girlfriend says "You need to come over here and look at this" He saw it not believing it, pulling out card after card trying to top what he sees. Dougie and Hutch are laughing hard at how many bags Dougie's got to carry with Hutches help along with the new jewelry he is now wearing asking "If there's a pawn shop in the mall" Walking next to the man's now ex-girlfriend who points out four of them. The man still in the store stunned with no jewelry or girlfriend and now paying for all Dougie's new clothes wondering how he lost that bet. The sales woman reminds him over the loud speaker "Because you didn't have enough on your Credit card ass wipe and next time you shouldn't judge a brother on where he shops!" but thanks him for the commission saying "We'll take an early lunch now. 17 thou in one day wow, Like that guy really needed it but glad he did!" They walk the arrogant shocked man out of the store and lock the door as he stand there no jewelry or watch looking at his credit cards as the women put up the "Be back went to lunch" sign on the door looking right at him. Laughing on their way out, saying to each other "Wonder if they could find the guy who won at lunch celebrating in his new clothes and bling!"

Walking to Hutch's Vehicle still getting stares from all the people as women would smile at them and the men would have frown up their faces at the sight of all those bags, filling every seat but the front two with bags from the store getting hungry and heads back in the mall to a restaurant to get something. Sitting in the booth Dougie wanted to know how much did Hutch have on his Credit card to make those women smile like that, Hutch looked at the woman sitting next to Dougie and told them "I'm maxed out my Credit cards that's why you are treating me to lunch remember". Dougie looked back at him and going "But this is" His words are cut by a big kick from under the table that makes him be quite for a moment and his eyes tears up. The woman looks at him asking "You alright?" Dougie smiles with tears in his eyes from the pain of being kicked saying "He just wants to yell for putting that loud mouth in his place" then she asked "It must be nice to have such unlimited funds to play with since I was there and saw the read out on the machine". Not fully understanding what she meant by that he told her "Saving up for a rainy day and spending my money wisely" That made the woman laugh telling him he was silly about what he said "Rainy day!" Before another word is said her now ex-boyfriend stand at the table looking at her, reminding her they were coming in there for lunch. He asked her "Could I speak to you" and begs for her to forgive him for being so stupid and promises it would never happen again he's learned a lesson about this and wants to be back with her dropping to his knees at the table. She looked at him then Dougie, he told her "You know you love him so why don't you go back to him, just look at him on his knees he's going to ruin my appetite". She shook her head but slips Dougie her number while her boyfriend was getting off his knees. The waitress came over and said "It looks like you need a little more time" looking at the man getting up.

Hutch smiles getting her attention and told her he'll have a "Drambuie and Gin with ginger ale on the side because with this going on I need a drink" she looks at them and says "Sure you don't want a double". The woman leaves with her boyfriend and motion back to Dougie I'll call me, Hutch looked at him going "Why you took that woman cell number, you know that's going to keep shit going with them". For a moment there's nothing said as Hutch looks over the menu then looks over at Dougie from behind the menu. Dougie was looking back at him shaking his head "yes" knowing what he's going to ask and they both laughed. Right before the waitress came back to the table with the drink Dougie gives Hutch back his Credit card before looking over what to order when she got there asking "Ready to order". Finishing their food asking for the check looking at it, Dougie was about to pay cash for it but Hutch told him "Put it on the card and don't worry" On the receipt there was a line on how much to tip the waitress so Hutch was going to tip her thirty dollars but Dougie wanted to leave the tip. Hutch marked the 80$ dollar box not noticing he did it and hands the waitress the bill and his Credit card. She came back to the table with the biggest smile on her face to him and asked him "Are you sure you know what you signed for?" He shook his head "yeah" putting the bill and Credit card in his pocket as they stood up. She hugged him thanking for the tip and shook Dougies hand thanking him also but sees the thirty dollars cash he slips her and hugs him for that too. They leave and head back to Hutch's house unloading most of those bags into Dougie vehicle which gets over loaded with bags. He told Hutch he'll call him so they can meet up with the rest of the guys and go back to the city as he left. Hutch goes in the house and upstairs to lay down for a little nap before he goes out that night. The phone woke him up out of a good dead sleep, Its Mack telling him "I'll be there in a short time so be ready" and Hutch told him the front will be open in case he's in the shower. All clean and getting dressed for that night with the new stuff he bought at the mall, he is looking at the little bottles of cologne on the dresser spraying just enough on his body so everyone would notice the new smell. When the G.D.M.4.L gets there some of them want to go see what's up with this club in the city and then eat after but this time everyone takes their own vehicle in case they get to take a date out of the club. Parking their vehicles and walking a couple blocks to the club and seeing all the good looking women lined up to get in the club. Once they got inside it's packed with lots of women more than men so they head to the bar for a drink and huddle, but Hutch is already on the dance floor pulled by this woman that smelled his cologne. All the guys are looking at Hutch as he dances with the woman then another comes up behind him and he dances with the both of them for a while. Thirsty he lets them know he's going to the bar to get a drink, one of the women asks him "What did you want and she'll get it!" Being the gentlemen that he is he told her "I'll buy you both a drink if we can get off the dance floor". When they agreed they followed him to the bar, he bought their drinks but was sweating from all that dancing. It had the cologne scent in every woman's nose close to him coming looking for the source and once they found it was Hutch, he was on the dance floor again. Some of the men that weren't dancing just standing at the bar with their heads tilted at the way the women were dancing with Hutch. From bending over forwards backing their behind on him to one woman had her leg around his hip holding him as if they were doing what it is they do in bed with no clothes on. Every now and then each woman would take his hand and put it on their chest, under their clothes looking him in the eyes strangely. Even the women that came there with their men wanted to dance with him. When the Dee Jay played something slow which gave him a chance to get off the dance floor as the lights got really dim, he could slip away in the darkness. Making it back to the bar and hearing all the comments from the G.D.M about how he was getting it in on the dance floor.

Steel told him "You better stop dry humping these women and take some of them over to that dark part of the club and get it in, because that's what they dance like they want you to do". Hutch was about answer Steel when this woman with the most hypnotic eye turns Hutch around and asked him "Want to dance?" He looks at her stunned by her beauty and body to match not saying a word till he get popped upside his head by Mack that snaps him out of the whatever trance he was in. This woman is 5' 7" about 160 lbs. toned body but 6'1" in her high stiletto heels. She take him back out on the dance floor were lots of women had been looking for the man they were dancing around with that smelled so good making them want something from him, as Hutch and the woman starts to dancing but gets surrounded by some women. The woman he's dancing with looks at all the other women ready to cut in and she takes off one of her shoes and welds it like a weapon telling the others "Back off!" One woman comes at her and she stabs her in the chest causing the bra to spout liquid silicone from it and deflate. That woman runs off, the one who stabbed her holds her heel high asking "Do anyone else want to see if theirs are real of fake?" This other big chested woman little shorter than her took off her heels and held them in both her hands. The tall woman with Hutch took off her other heel and grabbed another woman's scarf tying her heels together with the scarf welding them like nun chucks like Bruce Lee in the movie (Enter the Dragon.) The shorter woman attacked the taller woman, just like Bruce Lee the taller one is slapping this woman good with her shoed then popping both her water filled boob enhancers under her clothes. She runs out and the woman looks at all the others and says "Waa-haa" Doing Bruce's pose and the other women back away knowing they don't want to get hit those heel chucks. This one woman with no silicone in her chest but has long nails cut the scarf in two leaving the taller woman holding two pieces of scarf tied her shoes. She starts using the shoes to beat that woman like a drummer at a concert doing a solo set. Hutch broke it up and told them both they can dance with him if they call a truce, the scent over powered both women and they agreed to share. Hutch asked the taller woman her name first and she told him "Genova!" as she kissed him for asking her first. Looking at the other one and asking her name she told him "Shanice!" and she too kissed him. The rest of the time there they danced together as everyone else found a partner to dance with till it was time to close the club, the other G.D.M.4.L gotten dates to come with them to the diner for breakfast too. When they got to the diner and took up a lot of tables and had two waitresses working hard to get their food and drinks or coffee for some more beer and wine for the others. When the bill came again the guys would look at it, sending it around the table letting everyone get a look at how much it came to and said "Eldest". All the women wonder what they were talking about with this eldest word till got pass to Hutch. He goes in his pocket and pulls out his wallet and one of the women makes a comment "Why are they all letting him pay for everything there". Hutch laughs and says to her "I'm eldest and they all take turns paying for everything once a week, that way they can treat their dates special later." All the women went "Aww" Hutch looked at the bill and stood up angry asking "Who ordered the Damn cheese cake! They know how I feel about that!" The women looked at Hutch and starts wondering if he was going to start a fight about the bill. The guys laughed explaining to each woman Hutch has a thing for cheese cake and only wants Juniors Cheese cake, so now he's got to go and stop by Junior's to get some it's his personal crack. Long as he doesn't see it, hear it or pay for it he won't have to go and get some just to please his crave but when we're out everyone knows not to buy or order cheese cake. He once ballooned up to 327lbs on it wasn't pretty either he had to have a piece every day before work and two maybe three piece after with cream.

Hutch excused his outburst and told the waitresses to put two hundred on the bill for each of them as all the women looked at Hutch thinking "Wow" one of the waitresses asked him "What was his wife going to think spending that kind of money on breakfast!" Hutch laughed "I'm not married!" They made a comment about his woman getting mad, again he laughed at what they said. "I don't have to worry about one either" The waitress says "Good looking big man like you not married or hooked up with anyone. Why are you a playa or gay?" Mack heard what she was asked and told them "He works too hard and most women see that as a chance to cash in on his hard work, that's why we protect our older brother" Dave looks at them adding "My big brother has a good heart and as wild as he is with a gentle kind soul, we don't want any silly female playing with his feelings like that for cash!" The waitresses took his Credit card and saw what it read, they cheered at the big tip he gave them after they saw it and came back to the table as everyone was getting up to leave. They kissed him thanking him for such a tip and all he could say is "You've worked hard for it and I want to show my gratitude for it!" They leave and some of the G.D.M.4.L head to Hutch's house again and this time Hutch isn't alone, he's got both Genova and Shanice in his vehicle planning on what they're going to do him once they get to his house. On the way there Genova cell phone starts to ring and ring and both Hutch and Shanice look at her wondering if she was going answer it. When she does it's her man mad on the other end wondering where she is because he's on his way home and she better be there when he gets there. Over hearing all that yelling he was doing, Hutch offers to drop her home not wanting to fight over a woman that's another man's property. It was on the way he says, dropping her home and she gave him her number saying in case she ever leaves him give her a call. Hutch told her from the looks of her he's not going to do that and drives off. Shanice starts talking how some females are phony with theirs and have the nerve to have a man, wanting to get with another man but then her cell phone rang after bad mouthing women for a few minutes. At first she giggles a little looking at Hutch and they both looked at her purse as the cell ring tone played in the back ground of her man singing lil Wayne's (Lick you like a Lolly pop) Hutch looked at her and back at her purse then at her again and said "Well charms or is it Tutsi or blow pop. You going to answer it and do I have to drop you a block away from your door too". She laughs "You silly" The curse words overheard made him stop and let her out to take her call outside his vehicle, after a couple of "Please baby I'm on my way I'm in a cab now". Hutch lets her back in and drops her off at the corner of her block and watches as she runs to her door in those heels looking like she was going to fall over any second. Hutch looks at her wave bye to him and head in her building and he drives off then a commercial comes over the radio "Does your man have problem getting it up or doesn't feel like the man he used to be, that's cause erectile dysfunction is common in men over forty and in black men they have a good chance of it becoming more estuarine as they get older". The commercial goes on to talk about a pill men can take to boost their testosterone but Hutch turns down the radio talking back to the man on the radio advertisement saying "This is what your Ads should be asking women! Does your man ask you for the lip gloss before going out to hang with his boys with their pants down around their butts". "Or ever notice your man giggles before and after he laughs ending with a sigh of a woman and the smacking of his lips!" "How about your man singing, Lay your head on my pillow, in that high pitch woman's voice note for note or yodeling". "Having argument with him and his voice goes in a higher pitch than yours saying he's sensitive too". "Ladies ever notice your man wearing baggy boxers under his skinny jeans with that tight jacket on or how about those baggy sweat suit pants still showing his under wear but has that tight sweat jacket on".

"Be honest ladies, he hangs with other baggy pant men at parties in the dark and only dances with other guys hum makes you wonder if you don't see the sign!" "See women you can tell your skinny man that eats everything but gains no weight because food runs out of his body because his boy is secretly running up in him, making it easy for food to just drop out his ass!" "The quick easy access of him having his pants down around his butt allows his man he's getting banged by, uh hanging out with (yeah right)." "To cover their actions they have to get with every young woman they see to keep up appearances". Tired of hearing the joke told by all older men and some women about men wearing baggy pants, why does young men wearing skinny jeans on don't ever have to chase young women any more like their crazy and desperate (because he already got in her jeans and wears them better than she wears them!) or D.L Hugely changed his name to just Hugely so he's not associated with all those Down Low young men who wear their pants down around their butts liking that thug love they get from another man, notice him arguing with you at your time of the month. (Keenan said it best "MEASSAGE!!!!") Ladies you need to leave that man/woman alone or give him that man's pill to boost his testosterone, because every time you argue his voice goes up a few octaves making you look at him thinking he sound more like you or one of your girlfriend when he screams at you "So Whatever!" Hutch can't continue because he starts laughing at what he was talking about and drive on to get home. LADIES! "MESSAGE!! Again!"

Monday the alarm clock is going off and Hutch wakes to find himself sore and wrapped up in the covers with the body pillow again, struggling to get out of the covers so he can take a shower and get ready for he talks to the body pillow "From now on when I get a drunk work out and come to bed you have to get your own bed to sleep in because we can't keep this up anymore" after checking for holes in the body pillow and taken his shower then dressed for work he leaves out after he made up his bed and took the body pillow to another room. Stopping to get his breakfast sandwich after going to the garage and got his work orders for that day, he gets assigned to the same building again in Manhattan where Moni is the supervisor of the work crew coming there to do the demolition on the floors they have to clean out. Being there early Hutch eats his food and watches the women going to work dressed so nicely so he turns up the radio listening to the morning show of Doug Banks and how bitter brother is going on doing his part the word of the day which has everyone in ear shot laughing at how funny it sounds. The van pulls up and parks right in front of Hutch's truck, so he gets out and put on his coveralls to work in as Moni gets out the van and looks at Hutch getting into his coveralls. He just had to make a comment about why Hutch cut the sleeves out of his coveralls jealous how big Hutch's arm are to his. Paying him no mind like he does anyway Moni has to say something about him trying to get under his skin, since he gotten beat up by that old woman on Friday. He's been more annoying and persistent to make every one of the workers' pay for not helping him especially Hutch. Who had jokes about the whole thing trying to sell tickets to him for Smack Down wrestling show saying "He might learn how to fight or at least know how to take a good beating and get paid for it." Moni assigned who will be working on what floor and who would be bring down the containers to the truck and that morning thing were going steady for a good while then things slowed down. Hutch took the opportunity to go in the building again to see what kind of place this was and how come it has so many rooms with experiments going on in them. He was about to borrow one of the crews badge but remembering he got one of his own from the lab coat he found the other day, using it to get pass the guard to explore more floors in the building. Taken the elevator down and getting off on the second sub level the floor he sees this door marked hard ware and goes in looking at a lot of the gadgets on the tables and takes a pair of binoculars that look very interesting. Going around and looking at other things there, one of the lab techs came in as Hutch ducked out another door not to be caught by him but the lab tech knew some was just in there and saw the binoculars he was working on missing. He goes looking around for anyone that would have them not seeing Hutch get on the elevator with them but heard the elevator bell ding as the doors opens and closed. He goes to see who's at the elevator and gets there too late, pressing the button thinking he could catch the person if they just left. Outside by the truck Moni is standing looking for Hutch as he comes out of the building and hears him start that familiar rant about where and how come he always coming out of the buildings they work at and what's he looking for more things to take home. Going on about Hutch in the buildings and how he needs to be by his truck in case something goes wrong with it because he would be the only one to fix what's wrong with it. Then looking down seeing something in his hands and wants to know what it is. Hutch held it up and saw how Moni just looked at it so he looks through them and saw they were some special kind of binoculars that could see through clothes and starts looking at all the women walking around seeing them without their clothes on but he could hear how Moni still wouldn't let go of his trying to get on Hutch about his not being by his truck. Telling Moni if he gave him those binoculars would he just shut the hell up about everything because he's tired of his mouth, Moni held out is hands with that I got over on you smile on his face. When he gave it to him after putting white out on bottom half of the rubber part he's got to looks through, handing it over to Moni as he starts looking through them and heard Hutch tell him push that little switch there. Now he could see under the clothes of women and pointed it out where he could use it, figuring that would keep him distracted enough then heard someone asking the security guard "Did anyone come out of there with a pair of binocular?" The guard told him no but points to Hutch as he stood by the front door. When Hutch heard that he knew Moni would be distracted enough as Hutch walks over to the man in the lab coat. He asked Hutch the same question about the binoculars. Acting innocent like he didn't want to tell what he saw but comments about that little man outside side in front of the building that is looking through a pair. Asking the man not to say he heard it from him then says "I've got to use the bathroom" The man thanked Hutch and told him "Don't worry I won't say anything about the tip!" and heads out to the front of the building. Moni is looking at all the women he could see making comments about them loudly as the man in the lab coat walks up in front of him and he could see the man had on women's guarder belts and black stocking under his lab coat. Moni say "What the freak!" He snatches the binoculars right out of his hand about to yell at Moni but stops first to look at him with those white lines around his eyes. Moni wanted to know what was he doing because those are his but when the man in the lab coat says "These are the property of the government and could have you up on charges for stealing them from the building" Not give Moni a chance to tell his side about how he got them but getting reprimanded hard. When the man was finish scolding out Moni and went back in the building, he just knew Hutch set him up and was very mad about it going looking for him. Irate he gets on the elevator going up to the floor their working on looking for Hutch but there was no sign of him anywhere on the floors. Taking the elevator back down to the ground floor walking through the lobby noticing the men's room sign thinking he's always going in there and should find him there. Now even madder than before Hutch would come in the building to hide from him in the bathroom after setting him up like that, Moni's about to go in the bathroom and sees the fire extinguisher taking it off the wall. Going in the bathroom and once inside he stands there just listening as he hears a little chuckling coming from the only stall with the door closed, so he walks down to the stall and stands right where he hears the noise coming from. Without saying a word he kicks in the door (Boom!) and squirts the extinguisher in the stall all over the person in the stall then shouts "Ha! How you like that shit!" The mist clears he sees it was the big security guard standing there with a paper in his hands mad at what just happened. Moni looks at him as he yells "What the hell!" Moni looks at him holding the fire extinguisher asking "What are you doing in there?" Then looks at the big man going "Wow I thought you be bigger, is it because of the cold oh I see you have small feet!" The guard drops the paper and bent over to pull up his pants and charge at Moni who eyes got wide and sprays the guard again blinding him on purpose this time from fear of what he was going to do to him and covering his escape with that fog of CO2. The mist clears and the guard yells "I'm going to kick your shit colored ass all over the building with my small feet you dead man walking!" Moni came out of the bathroom heading towards the elevator and saw Hutch just coming off the car and he yells for him to "Hold the door." Hutch saw the fire extinguisher in Moni's hands but turns hearing the big guard covered in white power looking mad for some reason yelling "Where did he go!" It didn't take long for Hutch to get what happened holding the button to the elevator door and pointing at it. The guard runs in the elevator as Moni was pushing the button wondering why the door wasn't closing till the guard got on and then it closed with him screaming "Wait! Wait". The elevator goes up and Hutch heard screaming and a lot of bumping, he smiles and goes back out to his truck to finish loading it so he could go dump it then get back. Just about loaded the workers got radioed "There was one more container coming out it's being pushed by the security guard" It had Moni on top of the garbage in the containers out cold covered in white powder but it didn't look like he was knocked out because of the white circles around his eyes. The guard gave Hutch a fist dap "Good looking out with the elevator" and went back inside. Hutch and the workers are laughing taking pictures as he woke Moni up helping him out of the container then leaves for the dump. Moni in pain watches Hutch leave for the dump laughing about him. Going back in the building passing the security guard who stares and growls at Moni as he hold his head down passing by quick to go back up to the floors their working on blaming Hutch for everything that happened to him. While he was gone Moni came up with an idea to prank Hutch and get even when he gets back and comes in the building again. Coming across these big cans of goo and thinking of rigging it up to his trucks door so when he opens it the can will pour all over his head, a plan that he knows will work if he let Hutch go in the building for long as he wants so it could give him time to rig it.

Back from dumping the truck waiting to pull in the parking spots they have ready for the truck to load in front of the building, Hutch's truck was the last in line because Moni had to rig his prank and needs time to do it plus not have any of the other drivers see him do it. Things slowed down and Moni knew he'll want to go in the building, watching Hutch goes in the building like he was doing earlier. Moni goes over to his truck to hurry and rig his prank on Hutch before he's seen by any of the drivers. Hutch on the third floor already sees a sign on the door "Misc. supply room" and he goes in it, looking around he sees a lot of things they're going to throw out for garbage. One of the work crew that doesn't like Moni sees him trying to rig something on Hutch's truck that would pour out on him when he opens the door. Hutch gets told about it and thanks him and looks around the room seeing a few things he'll need and takes this inflatable raft, some white powder, duct glue tape and some nails with this grease can laying around plus some balloons and gets busy rigging his own contraption up for Moni.

Putting everything by the door he goes and looks for a container to put them in. Finding one he loads it with the stuff and heads out the building making sure Moni is busy trying to rig his truck up and doesn't see him heading towards the van they came there in passing the drivers smiling at them as he went by. Looking up the block where Moni is, Hutch puts the container in front of the van so it can't be seen and get to work quickly rigging the van up then getting back before he's seen by Moni.

The work day is over and time to head home Moni was outside when Hutch finished loading his truck and heads towards the door, noticing the wire Moni got rigged up so when he stood right at the door all Moni has to do is pull on it and those cans of stuff will pour out on to his head covering him in the stuff. Standing on the wire so it doesn't pull taking out his pocket knife cutting the wire taking the cans off his truck putting them in the container he looks at Moni and gives him a wink smiling "Nice try" getting in his truck driving away but turns the corner parking with his engine still running. Mad it didn't work Moni goes to the van and gets in slamming the door shut activating the inflatable raft which starts to blow up on the driver's side of the van. Reaching for the handle which comes off in his hands, he looks at it trying to put it back on but the grease on the handle makes it hard to hold steady. The van is filling fast with this bright yellow raft as people walk by seeing Moni fighting with it coming on his side of the parked van, but it's no use the raft keeps growing bigger filling the van. Looking around he then notices the nails just above his head and tries to pull them out, the way they're positioned with the points down wards like that. The grease on them makes it hard for him to pull them out and he's running out of space being pushed to one side by the raft. All he could do is look back at all the people now looking at him squeezed against the door and window looking up at the nails, letting out a yell "AHRR!" The raft fills the van then popping making a muffled "Boom!" Shaking the whole van, inside is nothing but white as people stand around there looking with all the workers wondering is he OK. The door somehow opens up and Moni steps from the van covered in white powder, even coughs out white powder then looking back at the people just looking at him covered in white powder. Hutch looking around the corner saw what happened and starts laughing then disappears back around it but not before he's spotted by Moni. Moni yells "YOU MUTHA FLOWER SOOKA!" He runs to the back of the van first then starts after Hutch leaving a white trail of foot prints and mist running to catch Hutch a few blocks away still driving. Hutch is laughing at what he did to Moni when he heard cars beeping their horns behind him and looks in the mirror to see Moni running in traffic to catch up leaving his misty trail behind him. Laughing at Moni running to catch his truck but when Hutch did a double take look in his mirror, he sees Moni got half a block away and noticed had a sledge Hammer in his hands over his head with this mad look on his face gritting his teeth getting closer and closer. Shifting gears as the light turned green knowing he can't catch him, Hutch smiles at Moni and drives towards the Manhattan Bridge that leads to the BQE expressway so he can get to the garage and not be there when Moni pulls up. Beginning of Sixth Avenue Moni stands there with a sledge hammer in his hands till the cop car pulls up next to him still covered in white making a comment to him "That's no way to make flatbread". Moni stand there for a moment staring forward with the hammer as the cop looks at him slowly turn his head towards him with a wild mad look in his eyes. Just then the cop eyes got wide realizing Moni was going to use that hammer on him. People watched in amazement and others video for U-tube as this little man with a big sledge hammer went to work on that squad car smashing it up. Moving so quick not giving the two big fat white cops inside of it a chance to even get out of the car as he hammers the car in rage they made fun of him. Leaving the car looking like it was in smash up derby as other cars go by looking and laughing at the cops now stuck inside as Moni walks back to the building with the hammer. The driver cop says "How we're going to explain a white powder little shit colored man with sledge hammer bigger then he is did all this damage".

Moni gets back carrying the hammer over his shoulder and goes to the back to open it up to wash off some of the powder still on him, but as he opens the doors which triggers another surprise as water balloons (4 of them) drop one by one on his head breaking open soaking his head and down. Moni stands there with all the workers looking at him not saying a word because he still holds that hammer, leaning back letting out a war cry the whole city must have heard. Dropping the hammer grabbing a towel telling the workers they have to leave before another of Hutch's trap spring on him.

Hutch parked his truck and was almost home when he gets a call from Mack saying "There at the Sea witch having a drink before going home so come through!" Fifteen minutes later Hutch is walking through the door meeting his brothers telling them good thing they called he was about to head straight home, they have a glass of beer waiting for him as he sat. About to drink their sixth round of beers when the door opens and in walks the first of three women. 2Soon, Dougie and Hutch sitting at the table without a woman by their sides unlike Mack and Goodie, LiL-Rob plus Jazz all have dates. Looking at the women walk right to the bar and took a seat. Dougie went to the bar to get another round of beers for everyone that was laughing having a good time, Sonia sitting at the bar next to him and he starts talking to her and breaks the ice as she told him "You guys look like you are having fun!" Dougie invites her and her two friends to join them because there's room for three more. Telling him she'll ask her friends and sure they'll be willing to join him and his friends seeing the fun their having, she leans over to her to them with Dougie shaking his head agreeing to join them. All four of the walk back to the table where the GDM4L brothers are sitting, Dougie made the introductions of Milaya who sat next to 2Soon and Sonia took the chair next to him since they talked first. Last was Elise that Hutch gave up his seat too excusing himself then walking out the bar to go in his ride. Everyone looked as he left out the bar, Jazz makes a joke about how fine she is that she scared him off and wonders if that happens a lot, she smile and laughed with everyone not knowing what to say about that comment. Hutch was out at his ride putting on a little cologne thinking he just came straight from work and didn't want to smell bad since he had been sweating a bit from work and now drinking. Walking back in the bar to everyone having a good joke and laugh about him being scared off by this woman. She looks at him and told him she don't bite and he could have his seat back and she'll take another chair somewhere else but Hutch told her stay there and grabs a chair and sat down next to her and introduced himself and asked her name again.

The rest of the time there they was laughing and joking about things and Hutch told his story about what happened to Moni and the women describing that big old woman and how she moved on him that had everyone laughing hard as he went on about her giving Moni his ass beating wrestling style. Mack and 2Soon had their own jokes about it which had everyone laughing even more and Elise was getting more and more of the scent Hutch had on, she already started to like him once everything got settled at the table but seeing how funny and generous he was because he would keep going to buy the drinks not giving anyone a chance to get up and pay for a round. The cologne was affecting her real good as she was giving him such seductive looks as he was still joking about the job and Moni.

It was getting late and everyone had to work the next day some earlier than others and not that everyone was nice and tipsy and still laughing about what Hutch told them it was time to go. 2Soon and Milaya had exchanged digits like Sonia and Dougie but everyone was shocked at how Hutch and Elise was kissing at the table like long time lovers, Sonia says "Damn! Girl we just meet them!" They stopped looking at everyone as if they just appeared out of thin air. Hutch just smiled like a school boy who had his first kiss and Elise told him "They better get ready to go" and grabs his cell and calls her number. Milaya went "Guess there's a 2nd meeting of you two in the future huh". Walking out to the vehicle and saw Hutch's big blue expedition behind 2Soons' green Navi right behind Mack's black Land rover across from Jazz's blue and gold Escalade and LIL-Robs white Lexus Jeep, behind Dougie's silver Altima. The women talked about how they look like good hard working men and could see why their brothers. Elise was driving a red burgundy Explorer as Milaya and Sonia got in waving bye to the guys and they drove off, it wasn't long after they left the fellas still outside they started talking about Hutch and Elise. Asking did he know her before they walked in the bar because they never saw him act like that with any other woman. Hutch couldn't explain it but just told them she's nice. 2Soon agreed going she was looking at him when he was talking about the job and Moni and Mack added "Yeah she wasn't hiding that you had her in a trance" even the girls with the other GDM4L said there something different about Hutch. When he was telling jokes he looks different like how he dances with confidence it gets every females attention. All the GDM4L and Hutch looked at LiL-Rob's girl for moment not saying a word then looked at each other all going "Nah". That was the cue for everyone to get in their vehicles and go home. Hutch is walking in his door when his cell rings, its Elise asking him "Are you thinking about me and where do you live". Elise was driving like a mad woman hurrying to drop off Milaya then Sonia not even giving them a chance to get fully out of her vehicle and say bye as she pulls off leaving them wondering what was wrong with her. Hutch gave her his address and direction to get there and a shortly just as he was getting out of the shower and dressed for bed his doorbell rang. It's Elise and she was wearing a trench coat with her hair up still having that seductive look on her face as she asked him was he going to invite her in. He invites her in and watches as she walks pass him with that sway women have when they want a man to just look at them. She asked him "What is in the glass on the table?" He told her something to help him sleep (Drambuie, Gin, Vodka, Myers Rum for color, shot of over proof for kick, Brandy, Cognac with lemon juice and pineapple soda with little of Pepsi topped with lime slices) she took a sip and went "WOW! This is strong and taste so good got anymore" He told her he made a few bottles for company when they want something different. She took that in his glass and gulps it and what little left she pours down the front of her then opens her trench coat slowly showing that sexy teddy with lace she had on. All his mouth could do was drop open at the sight of her 5' 5" frame so slim about 124lbs. blinking his eyes at how sexy and beautiful she looked standing in his house. She saw the remote to the Cd player and turns it on to hear Silk "Freak me" She motions for him to join her in a dance and they dance for a couple of songs then kiss like they did at the table in the bar and break with him looking at her intensely then carrying her up to his bedroom. The whole house is quite except for her moans of pleasure that get louder and louder but then she says "Why are you stopping" She wants more and he can't leave her wanting it so badly, he looks at her and tells her "Alright one more". Then he's done but don't want her hooked he needs his strength for work. He takes her foot and rubs it with the oil then cracking her toes so loud she moans "Oh yeah baby". When he does her other foot with each toe and the rest of the foot she moans loud "Oh Damn baby Yes!"

Every time he cracked a part of her foot and moved to her lower back she was now calling his name "Oh Yes Hutch baby right there! Harder baby! Pop it! Damn get it yeah get it!" This went on for a couple hours as the window to his bedroom was open and her voice carried on the wind to other houses in the distance. Down the hill in some of the houses women heard what was going on in Hutch's bedroom as the noise carried down to their bedroom windows. One woman listening for a while got mad looking at her husband, slamming in a clip to the Glock nine clicking back the chamber loading a bullet in it. Mad she's not having any like what she's hearing, holding the gun up thinking about shoot him for lack of sex hearing all the noise for a while coming through her window. Another woman sat in bed sharping her Crocodile Dundee knife on a stone as her husband slept giving him such a nasty sneer like Conan the barbarian. Another woman in bed next to her man was shaking the Viagra bottle then pouring them out and counting them wondering why the bottle was still full as she looked at her sleeping husband. Another bedroom where a woman just had sex with her partner was listening and writing down how long the sound she was hearing had gone on for compared to the short time she just had with her partner looking at the fire & ice condom wrapper on the dresser making a note he needs Viagra and red bull too. A lot of women were at their windows wondering where that noise was coming from and who was getting it like that.

Its Monday 4:30 in the morning and Hutch gets up to go in the other room to wake Elise up so he can get ready for work and thought she might want to shower there or get a jump on the traffic, so she can get home and dress before she has to get going for work herself. She wakes with such a smile on her face saying "I never felt a man do that to me before wow" She goes to kiss him but he turns to give her his cheek batting his eyes then says "You are beautiful but that dragon no matter how good you look come to visit everyone during the night". Handing her the mouth wash going "Don't be stingy I shop at Costco" Holding her hand to her mouth and breaths in it "Wow!". Her breath fresh like his now she kisses him and told him "Glad to see you are one of those men that don't have to be told about your goat breath in the morning that make women's eyes burn and roll up" Telling her he'll call her later as they both leave his house. She heads home and he's on his way to the garage to clean his truck and get something to eat afterwards. Hutch first one at the garage like always had finished washing and wiping down his truck and built up a little sweat doing so, coming across two of the little silver capped bottles of cologne he got from the building thinking it must have fell out of his bag in the truck. Going in the bathroom using some on himself before anyone came in thinking "Why not smell good for work today". Meepbo gets there and saw Hutch by his tuck and told him he'll be going back to the building but then Meepbo's daughters got out of his vehicle as he opens the office part of the garage telling Hutch "They're going to have to learn the business sooner or later so why not now" Hutch is a little pumped from the exercise of washing and drying his truck as they look at his arms and shoulders but that cologne hits their noses as they got close to him. Being hot from the work of washing his truck the cologne has an immediate affect when they go to shake his hand hello. Each one had a hello in a seductive way as they looked him up and down like a piece meat to be eaten right there licking their lips staring at him. Hutch didn't catch it as he shook their hands and got in his truck thinking they're too pretty and have nice bodies to get dirty in this business as he drove away.

At the sandwich shop where he gets his breakfast, three eggs and double turkey bacon and beef sausage sandwich with grapefruit juice. He runs into his old time friend and fellow truck driver Gerard as he was telling some other guys about the woman he saw the other night with a body that makes any man go after her with everything he's got. Hutch walks up behind Gerard as he describes this woman to the other drivers there talking about what would they do with such a woman. Hutch made his comment about that's everyman's fantasy having sex with the finest woman or having two or three but if you come of your pocket to find out she's cheating with the next man who can stay a while longer in the hole. Adding there's more to keeping a woman than just sex. A man comes in selling cologne for a high price even though he tells them it fell off the truck, so Gerard was going to get a bottle but Hutch told him he's got something better smelling he could have and went to his vehicle to get it. Coming back with one of the silver capped bottles he got from the building telling him he use it and it's better and last longer than any other cologne he ever had, so Gerard smells the cologne liking what he smelled wanting to know the name of the stuff. Hutch told him "Get some! It's new and to keep the bottle just don't take a bath in it like some of those people that don't wash using cologne to cover their body funk". (Talking to the reader "YOU KNOW WHO THEY ARE, MIGHT BE NEXT TO ONE right now") Leaving the sandwich shop and heading to Manhattan so he could enjoy his food before Moni the crew showed up, once at the building he parks the truck and turns up the morning show so everyone walking by could hear it. Done eating his food and getting out the truck to stretch he sees another friend of his coming his way all dressed up in a suit and tie but looking like he was in a rush. Hutch calls his name "Gary! Where you going to in such a rush man" He told Hutch he wanted to get to an interview before anyone else got there but didn't have enough to take the train so he left the house earlier and walked from Brooklyn. Hutch told him he got to be an hour or two early plus he looked good but might be giving off a little odor from walking like that, going into his truck and comes back out with that another sliver capped bottles of cologne. Gary was reluctant to use it till Hutch used more on himself, Gary liked what it smelled like on Hutch and knew it had to be good. Asking the name of it so he can get a bottle of his own but Hutch told him the name is called "Get lucky! and if you use it right you'll will be" Going in his pocket and give Gary Three hundred dollars saying "When you gets the job you'll need to go to lunch" and he could have his friend looking hungry while everyone else is eating their food. Gary proud didn't want to take the money from Hutch but knew he is right and wouldn't have it any other way. He told him he'll pay him back with his first check. Hutch told him take your son to dinner and buy him something for his uncle Hutch, with glassy eyes look and big hug from his friend Gary told him "Now I know I'm going to get this job man". Hutch said "A new woman too cause you smell so good you might be banging the boss on her desk if the secretary don't want join in on you two". Gary laughed at what he said telling him "You crazy man" and again hugs his friend saying "I can get breakfast and take the train home now too but I'll let you know how it turns out bruh" Gary turns the corner going to breakfast as Moni and the crew pulls up in front of the building. Hutch looks at the van rolling his eyes then goes to get his coveralls to put on so they can get busy with their work.

Gerard at work in another part of Manhattan he'd used the cologne before doing any work then goes in the building after working up a sweat to let the people know he got started and wanted to know if there was any more stuff to be thrown out in the garbage before he moved on. In the elevator he was sweating from the work he just did and two women just gotten on from the office on 2nd floor.

These two beautiful looking white women were talking to each other then start to smell the cologne coming from Gerard standing in back of them. One kept talking but backing up little by little till she rubbing against him and grabbing herself as well, the other one just couldn't take it and grabs him kissing him but the other one didn't want to be left out either getting her kisses too. Grabbing Gerard by his clothes and wants to take them off right there in the elevator going up but then gave each other a look saying "Conference room on the 14th floor" at the same time. The red head woman said "It's empty till 11:30am that's when the meeting is scheduled and it's only 8:30 am now" They head up there with Gerard and once inside the put the do not disturb sign on the outside of the door and lock it from the inside. Not knowing what to do as these two women strip him naked and go at him like there was no tomorrow, Gerard had the biggest smile on his face and didn't put up a fight to resist thinking he had to be dreaming but went along with it saying aloud "I'm not going to waste this dream".

11:15 and they're dressed sneaking out before anyone sees them going to the elevator, giving Gerard their cell numbers telling him he better call or they will find him as they go back to work. In the conference room people are walking in the room to have their meeting and smelling something as the boss sat down sniffing a couple time looking at everyone "This room smells like ass and good cologne" When no one said anything to answer him he adds "Who ever got some they could have sprayed but it smell like he tore that ass up so I'm going to let it slide this time!" The older women in the meeting whispering to each other "Some lucky woman got hers". Since there were more women older than younger men at this meeting and they were feeling the effects of the cologne mixed with heat plus sex in the air strong in that room. Giving each other a look as one went to lock the door after putting the do not disturb sign on the outside of it, the men wanted to know why they smiled and had that look in their eyes standing there for a moment before pouncing on all of the men shocked by the women actions. Outside the conference room some men are heard saying "Why are they stripping? Whoa Ms. Brickley where did you get that from and what are going to do with that thing?" (A crack of a whip is snapped!)

In another part of Manhattan Gary was sitting outside the office nervous and sweating a little since he heard the woman interviewer kick out the last two men in a nasty way, he was next in line for the job. The secretary called his name and sent him in the office where the woman boss was sitting behind her desk with her back to him as he came in to her office. Telling him to have a seat as she was going over his application still not turning around but starts to lightly smell the cologne he was wearing. She had a mean look on her face turning around but changed it looking at Gary thinking he is cute as she held his application paper in her hands then her facial expression turned seductive. Asking him his name again and moves closer to him sitting on her desk facing him opening her legs showing her skirt dark tunnel. Telling Gary she's got a test to see if he's the right man for this job asking him to "Stand up and come close to me". The closer he got the stronger the smell of the cologne was, making her have him stand right in front of her asking "Can you pass and physical before getting the job". Gray said "I can pass anything you have because I don't take any drugs or smoke plus I'm in great shape" She looks him up and down then leaning back clicking on the intercom telling the secretary she's going to have a personal interview with this one and to hold all her calls. She Lean up after giving him a good look at her on her back in that position on the desk, Gary for moment stood in front of her looking then licked her lips at him.

The noise coming from the office had all the rest of the applicants looking at each other wondering what's going on in there, then heard some grunting and the boss lady saying "Come on big boy that all you got". The secretary walks in the office and sees legs sticking up from behind her desk and grunting still going on as she clears her throat about to walks over to see the boss getting it from Gary. The smell of his cologne and sex went right to her head before she even got to look at what's going on, over the intercom the other applicants heard her saying "You all can go home the position is being filled now, we found someone to get the work done". Then she strips her clothes off and locks the door to the office walking back over saying "I know how to take Dictation too". Later on that morning right before lunch Hutch had left to go and dump his truck since it was loaded. Gray came back around where he was working to tell Hutch what happened to him but he wasn't there, so he left a message with Moni for Hutch when he gets back.

Gerard was walking out of the building back to his truck with that smell still emanating from his body every woman he walked by stopped and looked at him telling him he smells so good they could just eat him up. Thinking today is his day and his friend Hutch told him that it would happen just then the red haired woman came out of the building telling him she gets off at 4pm and wants to follow him to drop off that truck so they can have dinner and dessert.

Hutch got back from dumping the truck thinking to himself as he got out his truck where was his friend Gerard he didn't see him at the lunch truck or at the dump site. Moni breaks his thought coming over to Hutch telling him about Gary screwing up the message he was to give him. Letting Hutch know some man named Gary was talking about not being along anymore, he got the job thanks for loan and advice since he dug out two dimes going home to change. Something else Moni couldn't and didn't want to remember for Hutch. When he said Gary got the job Hutch didn't care what Moni said after that because he knew he would see him later anyways. Thanking Moni for his attempt to give him the message Hutch goes back to wait for the trucks to move up so he and the other truck can get into position. Looking at the trucks and thinking they're going to be a bit longer before they have to go dump he goes back into the building again and using that badge he got. Going back down into the sub level parts of the building to see what else he could find while down there. On the same level again where he got those little bottles of cologne from and going back in the room where they are and seeing there's still some left out on the counter he walks over to them and looks around making sure no one is coming and takes a few more of silver ones and just one of each of the gold and black capped ones there too. The closing of a door he heard and voices talking from the hallway makes him leave out of that room so he doesn't get caught and heads back out to the truck to stash the bottles he got. Not seeing Moni around Hutch heads to his truck and once inside he was putting the bottles in his bag but Moni jumps on the side of the truck sticking his head in the open window real fast "What you got there!" Surprised reacting with movement Hutch punched him back out the window and off the truck. Realizing he just knocked out Moni looking at him laid there on the ground, getting out of his truck going to wake him up to apologize but everyone saw him go flying off the truck and a fist sticking out of the window. They are holding up point card with 9.8, 9.9 10.0 approving what he done and some clapping that's what he deserves for sneaking up on you sitting in your truck. Hutch felt real bad because he didn't want to hit the little man even though so many time thinking about it but knew if he ever did, it would break something in his body and wasn't worth going jail for. Moni was sitting up and asking what happened so Hutch told him "Hit your head on the truck trying to stick it in my window man be careful!". Looking at the guys helping Moni to his feet as Hutch shrugging his shoulders at them for what he did. They were doing their best not to laugh keeping quiet about the punch off the truck. Hutch told Moni they need to squash the bad things going on the job, since its three day weekend why don't he come to the club and meet some of his friend and hang out with him having a few drinks and meet some women there.

Hutch knew he had to try and get on Moni good side for the sake of keeping his job if he ever found out about him punching Moni off his truck even though he did it accidently. Sitting up holding his head and jaw and thought it was some kind of trick Hutch wanted to pull on him. He agrees to what Hutch said about them going out and having a drink at the club and meeting some of his friends. Hutch wrote down the name of the "Gator club and the address to get there". Helping Moni to his feet and telling him wait there going into his truck and coming back with another gold capped bottle of cologne he got from down in the building and telling him to use this when he comes out that weekend because he's got to smell good when he meets the ladies. They go back to work when Kiamesha walks up the block wearing jeans that fit so good they looked like a second skin on her with boots that match her Giants Jersey (# 53 Harry Carson) which is just as tight on her showing she's has good padding in front, she walks right up to Hutch and everyone outside and around her watched her walk with the sway till she get right in front of him and stops. She moves close to him as he stood there looking at her thinking "Wow" she looks so hot and amazing as she took her foot and put it by his ear on the wall behind him pressing her body on his as he stood with his back against the wall. She reaches in her boot and pulls out some photos from it and hands them to him. All the men outside that saw this either stop walking by or at work watching holding their brief cases or hard hats in front of them as she was doing this to Hutch. Kiamesha takes her leg down off the wall and backs into him saying "These I took while waiting for you to call me and those are the friend I called when I got bored and wanted company waiting for you to call me!". Pictures of her in spandex her legs behind her head and some of her doing a naked side to side split, the others are of her with a another female with their legs in the air and banana between them and both in pretzel formation legs behind their heads. Hutch mouth opened staring at those pictures asking her "is that a pickle" in one of the photos. She answers with a passionate kiss to him and turns around backing up against him arching her back reaching for the back of his neck pulling his head down to her shoulder and says to him in the most sensuous way "Ah shuga you were supposed to be the pickle baby!" Everyman around watching them is weak in the knees seeing her wiggle on him and says "See feels like a pickle now!" Walking away having the workers and men around watch her as they bite their fists looking at her. After she turns the corner the worker and men watching close their eyes and shudder wondering if they had a chance at her, the workers and men look back at Hutch there with his hands in his pockets bent over slightly asking "What you all looking at" fanning himself saying "I need a cold drink" walking to the front of his truck, putting the cold can in coveralls with a sigh of relief hoping no one saw what he did with the can. Time to go home for the day Hutch helps the crew to clean up outside the building so they all can leave at the same time. When they get to the garage Moni asked Hutch was he for real about hanging out with him and going to the club. Hutch told him "yes" he was serious and there might be a special lady waiting to see his kiss ass self so he could kiss her ass in steady of the bosses, though the boss might get jealous of the new ass he is kissing being female and all.

Moni told him go ahead with that kiss ass stuff, he don't do that. Every worker there stopped what they were doing and looked at Moni as to say "Really! He just didn't say that!" Moni turns to look back at them asking them all "Do I really do that" They all said together "YES!" Hutch laughed and got in his vehicle saying "You have some issues to talk about with your crew see you". Leaving the garage and heading straight home and once there like he always does empty his pockets on the dresser and go take a shower then head to the kitchen to make something to eat so he could watch the

Animal planet followed by worlds most Dumbest or Shocking then go to bed.

Wednesday morning 4:30 he's up in the shower and dressed shortly afterwards looking at his stomach and sees the hard work he's doing is paying off by getting thinner. He put on a black tee shirt just a bit snug. Lifting it up and spraying a good dose of that silver cologne on himself then heads to the garage and take the bottle with just a quarter of the stuff left in it to use on himself in case he sweat too much. The sun is not fully shining yet and it's already hot and muggy. At the garage washing his truck sweating from the work, he sees Meepbo pull up with wife Toni in the front seat and daughters Sheila, Lorie and Carmella gets out behind them. He smiles at them and they do the same but a wind blows the hot air at the 3 women as Toni and Meepbo went inside the building. All three smelled him as the wind blew his scent in the direction they were standing. Closing their eyes taking a deep breath in hailing the cologne as the wind gave them a good whiff of that cologne he got on. Their noses wide open and feeling so hot for this man, they start to walk over to him. Hutch though it strange them looking at him so seductively after taking a deep breath but thought to himself they must not be around a lot of black men. Meepbo came back out the building and told them their mother wants to see them, just as they started towards Hutch. Meepbo looked at them and walks over to Hutch saying "Sorry about that, they never seen a big older black man like you in shape. Only the ones on T.V but they do get to see all the young white men in great shape. Like the wrestlers when I watch W.W.E or in those ads for under wears and colognes, half naked black men are watched when I look at boxing not seen up close like you". Making that comment bothered Hutch but when he said "Oh that's right you are not totally black you're light skinned, so that's not too bad" Then laughs about what he said handing Hutch his assignment. Looking at Meepbo wanting to knock the mess out of him for saying that, he just takes the paper and shakes his head walking way towards his truck. Meepbo's cell rings, it's his wife telling him their stuff is at the dock. They want so much to deliver it, how are they going to go get it and bring it to their home. Meepbo calls to Hutch before he could get in his truck, telling him he's got another assignment for him. Wanting him to take the lift gate truck and go get his delivery and bring it to his house. Thinking he's not going to pay that high price to get his stuff delivered, when he got his own trucks and big boy like him to bring the stuff to his house. Then calls his wife telling her he's got Hutch in steady of those meat heads to deliver his crates. Hutch just looked at him saying "Crates!" Meepbo says "You boys have that hidden strength and know how to lift stuff with that strong back" Hutch looked a Meepbo asking "Do you know what's coming out of that shit hole you call a mouth, how there could be a serious beat down for it!" Meepbo looked at him not paying attention to what he just said, on the phone with his wife. She was telling him she can't go with Hutch because she's got an appointment. Telling Meepbo send one of the girls with him to the docks and then home to let him in the gates, because she's not missing her appointment. Meepbo shouts "Those are my baby girls. How am I going to send them with" Toni cuts him off by saying "With a grown man that's lots older than your grown ass daughters, who's had boyfriends sleep over in the pool house and you knew about it!". Meepbo listens to how Toni scolds him out going on about their not little girls anymore but hot looking women who know not to get pregnant. Besides he's an older man you should feel safe about it, what could he do. Meepbo laughs telling her "You are right, even though he looks in shape. After he lifts those crates, his black ass won't be able to handle nothing but getting his black ass back here to work for me" Hutch had his back to Meepbo getting his bag out of his truck but when he heard what Meepbo said. He turns around mad after hearing that and goes to grab Meepbo with his back to Hutch. Galio pops out of nowhere stopping Hutch dead in his mad charge on Meepbo. He was still talking loudly on the phone with his back to him not knowing he was going to get crushed for saying those things. Galio stops Hutch saying "Hey my friend! Meh no ju wan na tere dis pees of chit a pot. Butt eez not wurt ju lose jur yob, trus meh men. No one don like dat pees o chit worse den meh. When eez took o-ber dis cumpani from da old boss Mic-hale". Explaining to Hutch he's a good man and person always been nice to Galio and he knows Meepbo is an asshole, but tells him get him another way not by losing his job over it and going to jail. (Not typing the rest of that the way he speaks, my fingers and head would hurt so imagine him saying his way) Hutch agreed to what Galio said calming down and should know better than to let him get under his skin like that. Saying "If I could find a way to get even with his ass I would" Galio pats him on the back saying "My mehn!" To the reader: (hey don't start, that was just one word Ok not whole sentence.) Hutch told Meepbo to give him a minute while goes to the bathroom and in there, he thought about the lift gate truck. Mad he's got to drive it because it has no A/C and he'll be sweating. Might as well smell good using the silver cologne he had in the bag leaving just a small corner left of the bottle on the sink. Coming back out the bathroom to get in the truck and wait for the address Meepbo was going to send him to pick up his crates. He does a double take looking at Sheila and Lorie as he walked up to the truck with them in it, Meepbo says "They'll go with you and when you get to the house just put your load anywhere they say to put it OK" Hutch looked at him and got out of the truck to say something to Meepbo but Sheila gets right in front of him, Saying to Hutch "I'm sure you can handle where I tell you to put your load like my daddy said". Giving him the same seductive look as her sisters did when they first got there. Paying her looks little attention he goes by her and gets the paper work so he could pick up the crate from the dock, coming back and tells them to get in the truck. Her mother was taken the vehicle with her as Carmella gets mad that she couldn't go with Hutch and her sister too. On the way to the Brooklyn dock from the borough of Queens in that hot truck with two more passengers made things only hotter inside plus from the heat of the day and the engine. Hutch starts to sweat more and the cologne he had one was really affecting Sheila and Lorie as they asked him about his personal life. "How come you're not married and why don't you have a girlfriend" Lorie asked. Sheila moving closer and closer till she was rubbing up against him while he drove. Hutch had other things on his mind and didn't pay any attention at how Sheila was taking his hand putting it on her thigh. Whenever he went to shift the gears he turns looking at her quickly and would say "Sorry" thinking he did it by accident trying to keep his eyes on traffic. Lorie would reach around the back of her sister and over to rub the back of his head and neck making it feel good. Sheila kept taking his hand putting it on her knee moving it up her thigh till he touched her there, quickly pulling his hand away realizing he touched her there. Then felt Lorie's hand rubbing his neck. He looked at them quickly turning back and forth to watch the road, asking them "You two alright! What's with the hands on treatment". Then he noticed Sheila had unbutton a couple button on her blouse showing more cleavage and Lorie was doing the same thing as he drove.

Sheila right next to him said "Wow it is big as it looks!" As she grabs his arm and leans her head on his shoulder then reach for his stick shift making him jump up hitting his head on the roof of the truck, grabbing her hand going "Girl don't do that I'm driving. What's with you two?" Lorie asked him "Is it true what they say about men with big hands and feet because your neck felt so thick" Hutch told them to act right because when they get to the dock there's going to be lots of other men there and the way they are acting, "Do I have to keep an eye on you both". They looked at him and shook their heads "NO". They get to the dock a short time later and both women watch as he loads the crates on the lift gate flatbed truck then secure the crates with straps. He worked up a good sweat doing that and got a little swollen from all that lifting which turned them on even more. On the way to Meepbo's house the truck was so hot Hutch was sweating even more making them more and more horny for him and he had to keep his eyes on the road and their hands off him while driving. Lorie putting her hands on him while Sheila kept putting her head in his lap, even other trucks going by them would look in and see how their blouses were open showing how nice and plump their chest was. They kept trying to get Hutch to touch them or touch their selves and truckers going by would blow their horns approving what they saw. Finally reaching the street where Meepbo house is, they have to use a code to get through the gates. They gave Hutch the code to punch in to have the gates opens as Sheila grabs at his stick again when he leaned over to push the key board. Banging his head on the top of the door frame this time as he jumped from being touched again, she had hands on his manhood and squeezed. Pulling her hand away holding his head from the pain he looks at her as she turned to Lorie with eyes wide biting her lip a little at what she felt mouthing to her sister "It's BIGG!!" Lorie just looked at her smiled and shook her head as he asked them "Where should I pull the truck". They told him pull it around back where the garage is, once there Hutch jumps out of the truck quick to get away from the hand mauling they were doing to him. About to tell them something but never gets a word out from what he saw coming from around the trucks passenger side. Holding his hand up pointing his finger at them but froze that thought looking at two hot looking women walking toward him and everything went in slow motion. One shorter than the other looking so sexy walking as they towards him, he really didn't look at them like that till now. The back yard fenced is a high wall for privacy guess Meepbo wanted it that way, but in the back ground as his daughter walks towards Hutch. It made them look even hotter coming around the flatbed truck with their blouses fully opened and letting down their hair doing that slow motion walk, they walk over to him now that he looks at them like the fully grown hot sexy looking women they are wondering how come he didn't see them like this earlier.

Back at the garage Meepbo walks around his vehicle making sure he got everything he needs out of it before his wife took it, then has to use the bathroom. He goes in to use it and finds the bottle of cologne there on the sink with a quarter left in the bottle as he smells it. Liking what he sniffed he sprays it one times on his clothes, then 4 more time under his shirt. It's so hot and knew he's been sweating a lot from the heat thinking he didn't want the smell to go away mixed with his sweat. Walking back through the muggy garage and it makes him sweat even more before going back in the office. While he was in the garage Carmella left the building walking down the street to the coffee shop, she wasn't in the office when her father walks back in there. Opening the door as the cologne scent with the heat goes in first to the cool office. Toni was on the phone with her girlfriend telling her what time she was going to be at their appointment, but as Meepbo stands there in the door way she got a good whiff of him from the heated air rushing in the cool office. She stopped talking in the middle of her conversation looking at

Meepbo like he was a piece of meat and she was the animal about to eat it. Her girlfriend was calling her name over the phone but she didn't answer only hung it up. Meepbo asked "Who was that you just hung up on". Her response was licking her lips then looking at him up and down while breathing heavy as he gives off the odor of that cologne making her so horny. She reaches for his remote lock and locks the door behind. Meepbo's raised his brows and eyes got wide from the look she gave him hearing the door lock behind him. When he turns to look at the door and turn back he's attacked by his wife so fast he didn't even see her move from behind the desk. She's all over him stripping his clothes off him while he asked her "Is today my birthday". She moves him all around the office knocking over things in the way till they get to his desk, where she pins him down climbing on top of him. He begs for more telling her "let the beast out". She growled "Yeah!" but stops surprised at how big Meepbo was, she had forgotten. Going "OH yeah! That big beast so I don't need to be gentle!" Grabbing him feeling it grow saying "Oh Shit!! I forgot you got black in your family baby!" Carmella walking back into the building, when she heard stuff being knocked over like a fight was going on in the office but then her mother growls aloud "EERRAAHHHA". Meepbo cry's out "Yes baby! Yes baby do it!" Rolling her eyes she can't believe it, their having wild sex now and here in his office at this time of day. Walking back to the receptionist desk with the coffee and tea she got for her mother sitting down and drinking the coffee picking up a magazine while hearing the commotion going on as the secretary came in for the day. Looking at her "Carmella what's wrong?" Then hearing a lot of banging which startled her and the look on Carmella's face of discuss, she explains what's going on with her parents so they turn on the radio.

At Meepbo's house Hutch watches as they walk towards him with their hair out, Sheila resembles Scarlett Johansson her hair flows in the wind with that look on her face. He's seen that serious look before on Kiamesha, as Lorie reminds him of young Bernise Richards as he sighs watching them walk at him. Backing up trying to talk to them but they're not listening to nothing he said to them, even when he says "I'm going to call your father". Sheila says "For what so he could call you boy again, well you are not a boy from what I see, so act like the man and stop moving away from me" The words she said to strike a nerve and not looking he backs up hitting the lawn chair and falls back in it. They pounce on him and Sheila lays such a kiss on him then sucked his neck in that spot. It makes him stop fighting to get her off, Lorie was taking off his boots unzipping his coveralls pulling them down his body. His cell phone fell out and hit the ground, the noise made him pushed Sheila off him and went to call their father. They just looked at him and Lorie told him their father gives them what they want anyways and right now they want him. Hutch didn't believe what's going on and calls the office putting it on speaker to get hold of Meepbo. Who is pushing his wife off him from on the desk top just to pick up the phone as it rang. He answers it "What is it! Better be good" he sit on top of the desk. Toni backed away from him and sat down on the couch looking at him across the room. When he realizes it was Hutch he got very annoyed saying "If it's about where to put his load now that you're there at my house, let my daughter tell you where they want it. Don't come back till you put it in all the places they show you no matter how long it takes" Hutch tries to tell him about his daughters and how their behaving but his attention gets diverted to his wife moving at him. She leaps at him taking them both over his desk. Hutch is calling his name but hears growling then the phone went dead. Meepbo is being attacked from his wife again because the smell of that cologne mixed with their sex in the air had her really horny saying to him "It's been too long I felt this way about you". Raising up from behind the desk going in his draw pulling out his Viagra bottle but gets pulled back down causing him to spill the pills up in the air, not before he catches one quickly swallowing it down "In ten minutes I'm the man again". Toni's hand comes up feeling around the desk top till it feels one of the little blue pills, snatching it off the desk saying "Here take another one and be a better harder man longer, I'll keep time on you". Hutch looks at Sheila and Lorie nervously laughs but they didn't wait for him to cut off the cell taking it from his hand. Telling him if he doesn't do what they tell him, their fathers going to hear a story about what you tried to do to them. If you do us then he'll hear another story how helpful you were. Hutch looked at them

"Are you serious!" Lorie's answers "Serious as this". Dropping her skirt and showing her meshed see through panties and toned legs and flat stomach as she ran her hands up and down her body. Sheila said to him "Did my father ever do anything to make you mad and you want to get even with him for something." Hutch just smiled and looked away for moment, she then says to him in a sexy voice while twirling her hair looking at him with hungry eyes "Umm why not get even by knowing you did the bosses daughters for every time he made you mad!" Again Hutch smiled this time given her such a look her eyes got wide watching him sneer and she knew she got to him and gasped when he licked his lips.

Meanwhile Meepbo and Toni now taking a break try to clean up his office but could get far because Toni would still smell that cologne in the air and now mixed with sex odor would be even more hornier. Getting back at him with renewed energy, he would try to fight her off but given in from being over powered by her. Down stair the receptionist and Carmella were going over things about the company her father wanted them all to know and would have to stop from the noise going on in her father's office above them. She would get embarrassed by what they were doing and noise they're making. The receptionist was blushing hearing this activity go on for so long in the office like that so she turns on the radio to help cover the noise of them upstairs. She turns to Carmella asking her "What did your parents take this morning and where can I buy or order it from. It sounds like a wonderful product for her to try with her husband. Hearing how it gave a person that kind of stamina to go that many times!" Carmella would try to explain her mother isn't on anything, getting interrupted by the sound her parents were making noise. Then said to the receptionist "If there is anything, I'm going to find out because most of the men I've dated didn't even last the first twenty minutes and that's including 15 minutes kissing and 3 minute of foreplay". When the noise stopped early in the afternoon because Meepbo told Toni he wanted to continue at home and stop on the way to get a red bull plus a monster energy drink, she wondered if she made an mistake given him the extra blue pill. Meepbo said "If I don't go down in four hours I'm not calling a doctor just going to keep on tip drilling till I strike oil or till you know who's it!" Telling her better pick up a case of red bull with monster energy drink and some Mega man vitamins, opening a window to let the place air out for a minute. They're both are so winded tired from the activity as they got dressed to hurry and leave. He puts on her blouse and she put on his shirt with one of the others shoes and hair looking like they were in a wind storm. They come down stairs first is Toni passing the receptionist and Carmella both looking at her. Toni's hair all wild looking and in her father's shirt with her make up faded and smeared all over her face, going up and down from the one heel she has on trying to wave bye like there's nothing wrong with her. Meepbo comes behind her with a woman's blouse on with a tie and his hair look no better than Toni's with makeup smeared all over his face.

Going up and down as he walks because he's wearing his wife's shoe trying to smoke a cigar as he stops and tells them to "Handle things because I need to go home for body positions uh business purposes!". Carmella tries to talk to her father but he cuts her off saying "This is a good time for you to know what the business is all about". Then says "Receptionist will help you with all that you need to know and if there's a problem you can't handle, leave it till tomorrow then I'll deal with it!" They get in his car and drive off leaving Carmella and the receptionist looking at the car drive away then each other.

Early that afternoon Hutch was getting dressed looking at the two naked good looking bodies stretched out on the bed in the pool house, passing a mirror looking at himself asking the reflection "Feel guilty at what you did". Reflection shook it's head no and hi fived him saying "She should have never said that" He takes his cell phone then takes a couple of pictures of them out cold laying there looking like that, forgetting about the expressions on their faces setting photo cam so he could get in the picture with them sleep. Going out and unloading the crates off the lift gate truck and leaving to get out of there in case Meepbo did come home. Hutch emanating sex and cologne gets back in that hot truck driving back to the garage. Going over the way he had sex with them both helping them reach that goal. Showing them new ways they could get there with him doing it, while calling his name carrying on that way. Thinking it's a good thing they're a good ways from the neighbors with all the noise those two were making hope wondering who taught them about sex. On his way back to the garage he thought to himself "I should have taken a dip in that pool and then showered before going back!" He wanted to get back fast so in case Meepbo showed up there looking for him and didn't find him with his girls like that. Once he got into Queens stopping a local Jamaican food store picking up two sea moss mixtures, peanut drink, 2 red bulls drinks and eight beef patties. Time he reached back at the garage everything was eaten and he was sweating more being in that hot truck. The traffic was so backed up due from a couple of accidents on the Expressway and Meepbo didn't even notice the flat bed on the opposite side of the expressway he passed. Toni had her hands on his legs giving him that look of she wasn't finished at what they started in his office now. Hutch finally gets to the garage backing the truck in parking it and just as gets ready to get out Carmella was standing right at the door telling him her father left and she's in charge, when he got out she asked him for the paper work. He reaches back in the truck to get it for her and that aroma hits her nose. Remember what it smelled like that morning and now more intense with the odor of sex strong on him she looks at him as he gives her the papers from the delivery he made with the crates to her father's house. Asking her "Was there anything your father left for me to do". Giving him a sexy smile biting her lip with a shake of her head "No" He went "Ok". She watches him walking towards the bathroom in the garage. Not wanting to be disturbed for what she has in mind for him, she two ways the receptionist and told her since it was late in the afternoon she could go home early. Then Carmella goes into the bathroom where he was washing his face with top half of his coveralls off his body. Hearing a clicking of the door being locked and felt a pair of hands grab his chest from behind. Saying "I'm going to put a hurting on the joker that's thinks this is funny touching me like that!" Cleaning off his face turning around seeing Carmella there with no clothes on looking at him the same way Sheila and Lorie did. Telling him "Big as you are, you better put a hurting on this" From the looks of those little bite marks on his chest she knew that's Sheila trade mark and knew she got there before her, saying "Good I feel you need some overtime anyways, what better way to get a bonus then from the boss huh!" Her eyes widen at what she felt in her hands and Hutch thought to himself maybe he should let Meepbo get him mad a lot more if this was going to happen.

Meepbo and Toni make it home as he finished his two red bull drinks and took his vitamins and didn't even make it in the door, as she tackles him on the couch knocking it over. They continue on the floor behind the couch with him saying "I drank red bull, got 3 hours left. I'm going to make use of all of it!"

It was getting late in the afternoon towards evening time and the truck were pulling in to the garage with all the driver getting out and going to their cars not even stopping to head towards the bathroom wanting to get home. They were leaving and could hear the faint sound of what they thought was Galio watching his porn again laughing to themselves saying "He must be watching a good one the way she is moaning" as they leave the garage. Sheila was the first one to wake up seeing its dark outside thinking to herself "Wow she never felt anything like that, even when she had two guys at one time!" Feeling good but very sore thinking she better take a shower and get cleaned up. When she went into the bathroom turning on the lights looking in the mirror. She got the answer to why her face was feeling so strange. Her face froze in a big smile and lips red covered in dry glazed semen having her look like the joker from Batman. She gets startled by her sister standing in the doorway looking like clay face or she had a stroke one side of her face slid down with dry glaze all on it. Feeling their faces and how hard they were along with the soreness their bodies felt, they knew a hot shower would make them feel better and get rid of what was making them look that way. After a nice hot shower Sheila was standing there in her towel and noticed the big hand print on her shoulder. Standing in front of the mirror opening her towel to see all those big hand prints all over her body on her chest to her thighs and turning to see them on her butt telling which way he was holding her while he was doing it with her. She goes to show Lorie but sees she already knows after her shower, they laugh comparing big hand prints and putting their hands in place.

Hutch told Carmella in the bathroom at the garage to let him go first to see if the cost is clear so she could leave without being seen by anyone that might be around the garage, when he came out of the bathroom there was Moni about to leave and sees Hutch. He just had to come over and talk about how hard his day was from him not being there. Hutch didn't want to hear it but listened to whatever he had to say just to get rid of Moni, that way he could get Carmella out of there without Moni seeing her. Watching Moni leave then going back to the bathroom getting Carmella letting her know she can leave but not before she told him their secret's safe with her and no one will ever know about what they did. He couldn't believe the day he was having on the way home, so when he got a call from Mack to meet him and some of the GDM4L at the Sea Witch he agreed. A drink would do him some good right about now, short time later he's sitting at the table telling them about his day with the boss's daughters and what they did. Sitting at the table he puts his cell phone down and 2Soon picked it up to call Sonia to see what she was up to and if she wanted to hook up later. Done with his call he starts going through Hutch's phone coming across the photos Hutch took of the boss's daughters and bust out laughing. Everyone at the table thought he got a funny call or something, till he shows the photos having the rest of them laughing at the way the ladies faces looked. Byron asked "Man what's that on their face!". Everyone turned and looked at him and Mack goes "Skeet! Skeet! Skeet!" Douige says "Nah bruha more like Gush! Gush! Gush!"

Tyrone said "See that's what happens when a man hasn't been with a woman in 15, 20 years or so and works all the time. Hutch you got to get out more man and let some of that back up go or you're going to drown some woman!" They looked at Hutch laughing at what Tyrone said. Hutch changes subject by asked them to help him with Moni, explaining he invited him out on Friday. Needs to show him a good time or he's going to hurt his little kiss ass always in his business at the job. Dougie told Hutch sure they wouldn't mind helping with Moni asking "Where should they take him?" Mack went the Gator club man in the Village that's where a lot of honeys would be and they might find him one. They all agreed to meet on Friday as Hutch ordered another round then two, then three and 4.

Back at Meepbo's house Carmella had come in and not seeing anyone went to take a shower to get the sex smell off her so none of her sister would know what she did with Hutch. Now cleaned from a good hot shower walking to her room she hears Sheila say "Carmella is that you? We're in the living room come here!" Sheila wanted to know how her day went at the garage and to tell her about what happened with the both of them and Hutch. Carmella walks into the living room towel wrapped around her, Sheila and Lorie starts laughing seeing a hand print on her shoulder and finger marks on across her face that showed after showering. Trying to compose their selves Lorie asked her "Explain again how your banging day went. You clearly had someone get a good grip on things for you!" Carmella wanted to know what was so funny so Sheila took her to the bathroom and told her to open her towel and look into the mirror. Her jaw dropped at what she saw all those hand prints on her body then Sheila raised up her big night shirt revealing hand prints on her body too saying "Umm he's got a good grip doesn't he?!" They go back into the living room and Lorie just said "Me too!" The rest of the night they compared and talked about what he did with each of them wondering how can he keep going like that.

4:30am Friday Hutch is up and got to the garage and pulls his truck out hoping there wouldn't be much mentioned about what happened the other day. The receptionist pulls up and head to the office and comes out with the route schedule saying "The boss wouldn't be in toady because she got a call from Toni (his wife) that he's wiped out and still sleep and would need rest. (Picture Meepbo sleep in the bed on is back with a stiff one under the sheets, snoring like a lumberjack after a hard day work in the forest) Hutch gets assigned to the building again in Manhattan so he goes to get his breakfast first before he heads there and wait till Moni with the rest of the work crew gets there. Like usual he's there listening to the radio and people are walking by grooving to the morning show. Finally they show up and the day begins and like usual Moni has to try and get on Hutches nerves by commenting about where he should be and what he's wearing. While in the building Moni got a chance to get to the only windows on the lower levels no higher than four floors where it was just over Hutch and wanting to get even with him for the balloons dropping on his head that time. He got hold of one and fills it up then going to the window and waiting for the right time to drop it on Hutch's head. Hutch was grooving and throwing things in the truck crushing them up, when these two nice looking women walking towards his way watched him lift something heavy throwing it in the truck with a boom! They were impressed with that. They wave and smile at him making him stand still long enough for Moni to drop a big water balloon out the window on his head. They looked at him all wet and laughed at what happened. Looking up and seeing Moni laughing then wave from the window at Hutch standing there wet from the balloon he just dropped, he couldn't just let Moni get away with that so easy even if today was Friday.

Waiting just right after lunch to make his move but didn't know what he was going to do till he went in the building to let him know he was loaded ready for the dump. Walking around asking the men "Did they see Moni anywhere on that floor they were stripping". One of the work crew answered he might be up two floors up yelling at the crew about to start pulling out the old bathroom on the 26th floor. Hutch went up there looking for Moni and one of the men say "He just went into the bathroom". Going into the bathroom hearing Moni say "Whatever it is it'll have to wait till I get out of here!" The smell and noise he was making had Hutch holding his nose then turn around and go back out to see the men banging to strip out a big part of the wall on the other side of the bathroom Moni was in. Hutch got an idea when he saw the big hose and the pipes exposed in the wall that came down, so finding the right big pipe he gets a wrench and opens the big pipe and stuck the hose in it. Going over to the control value and turning it on full blast and heading back down stairs. Moni sitting on the bowel hears this low rumbling noise at first and then louder and louder. One by one the bathroom stalls is heard gushing like fountains till it reaches Moni. He sat on his toilet trying to figure out what is that noise, all the water in his bowel comes up and wets him first. It gushes up holding him against the ceiling for a few seconds as he screams fighting with the gushing water. Falling back down in the sewer water now ankle deep on the floor, getting up wet from it. He wonders why it's building up that way as he heads towards the door to get out and finding it hard to open. Finally getting the door open letting the water rush out and on the other side is something that was blocking the water from going under the door. Screaming for someone to shut off the water standing there soaking wet, Moni looks around to see who could have done this to him. Smelling from the pissy toilet water as small pieces of terd and paper lay on his shirt he screams "Where is Hutch, because that mutha sooka is the only one that could have done to me!" They told Moni they just saw him going down to the truck and Moni goes down after him but is too late as he watches Hutch pull away and turn the corner heading to the bridge so he can go dump his truck. Shouting "I'll get your ass when you gets back here!" Moni goes to the van to get some dry clothes from his foot chest in the van but when he goes to open it up he gets blast of some stuff "POW!" that knocks him back off his feet. Getting up and realizes its horse shit that blew out knocking him off his feet, he's lying in on the street. He's so mad screaming Hutch name like a banshee and goes for the water hose their using outside the building for the truck to keep the dust from clouding up while they dump the debris in the back of them. People hold their nose walking pass Moni dripping wet standing next to van smelling like horse shit mad at what just happened as he washes up. All clean of the shit now going back to the van getting in closing it's door so he could change into dry clothes and wait for Hutch to get back.

Later after dumping the truck Hutch is pulling up in front of the building and Moni had gone back in, he heard that Hutch was back and came out to yell at him for that stunt with the hose in the bathroom because he just knew it had to be him. Hutch calmed him down by reminding him of the peace offering invite to the club saying "You did get me good with the water balloon out the window drop in front of the women". Which made Moni laugh he got Hutch real good with that one, thinking it don't compare to getting blown back from the toilet and smelling like shit. Asking Moni for a pen to give him the address to the Gator club and told him to wear something sharp looking because all the women there are going to want the new face that's with him and his guys. Moni got excited wanting to know how many women would be there. Hutch told him so many women that they would have to protect like a movie star from being the new face so clean up dress sharp and smell good.

He might get to choose one or two maybe three to go home with. Nobody would think he's a lesser man and the more Hutch went on about the women at the club and how they were going to be dressed in their short and tight clothes showing all that body. Moni likes that idea Hutch had told him and they went back to work making so they could get off early enough and he could go home and get ready for the club that night.

9 pm that night things are jumping at the Gator club, Hutch with some of the GDM4L who got there early to wait for Moni to show so they can have a good time with him so he'll get off Hutch's back, they're in there having a drink and dancing with some of the fine women getting things set up for him. Moni is getting out of the shower dancing around thinking about the time he's going to have with Hutch and his friend plus all the women he's going to meet. Grooving around singing the Rap song by Heavy D "Got me thinking" Then playing another By Heavy D "Big Daddy" saying to himself in the mirror "Those ladies won't be able to keep their hands off me, even fight each other to get at me" keeping the paper on the counter near the sink when he got out and not noticing he knocked it in the sink swing his towel around when he was dancing. After drying off then starts to brushing his teeth spiting in the sink he looks over to get another look at the piece of paper with the address on it. But it wasn't there so he looks around for it and then saw it in the sink where he spat the tooth paste out. Grabbing it out and wiping it off tearing the soft paper apart with part of the name of where he was supposed to meet Hutch. Getting dressed and then looking up the address in the phone book finding the first one he saw which matched that part of the paper "Two Potator 375 Village Street". Holding the piece of paper next to the address in the phone book, it was close enough for him. Knowing Hutch would

be there then using a lot of the gold capped spray cologne Hutch gave him so he would smell good. Getting out the cab as the driver is laughing at Moni with his hair slicked back in a salt and pepper suit jacket with a green shirt on under it wearing a purple, black and yellow tie with orange pants. Gold belt to him looks nice with black white tops Stacy Adams shoes with red socks, Moni just knew he was sharp looking going catch any woman that was in the club. He walks to the entrance of the Two Potator club in the Village where everyone outside is looking and snickering watching him good in the club. Making a grand entrance the security guard just inside the door and everyone else was looking at him. Being stopped by the security guards and told it was ten dollars to come in. Moni told the security guard he was invited by his friend Hutch and told to dress sharp to meet the honey's. Security guard went still have to pay but then guard adds "You must be some special friend to be invited here dressed like that" Moni told the guard his friend Hutch is sharp like him and should be in there already. The security guard laughs and went "There's another one of you in here? How'd that walking cereal get pass me, I'll never know but your still going to pay 10$ or you don't get in. What's that smell, is it you?" Moni went "It's the latest shit you couldn't afford it". The security guard laughed then said "You're right and wrong. You smell like something else but I could afford to get dressed by turning on the lights" Moni held up his hand going "Hater! My gear is tight!" Handing out 10$ to the guard then walking on. The second security guard goes "That's the strangest thing I ever seen, walking fruit loops with attitude". The first guard answers "No! It's not" Pointing to the man covered in silver from head to toe wearing spandex to match with his silver suit jack dancing the Vogue with another man covered in blue from head to toe in blue spandex with a blue suit jacket on pausing to look back at the two security guards that look at them. The first guard tells the second one saying "You were saying what was strange again".

Moni walks up the bar getting strange looks on the faces of people in there, as he orders a beer and two women in there came up and stood next to him just looking at him. They ordered what he was drinking and asked "What made you bold enough to come out looking like a rainbow threw up color?!" The place was hot and getting hotter Moni was a little nervous and starts to sweat wondering where Hutch was and how come he didn't get there yet. Moni tries to meet some of the women on his own. At first they would laugh at him but with him moving around in the hot place in that heavy jacket making him sweat more they would look at him with an angry look on their face when he got close to speak to any of the women in there. Then he starts to notice the men in there are dancing with other men in the place and they were dancing a little too close in his opinion. Then as they start to kiss each other and holding hands, Moni moves on till he went around the whole dance floor looking for Hutch in the place. Back at the bar he orders another beer and this woman came to get a drink, he said something to her but was sweating more fanning his shirt to cool off. The woman took offense not understanding what he said and starts to cuss him out. Her friend saw what was happening and came over only the scent got to her nose as well and she mad at Moni telling him to keep away from her piece, taking a swing at him missing but grabs him and slams him to the floor. Moni got back up looking around the bar saying "There's no cake or pie here and if you wanted a piece you better go to the bakery first!". Then he sees the two women kiss and noticed more women kissing other women and more men doing the same. When the music dies down a little he's heard talking about what kind of place lets this type of thing happen here and those people should be ashamed at their actions. One woman told him he didn't need to be in there if he felt that way, so Moni said "I need to by her one, for bumping her glass" but to her it sounded like "She need to mind her business before he whoops her ass" With the smell of his cologne it sent her over the top and she grabs him and starts to fighting with him. Pushing him into another couple at a table and they got mad at him and starts to beat on him. It seems the whole place wanted a piece of him from the cologne smell they had got a whiff when he circled the dance floor. While struggling with this one woman she manages to tare open his shirt letting the full odor of the cologne he got on out which made every woman and men in there want to get their hands on Moni. They even starts fight each other to get to him. The security guard heard the commotion going on in the club and saw it was Moni they were after, saying to the other guard "Why am I not surprised". The other guard says "It's always the loudest dressed one with the biggest attitude". They rush in there to get Moni out as he was being slapped and punch by the women in there, but the women and men wouldn't let them get to him as they were beaten up for even trying to get protect him. While they were beating on the security guards, Moni thought he had a chance to get out of there and ran towards the door. He gets clothes lined by this skinny old gay man "Where you going Bitch!" He looked up from the floor seeing who hit him with that clothes line from hell making flip on to the floor. The old man was picking him up to beat him some more, when this heavy women came over to take Moni from him. They got to fighting and she got her ass beat for trying to take Moni from him. The whole place is on full riot trying to get to Moni as they chase him around in the club slipping and falling on the drinks he grabs from tables throwing them on the floor behind as he runs for his life.

Hutch is outside the Gator club waiting for Moni wondering what happened to him hoping he didn't think it was a set up and not show up as three police cars went by with their light on, then four more cars went racing by but he didn't really pay it too much attention.

2Soon and Mack came out of the Gator club and found Hutch standing outside looking around asking him "Why is he out there?" He just answered "Moni! He should have been here by now!" There were eight more police cars and three ambulances plus four fire trucks and two swat trucks and five riot squad vans rushing by with their lights & sirens blaring. They all looked and wondered what was going on that all those vehicles went by like that, four people standing in line to get in the Gator club starts talking. They just got a call from one of their friends hoping their not at the two potato club some nut started a big riot over there it's a mess. Mack over heard them talking and gave the information to Hutch and hoped Moni didn't go there. Hutch told him he wrote down the Gator clubs name and address and what it's next to on a piece of paper for him saying "He have to be a moron to go there with all that fighting going on". Mack and 2Soon went back in the club saying "They're going to be in there with lil Rob and Byron and Jazz but they're going to send Dougie out there to check on him till Moni shows up" Hutch told "Go head back in and he'll be out there not for long, because if Moni isn't there in the next fifteen minutes he' coming back in to get in his dances with some of the honeys in there too".

Moni is running from two women and one man ducking through all the other people fighting in the club so they can get a chance to beat on him. The police came in with the beat up security guard as he points out Moni saying "There he's the cause of everything" They break through some of the people fighting to get to Moni who's getting beat on by two women. The cop went to grab him away from the women and they jumped the police shouting "Their not finished with his ass yet!" They all starts to fighting and the women police officers grab Moni to get him out of there, they starts to the door and his cologne odor get to their noses. They look at him mad "You're the cause of all this. If it wasn't for you they wouldn't be there". They beat on him and cussing him out while doing it. More men police see what they're doing and try to stop them, they wind up fighting with the men police to get at Moni as well. One cop shouts to three officers "Get him out of there" and one cop asks him "What the hell did you do to have all these people want to beat your ass". One cop says "Look at what he's got on that would cause anyone with good fashion sense to want to beat his ass for coming out of the house like that". Another cop looks at him then says "Shit color man dressed like fruit loops that'll do it". The fighting spilled into the streets and the fire department had to use the hose to cool everyone down. The riot squad surrounded them to keep them in a tight circle, Moni is all wet and beat and bloody as they put him in a car to take him away. Most of the women saw it and starts to go after the car. The News vans with reports were there to report what was going on and tried to get a good shot of Moni as the police took him in the car, and it was being chased by all those women and some gay men still wanting to get their hands on Moni too. The news story was on the TV and other broad cast stations about the riot and how one man starts a big riot for what reason they're not sure. Whatever the reason it was for, there were lots of people hurt as well as fire men and policemen plus women saying "There'll be an investigation into the of this riot" Hutch standing by the electronic store saw the news on the TV sets in the window but didn't see the who cause it while he was waiting for Moni. He decides to go in the club because he's waited long enough and sure Moni is making his own plans doing who knows what.

At the hospital Moni is being examined by a nurse on the table when she hauls off and punches him off the table, then starts cussing at him while he lays there on the floor. Another intern saw what she did and wondered what was she thinking doing something like that and takes her out of the room, then comes back in there and helps put him back on the examine table. Saying they need to wash him up to clean off all the dirt and glass off his body to see what's wrong with him internally.

Hutch and the GDM4L had a good time in the club with Hutch buying drinks and food for everyone with them and the new women they met in the club. Making sure everyone in there really had a good time with them plus giving out big tips to the waitresses and barmaids and bartenders. They were closing the two potato making arrest and had Moni at the hospital cleaning him up to exam him.

Leaving before the club closed most of the GDM4L had a woman they met in there on their arm going elsewhere and Hutch had got a call from Elise and she wants to come over to his house. He left them and went home to meet up with her but first stops at the bank to see what kind of damage he did to his account. He gets to the bank takes out his card and looks at his account and shows there was not even one penny taken out of his account. Scratching his head thinking after all those drinks and food for all those people there must be some kind of mistake, he spent a lot and wanted to know exactly how much he had to work hard to put back in his account. Thinking maybe they'll take it out later he leaves the banks not wanting Elise to have to wait for him that long, he hurried home to find her waiting in her vehicle as he pulls up. She wants to know where he's been so long and who did he go out with. He explained about Moni his co-worker at the company and how he wanted to take him out and show him a good time but he never showed so he had a good time with the

GDM4L. She asked him "Do you always have to have them around and do things with them". He explained they're his brothers plus their tight like that. Opening the door to his house letting her go in as he disarms the alarm closing the door behind them, she looks at him and could see he's still tipsy. Suggesting to him they need to talk about the other night and what happened, that only triggered something in his mind as he told her wait there and left the living room. He came back holding something behind his back as she sat on the couch in the living room. He gave her a big sneaky drunken smile and stood there for moment having her wonder what he has behind his back. She threw her head back closing her eyes biting her lip at what he showed her and what she wanted to talk about was for gotten as she looks at the DR.Scholl mint foot cream and nail clipper with anti-fungal liquid with a face mask.

Hours before day light his window is open and coming out of his house is loud moaning of "YES! OH BABY! RIGHT THERE! HARDER YEAH BABY HARDER!" Again lights coming on in house in the distance as Hutch has her calling his name but stopped for a moment when he thought he heard what sounded like two gunshots faintly (POW POW!) and a man's voice going "Honey no wait don't, ah Shh-unck!". The sound of a big knife slicing into meat is heard another sound like a shot gun being cocked back, asking Elise "Did you hear that?" He gets up to close the window and hear a woman's voice shout "These shits don't work and neither do you! BOW!" another shot gun blast come from somewhere in one of the house down the hill as he looks to see exactly where then closes the window. Turning back to look at Elise who is fast asleep and snoring like a big lumber jack, he shakes his head and picks her up and puts her in one of the other bedroom then comes back and lays in his own.

4:30 Monday morning the alarm is going off and Hutch jumps up to cut it off looking around with a daze from over sleeping for one day, he sees a pair of lady shoes on the floor by his bed and thinks where did they come from but couldn't remember so he goes to take his shower.

Elsie heard the water and starts to wake up and see that she's not in her bed and wonders where she was as she got up and walks around. Coming out of the shower a towel wrapped around him, running into Elise as she walks in his bedroom hearing the news report on the radio. She thinks "HOT DAMN! He looks good for a big man!" Looking at him without his shirt on surprised to see very little fat on the upper body of the big man. Then she looks down at the towel to see it slowly rise poking straight out at her as he blushes and says "Excuse me I got to get dressed" keeping her eyes on that spot wondering as he move pass her, she just smiled at him as he closes his bedroom door. Hutch comes out dressed for work and asked Elise "Do you want me to cook breakfast" She laughed at him asking "Are he serious. She rarely knew that men cooked unless it was nuked from a box". She told him she'll pick up something on her way to work after she goes home and gets her shower and dressed but she'll call him and talk to him later to see what he was doing. A little peck to his cheek they leave his house and head on their way. Hutch gets to the garage like usual and gets his assignment to go back to the building in Manhattan and stops for his food like usual, inside Gerard who hands him a cigar and tells him about the day he had with the two women thanks for the advice. Hutch didn't believe him at first and thought it was a joke but then thought about his own day with the boss's daughters. Thinking there's something going on but can't put his finger on it because he's got to get to the building so he let Gerard know he'll talk to him later and gets his food and leaves. Getting to the building early eating his food and listening to the radio Doug Banks Morning show like he always does and the music plus comedy bits they do. Hutch sees the Van pulling up and gets out his truck wanting to talk to Moni and found out what happened to him and why he was a no show at the Gator club. Standing there and seeing Hernando get out of the Van another of the company's foremen and Moni's cousin, wondering where Moni is and thinking it must be serious for him not to even show at work. Hernando told Hutch Moni isn't feeling well and he'll be taking his place till he feels better, Hutch hoped it wasn't anything that's going to keep him away from his work. Explaining that he and Moni have their differences but he doesn't want to see any man out of work like that. Hernando thanks Hutch for the thought and tells him when they get a chance to talk he's got something to him about Moni. Shaking his head he understood looking at the paper in his hand as he turned to walk in the building. Hutch asked him could he read it since he forgot to pick one up. Hernando handed him the paper and walks into the building, Hutch looked at the Headlines which reads "Unidentified man causes riot" Thinking to himself thank goodness it wasn't over at the Gator club but looking at the fuzzy picture thinking that man look so familiar in some way.

Mid-morning the elevator breaks down from the heavy material put on it to be taken down to the trucks the workers and drivers are given a small break. Hutch goes back into the building to explorer some of the rooms he saw down on the lower level and takes out the badge getting on the elevator going down again being nosey. The elevator door open on another level where some people were waiting for it, Hutch gets off as they get on and he watches the door close. Turning after hearing a "Bang" and saw the whole floor dark and empty then heard these growls from something that sounds really big and angry in darkness. He thought better get out of there in case something wasn't fed, because someone didn't pay it any attention. Hearing it again louder and sounding very angry, he presses for the elevator and gets on when it came. Getting off the elevator he runs into Hernando in the lobby of the building and was told the elevator is down so they have to come back tomorrow that's when it'll be fixed. With no on around Hernando told him about Moni and how he's in the hospital and blames Hutch for it.

Hutch looked puzzled at what he said wondering why Moni blames him for being in the hospital. Hernando told him "It was Moni people tried to get causing the riot at the two potato club that night. He went there to meet you" Hutch puzzled and wondered why would Moni go to the two potato, explaining to Hernando how he and some of his friends went to the Gator club and waited for Moni to show. Plus they had some women he wanted Moni to meet there, showing him the pictures. Understanding now why all those police cars and riot squad, fire department went racing to the place.

Hutch and Hernando talk a little more ending with Hernando giving Hutch the hospital and room where Moni was, Hutch told him he would go up there to find out what happened and get to the bottom of it. Hernando felt better talking to Hutch thinking he's not like that and knew once he seen Moni they would figure out what was the cause of those people wanting to get after Moni to hurt him.

When Hutch got back to the garage and parked his truck Meepbo came out with a serious look on his face walking funny as if his whole body was sore from something. He calls Hutch's name wanting to talk to him for what he did at his house with his daughters. Thinking they must have told him about what happened and now he's going to get fired for what they did, he starts to explain he didn't mean for it to happen like that. Meepbo came over smiling at Hutch not even hearing anything he said and thanking him for leaving those crates right where he wanted them. Trying talk slang to Hutch saying "I knew you would've banged each one of those pieces out and knew his daughters couldn't move those things even after they went to the gym getting a good workout". Hutch asked him "Is that why you're sore too, you worked out?" He laughed going "I had her work it out all over me and had to put it down on her ass". Hutch looked puzzled at what he said and shrugged his shoulders "OK" Meepbo told him "You wouldn't know nothing about tapping that ass so good she wouldn't walk right for a week" That's when Toni pulls up to the garage and got out of the car walking like nothing was wrong with her. She smiled at Hutch hello. She walks over to Meepbo telling him she's going to the beauty salon and she's going to give him a one day so he could get the soreness out but he needs to go to the gym like his daughters. They look so sore now walking around happy. She looked at Hutch asking "You have a woman Hutch?" He told her "No one right now, I'm still looking". She went "A woman would put a smile on your face too, if you got some but big as you are you would need more than one woman!" Hutch coughs told her he's got to go visit a friend who isn't feeling well and leave them, walking to his vehicle his cell rings. It's his mother with news about her visit up there to his brother Cordell's house and how long she's going to stay. Letting her know he'll be ready when she gets there and wonders what's going on with his older brother that their mother has to come up and stay a week. Hanging up and turning his thoughts about

Moni and going to see him at the hospital to figure out how did he end up at that club, then starts laughing about how annoying Moni can be and thought about what kind of club the two potator is then really laughing more about it. Picturing in his head Moni walking in the club and seeing some of the people carrying on and having something to say about it with his annoying ass, Hutch laughs harder thinking how he must have really got on their nerves. After pissing them off knowing how much of a coward Moni is and how he must've been running for his life in there. Pulling in his drive way Hutch sees Goodie, Steel and Mack they were leaving something in his door. They walk over to Hutch and Steel starts explaining they were leaving the money they owed him for the other night but Hutch has a hard time understanding Steel sometimes when he talks so fast and short.

He looks Goodie who shrugs his shoulders "Didn't catch that" Then looking at Mack who translates what Steel said. Hutch asked "Where's the owner's manual that comes with Steel I've been asking for" Mack just laughed. Hutch told them he wasn't worried about the cash and asked where were they going after leaving his house? Mack told him they were going to the mall to pick up a few things. Hutch asked "Would they mind coming to the hospital first with him to see what happened to Moni, he'll explain on the way". First he wants to change and get out of those clothes too so why don't they can come in and have a beer. Hutch took a quick showered and while getting dressed looked at the little bottles of cologne on his dresser and thought, Moni liked the gold capped ones asking Mack, Goodie and Steel "Should he bring him one as a gift". Steel asked "About the silver capped ones" Using just a little bit. Hutch said "see you already put it on!" then grabs one before leaving the house. Getting to the hospital and stopping to get some flowers and balloon before going up to see Moni. While in the elevator Steel was looking at this nurse who kept smiling at him smelling the cologne he was wearing. Mack nodded his head to Goodie and they both shook their heads at Steel and gave Hutch a slight elbow to the side to look at Steel and the nurse flirting with each other on the elevator. Reaching the floor where Moni's room was they get off the elevator and notices the nurse following them, so Steel nudges Mack to tell him he's going with the nurse that's waving for him to come over to her. Mack shook his head "Go head man! I'll tell Hutch" Watching Steel go in the room she stood at the door waiting for him. Mack and Goodie follows Hutch in the room where Moni is lying there in a body cast with his jaw wired up with his neck brace on looking at TV channel surfing. Seeing the news broadcast with him running for his life and the cops fighting to get him away, other news channels plays what happened that night until Hutch knock on the door and came in the room. He heard Hutch's voice trying to turn his head shouting at him "What the frock are you doing here! You sent those people to do this to me!" Hutch let Moni rant on about how he set him up for that. Goodie leaned over to Hutch looking at how Moni's jaw is swollen and his eyes are blacken, with knots on his head in the neck brace wearing that body cast asking "Was this the guy from his job they were to meet that night?" Hutch went "Yep he's normally not this ugly but annoying as hell". Goodie went "Damn they really FURGD him man huh!" (F--ked UP Real Good Dude) Moni say "I'm still in the room and how are you two going to talk about me when I'm right there in bed". Hutch asked him "How'd you end up at the two potator club?" Moni explained he called a cab to take him were Hutch told him he'll be. Hutch took out his cell and showed Moni the women he was to meet at the "Gator club" asking him "Why would I send you to a gay club. I wouldn't do that to those innocent gay men and women there by sending something like you to make their club time miserable". Moni laid there not saying a word after Hutch said that little joke to him, he then said "I guess it is my fault!" Hutch asked "Remind him how you got there again". Moni tells it again as Hutch listened because he now knows he should have called. Thinking he could have gotten Hutch's from Meepbo, then he goes over again what he did before getting dressed. How he got the paper wet trying to remember name of the club and address on the wet torn paper. Hutch told him never mind that just get well and get back to work they miss his annoying ass and here's some plastic flowers from him and the guys. Moni told him no one other than Hutch has come to see him, watching Hutch put the flowers in a vase. Going in the bathroom with it and spray them heavy with the gold capped cologne he likes without getting none on himself. Placing the vase in the window so he and anyone who comes in the room could smell them, Hutch told Moni now that he's got the story straight could he stop telling his cousin he set him up like that because it's hurting his feelings.

Moni looked at Hutch and told him he would, but that doesn't let him off the hook. When he gets back to the job it's on again, he's got some pay back to give him for toilet water bath he got. Hutch laughed and Mack said "You tell me you didn't flush him down the toilet already?" Hutch laughed told Mack "I'll explain on the way to the mall" then noticed Steel was missing. Mack said "Oh yeah about that, you know how Steel is right now playing Doc with some candy striper". They go to the room on the way out to find Steel taking the nurses temperature with his own thermometer behind this curtain. Mack coughs "Do I have keep my head turned too". Steel came from behind the curtain asking "Ready to leave".

Hutch laughs "If your personal examination had cum to a conclusion or can we just Skeet-Skeet out". Steel laughs too "I wasn't finished but guess I have to treat candy striper like now and later". Goodie say "I don't get that one" Hutch said "Mack want to interpret?" He looks at them both and said "Nope" Leaving the hospital a short time later their walking through the mall, Goodie wants to pick up this sweat suits he wanted. Hutch decides to get some things as well and Mack and Steel did some shopping too. They were walking around and hearing this faint voice calling "Uncle Hutch", but didn't see where it was coming from until Cheryl and two of her friends came down from the upper level. She hugs her all her uncle asking them "What are you doing in the mall". She didn't think he was the type to do the walking around mall thing. He just told her he's here with her uncles Goodie, Mack and Steel they were picking up some clothes and other things they needed. She looked at him with that could he buy her something look and he starts to give her cash, she told him if he lets her get things with his Credit card it'll be some percentage off and promises not to go over any amount he tells her not too. He looks at her with concern on face but she nudges her two friends, who also helped her give him the puppy sad face. Taken a deep sigh he goes in his wallet not looking at what Credit card he took and gave it to her, then saying "I trust you to use your best Judgment, beside you know your grandmother is coming up to visit right!" Then add "Don't forget your girls get something too". Letting her know he'll be at the food court with the rest of them waiting for her. They all hug their uncle Hutch and give him a kiss on the cheek as the guys coughed "Mistake!"-"Broke!"-"Bankrupt" for him doing making him look at them, when he turns back around to say something else to Cheryl they were gone. Goodie said "That girl got you wrapped around her finger uncle bank roll". Mack sides with Hutch saying "She good in school and not running wild either". Steel said "Do you see the body on that other girl!" Hutch pops him upside his head going "That's your niece fool!" He said "Not Cheryl the other two. Damn they didn't have bodies like that when I was growing up!" Goodie said "Man you want to go to jail or worse deal with that!" Pointing at Hutch standing there mad what Steel just said, then grabbing him by the back of his coat collar "Bring your ass on!" Cheryl and seven friends went into this one store picking out one or two outfits, at the cashier handing what she thought was her uncle's Credit card to pay for everything. The cashier swipes it and Cheryl and her friends noticed that it read unlimited funds as it cleared, she looked at them and they looked at her with wide eyes and big smiles. The store music starts playing "All about the Benjamins!" She hears her uncle Hutch's voice "To use her best judgment right" She knew what that meant and they went on a serious power shopping spree.

Hutch had finished getting some new clothes and sneakers he wanted sitting in the food court with Goodie, Steel and Mack looking at the women there while eating their food. Cheryl and the same two young friends of her came over to him holding these small bags since he been there a while waiting for her, "I bought you something too uncle!" Hutch looked at Goodie, Steel and Mack telling them "See you were worried she might leave me broke and crying huh!" Cheryl giggled "I would never do that to you, but I did buy me and my friends a few things if you didn't mind. Plus in the bag are your favorite wrist bands" He told her "That's what I wanted to get too, keep up your school work and make me proud of you all".

They all gave him a kiss saying together “Thank you uncle Hutch” and walks back to the rest of the friends sitting down under the food court with all those bags they have trouble carrying around. Steel still pointing to the two friends of Cheryl saying “If those two would have kissed him he would”. Hutch cuts him off again saying “Why you got to be this way”. Goodie added “Well they are healthy young women and we can’t protect them forever”. Steel looked back over the rail to see some young ladies with lots of bags having trouble carrying all of them because there are so many. He calls over Hutch, Mack and Goodie to look at the girls making comments on how their fathers must be feeling light in the ass each time those girls come to the mall. The stores must know each of them by their first name having all those bags like that, Hutch went “It could have been Cheryl” but looking at the girls not seeing their faces from behind. It was Cheryl and her friends having trouble carrying all those bags of stuff as their leaving the mall heading towards the exit.

Back at the hospital Moni is trying to scratch an itch with his unbroken good right arm as this little boy looks at him lying there in the room on the bed with the door open. Trying to get to the itch he hears the little boy laughing at the way he’s trying. Calling the little boy over to him and asking him to hand him the flowers in the window, the little boys does what Moni asked him to. Thanking the little boy as his mother calls his name for him to come along and leave the nice man to get well. Moni takes the plastic flowers putting some of them under his covers for spares and using the other wire cover in plastic to scratch his itch under the body cast getting the scent of the flowers on him as he starts to sweat. This candy striper comes in the room to check on him but smells the cologne mixed with his sweat as she leaned over him. Moni smiled at her and “POW!” Gets slapped and called fresh saying “She’s not doing a dam thing you and he could just get his own water or anything else he wants and better not call her for nothing again”. Moni in pain puzzled from what just happened as she leaves the room and he’s blinking his eyes from being slapped that hard for nothing by the young woman. Trying to figure out what just happened, the door opens up as two hospital orderlies wheels in what is to be his roommate and lets Moni know he's got company for now. Hutch was ready to leave with the guys when Goodies name was called and he looks to see who was calling his name, he saw Becka and Linda with some friends coming over to him asking "What brings him to the mall?." Explaining he's here with his brothers picking up few things, introducing the women to all of them again. Mack says "They look familiar" Goodie went "That night at the club we met them there." Telling Goodie they're going to Red Lobster in the mall for a drink and wants to know if he would like to join them, he asked her would she mind if his brothers came along too. They shook their head "No". Mack said "I don't have any place to go right this minute" Steel and Hutch said the same following them as they walked towards the other end of the mall to the Red Lobster. They pass one of the malls entrance ways, looking out the door at those same girls carrying all those bags walking towards parked car. Mack and Hutch make jokes about the girls daddies must be bankers or in the stock brokers the way those girls are shopping, either the banker or broker is going to sell some shares or get the right stock that's paying off to cover the debt of the credit card their using. Hutch said "I can just imagine the banker going to his daughter, sweetie we have to Viking aunty Angus in the back yard to cover the bill of that Credit card you're charging things on. That's why the big pile of wood is out back now repeat these words "LOW DO I SEE MY MOTHER. LOW DO I SEE MY FATHER" Steel joins in "THEY CALL TO ME. SAYING NOT TO PAY FOR A BIG FUNERAL, CHEAPER If YOU JUST BAR BEE QUE MY ASS YOU SPENDING FOCKER" Then explaining why they have to lift uncle Peter up and down, it's not that we don't like him but he's going on a hot ride with your aunty Angus. Mack asks "Where would he go daddy" Hutch talks in a deep voice "TO THE HALLS of VAL HALA or MOB HEAVEN TO PUT A HIT OUT ON YOUR SPENDING ASS". They start laughing at what they're saying and Goodie told them, they are silly for making jokes about a banker Viking his relatives because they really do think like that. Making to red lobster sitting in a big booth they all were having a drink and laughing as Steel was talking about Hutch giving his niece his Credit card dodging a bullet like that. Dougie and 2Soon walks in with their ladies Sonia and Milaya, they see Goodie sitting in the booth but walking closer they see Mack, Steel and Hutch with some women. Sonia and Milaya see the woman that's sitting between Hutch and Goodie, they look at each other then excuse themselves to go the ladies room. They call Elise and tell her about what they saw with Hutch and how the woman was all over him making seem like they were a couple and might be getting it on. Elise was furious about what she heard them say describing how Hutch had this woman in his arms with the others there having drinks. Telling them all those times at his house which shocked Sonia and Milaya about her being at his house not telling them she was over there, then going in to some kind of flash back about not letting another man take advantage of her again. Something snaps in her mind as she plots to change Hutch and make him what she wants him to be to her. They hang up with her and go back out to the booth where Dougie and 2Soon talked to the waiter having him move them to a bigger table so they all could sit together. Coming in on the tail end of the same conversation again about Hutch giving Cheryl his Credit card and how she used it to get herself and two of her friends something. Just listening to how they were talking about Cheryl and how she and her friends kissed Hutch for the things he bought for them. Getting the wrong idea thinking this was another woman that Hutch has on the side that has him wrapped around her finger and not his niece, Milaya and Sonia got mad at Hutch.

Cheryl is walking in the house asking for help from her sisters and brother so she can get those bags to her room. Each sibling had four or five bags struggling up the stairs to her room as Bernise watched from the couch as they came in the house with her stuff. Up in her room she had them put the bags down and told them to wait as she look through some of the bags to get the things she bought for them when she was at the mall power shopping. She gave Jordell an instant loop playback recorder with two speeds with sneakers and her sisters got clothes and shoes. Bernise was just lying on the couch and heard them laughing and thanking Cheryl for getting them their new clothes and shoes, Jordell kissed his older sister for the new recorder plus new sneakers he really wanted. She opens the door to see Cheryl with all this stuff and wondered where'd she got the money to get all that stuff, she told her mother "Uncle Hutch bought them for us and he didn't mind because he's got money to buy the whole block and more!" Bernise looked at all the stuff and wanted to know what she got for her, but Cheryl told her Mother "That's for daddy to get you something". Then Bernise asked "Where is your daddy?" Cordell was sleep in the family car because Bernise rarely goes out of the house unless there's a party going on and she's being picked up by her one and only friend, otherwise she doesn't leave the house and Cordell knows it. That's why he sneaks away from her during the day and sleeps in the garage.

Bernise knew Hutch had money but didn't know he had that much cash on him, but looking at all the brand new stuff Cheryl came in there with. Her kniving ass had to figure a way to get her hands on some of it, even if it meant using his brother to get it. Calling Jordell and telling him she would give him a dollar if he found his father because she knows he could. Jordell stood there looking at her and waits, she looked at him and asked "What you waiting for go find your father!" He replies "Mama what you always says, this is not the post office and I don't take C.O.D's pay now or no service!" She looked at him with a threating expression on her face "Boy! If you don't go and find your father!" He looked at her and says "Look ma, you can't catch me and when you do your always out of breath because you smoke like a factory in overtime. When you hit me it takes what two hits then your breathing hard again, so why don't you just pay me cause I know you keep cash on you for cigarettes" Holding out his hand she knew he was right and pays him. Jordell pulls out this bigger that she's got knot of cash he keeps and adds the one to the bills in his pocket. She looked at him do that and asked "Where did you get all that from?" He told her "Who else is going to pay for my college, lazy as you two are a kid can keep a wade of cash playing his cards right!" He goes to the garage and shakes the car telling his father his mother is looking for him, the window is rolled down and two dollars are handed out of the window as a voice says "You thought I was outside but I'm not there!" He takes the bills and starts to walk away but stops and starts back to the car, his father shouts "That's all I got!" Jordell turns back around and heads back into the house to let his mother know what his father said and maybe see if he could get a little more playing the both of them against each other. Bernise wasn't giving any more money up but knew she had to talk to Cordell because she could use a few things around the house plus some cash for her pocket. That way she can get the brand name things she wants like beer, cigarette, liquor she like to drink and wouldn't have to cook for a while.

After some time Hutch had to get up and wanted to leave but the guys wasn't ready to leave so the ladies sitting next to him offered a ride, saying "she had to get up early as well" and he took her offer with all the guys giving him the wink look as to say get lucky. Once they were out of the mall Hutch explained to her she didn't have to do that, because it would put her out of her way. He told her where he lives and thanking her for the thought and offer but pointing to the cabs outside the mall already, so it can take him home and she doesn't have a long drive home. He gives her a nice hug and thanks again saying "You're nice and hope you find the right guy for you" as he gets in the cab. The cabby is thanking Hutch for such a big tip before he pulls away, Hutch is walking up his walk way after getting the mail out of the box. When this vehicle come screeching to a stop in front of his house. He looks at the vehicle not worried because he knows who is driving but puzzled at how she was driving it. Elise walks over to him asking about the tail lights on the vehicle she barely got a look at as it turned the corner, thinking about chasing her ass down. He told her it was a guy driving a cab, but she didn't listen to what he was saying. She was too mad about him being at Red Lobster with another woman and telling him "I know what happens when men bring a woman to Red Lobster and she better not had a doggy bag either!" Hutch turns his head holding the laugh in thinking (Um where did she hear that from.) He told her he was there with his friends and they are still there, he's got to get up early for work in the morning is why he left. He doesn't remember the name of the woman that wanted to give him a ride home but he didn't, she cuts him off saying "Want to get caught by me huh!" Hutch tries to explain more but she isn't hearing it, he walks to the house with her behind still going on about the woman.

Going in and closing the door after he walks in the house first right in her face cutting off her conversation. She stands at the door surprised he would do that and pounds on the door for him to open up. Thinking he's hiding her in his house somewhere he doesn't want her to see. Hutch opens the door looking at her like she lost her mind going "If you find a woman other than yourself in my house I'll give you the house!" Elise folds her arms and looks at him for a moment then takes off running passed him saying "She can't hide from me. I know where a woman could hide in this place". He pays her no attention as he gets his things ready for work and she goes through his whole house till she come back to his bedroom. Hutch took his shower and put on his night clothes watching her come in the bedroom breathing heavy from running through the house and finding nothing. He listens to her talk about she knew there was a woman in his house as he walks her to the front door and opens it for her to stand there at the door, then closes it behind her as she still goes on talking "There had better not have been a woman in your house" walking to her vehicle by herself then turns and noticed she was outside and the door closed. Looking up and watch as the lights went out on the second floor, she stand there for moment then it hits her he threw her out of his house and turned the lights out on her too. She gets in her vehicle now mad at what he did and shouted "You got to call me sooner or later FOCKER!" Hutch is snoring already sleep and didn't hear a word she shouted.

That morning Hutch is up feeling good and decides to wear his black tee shirt that fits snug on him, he puts on the shirt after using some of that silver cologne that he really likes. Putting on his black sweat bands taking a look at himself in the mirror liking what he sees and goes to work. Getting to the garage first like he does and pulling out his truck and cleaning it and for some reason feeling really good about the day. Meepbo's car pulls up with him and his daughters as they get out of his car and look at Hutch cleaning his truck. He waves hello hoping they won't say anything more to him about that day, but they all just look at him and then go in the building with their father. Thinking he just needs to get out of there so he doesn't feel so uncomfortable around them as Meepbo tells him his daughters will be coming around checking on the driver to see how the rest of the business is going. He's got a couple small jobs which he needs done. Hutch wondered if he was going to get pulled off the building and Meepbo told him he doesn't know because Moni is still out and Hernando is taken his place till he comes back. Telling Hutch just go to the building in Manhattan and he'll send word what he wants him to do. Before Meepbo could say anything else he heard the door close and engine start revving as Hutch is in his truck and pulling off. Thinking "Wow that man loves his work if only I had a few more like him". Hutch is working hard and swelling up from it, not even close to lunch time when Meepbo's car pulls up and Lorie and Sheila get out. They go over to Hernando and tell him he's got to let Hutch come on the other small job and give him a piece of paper with the address on it. Hutch is sweating heavy under the coveralls he's got on when Hernando comes over to him and tells him he's got to follow them to the new small job Meepbo wants done today, he'll be along soon as the other trucks get there. Hutch did what he was told following Lorie and Sheila to the building where the guys will be cleaning out this one whole floor to be redone. Hutch pulls up and sits in his truck but there's a knock on the passenger side door and he looks over to see Sheila standing there waving for him to come out of the truck. Turning down his music and asking her "Is there something wrong?" She laughs at him and says "I need you to come with me to see if they would need another truck there with all the stuff that has to be thrown out."

He gets out of the truck and stands in front of her looking at the building as the cologne he has on mixed with his sweat in his clothes hits her nose making her close her eyes and take a deep breath telling him he smells so good. He thanks her for the compliment and walks with her into the building as she hold his arm smiling at people as they get on the elevator and she leans her head on his shoulder. They reach the floor to get off on and she pulls him by the arm saying "This way". He looks at all the offices that are empty and says to her "There's no one here!" She pulled him in this big office with the big double doors and a voice says "Well I wouldn't say nobody." Lorie spins around in the big chair and she's got on just her bra and panties looking very sexy with her hair down like that. Then he heard what sounded like the doors being locked and turns to see Sheila in her bar and thong saying "They don't have long and he doesn't want them to tell their father so he better comply". Hutch thought this could only happen in the movies, since this is his life he can't wait to see the movie on it. They unzip his coveralls and the smell of the cologne in his shirt has them really horny for him as they both attack him all over the office.

Its 1:30 and Lorie's cell phone is ringing, it's Hernando on the phone saying they'll be there in a half an hour which gives they time to use the shower that's right next to the big office so they can clean up. Hernando arrives with the crew and sees Hutch sitting in his truck listening to his music. Hernando knocks on the door and tell him to get ready for the stuff to come down so they can get out of there early. Fifteen workers are standing outside the van as Hutch starts up his truck and looks at them thinking they look very serious about what they're going to do as they follow Hernando in the building. Hutch went back up to the floor to see them working like little cartoon Tasmanian Devils going through everything and tearing it out ready to be taken down to the truck, when they go to the couch most of the crew was standing around talking about it and the chair on it too. They were saying "It smelled like some people were up there doing their thing on the couch and chair in the office from the odor and sticky wet spots and it wasn't that long ago they left. Hutch's eye brows raised as he coughed clearing his throat knowing that was his cue to go back down stairs and wait for them to get there. In the bathroom Sheila and Lorie was trying to cover up the hands prints on their body left by Hutch's big hands again. Hernando knocked on the door to tell them they were ready to get in there, Sheila and Lorie checked each other one more time before they walked out of the bathroom trying not to show they were walking sore. Hernando and the rest of the work crew stopped working and just looked at Sheila and Lorie as they walked funny to the elevator, but Hernando trying to keep a straight face stops them. He told both of them "Look what you do when your home is one thing, I can't let you two leave like that!" They ask him "What is he talking about?" Showing them in a mirror the hand prints they tried to cover up and the way their walking, like they just got off a big horse bow legged and stiff back. He sends one of his workers down to the van to get two of the white cloth dust jump suits and tells them next time they have a men up there make sure they have the right clothes to over all those hand prints, so their father won't think it was him or one of his crew. Hernando come down to the truck as the men starts bring down the stuff to the truck to be thrown in, he asked Hutch did he see any man that came in the building with the boss's daughters. Explaining "They have big hand prints on their body and walking funny like they've been rode good and hard". Hutch coughs at what he just heard and quickly said "They walked in with two guys but I didn't see them come out when I was sitting in the truck". Hernando said "Two he could have sworn there had to be more than that from the way they were walking and had prints on them" Hutch coughs!

Hernando told him "I gave them the white jump suits we use because of dust so their father wouldn't see the hand prints." He knows how Meepbo would get mad about his girls. Hutch agreed saying "Good thinking" Hutch's cell phone rings and his mother is calling to make sure he's ready for her when she comes up there for her visit tomorrow. He told her there shouldn't be any problem when she gets there because it's going to be a three day weekend for him starting tomorrow and he'll pick her up.

Early that Thursday afternoon Hutch was back at the first building and the last truck to be loaded late that afternoon. Standing outside his truck while the music is playing watching people go by grooving to the radio Dee Jay mixing music pumping out his system sounding good to them walking by. The work crew and Hutch was talking and laughing about Moni and how he got dusted with white Co2, when eye candy (Kiamesha) walks up to Hutch standing there. She's a little mad at him, it seems he's avoiding her and she doesn't like it. She always used to getting what she wants and most men do anything she wants, but she's got this thing for him ever since she smelled that cologne on his body. Showing cleavage enough to have every man stare at her dressed so sexy but classy in her woman's suit that shows her nice rounded butt and muscular thighs, looking like the executive of a big business as she walks over to him. She stands so close pushing her chest just under his and wants to know what she's got to do to him to get him to come with her. Pinned against the truck and her Hutch looks down at her, before he could say anything she took her hand and with no one noticing puts it in his pocket feeling what she wants to feel. Pulling his head down a little so she could tell him in his ear "Your body wants to come with me, I could feel your pulse in my hands growing," Closing his eyes and swallowing melting in her hands and tries to say something, she pulls her hand out of his pocket and turns her back on him leaning against him. She says "I'm going to catch you one day away from your job and when I do" taken his arms wrapping them around her like a fur wrap engulf in them. She wiggles a little against him feeling him throb then she turns quick and about to kiss him, but licks his earlobe and says "Till then watch your back, I'll find ya". She walks away with all the work crew plus Hernando and three security guards from the building watch her body twist in that suit till she turns the corner. They look at Hutch as one of the older security guard walks over to him "I got a couple questions son, if ya don't mind." Hutch just looked being asked "Are you married, in love, have a jealous woman, saving yourself for a special woman, scared of wild pu-tang, because she looks like it is some wild Pu-tang or just plain GAY!" Everything the old man asked he shook his head "No, to". Then the old man said "What are you waiting for man? That's a BFG-VNAD for me!" He looked curiously at the old man as he explain what he meant by that BFG-VNAD (Bumpy Face Gin, Viagra Night, Aleve Day) "After drinking the gin and taken the Viagra, doing what he knows she's going to have him do. Then taken the WHOLE! Bottle of Aleve the next day from being sore from that night" They both looked at each other and laughed then Hutch told him "There's something about a woman like that who looks like she uses men only like gum till the flavors gone then she gets another stick, so why I don't want to just bang that out and be at her whim when she wants a toy to play with. Just not feeling it that's all" The old man looked at Hutch saying "That's what you're going with uh" He turns telling all of the guys watching them talk "He's whipped! Not wanting to be another

Tiger, Kobe, Sanders, Justice, Fox, Humphries, McCartney, Cole, Jeter, Jordan or Trump!" The guys shook their heads going (AH!) agreeing with that, thinking she does look a woman that would take half of his half too.

Back at the garage Sheila and Lorie were getting out of the car still in the white cloth jump suits as Meepbo came out to see them walking a little stiff, he said "I'm so proud of my daughters for getting down with the men banging out some hard work, giving it up good for the business". Carmella looked at them saying "You were to take charge of the work, not get a work out!" Telling them need to get out of those dirty cloth suits so they don't get dirt all over the carpet in their father office, Sheila Says "No need to". Lorie and Sheila head to the car as they told their father they were going home to get cleaned up from working so hard on the floor in the building learning the business. Sheila whispers "You mean getting the business on the couch, chair, desk, end table" Carmella watched them laughing and drive away but then thought about how they looked and walked, knowing she saw them walking like that before. Then she gets it why the suits they were wearing wasn't dirty and why was their hair in pony tails. Carmella told her father she was going home to help Sheila and Lorie in case they needed anything and races to her car to speeding away.

Hutch is pulling up the garage after dumping his truck and quickly washes off, when Meepbo came out thanked him for working hard on his daughters, next time don't work them so hard in those positions because they were so sore and stiff when he saw them. Hutch stood there for moment looking at Meepbo trying to figure out if he somehow knew what happened in the building, thinking there was no one around telling Meepbo. Saying to him "OK, I didn't want to but you know how I work", Meepbo answered "How else was they to learn it take it from a big man, to help them reach the satisfaction of being worked like that. Guess they now know they would get sore from that much hard work!" Hutch looked at him. Then Meepbo says "Hope you didn't have them all over the place knocking it down or digging their backs out. Right that's how you bros say it?" Hutch shook his head and went "Yeah I was knocking 'em down, busting them both out" Meepbo went "Good! Good that's what I want to hear." Then stops to think about what they both just said, but Hutch breaks his thought and told him "he's out of there" and grabs his bag out of the truck. Not noticing one of the silver capped bottle fell out on the floor. Meepbo watch him leave and noticed the bottle on the ground half full, he smelled it and thought he saw one like that in the bathroom so using some thinking Toni should like the way he smells now. Carmella gets to the house and looks for Sheila and Lorie but find Sheila steaming up her bathroom in the shower and Lorie soaking in her tub with lots of bubbles. Carmella asked Lorie "How come she's in the tub this time of day, she normally gets in before bed" Standing there at her bathroom door she hears Sheila coming out of the shower and goes to her room. With two towels wrapped around her body she stands there looking at Carmella asking "What are you doing here so early, thought you were helping dad!" Carmella doesn't say anything but reach for Sheila towel, she gets her hand pushed away by Sheila "What are you doing trying to take my towel" Carmella told her she want to see underneath it that's all. Wanting to know why she never was interested in her body before then asked "Are you turning funny". Carmella doesn't answer and turns to walk away but quickly turns back catching Sheila by surprise and snatching her towel off. Sheila stood there with her hands on her hips "Going happy now!" Carmella saw the hand prints on her body and shook her head saying "From the looks of those hand prints, I could tell how many positions you were in with him". Looking at her up and down seeing prints on the front and back even on her feet. Then asked "Lorie too". She shook her head "Yes" going to see Lorie but she was fast asleep snoring hard and loud under her cover in bed.

Going back to talk with Sheila and finds her in the kitchen eating up a storm attacking the food as if she never ate before. Carmella sees her and goes to watch TV in her room.

Hutch is on his way home to get in the shower but talking to Dougie about going to the club since it's a three day weekend. Arriving home having a beer up in his bedroom when Mack and Steel knocks on the door, he uses the intercom and told them to come in because he's getting in the shower. After his shower he dried off got dressed and went down with them having beers as the rest of the GDM4L came over dressed and ready to go out that night. The guys were walking around the house and LIL-Rob saw Hutch putting on some of the silver capped cologne getting a whiff asking "Where did you get that from, I likes the smell". Handing him the bottle saying "Here use some and tell me how it holds up for you at the club!" LIL-Rob was putting some on and the others smelled its scent that carried over to them, they knew that smell from before came to get some more sprayed on them except 2Soon. He used the black capped one just a little bit saying "I don't want to follow the crowd!" Byron asked "Hutch you should be tired from work?" He answered "I'll be alright!" as they all had a couple more drinks before heading out to the dance club. They get to the club there's a lot of women looking very good to them as they drove by to find a parking spot for all the vehicles. Walking back after finding some spots for their vehicles looking like a musical band walking towards the line of women waiting on line to get in the club. At the door 2Soon, Derrick and LIL-Rob all know three of the security guards so they don't have to wait in line when their guys are on the doors, paying the fee to get in they all head right to the bar for one more drink to add what they drank at Hutches house. The music has people grooving but no one is on the dance floor just standing there listening to it, all the women were waiting for some men to ask them to dance but it looked like they didn't want to work up a sweat. No one was on the dance floor till the GDM4L came in and had one drink then branched out asking the first female they came across to dance. The music was sounding too good for them to say no and every Grand Drunken Master 4 Life had one or two ladies dancing with them. Things got hot for the GDM4L having those drinks and moving to the music. The club's so big there's a section where the light is out and if someone was to be in that darken arrear they could see out into the dim lit club but no one could actually see who or what is in the dark arrear. Lots of people go in there to do whatever they don't want anyone to see them doing to each another in there. The dance floor is getting crowded with more new people that came in the club and wanted to dance. The place gets hot and all the GDM4L are starting to sweat from the combination of heat and moving around with the drinks they had going for more plus the women they are dancing with at the time. The only one not dancing and having a good time is 2Soon because it seems every woman he says something too gets afraid of him and can't understand why. He would get to talking to one all of sudden they would start looking at him like he was going to eat them up and move away quickly. The music was pumping and Hutch was doing his thing with this woman when Elise walks up behind him, getting the woman's attention mouthing to her "That's my man" and shooing her away. The woman found another partner to dance with quick as Elise just stood there. He turns around doing a dance move to see her just standing there. She wants to know who in the hell that woman was he was dancing with. Hutch surprised asked "Where did you come from, I didn't know you was in here?" She answers "I just happen to come there with Sonia and Milaya, they wanted to come there to have a girls night". Sonia had cut in on Dougie plus Milaya was already dancing with 2Soon, they were just having fun with their men.

Elise was giving Hutch the third degree about him not calling her to see if she wanted to come to the club, and what was he going to do with that woman once they left there. 2Soon was trying to figure out why Milaya was not trying to stay by him after a short dance, she was scare of him for some reason. Sonia wanted to know what he done to her girl, he explains nothing but sees she's really afraid of him. Elise came over to them and wondered what was going on as well. Hutch came over to help by taken 2Soon back to the bar and try to figure out what happened. He didn't want things to turn into a scene as people starts looking. Telling 2Soon to stay at the bar and he'll go talk to Milaya to get her side of what's wrong. While Hutch was walking back to them, he gets these pair of hand come from behind him and takes hold of his chest. He looks down at the hands feeling a body in back of him thinking "Who can it be". Elise saw what was going standing there with Milaya and stares at him with such a look, like she could beat his ass. Hutch turns and sees Sheila standing there and asked her "What are you doing here?!" She answers "One of Lorie's friends wanted to come to this club, since they had a good nap thanks to him they were ready to go out!" Elise was over there fast and looking at Hutch with eyes that could burn through him then wanted to know "Who is this now?!" He answers "My boss's daughter!" Elise said "Looking like that?! Boss's don't have daughters that look like that!" Sheila took offense at what Elise was shouting at Hutch about her looks she said "White girls with black girl booties not going to flying with her. They supposed to be flat butted skinny and have bleach blond hair not looking like they could star in a Ludacris video of how low could they go!" (He turns away with thought, she must have not seen the video; White girl with black hair has got a BANGIN ASS BODY & HIPS too.) Sheila took what she said as a compliment and told Hutch she'll see him Monday at the garage. She walks away with a black girls swagger looking back over her shoulder at Elise and rolling her eyes flipping her hair going back to her sisters and their dates. Elise said "I should go over there and kick her ass for being so bitchy. So what she's the boss's daughter she still can get as ass beating!" Hutch went "Careful she looks like she does a lot of platies and hits the treadmill too from the muscles in her legs, hips and stomach!" Hutch told Elise "see all three of them, they are Meepbo's daughters and he's my boss. They have dates with them so why are you like this?" Elise looking at Sheila and her sisters said to Hutch "OH so now your checking out her body, now your into women like her and Jessica Biel and Scarlett Johansson, Alyssa Milano, Rose McGowan and Michelle Pfeiffer or all those hot white women huh!" Turning to say something else to him but see him writing something down on a piece of paper she asked him "What are you doing?" He asked "What was that last two names you said McGowan and Pfeiffer?" She gets really mad at him and goes back to Milaya and Sonia telling them they need to leave, Hutch just got on her last nerve with that white girl and they need to be somewhere the men aren't so stupid. Sheila saw that Elise was mad for being next to Hutch and walks back over to him to make her even more jealous by asking him something softly to make him bend to hear her over the loud music playing. She puts both her arms around his neck and making it look as if she was going to kiss him and says in his ear "Hope I didn't get you into trouble with your girlfriend" As she was doing that Elise turns to look back and saw

Sheila with her arms around his neck and got really mad leaving the club with Sonia and Milaya. All the rest of the Grand Drunken Masters 4 Life were being taken into the dark spot of the club by most every woman they were dancing with except 2Soon at the bar till a woman threw her glass of beer on him for scaring her like that. Hutch saw what happened to him and rushes over to him before he got mad. He follows 2Soon in the bathroom and they talk about what happened. How come every woman he talks to got afraid of him, telling Hutch he don't want to smell like beer as he rinse off his shirt in the sink and blow dries it with the hand blower. Hutch was trying to figure out with him why that was happening, remembering the silver capped cologne in his pocket handing it to him. Some of the Grand Drunken Masters came in the bathroom to clean up from their experiences in the dark spot of the club. Asking "What's going on with 2Soon" blow drying his shirt, Hutch explained he's having an off night that's all but thing will get better the night's still young. They all talk about how there must be something in the air tonight, every woman they are dancing with starts getting very really horny and wants to take them over to the spot. Then they hear what sounds like Steel and a woman moaning coming from one of the stalls there. Looking at each other and asking has any one of them seen Steel since they got in the club. Mack goes over to the stall and bangs on the door loudly saying "Hey man I really got to go or move over I won't peek". They all starts snickering like little boys in school at what Mack said standing by the stall. Steel answers "Hey this one is full there's other in here". Mack answers back "That's it I'm get security". The moaning stops and couple second the door opens up as they all stood there watching, first the woman come out with wild hair then Steel fixing his pants and shirt. They clap for the woman as she runs out and then for Steel as he looks at them mad they interrupted him. LIL-Rob told him "While you are in here with just one, we were getting two and three at the dark spot of the club man" Steel laughed at him because he didn't believe him till D-train bust in the door with two women saying "Oh sorry we thought there was no one in here!" Letting the women go back out to the club saying "I needs to talk to my brothers". D-train stand in there with all the G.D.M.4.L as 2Soon got dressed and Jazz said "I don't know what's going on here but I'm not leaving till I get a few more in". That's when Dave said "YO! Let me see those tip drill covers!" All of the G.D.M.4.L go in their pockets pulling out and unrolling their covers and holds them up. Dave says "Hold it there's something not right here!" He walks over to this one guy holding up two condoms that's not magnum asking "Who the hell are you man?" Smacking the condoms out of his hand yelling at him "See With those little ass shits that's why you're not a G.D.M.4.L, now if you don't get your ass out of here!" The man gets slapped up his head by all the G.D.M.4.L as he goes through the gauntlet before leaving out the men's room. Putting away their covers and heading back out to see there were more women on the dance floor, they spread out to go get one. 2Soon heads back to the bar to get another drink first and some of the women remember him moving away afraid, but then one woman smelled the cologne Hutch gave him to put on. Tapping him on his shoulder he turns around and sees her smiling at him, with a little attitude he goes "Don't tell me you want me to move right!" She told "Yeah your ass right on the dance floor with me". The DJ played SWV's "Right here!".

Everyone in the club was dancing or moving as the Dee jay was mixing the music things were getting really hot. Hutch looked around at his brother and noticed how they were dancing so close and moving as one on the dance floor with the women. Looking around at the bar arrear for 2Soon but then sees the back of him on the dance floor with this woman, then she walks him into the darken arrear of the club like everyone else. Everyone was dancing for a while and then the music starts to die down and all of sudden everyone heard "OH Shhiottt!" Followed by a big splash sound with a few sputters then quiet. The clip clop of high heels on hard wood floor is heard as this woman walks out of the darken arrear in a black dress drenched in this liquid from top of her head down the front of her dress. All the G.D.M.4.L looked at the women run pass all the people on the floor and Mack says "Hutch! Where are you bruh, this looks like you're doing!" Hutch taps him on his shoulder standing right behind Mack saying

"Why! I haven't been with a woman in over 15 years!" Things got even more quite as everyone slowly turned looking at Hutch after he said that to Mack. Hutch looks back at the people "What a brother can't go through a dry spell?!" A voice came out the crowd "DAMN! Man that's not a dry spell it's an era, you must've been locked up good!" Hutch held his hands up to his head to block the light in his eyes searching, growling "Who said that Sh!" A man being nosey walks by the dark arrear slips on some liquid hitting the floor with a "BOOM" Landing on his back lying there in pain. The orange glow of a face as this cigar is lit and starts coming out of the dark. 2Soon blowing the smoke out tipping his ashes on the man lying there then stepping over him on the floor, flicking ash again nodding his head the Dee Jay plays "Damn" (by Young Bloodz) Hearing LIL john's signature sound "YEAAAAAHH!" As the music plays and everyone starts dancing again, as the night went on Hutch got a chance to dance with his boss's daughter and show the rest of the G.D.M.4.L what they looked like before they all left the club. Still in the mood to party but hungry and wanting to get something to eat first, some of the G.D.M.4.L leave the club with a woman or two except Hutch, Dougie and 2Soon. For some strange reason and Goodie left with the two women he knew Becka and Linda. They all head to the diner they always go to after the club and when they get there the waitress asked "How many" Hutch turns looking at everyone and says "28." She looked at them and leads them to the other side of the diner where they just fit. On the way to that side Hutch sees Elise, Sonia and Milaya at a table. Milaya looks at 2Soon as he walk over to her and they get to talking only this time she's not afraid but get more attracted to him and Dougie and Sonia are already sitting together. Hutch walks over to Elise, he wants her to join them and they can talk about her being mad at him. She wants him to beg her first because she's still mad about what happened at the club. After some begging she decides to join them and sat next to Hutch as all the G.D.M.4.L went "Ah" and 2Soon lead the choir of Billy Ocean song Suddenly!" with the others joining in having the whole place wonder what was going on in that part of the diner as the guys sung a little loudly on key surprisingly. The waitress had her hands full with everyone on that side of the diner, she had to get help and with two more waitresses they still had a hard time keeping up with everyone's orders. The bill came everything was on one check. It got passed around having everyone get a look at the bill till it reaches Hutch. Elise eye's got wide at the cost of everything sitting next to him looking at the bill, telling everyone to meet him at his house as he pulls out his wallet and hands the waitress his Credit card. Looking where it reads how much he want to tip them, so he checks in 150 dollars for all of them before handing it back to her. She looks at him after she saw what he checked for a tip, asking "Are you sure?" Hutch smile and told her to charge it and Elise wanted to know why she asking him about the charge? He told her not to worry about it as he puts on his jacket and gets ready to leave, but the waitresses were at the cashier swiping his card seeing what it read and hugging each other for getting such a big tip. They come back to him and thanked him for the tip kissing him on the cheek watching as he signed the receipt then putting his card back in his wallet. Elise snatches the receipt and saw what he tipped them and got really mad for him doing that saying "They didn't work that hard for so much it's their job to serve us". Hutch told her "They worked very hard and the food was hot and good besides it's not your money, I worked hard for it so I can spend what I like on people treat me good". The waitress smiled at her being put in her place like that, Elise got really mad because she couldn't say anything to what he said to her. Mad she told him "I'll see you at the car." Walking out the diner very mad looking back to see the waitress kiss him again on the cheek. They thanked him for the tip and told him "Hope they didn't start anything with his wife."

He smiles and laughed "I'm not married to her." The first waitress said "Your girlfriend or finance?" Hutch said "Nope! I just met her not to long ago." and walks out of the diner and Waves bye to the women. The two waitress looked at each other, the first one said "How come all the bitches get the good ones." The second one answered "Well if you get very bitchy who knows you might come across a good rich one too, but who wants to be a crazy woman with issues when he finds out about that. She'll get dropped faster than a Britney spears back up dancer or married best friend maybe even a J-Lo's ex-boyfriends." They laugh and go back to cleaning up the tables.

Hutch walks to his vehicle still a little tipsy looking at Elise who is leaning up against it mad at him for saying that to her. She wants to know what was he proving paying those waitresses like that and then saying that to her in front of them. He explains he didn't mean nothing by it except he works hard for whatever he's got and not even his own mother would tell him what he could do with it, when someone gets on him about taking care of the people that took care of him tends to get a little defensive. Then asked was she coming back to his place or not? She rolls her eyes still mad about what he said to her and told him "No! Got something to do" He said "If you change your mind the door is open" Getting in his vehicle to catch up with the others because he knows they'll be waiting at the door for him to open it, they don't know how to disarm his alarm system to get in his house. Reaching his house quick from the short way he took and sees the cars pulling up as he opens the door and disarms his system. Everyone came in tired from the food and drinks plus drive back to Staten Island and a short time later they are looking for somewhere to lay down or left to go to their own home. Hutch took his shower tired from working earlier and then dancing most all that night he just put on his boxer under his towel. Becka came knocking on his bedroom door because Linda threw up on her from the drinks and food that didn't agree with her, she told him the other bathrooms are full and would like to clean up from the mess on her clothes too. He told her "Sure don't mind me, got to get dressed anyways". He gave her one of his shirts and sweat pants to put on when she comes out of the shower. She went in as he was looking for something to put on himself but doses off to sleep being so tired and lying on the bed. Because he's got one of those beds if you sit on it for too long you are going get comfortable and lay down drifting off to sleep. Elise had changed her mind and came to his house so she could talk to him, feeling she didn't get in the last words with him. Finding the door open like he said she walks into the house and heads up to his bedroom seeing some of the G.D.M.4.L on his couch and love seats with women sleep. Opening the door to his bedroom she sees him lying on the bed and a towel around him sleep, then Becka came out of his bathroom in the shirt and sweat pants he gave to her drying her hair saying "I really need to get all that sticky stuff on my chest dripping down the front of me like". Her words are cut startled by Elise standing there looking at her then at Hutch again shaking her head turning around to leave the room as Becka says "Wait!" She yells back at her "Save it Bitch! I could see why their brothers they share everything like brother dogs do!" Running down stairs upset almost running over Dougie as she leaves the house mad at what she just saw. He looks at her wondering what was all that about and goes up to Hutch's room where Becka was trying to wake him lying on the bed in his towel. Becka explained to Dougie what happened and he told her she's not going to wake him, he's in an Odin type of sleep best wait for him to wake then explain it to him. She asked "What about Elise?" She thought the two of them did something and now she's under impression they had an affair. Dougie told her "Elise could think all she wants we don't get down like that." Telling her to come on and leave Hutch sleep, Dougie turns to leave the room and Becka was about to get off the bed and looked at the towel wrapped on Hutch.

She starts to take a quick peek at what's under it being curious. Dougie clearing his throat stopping her "Hey you really want to risk taking a peek, you in enough trouble as is!" She gets up saying "If I'm going to be accused of something it's best to at least see what I'm in trouble for." Before Dougie could stop her she lift the towel "HOLY SHIT! What happens when that thing gets big!" Dougie turns his back not wanting to look and grabs her off the bed then tells her "Got your look, now what happens after is on your ass. If that was your man what would you do to the woman who looked at him?" Becka said "Besides hi five the chick, then bragging about what I got or the thing he's got and does with it to me!" then smiling big. They head down stairs to let Hutch sleep. While Elise was driving home something in her mind snaps even more about what she thought happened. She starts talking to herself about how she's going to make him pay for cheating on not even giving her a chance to sleep with him before he gets with some other bitch. Her ranting to herself continues all the way home about how he gives everyone else his attention but her. She's going to make him along with all the other men that ever cheated on her pay for their betraying her, as she stares at herself in the vehicles rear mirror listening to her other side tell her things to do.

That afternoon Hutch was waking up finding himself in towel then jumping up remembering Becka was in his shower. Hurrying and finding some clothes to put on, he looks in the shower to see she's not in there. Going down stairs to see who is still there and what are they going to do or later. Mack told him Cordell came by then asked "Why was he holding his head like that when he came back down stairs from talking to you." Hutch had to try to remember if he spoke to Cordell because he was still sleep when he came, answering Mack "Guess he done something stupid to get hit in the head." Saying "I can't remember what it was or maybe it'll come to me later." Some of the G.M.D's were still sleeping and others had got up and went home. He went to get a good working out first and then to washing his clothes since it's the weekend. He always go the laundry mat on weekends when he got time, thinking he'll shower after he came back from the laundry. Putting on some of the sliver capped cologne to cover the smell of him doing a hard working out then gets his clothes and heads out. Getting to the laundry mat in those same clothes he worked out in, opening the door and a breeze blew in carrying his scent in the place where some old and young women were washing clothes. Catching a good whiff of what came in there with Hutch having every women looking at him. Going over to one of the medium Machine and putting his clothes down giving back a friendly smile to all the women in there looking at him as if they were lioness stalking a kill, with some slowly peeking their heads up from behind the Machines one and two rows over. Making him feel he was the target of the day as he saw nothing but the top of their heads and eyes follow his every movement. He took off his sweat jacket still swollen from pumping iron letting the scent out even stronger. The women look at him standing there at the Machine trying to find quarters. Leaving his clothes by the Machine he heads to the front counter to get change but gets cut off by one of the women holding four quarters in her hands saying "I've got some change if you need me!" He didn't really catch what she said and told her "Thanks but I couldn't take your money." He walks around her and met by two more ladies saying “They can wash him if he likes.” Again not paying close attention to what they said he answers “Thank you but I can handle this load I’ve done it before.” One of the ladies says “I know you got more than just one load!” Looking at him seductively smile standing on his side. Still not catching what they are saying to him, smiling back at them he goes up to the counter.

The young lady was behind the counter putting on the shelf a bag of clothes she just finished washing to be picked up by the owner and hears Hutch ask her for ten dollars of quarters. She turns and looks to see the big man holding a ten dollar bill in his hand as the scent of the cologne hits her nose, making her take a deep breath as her eyes got wide and she leans over to show her cleavage even more to him. Asking “What did you want?” He said “Ten dollars of quarters please.” She looked at him licking her lips sizing him up handed him a roll of quarters and she took the bill “Don’t you need something else?” He smiled at her and replied “I’m good.” The young woman watched him walk back to where he left his clothes, another woman there telling him she put his clothes in the Machine and started washing them for him. Another younger woman than her told him she put in his whites in the Machine next to his colors too. He thanked them both for what they done but the first older woman said she was going to do both till this youngster wanted to try to get her hands on his white things. The seconded younger woman said “Listen gran ma, he’s too young for you so let a woman that could handle him get at that!” The older medium size woman looked her up and down replying “Don’t you have two crumb snatchers over there playing on the arcade Machines. He doesn’t need to be the third baby daddy in your circus!” The seconded heavier sizes younger woman went “You are pass your prime you old dried up hole and he wouldn’t want something that needs to be watered every 2 minutes!” The older medium sizes woman got really mad and rolled up her sleeves saying “I dropped two kids years ago and kept myself in banging good shape, so kicking your ass and have enough to have a man his size screaming my name in four languages and sucking his thumb afterwards!” Hutch didn’t know what to say about that but just looked. The younger heavier sizes woman told her “If you got it like that then let's get at it and see who still got what left for him, you old bat!" Before anyone could say something the two stared at each and the younger woman charged at the older one pushing her into the bathroom, where it sounded like there were two big cats cussing and yelling banging and booming in there. A few minutes later the noise stopped, the door opens and the older medium sizes woman came out with her hair a mess and clothes a little torn fixing herself. Leaving the door open for all to see the heavier sized woman lying there all beat up out cold on the floor. The older woman smiled at everyone then realizes her upper teeth were missing and goes back in the bathroom to find them in the hair of the heavier woman lying there on the floor. Hutch was wondering what the hell is going on here, then gets tapped on his shoulder by the counter woman asking "If you wanted the small bottle of bleach could you help me reach some from the back storage room, the boxes are too heavy for me." Being the gentlemen he is, saying "Sure lead the way." Walking in the back storage room she closes the door looking at the other women watching by their Machine mumbling about how she thinks she so slick getting him to go in the back like that. In the room she walks towards him tripping on a box falling into his arms getting a real good whiff the cologne and feeling him up. Helping her stand up right trying not to look at her nipples, they wasn't visible before and now seem to be staring back at him like buttons to be pushed. She points to the boxes up on the shelf asking him to hold her steady as she steps on a foot step to get the bleach from a top shelf. Standing in back of her first but she kept bending over and her behind to touch his chest and in that short skirt, he felt uncomfortable so he gets in front of her where her chest was so close to his forehead brushing up against it and down to his nose. She twisted back and forth, up and down making her nipples rub his head and nose then close to his mouth as he jerked back trying not to touch them feeling how hard they were. Grunting and groaning to get the box having the women on the other side of the door the listening think there was something going on.

The wobbly step ladder was shaking as she tugs and pulls the box out but the momentum carries her backward into the shelf behind,

Hutch tries to catch her but only manage to grab her lower legs as she bent back hitting her head on the shelf and knocking over the liquid soap above her on the shelf. From the other side of the door all the grunting and moaning heard had some women by the door really thinking naughty things, till they hear her go loudly "Oh! Oh! I'm going too." He's heard grunting then there was a bang boom. They open the door to see him standing there over her holding one of her legs as she's on the floor with what looks like globs of white thick liquid on her chest down the front of her skirt. Some of the same liquid was dripping from the front of his sweat pants, when the bottle spilled liquid on them but is not seen by anyone staring at him. Hutch says "Could someone get some ice or something I think she hit her head!" One of the ladies go to the machine and gets a can of cold soda, the others want to see what happened in there. One lady comments "Hot damn, he's a big gusher. I heard about his kind never seen one in person till now." The others go over to see for themselves and saw the counter woman out on the floor in the storage room. They all smiled at each other nodding their heads and wondered who's next. Hutch uses the cold soda to wake the woman up and make sure she was alright, with all the other women looking and listening to the laundry attendant says "I had no idea it was that big and heavy but it was a tight fit in there. Her legs and butt are going to be sore for a while after this." Shaking as she stood up. Seeing she was alright and didn't need to call an ambulance for her, he goes over to where his clothes are folded and in a bag ready for him. He looks around and tires figure out who did his clothes that fast. This older woman told him she did while he was messing with amateurs, she know how to do a lot more then get clothes ready fast. Just because she's a little mature doesn't mean it stale and can't get loose especially from a good dose of vitamin E out of big bull like him. His cell phone rings saving him from an awkward moment, its Mack he's wondering when Hutch is coming back because his mother call and wants some things picked up from the supermarket for the BB-Que. He smiled at the woman grabbing his clothes and thanks the woman as she pulls out her teeth for him saying "Nothing like having that thing gummed by an expert!" Smiling at him as his eyes got wide with a shock look on his face he runs out quickly.

A short time later he walks back in his house, that's when it hit him what Mack was asking him "Why was Cordell holding his head". Then remembers Cordell coming there asking for a loan to get something for his house and Hutch told him take some from the envelope of cash Mack and Steel left for him. He never took it to the bank putting it on his dresser draw. Cordell the amount he needed was in the envelope but Cordell tried being slick getting more than he needed that's why he got hit upside his head. Asking Dee, Mack and Steel to give him few minutes as he jumps in the shower to wash up and then get dressed. Afterwards he got dressed using more of the sliver capped cologne before heading out to the supermarket with them to get things for the BBQ his mother was going to be doing the cook for. They get to the supermarkets Steel was commenting to Hutch how he likes his shirt and want to borrow it, so Hutch switched shirts with him before they went in just to keep him quite. Steel starts to complaining how the shirt has just a little too much cologne even though there wasn't. They walk through the supermarkets looking for everything they'll need for the BBQ, splitting up going down different aisles meeting back at the cart with the stuff they find to get done faster. Hutch was pushing the cart going down an aisle looking for some things and saw these women at the other end coming down his way.

Thinking they need to be on the shelf because he would put all three in his cart to buy and take home as he starts to pass them giving a friendly smile saying "Hello ladies" All three smiled back "Hi" The cologne scent hits their nose and had them turn and look at the big man as he turns the corner heading down the next aisle over. Looking at each other each one biting their lips and giving a sneer smile, they rush down the aisle to head off the man at the other side that just passed them smelling so good. They want to see him again and get a better look at the big man. Steel saw the back of them from the beginning of that aisle they just rushed down and turn to the left thinking those were some nice ass women turning that aisle. He wanted to head them off so backing up fast down the aisle he starts to turn around but runs into Marveece hard falling backward to the floor. Marveece 6' 5"and 315lbs stands there for a second startled then goes "Oooh Marveece! I'm so sorry shuga I didn't!" Her words cut short as he/she was helping Steel to his feet and got a good whiff of the cologne in the shirt Steel had switched with Hutch earlier. Steel says "That's Ok it was my fault turning so fast not thinking there could be someone behind me. Are you OK, I didn't hurt you or anything?" Marveece thought "Wow he's so fine. Ooooh Marveece he's concerned about me" Steel backed up and looked at the big person he just bounced off as it registered to Steel, this is a man dressed like that not some over grown woman speaking in third person about herself.

Hutch was checking the stuff in his cart and what they got so far then starts down the aisle, stopping as he sees the same 3 women gauntlet spread down the aisle looking at him. Erikaa dressed in burgundy sweat suit was first standing on one side as he starts to pass, Donna's wearing a Canary yellow sweat suit as she stand in the middle and Janet is wearing a powder blue sweat suit with "Baby" printed on the butt being the last one. Her back is to the shelf as she turned asking Hutch walking down the aisle "Excuse me but could you reach that box of stuffing over my head and hand it to me, I can't reach it and don't want to climb and get hurt" He looks at all the boxes of stuffing over her head and says "OK, I wouldn't want to see you hurt either." Stepping toward her but sees she's not moving and thinking he can just reach over and get the box. When he does she gets another good whiff of his cologne that close to his body and squats down while he was reaching the box. He didn't see her as she was squatted in front of him till he looks down about to ask her which one she wanted. She looked up at him answering "Whichever one that would fit in a hole and taste good." When she said that (POP!) she gets rained on by stuffing bread crumbs as the box gets crushed in his hand "OH sorry about that!" He brings down another box as she stood up with bread crumbs in her hair. He asked her "What was she doing down there?" Janet held up a can of gravy "With all that stuffing going to have to see gravy come out, uh with it." That's when Erikaa came over and says "We need dessert too where's the Jell-O?" and she walks down the aisle letting him see her jiggle. He asked Janet "Are they eating dinner together?" Donna answered "Yeah we're eating you, err it together" catching her words then asked "Which do you like better, our hot buttered rolls or our hot buns?" Hutch looked at her and got speechless. Janet asked "Well which one would you like to bite into out rolls or our buns?" Hutch shook his head out of thought he was having looking at them saying "Err buns or always better." Donna looks at him over by his cart "All that meat and no potatoes. Wow I see why you are such a beast" Hutch explains we're having a BBQ for my mother she's here to visit me and my brothers. Erikaa came back saying "I don't find what kind of Jell-O I wanted." Hutch looked at her and suggested pie is always good to. Donna asked "What kind of pie does he eat?" He told them "Peach is always good, but peach with cherry and ice cream never fails." Then says "If you ladies aren't doing anything you could come to my BBQ there's going to be a lot of people there, it'll be safe that is if you don't feel like cooking." About to answer when Dee came over to Hutch with more some stuff to put in the cart trying not to get in the way of his conversation but asked "Where Steel?" Hutch shrugged his shoulders then let them know if they change their minds he'll be in there till they're ready to cash out and went with Dee to find Steel. Pressed for time to get back and set things up for the BBQ not to mention having to get beer they go looking for him. Steel was standing there looking at Marveece with blond hair braided shoulder length dressed in black and yellow spandex with button down light green shirt and pink scarf and silver and gold bracelets on his arms wearing pink flip flops with gold and silver rings on each finger. Telling Marveece he had to go find his friends because they would be looking for him by now then hears this "Oooh Marveece!" Come out of him again as he/she says "You are not in here alone baby?" and asking him "Oooh Marveece! Where did you get that shirt?" Explaining he likes the way it fits on Steel and the color looks so nice on him with plus smelling so good like that too, it's driving her wild. Steel stands there and blinks as Marveece flicks her hair around while talking to him. On the way to find Steel in the supermarket Dee and Hutch kept hearing this "Oooh Marveece" sound and wondered who was making those noises and starts making jokes about it. just as they turned the corner of an aisle and heard another "Oooh Marveece" again, Steel saw Hutch and Dee and they saw Steel and Marveece at the same time. Steel about to point over Marveece's shoulder going "There they are." Dee turns looking at Hutch and jumped into the cart and Hutch pulled back the cart fast around the corner. When Marveece turns to see no one there he turns back and laughs at Steel "Silly there's no one there. Baby you trying to get away from Oooh Marveece!" Hutch left Dee in the cart and went back to peek around the corner of the aisle and took his cell phone camera and starts to take pictures from around the corner. Thinking he's need proof of what they just saw Steel with. Taking the flash off so he wouldn't get noticed Hutch snaps a few shots of Steel with Marveece standing there together as Marveece puts her hands on Steel laughing with him. Hutch knocks down a can while taking snap shots getting their attention which gives Steel a chance to runs the other way when Marveece looked to see who knocked down the can rolling towards them. Turning back not seeing Steel there he lets out a loud "OOOH MAR-VEECE! Where my next husband future baby daddy get off too!" and went looking for him. Saying "I didn't even get a chance to get your name to be call in the night baby!" Steel heard what Marveece said about him and ran even faster just to keep on the other side of the aisle away from Marveece. He saw Mack standing there with stuff in his arms wondering where he came from in such a hurry, Steel get behind him saying "Don't let that thing get me." About to ask him what he was talking about when he saw Marveece coming at him asking "Did you see the most delicious looking man in a blue and white shirt that smelled like I could eat him whole or make him my man for life?" Mack shocked at what he heard and tries to keep in his laughter saying "I didn't see him but if I do". Marveece says "Oooh Marveece just call Oooh Marveece and I'll come running OK!" Mack shook his head and goes "uh O-K!" Trying to get over the looks of what is after Steel as he went by and Mack turns slowly shielding Steel from his view as she turns the corner. Mack asked "Steel! What the hell did you do?!" Steel explains all he did was bump into it and get knocked back to the floor now it wants to be, Mack says "Mate for life STUPID! I heard." Then busted out laughing because it call him delicious and asked "How you going to let another man call you delicious! Did you hear CEDRIC the

Entertainer! What he said about that and you're going to let another man call you that and not whip his?" Cutting his words looking at Steel sizing him up compared to what's after him, going "You are going to need help and I'm fresh out on this one bruha!" Turning to leave and asked "What you going to do?" Mack went "listen to that!" Oooh Marveece" is heard in the back ground. Then say "From what that sound like, you better run for your life man. Because if it catches you, Steel won't be your name any more aluminum will be it cause it's so sparkly and bendable haay!" Steel went "That's not funny man!" Then "Oooh Marveece" is heard again coming that way. Trying to think of a place quick where should he go. The bottom shelf was empty and he could just fit. Diving on to it just as Marveece starts down that aisle again. Mack shrugged his shoulders "Still didn't see him." Hoping she didn't look down towards the floor passing in a hurry. Not looking down as he walks on turning the corner then quickly looking back at Mack wondering why is that man just standing there. Mack notices Marveece looking back at him then looks at the things on the upper shelf. Marveece thought for a second and looks up at the top of the shelves and shook his head and kept walking, Mack told Steel "Now man! Get the hell out of there before it comes back, I'll let Hutch know." Mack finds Hutch and Dee laughing hard in one of the aisles and wants to know what's so funny. Hutch shows him the pictures of Steel with Marveece, then Mack told them what "It! Said about Steel". They all fell out laughing making jokes about calling Steel his new pet names, Copper or Rusted Steel, Rot Iron and the best one of all Aluminum. Hutch thought about the shirt and said "Good thing I gave Steel that blue and white shirt or it could have been me!" They all fell out laughing because it could have been Hutch instead of Steel. Marveece over on the aisle heard them and said "That's his name? Steel!" and repeated it in such a nasty way "STA-EEEEL huh!" Asking aloud "Where's the BBQ again and is that where he's going to be" Knowing they're going to be in trouble with him once he find out they let it know his name. They hurry and get the rest of the stuff for the BBQ, but Dee says "let Steel sweat it out a bit" and they make a bet on how long Steel can keep away from it. Heading to the checkout line Hutch didn't notice Donna, Erikaa and Janet are right behind him as he stand there talking to Dee and Mack, but they do and make comments about what's behind him. Dee and Mack help with bagging the stuff after it was paid for and loaded it into another cart, as Hutch was talking with Janet about how much food they have in their cart and wondered if they can cook. Donna asked Erikaa "Do she think they have enough for all the things in their cart?" and Janet stopped talking to Hutch when she heard Donna said that. Hutch asked "Was everything alright" as the last of his stuff was on the belt to be totaled up. Janet looked at him and said "They don't have enough, going to put back some things back". Hutch looked at them asking "Is this some kind of hustle to get him to give them money?" Janet looked at him and told him she's almost finished with her LPN training in another year and a half, Erikaa is 2 more years from her law degree in corporate law plus Donna is graduating next year from accounting school. Hutch already attracted to all of them anyway hoping this wasn't so kind of scam. He told Mack and Dee to take the stuff and load it in his vehicle, he'll be right there, telling the cashier to charge all their stuff to him too. They went "You didn't have to do that!" He smiled at them "I'm like that". Derrick and Mack took the stuff to the vehicle and came back in because Hutch had the keys, they heard Steel calling to them saying "He can't keep running from that thing much longer so if they wouldn't mind hurrying it up!" They all turned when they heard "Oooh Marveece. I know he's close I could feel him." Hutch threw his keys to Dee and told him to open the door so Steel can run and get in the vehicle so they can save Steel from becoming the rotor rooter man; Donna asked "What's that all about?" Hutch laughed going "Long story" and starts loading things on the belt to be rung up and when the cashier told him the total he hands her his credit card. He was laughing with Janet about Steel and giving him that shirt, Donna and Erikaa along with the cashier saw the read out "Unlimited Funds" flash across the screen.

They looked at each other not believing what they just saw as the cashier hands Hutch back his credit card and the receipt to sign. He looks at them staring at him asking "What? Is everything alright you two look like the bill was so enormous it took half my money, but don't worry it didn't make a dent in it. I always work hard to put back what I spend OK!" Donna amazed asked Hutch "What do you do for a living, if you don't mind me asking?" He laughs a lil "Ok you caught me, I'm not a business man or white collar worker I'm just a normal" Steel cuts him off calling his name "Hutch! Where are the others?" He told him there out by his vehicle and he forgot to let him know, all he's got to do is make it out the store. They're waiting for them to leave. Steel mad now says "You here talking with some ass. I'm running around here trying to save mine!" Janet took offense at what he said ducking behind Hutch making the "Oooh Marveece" sound which made Steel think it was him again and take off running. Hutch knew it was her looking at her shaking his head going "I like that. See I can take you anywhere." Huddling the ladies together after getting a good idea of how he's going to get Steel out of the store to save him. Hutch grabs some bags and with their help when Steel came back again they all stood shielding Steel from being seen by Marveece with Hutch holding the bags high up and the ladies walking close together to the exit. Outside by Hutch's vehicle Steel start to cussing at Hutch for having him wait so long in there so Donna and Erikaa asked loudly together "is that the thing you are running from?" Steel didn't even look as he dove in the back of Hutch's vehicle and closed the back door down covering himself with bags. Hutch looked around and Marveece wasn't nowhere in sight, he told them "I'm going to fall in love with you women keep having my back like that." They all laugh but then Marveece did come out calling and looking around "STA-EEEL! Honey baby! You can't hide from love!" Standing by the back door of his vehicle Hutch could see through the tinted dark window and saw the darken shadow of a head pop up shaking a fist at him with muffled cussing going on about how did it find out his name. Mack came to Hutch and told him there's no room in there unless he wants to lap up with Derrick (Dee). Donna said "That's Ok he'll get to ride home we'll take him, it's the least we could do for buying our food like that". Hutch said "I can get in the back with the food". They grab him and walk away from his vehicle as Marveece came up to them remembering he was talking about Steel, saying "I can't find my Steel. Wish I could get some in me because Steel don't bend or brake but it would be fun to see if I could Oooh Marveece." Erikaa points "He's in the little blue car going around that corner, girl you better go get your man before another woman like Lois Lane comes looking for her man of Steel with kryptonite in her hands". "Oooh Marveece, girl you right" He runs to his vehicle and drives off trying to catch that blue car and Hutch, Janet and Donna turn looking at Erikaa who shrugs her shoulders "I got him to go away right!" Hutch was the first to start laughing and then the rest joins in. He looks at them asked "Where are they parked and could he fit in it." Donna point there and starts walking towards this little hatch back vehicle. He looks and says "Well looks like I'm going to be packed with the food anyways." As he takes the walk over to the vehicle but then he see them walk pass that vehicle and opens the side door of the leisure van and says "Well are you getting in and sorry about the A/C it needs recharging". Hutch said "I can have that fix too if they don't mind stopping so I could get some cases of beer from the distributor and stop at the liquor store too." She said "Well I'm driving if you are buying." On the way there the heat of the van makes him sweat and the cologne on is body makes all of them very horny for him. Janet is looking at how big his arms are asking "How much can you lift?" A car cuts off Donna and she turns and hits the brakes causing Janet to wind up in the arms of Hutch, not being able to control herself anymore from the way he smells to her.

She laughs about being in his arms after Donna nearly had a crash and start kissing him, Erikaa calls her name and when they stop for moment she rushes back there and picks up where Janet stopped. Donna calls for the both of them to stop because she didn't want him to get the wrong message about them. All she could hear is moaning coming from back there so she finds a spot near the distributor closing the front curtains and heads back there too as the van rocks back and forth. At Hutch's house the G.D.M.4.L are getting things ready for Mama Betty to come over from Cordell's house and wonder where Hutch could be with the liquor and beer. Cars were going by the van still rocking but not hearing the low moaning going on in it as time went by. Hutch comes out of the van and heads into the beer distributor to get what he needs then comes back to the van with a U-boat of beer. Knocking on the door first and getting no answer he opens it to see the ladies now sleep on the bed in the back of the van. Loading the beer in the rear where the bags of food are then folding up the U-boat and heading to the liquor store, shortly after going in and coming out with the same U-boat boxes of liquor on it. He again loads the van with the boxes and U-boat then drives off heading back to his house. By the time he gets to his house they are up and dressed, wanting to help unloading the beer on to the U-boat with the boxes of liquor on top of them. He asked the three of them to come in to meet everyone at his BBQ plus his mother is there and how can they not want to meet his mother. Donna asks "How you still got energy and we're drained, you must do this a lot huh?!" Hutch shook his head "Nope!" Janet asked "When is the last time you been with a sista or two or three at one time you can be honest?!" Hutch smiled at them and asked "What year is this again?" Erikaa goes "year?!!" Donna went "Tell me you are not a virgin?!" He looks at her "No I'm not a virgin. It's just been some years since I've been with a sista not to mention three at one time." Janet asked "What year you stopped being a virgin?" Hutch went "21" and Janet asked "How old are you now?!" They all looked and waited for his answer as he said "41" Erikaa asked "How many time when you were 21 did you have sex?!" Hutch turned red saying "Once but it wasn't that long." That's when Mack and the others came out to greet him and say hi to the ladies, asking were they coming in. Donna said "They were tire and have to get their food home before it spoils." Thanking him for the invitation exchanging numbers and telling them they know where he lives and the door will be open. Watching as the Van pulls away Hutch goes inside to join the BBQ and see his mother who is waiting for him, but after he takes a quick shower changing his clothes.

In the van Donna, Erikaa and Janet discuss in amazement at how Hutch could have gone so long without having sex or a girlfriend. Janet says "That's a lot of jerking off or he's backed up so much it would explain how he's got so much energy after all of us are drained. DAMN! He's got brains knows how to talk intelligent, polite understanding, good looking, not conceded, has a job, his own home and don't live with ex-girlfriend or his Mama but most important no KIDS OR baby mama drama physco's women. Girls we found the white unicorn!" They laughed at what Janet said and talked some more on their way home about Hutch thinking they should show up to his BBQ.

Marveece had caught the little blue hatch back car and found there was no Steel in it, but he remembers the license plate of the vehicle Hutch and those women were standing by when she told him about this car. Marveece calls her friend Davona who has a cousin that works for the DMV to track down the vehicles owner and address for her, telling Davona about Steel and how he's the one that's going to make Marveece happy.

Hutch clean now after his shower goes and greets his mother and brother Cordell and his kids with their mother his brother's pet Bernise. They are laughing about the story Derrick and Mack told about Steel and the thing he met at the supermarket that chased him around the whole place calling itself in third person. Hutch noticed that he was missing and pulled Derrick to the side asking what happened to him. Dee explained he wanted to be dropped off at his house, something about getting rid of that shirt so he could change and bring it back to you after what happened at the supermarket. Everyone at the BBQ was having a good time when Erikaa and Donna showed up and came in, they had all of the men looking at them wanting to know who these two fine looking ladies are and tried to talk to them not getting anywhere. Derrick remembered them from the supermarket. He let the guys know they were there for Hutch because he was the one that invited them so he introduced them to his mother and they stayed close to her as the BBQ went on. Steel was on his way to Hutch's house for the BBQ after changing his shirt and know they must be having a ball laughing about what chased him. He got close to Hutch's place and saw something very familiar at his door way so he ducked in the bushes not to be seen by Marveece standing at the door. Cordell opens the door to see this big dark skinned person standing in black and yellow spandex with white shade and pink scarf wearing a light green button down shirt with a bright colors blond hair going "Oooh Marveece could I speak to the owner of the blue Expedition that's parked out front."

With a blank expression on his face at what he looking at, he tells Marveece to wait there he'll get the owner. Calmly he closes the door then tare ass over to Hutch and tells him "There's some person thing making sounds he's never heard before asking to see you at the front door bruha." Hutch goes to the front door opens it to find Marveece standing there, trying to keep a straight face asking "Can I help you?" Marveece went "Oooh Marveece can you help me find Steel. I needs my man!" His eyes got wide at that question. Marveece said Oooh Marveece. Me and Steel were meant to be together because fate brung him to me in that supermarket." Hutch thinking fast "Uh huh, well I haven't seen him since the market earlier but I will gladly give the address where he could be found in the Bronx and his cell phone number to reach him!" Glad to get it and went "OOOOH Marveece!" Marveece clapping her/his hands together like a little kids happy to get a prize giving Hutch the biggest smile. Hutch asked it for something to write on. Watching Marveece digs in his purse to get something to write on. In the bushes Steel heard some of what Hutch said about giving up his address and cell phone to Marveece so he could contact him. Then saw him writing something on the piece of paper as he was moving closer to the house trying not to be seen then watching Marveece extended his hand to shake. Hutch said "Not really a hand shaker." Marveece goes "You're a hugger then." Grabbing Hutch and gave him a hug. Mama Betty came to the door to see what everyone was trying to get a look at from what Cordell was telling everyone about something or person at the front door to see Hutch. Opening the door wide and seeing Marveece hugging Hutch she screams loud "AH HELL NAH! What the Foosball is THIS?!" Hutch finally broke the hug looked at his mother as she was standing there with her hands on her hips and face all screwed up. Hutch tried to explain he was grabbed by this uh, his words are cut by Marveece saying "My name is Oooh Marveece! And I was just thanking him for the information he gave me, thanks again baby!" He turns to leave going back to the vehicle to drive away and waiting for him just by the drive way was Steel. Hutch's mother went "You better tell me something because if you are seeing things like that I can make a few calls and have a few up here dropping it like it's hot with booty so round they look fake. They'll put it on ya having you call me every night to thank me right before you suck your thumb and go to sleep!"

She went on about how she never saw him with any woman or heard about him seeing one and wondered why but hoping it's not what she just saw. He assures her it wasn't what she thought then heard someone cough from behind them, turning to see everyone in the house bunch together trying to peek at the front door. Looking and listening how it sounded and heard what Mama Betty just said to Hutch. He turns and says to everyone "I'm not seeing nothing like that and it wasn't my secret lover so you all can relax. I like women" nobody moves as the whole crowd even the kids just looks at Hutch with blank expression on their faces, he turns back to his mother and says "Mama! Would you tell them I'm not gay I'm straight." She looks him up and down with her arms folded then lean towards him saying softy "You better not be one of those down low under cover skinny pants around your ass wearing men, calling yourself a thug and yodel while singing!" "Let me hear you laugh and you better not be giggling before and after you do in a high pitch or sucking your teeth" Pointing her finger at him then turning to everyone saying aloud "Alright yall break it up my baby aint gay, he's just womanless, girlfriend deprived, no wife having, booty call line disconnected, no jump off to jump on, no hole to tip drill in and nor back to get dug out" Hutch yells "Ma! They get the point!" One of the little kids there said "I thought that MADONNA like a virgin song was a myth never thought I see the male version in person, I was wrong!" Hutch "Who kid is this?" Derrick, 2Soon, Goodie, Herb, Jazz looked at each other as LIL-Rob asked them "What was all that talk about him being with the boss's three daughters then." They all looked at LIL-Rob and shrugged their shoulder as Doug went "See what happens when you work out and take that shit for too long, you imagine shit" When Steel snuck back to the street walking up the other way so he wouldn't be seen by Marveece. Mad thinking his brother in arms would give him up like that to make a joke out of him. Everyone was having a good time eating and drinking as the music was getting everyone to start dancing and making noise. Erikaa and Donna in the kitchen feeling uncomfortable till Derrick came over to remembering them from the supermarket telling everyone there, seeing how good they looked and they came for Hutch and only Hutch. Derrick also reminds his mother of them in the kitchen and they were there for Hutch she raised her hands thanking the "LORD" saying "I knew my baby wasn't gay." Telling them about the scare at the door and what it looked like, they laughed and told her they know it was at the supermarket earlier. Erikaa and Donna had a good laugh with Mama Betty as they told her about Steel and it was after him. Steel was walking into the house and looking for Hutch with a mad look on his face. Mack asked him "Everything alright" and told him Hutch was out by the pool following Steel out there to see Hutch laughing with 2Soon by the water. Steel didn't say nothing as he pushed pass 2Soon then struck Hutch knocking him in the water shouting "How could you give me up like that man, I thought we were friends." Mama Betty saw that and grabbed two pots one in each hand and ran out to the pool "Bing, Pong Poink, Ping Pong Bing Poom Ping Ping Pong, thump Ka-Splash" Steel goes in the water and Mama Betty stands by the edge yelling to Steel "You don't come in a person's house not saying Hello or nothing but go to punching out my baby at his own party how rude is that!?"

Cheryl was posting what she just seen on U-tube saying to the other kids "My gran-ma Betty don't play did yall see that round house kick she did wow!" Steel was getting out of the water along with Hutch as 2Soon and Dee was trying to hold Mama Betty back explaining to her Steel was playing with Hutch. She's got it all wrong about him because all she's got to do is looks at Hutch to Steel, he would break Steel to pieces then he might eat those pieces.

Hutch asked Steel "You having a bad day, because there better be a good reason why you did that?" Steel explained he was in the bushes and heard Hutch give that thing his address and cell phone number, wondering if he was going to make him out to be a big joke. Hutch laughed at him and asked Steel "Since you were in the bushes, did you hear what address I gave that thing or the cell phone number?" Steel couldn't answer that and Hutch asked Steel "How long we've been friends and how many time I covered for you?" Steel answered those two by saying "Over 20years and so many times he lost count but what's that got to do with what he did." Hutch reminded Steel about the little place he use to have in the Bronx that took them forever to find because they would either go pass it or be on the other end of the Bronx. They would have to call him to get direction to the place on the old cell phone number he never cut off but just got with a new company. Steel thought about what Hutch said and felt bad he should have trusted his friend that had his back for a long time, coming up with something to get that thing off his ass. What better way to than to give him an address and phone number it could leave all the messages it want on but will never get answered. Mama Betty saw Steel hug Hutch and she went over to apologize for beating a drum solo on him like that and spin kicking him in the pool. The BBQ continues as Milaya and Sonia curious asked 2Soon and Dougie who were the two good looking women that came there to meet Hutch. 2Soon said "I didn't know but they just might be friends he met somewhere you know he's just friendly like that." Donna and Erikaa were laughing at how funny Hutch's mother was as she talked about him not having a woman for so long because all he did was work and lift weight and come home to hang with his brothers G.D.M.4.L She worried on how to set things up for him to be with some of the young women down in her home town if he was turning to the other side. Never seeing any pictures of him with or talk about any woman when he use to come up there and visit before. The music was sounding so good to them they'd excuse themselves to get Hutch and dance with him out by the pool along with everyone else there dancing with a partner. All the guys felt it was about time Hutch showed everyone he could have fun with a woman but liked that there were two around him and nothing strange was happening keeping an out for something any ways because they know him. The BBQ winds downs and everyone starts to pitch in to clean up before they left. Hutch was telling everyone they didn't have to help he's got it even when they wanted to anyways because they're family and appreciate him having the big BBQ at is place.

While cleaning up by the pool Donna was very tipsy like everyone there, she slips and falls in with everyone one laughing including her at how it look when she fell in. Erikaa went to grab her to stop her from going in but the biggest laugh was when Erikaa call herself helping Donna get out of the water trying not to get pulled in and snatched on Herb standing real close by her eating his plate of food. They both got pulled in by Donna as Herbs plate went in the air and was caught by Mack standing next to him by the edge of the pool without anything falling off the plate. Hutch rushed over to the pool and pulled out Erikaa and Donna as everyone was laughing then helped Herb out as Mack walked over to him with his plate, seeing how mad Herb was he asked "want your plate back?!" Everyone laughed even harder when Herb stepped to take his plate back and Mack spun to keep him from getting it causing Herb to go back in the pool. Everyone had left except Bernise and Cordell who was the last to leave after packing up half a tray of BBQ and fixings along with two bottles of Castle Cream for herself and bottle of gin for him.

Hutch was in his room with Erikaa and Donna telling them to take off those wet clothes and points to his shower while he looks for something dry for them to put on. While they washed the pool water off them he checks on his mother to make sure she was alright and locks up his house. Coming back into his bedroom still feeling tipsy himself, he sees Donna on the bed looking so sexy in just the top half of his pajamas calling him over to her using her finger. As he walks towards her he hears this clicking of the doors lock as Erikaa stood by the door in a tee shirt of his looking sexy as well. Hutch told them not to move an inch as he goes in one of his draws and pulls out two pair of plastic vampire teeth and gave it to them asking to wear them saying "Show me our teeth because I always wanted to get bit by vampires." That turned on Donna first as she said "Freaky too?!" Erikaa excited said to Donna "Let drain his ass!"

The next morning Hutch was the first one to wake to the smell of cooking and goes down stairs to the kitchen to see his mother setting four plates at the tables. Saying to him "Good morn, I know how to get you up and those two shouldn't be far behind you." Hutch smiles at his mother and kisses her good morning then sits at the table just as Donna is the second one coming into the kitchen. She says "Good Morning Mama Betty" kissing her on the cheek. The yawn of

Erikaa saying "Good Morning Mama Betty." Then kissing everyone, his mother looks at them dressed in her sons shirts saying "Times sure are changing, I remember when a woman dressed in a man's shirt meant it was a good night but I see two women in his shirts HOT DAMN!" They all sit at the table to Turkey Bacon and sausage, eggs and grits with Orange juice for the women and Hutch gets water with his small cup of pills. He looks at it and then the glasses of juice the girls got wondering where's his juice. His mother in such a good mood said "What? I know what goes on in the morning after. Well there wasn't another woman with me but from the looks of these two. Moving like you must have dug their backs out good and needs to put some of that back in ya. Even if it's been years you haven't tip drilled son!" Hutch almost chokes on his water and looks at his mother yelling "MA!" Both women faces are red from blushing as the try not to laugh at what Mama Betty said. She let the girls know how proud of her son she is and it does her good to see he's with not one but two very good looking healthy women that like her son. Then saying "it's better than none or what she seen at his front door yesterday." "GOD knows if he were with that thing she would have to cap him a few time out of love for her son of course, but can't see a good big man go to waste in her family!" She toasted them for being with him and for her still alive to see it feeling like celebrating. Donna leaned over to Erikaa saying "Wonder what she'll do when she finds out about Janet making it three of us that's been with her son" Erikaa reply's "If she cooking like this (eating her food) and last night's BBQ, we'll tell her after breakfast and see what dinner's like." Donna shook her head agreeing and they clink glasses and finish enjoying her food. Mama Betty told Hutch she was going over Cordell's to visit with the rest of her grand kids in a little while after they ate breakfast and she would need a little cash from him to hold her over. He told her she didn't have to ask for that. He'd give her what she wants because she's his mother and shouldn't have to ask for anything from him. Donna and Erikaa looked at him with such feelings to hear a big man say that to his mother, smiling at him and gave him a kiss at the same time on both cheeks. Mama Betty saw what they did "See told ya you are going to need those vitamins and incase he goes limp girls, I got stay hard cream for that too!" Hutch yells again "Ma!" She looked at him and said "What don't think I don't know about tapping dat ass or fire and Ice skins, taking a blunt to the head. I watched 106 & park enough to see how the young ones don't know shit from shampoo.

Before there was gin and juice we use to have MSNG and women got ours a few times before men ever nutted so they had to come back for more" Hutch screams "Ma! No more 106 & park for you!" Donna curious "Excuse me Mama Betty what's MSNG?!" Mama Betty leans to her "MOON SHINE NIGHT TRAIN GIRL! Both of them kept his ass from getting his before we got ours a few time and he worked hard for it too!" She remembers the good time with that and it makes her laugh as goes up stairs with them to get ready for Cordell when he comes to take her over his house. Later Donna and Erikaa told Hutch they have to leave to get ready for work that night so they told him he's got their numbers and kept on the throw back Giants jersey they were found in his bedroom closet (Donna with 56 Lawrence Taylor and Erikaa 53 Harry Carson) and he gave them # 58 Antonio Pierce all linebacker jerseys and said "Tell Janet need the whole team next time." watching as they drove away he went back in the house to get dressed himself and with his mother for his brother to show up. Cordell didn't come as usual and Hutch dropped his mother off at his house. He and Bernise were still drunk from last night sleeping it off so Hutch took his mother over to see her grand kids who were happy to see their gran ma Betty and uncle Hutch. Jordell the only boy and next to the youngest girl Javon gives his uncle Hutch a big hug and slaps his hand five saying "I want to grow up big and mus-killer like you." Which makes his uncle smile as he hold him in the air and Jordell pats his uncle's arms. Cheryl the oldest girl gives her uncle a hug and says "Shouldn't you be sleep because you have to work." Hutch looked at her and says "See that's why I don't have a woman Ma. I'm being bossed by my niece who acts like my older sister or mother." Mama Betty said "Not any more" Hutch tries not to discuss his dates and gets ready to leave after giving all the kids pocket money (Kayla, Kita are twins and youngest girl Corie) he then saw a grown hand being held out. "What's this?!" He looks at Bernice's hand in front of him she said

"If you are going to give the kids money you could give me some too!" He laughed at her and told the kids to run along and hide their paper before shredder here comes along and wants to use her foot hand to take their money. Bernise got madder at what else Hutch said next her "I'm not your man better get that lazy other half of the baby making Machine to get some work done and get you some!" He also gave the dog five dollars and Bernice went to take it from the dog. He growled and barked viciously sneered at her showing all his teeth. She asked "What the hell is the dam dog going to do with five dollars?" Hutch laughed and said "More than what you can do with it." He looks over at the dog holding its paw up and he gives him pound. Before leaving his mother there she asked "What was he going to give her?" He goes in his wallet and pulls out a credit card and told her what her she spends don't worry about it just don't lose it or hit it too hard where he has to sell the house. She kisses him as he gave her the key to his house and told her any time during the week she can always come back to stay at his house, she's got the key just don't bring mooch and drink Smokey there "I like the way my house is and those two leaches would suck it dry." She laughs hugging her son before he leaves. That same day Hutch dropped off his mother at his brother Cordell's house. Six women are having two different conversations but similar about the same man, how he had two women at his BBQ and had lots of fun with them while everyone watch not objecting about it.

The first conversation was with Milaya and Sonia to Elise telling her how these two women showed up and Hutch was dancing and laughing having a good time. Even introduced both of them to his mother and his guys were catering to them, getting their drinks and food. Elise asked "How did they look?" Sonia told her they looked a cross between hood rats and ghetto fabulous in their sweat suits with words on their big asses (FU-BU and BABY PHAT) shaking it for all the guys to gawk at. Milaya told Elise "They had fake hair and looked hungry as they ate everything in sight and drank like Viking men. She thinks one of them had a mustache trying to get close to talk to every man in the place." Elise said "How could he invited such things to his BBQ and not give me a call to come there. Not that I would have gone because I had other better things to do!" She looked really mad after saying that.

The second conversation going on was with Donna and Erikaa and how they had a ball at the BBQ with Hutch and his friends and even met his mother. She's down to earth about him being with them. She told about him not being with a woman so long she thought he was turning gay, they laughed telling Janet about it.

Then telling her about the pool and after they had to take showers, Janet cut in saying "Not to leave out one details." They didn't explaining how it went using vampire teeth till they fell asleep with him in the middle of both of them. Donna told Janet about the next morning his mother had breakfast for them talking about things that made them blush, because she's up to speed on relationships and don't have problem with her son with two females. Matter a fact she was proud of him and they thought she was going to throw another BBQ if they would have told her about (you) Janet being the third one. Janet was excited and mad she had to miss the BBQ because of her of her classes but said "I'm not going to miss the next one he has." They continued to talk about his house, what it looked like from the pool to the Jacuzzi tub in his bathroom. How he said he always wanted a tub big enough for him to have room. They talked about Hutch excited to have met a man that works hard for everything he's got and not be the type of man the shows off but shares with his friends old and new. Something bothers Donna about how come a man that rich would live like that and not big like other rich men do.

At the same time in another part of the city where Elise was telling Sonia and Milaya, she was going to make sure Hutch shares everything with her and not give it away to his friends anymore because he is the type of man that needs to be controlled on his spending his money with his friends. She knows this from all he times she was out with them, he needs a woman to give him direction and purpose in is life. Then she starts to explain how she was going to do that by first getting rid of the G.D.M.4.L and all the weekend partying they do. Sonia asked "How were you going to do all that, you haven't broke him off a taste or put it on him to have him wanting to do all that you want him to do?" Elise told her "No not yet! He the type she's got to pick the right time to do that and show him who has control between them." Sonia and Milaya looks at Elise wondering if there was something going on up in her mind from the look on her face as she was telling them of her plans.

At Cordell's house Mama Betty was looking at Cheryl saying how nice she looked in her clothes and she told her grandmother "Uncle Hutch bought them for me." Mama Betty asked "Didn't he buy the other kids some clothes too?" She answered "Yeah some but she didn't have time to get them all the things she wanted too" explaining it was her that did the shopping. She was at the mall with her friends and saw him there so he gave her the money to get something for herself so she bought something for her Jordell and her sisters too. Mama Betty looked at the kitchen heading in there to fix coffee and food and told Cheryl to wake her father up so he can eat then they're going to the mall to pick up a few more things for her sisters and Jordell too. She woke her father up telling him his mother wants to go to the mall shopping for the kids. While fixing the food she looks at the rest of the house and how it could really use some things too but she didn't know what. The kids got cleaned up and ready to go with her and Cordell to the mall to get whatever she wanted them to have, thinking Hutch wouldn't be too mad for going a little over spending on the kids.

Hutch was back at home getting his work gear ready for work the next day. Then starts to do a work out but felt something as he worked out hard but couldn't put his mind on what it was he was thinking about. It was his mother at the mall and she was about to be shown by Cheryl why he gave her that credit card. Mama Betty thought to herself, she would be fare getting the girls clothes first they're the hardest to shop for being women. Jordell was easy there was one of him. At the cashier Cheryl said "I just remembered what I wanted to say about uncle Hutch giving you his credit card gran ma!" They stood right by the counter and Cheryl showed her what the read out showed when the cashier swiped the card. (LIL Kim's rap starts playing "MONEY POWER RESPECT!") Mama Betty's eyes got wide at the words flashing across the screen "UNLIMITED FUNDS" and she looked at Cheryl puzzled "When did all this happen? I knew he was saving but didn't know that much." It didn't take long for her to get shopping, first with the girls all the clothes and shoes they needs for school and after. Getting them all new wardrobes as Cheryl and the twins picked out all the clothes having their own fashion show at each store they went into. Picking out what they wanted and liked first, but when it came to picking out Jordell's clothes he was alone with his crowd of sisters watching him come out in the latest little boy clothes. Cheryl picked out very good things for him to style in as they would clap and Corie had the loudest whistle for her brother as he modeled everything picked out. They would have so many bags at one time Cheryl made the suggestion to leave them in the station wagon and come back in and finish shopping. Mama Betty told her that was a good idea, the first time they went to the car Cordell was sleep in the front seat when they unloaded the first group of bags and went back in. By the time they came out with another round of bags it filled up the entire back of the station wagon and some of the back seat as they went back in again. Cordell wanted to get comfortable adjusting his seat and looked at the rearview mirror and saw the bag filled the back of his station wagon then closed his eyes again going back to sleep. Opening one eye first at what he just saw in the rear view mirror with his head tilted on the window then opening both eyes looking in the mirror and turning his head quickly to be surprised it's real looking at all of those bags in the back. Getting out the car locking it up and goes in the mall looking for them to find out what's going on. When he catches up with them Cheryl let her gran mother know if her daddy found out about the Credit card he would try and take it from her so it's best they keep it a secret. Mama Betty told her she knows and would have to find and dig him up from all over the country buried in little baggies if he took your uncles Credit card. Instead they convince him to let them buy his clothes and make him look good too. It wasn't long before he was doing his own modeling for his kids and mother, they were loading more bags in his station wagon then going back inside this time at the food court trying to pick out something for all of them to eat after doing all that shopping. Standing in line to get food for the kids Mama Betty heard this woman with three kids say to them

"They had to share a meal because she couldn't get all their clothes and feed them too." She heard another mother say to her four kids "Just one thing I don't have a lot of money." Another woman told her two kids "Their father didn't send and child support for the last two months so they only could get a pair of sneaker each that's what she can afford."

Thinking glad I didn't raise my sons like that but got an idea. Cheryl watches her grandmother go over to these women and say something to them as they shook their heads "Yes" to what she was saying. Then walk over to the empty section of the food court with a twenty single mothers and have them seat their kids and huddle together break like a football team at a game. Cheryl watched the women go to their kids talk with them and come back to her grandmother and watches each woman order food and when it came time to pay for it, her grand ma would go over to the woman risen her hand at the counter where they ordered food. Paying for the food and watching the woman go back to her kids and say something to them before coming back to a huddle with all the women, then watches them leave their kids in the food court eating their food being watched by one of the other women she talked with. Cheryl and her sister with Jordell was eating their food and looking around wondering where her grandmother could have gone to but then all of sudden one of the group of kids was jumping up and down cheering as their mother came to them loaded with a bunch of bags. Then another group starts the same thing and one by one the kids that saw their mothers coming loaded with bags jumping up and down cheering. That section of the food court was cheering and shouting for Mama Betty as she gotten all the things plus some extra toys and gadgets for them making them promise to keep up their grades in school. The women were crying and hugging her thanking her for everything as she told them "Women got to stick together no matter how dead beat the men are in their lives. If they only knew how much they control everything if they would only stick together." Each woman made sure their kids knew it was a woman that did for them not their dead beat ass fathers who would come up with excuse on how things were tough for him and his new family or girlfriend that week or any week so he wasn't able to help out with clothes and money and time with his own kids. Before each woman left they made sure Mama Betty had their names and numbers to keep in contact with her and Cheryl caught on to what she had done and starts the starts chanting "GO GRAND MA!" All the kids and their mother chanting it too for a while before all left their separate ways. Cheryl told her that was nice of her to do that and now sees where uncle Hutch gets it from but promises not to tell him anything as they cleaned up their table and took their bags out to the car making sure Cheryl picked up just a few things for her mother too because they know Hutch wouldn't like that they did so he got a few things. On the way out she comes across a furniture store and walks in wanting to see some things she would like them to have and asking about deliveries.

Hutch was getting a very strange feeling like he was doing something for a lot of people but couldn't think of what it can be, at the same time his mother was looking over all the new furniture she picked out and just bought for Cordell's house. Asking if the store could deliver the things she bought on the same day. Hutch was having second thoughts on if he should have given her cash instead of his Credit card that way he wouldn't have to worry about her over spending on his card, but then had another thought about her not going over too much where he couldn't handle it and would make Cordell work it off somehow with him.

They come out of the mall with more bags of stuff and looking at the small station wagon wondering where they all were going to sit with the car filled with bags of clothes and stuff for them. Mama Betty was looking at the car when this car dealership caught her eye and she looks at Cordell's and told the kids to wait by the car taking Cordell with over to the dealership.

An hour later they pull up next the station wagon with a brand new Chevy Tahoe fully loaded and have the kids start loading up the Tahoe with half the bags, Cordell asked "What about the station wagon?" His mother told him he's going to drive it home and he said "I thought I was going to drive the new vehicle home." She laughed at him "Just because I put you down as owner doesn't mean you was going to drive it when I can" Cheryl said "Grandma I can drive too uncle Hutch taught me how" she smiled at Cheryl and said "Show me baby."

Hutch was at home when he gets a call from Elise and she wants to see him so they can talk about him and where he needs to go with his life. He asked her "What's wrong with his life?" She told him "You lack focus and needs direction. I'm the woman that could turn it around for you. Just give me a chance when I come over there to talk and your friends better not be there either". He let her know he's in the house all by himself and getting his stuff ready for work but she could come over anyway, she told him she'll be there a while so have the door open when she gets there.

At Cordell's house the kids are running in the house with bags shouting to their mother grandma Betty got us new clothes and things mommy. Taking their new stuff up to their rooms then coming back to the new Tahoe to get the rest of the stuff plus stuff out of the old car too. Bernise come out the house to see the new Tahoe and looks at it then looking at all the bags the kids are getting out of the vehicles. She asked "Cheryl did you get anything for me?!" Cheryl told her "Yes! Grand ma paid for some things for you too." Bernise starts to go through the bags and Mama Betty grabs the bags out of her hands and told her "If you are going to look through them, then carry some in the house." Loading her hands up with bags watching her mumble something s she struggles with them going into the house. Cheryl looks at her sisters and says "Grand ma Betty's ruff! Don't step at her cause she'll get at ya!" Inside the house Bernise is looking at Cordell asking him "Why you let your mother spend all this money on them like that. Hutch is going to be very pissed at you and me for this!" Cordell answers "How could I stop her, it's hard to say no to my mother when she's like that!" and he goes back out to the station wagon to get the rest of the bags in it. Bernise looked at him coming in with the bags and went upstairs to their bedroom talking to herself saying "Good thing I was talking to one of my friend and they let me know I should have insurance on his ass, just in case of something like this! Least we'll have enough to burn his ass after his brother kills him!" She goes and gets some papers from under her bed in the box where she kept them. Coming back down to get back on the couch and waits to get him alone so he could sign them and not let his mother know what she did.

Meanwhile Elise came over to Hutch's house with such an attitude about what she thought she knew he did with Becka that time she caught her in his clothes. Making it clear she was there to straighten out a few things if they are going to be a couple and who needs to lead. That evening she was looking at the house judging his taste on everything he got in the place, walking around starting in the living room looking at him sitting there watching TV in his big chair. Elise begins her conversation with him. Hutch thought she might be having a bad day and needs someone to take it out on someone so he ignored her in her attitude. She again got in her snobbish way "Well don't you want to offer me something to drink it would have been nice to see it here, but I guess I'll have to wait till you fetch it for me huh!" He looks at her wondering what's gotten in to her, she wasn't acting like that at the bar they met in. He starts to the kitchen then turns back sounding like a french butler asking "Would Madame pre-fer H2O or something with a bite to its hops and barley bubbly liquid surroundings" She looks at him not understanding what he said, then he just says "Bud or bud light baby I aint got all day." Angry now saying to him "That wasn't funny and it was low class" Now he acts like German butler bowing clicking his heels saying "Heir fur-line' Zee Master of Za ha-Ouse had his friendz over, dey appear to have drank Za good sh-stock of Mer-lo and all sh-sparkling vine!" Frustrated he's acting like that she waves her hand at him and told him to come back so they can talk. She starts by getting on him and the way he spends time with his friends, how much time and money they take from him. He looks at her wondering what she's trying to say but listens to her go on about him being too generous with his things and money. Just then Dougie walks in "YO! Fam you up or knocked for the night?" His words are cut short at the sight of Hutch and Elise sitting on the couch. Dougie came over to see if he wanted to watch the game and drink a couple of buds figuring he couldn't sleep and would keep Hutch company "I see you have your own, so he'll be down in the club house so I don't interrupt you and your piece!" Going to the refrigerator grabbing a couple of bottles asking "Did you want another one before I went down in the basement to watch the game fam."

Elise was furious at how Dougie just came in the house and said "What if I would have been in my under clothes or something sexy for you and he walks in looking at me like that!" Explaining she would never be able to face him and would leave Hutch because his friends just walk in his house whenever they want to. Telling Hutch "Go be with your friend" but putting a few more thoughts in his head before she left. Acting very upset about what could have happened, making him think about it and how it affected her. After she left he goes down stairs and talks with Dougie about what happened. How she could have been in her underwear in the living room. Dougie said "Didn't meant to make her upset or bust in like that but don't you always leave your door open for us to walk in?" Hutch told him "Good point, never mind." Then asked "Want another beer I'm buying." They sat and watched the game.

At Cordell's house Mama Betty told the kids "Now that you've put away all your clothes, toys and new games and phones. I'm going to take us out to dinner, so go put on something nice so we can go eat and tell your father he can drive the new Tahoe but he's not drinking at dinner." Soon all the kids are dressed and ready to go, even Bernise put on something nice Mama Betty bought for her with the help of Cheryl. The kids were in the Tahoe playing with play station2 and X-box games looking at the screen in the back of the seats and the one in the roof. Cordell had started the engine looking over the vehicle again when Cheryl gets in next to him and he told her "Now you know your mother always sit next to the driver." Making her get out and get in the back with the rest of the kids. Mama Betty heard and saw what her son did as Bernise walks out the house and got in next to Cordell. Mama Betty walks over to the passenger side of the front as Bernise turns and said to the kids "Yall make room so your." Her words are cut as Mama Betty says "You!" Bernise turns looking at her as if she had two heads and said to Mama Betty "The woman of the house always rides next to her man." Mama Betty said "Where's the receipt the woman of the house can show she paid for this vehicle?" Looking at Bernise to show her one, then Mama Betty said "Well the woman of the house better get her ass out the Mama of the vehicle she paid for seat or get a vicious beat down!" Bernise turns to look at Cordell to say something but he gets out saying "I forgot to lock the doors to the house!" Getting out quickly and heads back to the house. Mumbling to herself Bernise gets out of the front seat. Mama Betty says "Better sit back there in the third row with all that mumbling you're doing.

I might think it's about me and back slap the shit out you for G.P setting an example!" Bernise looks at her again and thought about it, knowing she would do it too and went to the third row mumbling even cussing under her breath sitting in third row. Jordell says "AH HA! Ma got to sit back here with us." "SSSLAP!" Followed by him crying as Bernise covers his mouth and said to him "Hush!" Corie saw what happened asking her mother "Why you hit Jordell. What if I told grandma Betty." Bernise said "I'll hit you too." Corie looked at her and took a deep breath but finds a hand over her mouth that quick. Her mother told her to be quite. Corie held out her hand, Bernise wanted to know what she's doing that for, Corie said in the cutest way "It's for hush money mommy. You do it to daddy so if you don't want me to tell grandma Betty better pay up or else." Bernise looked at her with a mean look on her face and Corie just cheeses a smiled at her, seeing she wasn't giving up no money Corie went "Oh well." In hailing another deeper breath this time about to let it out Bernise said "Alright!" and hands her a nickel. Corie looks in her hand for a moment frowning then looks at her mother and said "Where's the paper, I know you got paper?!" Bernise asked her "Where you learn how to say and do that?!" Corie again in the cutest way she says "You mommy! I watch you with daddy all those times when he does something you say what no paper." Bernise told her "Stop watching and doing what I do!" Corie said "Ok after I get my paper!" Holding out her hand, wait for her mother to put a dollar bill in her hand. Cordell comes back and gets in the vehicle asking his mother "Where are we going?" Bernise said aloud "Hope it's somewhere I like." Mama Betty replied "You got some where you like money!" Waiting to hear a response, but nothing is said. Mama

Betty looks at the GPS and told him to type in Olive Garden and follow the directions. The Tahoe hits a bumps in the road on their way and bouncing Bernise up making her hit her head on the roof hard just as she held her head mad it happened asking “Where we going again.” Mama Betty said “You need to worry about putting on your seat belt instead where we’re going to eat case we hit another pot hole!” They make it to dinner that night and ate good then came home afterwards to get ready for bed.

It’s Monday and like usual Hutch is the first one at the garage getting his orders, leaving to get his breakfast and heading to the building in Manhattan. While Moni was out Hutch came across a few more things being thrown away coming out of that building and though of some new pranks for him when he comes back.

A few days went by quick and Hutch hadn’t heard from Elise at all, even though he’s been talking to either Donna or Erikaa but always finishes with Janet last those nights they called to check on him. He would have them laughing hard about something either he did or something that happened on the job or still bring up what happened at the supermarket with Steel and Marveece. When Donna asked him “Why don’t you have a girlfriend in your life?” He told her “Just started to talk to this woman right before I meet you three.” Explaining this one woman he likes but there was something strange going on with her and he didn’t know if they would really work out. They took turns asking “Why not?” “You seem to be the right type of man that would have any woman happy to be with you.” “How do you know we didn’t get in the way?” Then Donna asked “Was there a connection between the two of you and if there was, you should really give it another try.” Janet and Erikaa looked at her when she said that to him wondering has she gone stupid for saying something like that. She explained maybe that woman was the right thing for him and they kind of got in the way.

After all he said he did meet her first. How would they feel if he was stolen from them by another woman. Explaining to Hutch they are a little younger than him and can always find a man, but good men are hard to find. If he was to be talking to her first, then maybe he should give her a call. See how it would goes, because she could have been the one for him. Hutch didn't know how to take what she was saying. Making him think he really couldn't be that lucky to be with three beautiful women like them and have nothing go wrong. Thinking hard on what Donna said about him meeting Elise first that night really feeling something about her. Agreeing he did feel something a little and always wondered something about that. Telling him they will always be his friend but with school and everything they really didn't think about having a man in their lives at this point, with Janet doing the nursing classes and having to be on call. Erikaa needs to get to her studies having lots of exams trying to be that lawyer and her with accountant courses where would they have the time to have a man in their lives. Saying she was just being honest looking the fact of everything and not to have had a good time and great sex with him. Hutch didn't want to agree with what she said but knew himself she was right. He tries to make light of the situation by saying "You are not going to forget me when you get ready to get married are you. I just have to make sure Steel isn't chased in your church by Marveece wanting to get married there too." They laughed a little telling him he's silly, staring at the speaker and each other trying not to let the other know it was hurting for what they are doing in letting him go. Hutch let them know, if they ever needed him they can always call him. They don't have to stop being friends even if things work out between him and Elise. Donna told him "They know." Janet and Erikaa agreed then made up some story about how they can't stay on the phone because they have to study now. They all said "bye" to Hutch before hanging up the phone with him. He sits by his phone looking at it trying to wonder what just happened and not sure but feeling lost about the whole conversation. Donna looks at Janet and Erikaa as they look at the speaker then each other feeling the same way Hutch does. Erikaa says "It's for the best right?" Each one has glassy eyes looking at the other one and trying to smile. Janet lets a tear run out the corner of her eye grinning so hard trying not to let out her emotion about the situation and how it feels so bad for her to have let him go like that. Thinking he's a big loveable man who's heart is in the right place, so caring about them. Hearing her sniffle once and wipe the tear away, Donna and Erikaa look at her give a little laugh batting her eyes holding back what wants to come running out. They walk over to her and give her a hugs to say "It'll be alright and they'll be fine too and so will he. She holds them tight for a moment break quickly and heads to her room to cry alone about him. Donna and Erikaa just look and nod to each other then head to their own rooms not saying a word about it anymore but knowing they will do the same as Janet and have that cry about giving him up.

For the next couple days that week Hutch seems to be walking around like something is very heavy on his mind. Thursday night he gets off from work, his mother came back to his house needing a break from Bernise and the kids plus wanted to talk to him about his money and where did he get such an amount from. While at his house they got interrupted by Elise's surprise visit and how she came walking through it talking to Hutch as if he were the servant. Hutch was talking with his mother and had a couple of drinks when Elise starts getting on him again. Mama Betty wants to know who this woman was walking around his house. Saying what she likes and don't like about it and what have to go. Elise gets a little snooty with his mother assuming she was a cook he hired to come there, mentioning it to them as she dips her finger in the pots cooking.

Mama Betty looked at her said loudly "COOK! Is this heffer out her mind calling me the GAWD DAMN COOK!?" Hutch knew he better stop Elise from talking and showed her this is his mother. Elise looked her up and down at first and said "Yeah right! Your mother wouldn't be caught dead in those clothes tacky as they are." Hutch eyes got really wide as he turned to look at his mother putting her drink down about to charge at Elise from behind. Giving Hutch a stay your ass out of this look as her hand grab a fist full of weave snatching backward Elise to the floor. Before hitting the floor all she heard was "Heffer your ass really need to be taught some manners!" Hutch tries to get his mother to let go of her hair saying "Ma! She really thought it was a joke, like Steel at the pool now let go of her hair Please!" Elise is screaming in pain as Mama was heading for the front door dragging her. Elise got loose and now believes this is his mother as she gets up off the floor saying "I was mistaken thinking you were the cook, I see now he was telling the truth you are his mother of course who else could you be." Holding her head in pain trying to fix her hair asking Hutch "Well aren't you going to introduce me to your mother?!" He looks at her and says "Ma this is Elise you were dragging to the door like a bag of garbage about to throw out on her ass. Elise this is my mother Betty! Who was going to whoop your ass outside if I didn't stop her!" Elise went to hug his mother but get stopped as she holds her hand up. They both look at all of the hair in between Mama Betty's fingers. She waves her hand around then pulls out the hair from her finger and hands a big ball of it back to Elise "Here you might need these back!" Elise told her "That's Ok Hutch would cover what damage I suffered from this misunderstanding." Mama Betty standing close by Hutch looks up at him asking "Where this one came from and are you serious about her?" Asking him "You hit that yet! I hope you bagged it up and she's not toasting right now!" He cuts her off "MA!" Elise turns going "I'm sorry did you say something Miss Betty." Hutch told Elise "Yeah." His mother said "It was late and she's going to bed to let us talk about why your here." His mother had this look on her face of "Are you crazy!" He asked her to be alone with Elise so they could talk. She rolled her eyes at him not happy at what he just asked and heads to the kitchen saying "I've got to put away that food and clean those dishes." Watching her walk in the kitchen Elise sat on the couch and asked him to join her because she's got something to say. Coming right out with how she knows how things could work between them. Letting him know she's looking for man that will bring her more than material things to the table, not a bunch of free loading friends that will be in the relationship or some needy women that doesn't have a man in their lives. Needing to come over to their house wanting to talk about being extra's at his BBQ pool party. Saying there comes a time in a man's life when he needs a woman in his life like her to come before his friends and all others, she doesn't want her man not to have his brothers and sisters or stop being with his family. The only thing she wants for him to stop having lots of people over to her house because of what happened and doesn't want it to happen again. What would the neighbor think about them. Hutch was thinking "Nothing their usually here too." Telling him under her guidance she knows he could be the faithful type of man that would put his wife first above all women, even if they have children making her feel like she's the most important woman ever in his life. Saying he better come to her about everything even if he wants to try new things but can't sit in a rut or sulk about her denial of him not getting what he wants. She also wants to know he can handle any problems they would ever have without her having to lift a finger, because she's the Queen of the house and that's the man of the house problem to handle. When it comes to him bringing in cash to the house it must pass through her to make all the decisions on what she wants to spend it on something that suits her expensive new life style that she deserves.

Not to say she'll let the bills pile up of course his share will cover them like it should be. All the while she was talking Hutch was looking at her trying to figure out if she was on something or drinking something stronger than anything he'd ever mixed together, feeling her head asking "You feel OK?" Mama Betty was in the kitchen listening to what Elise was talking about thinking her son better say something before she comes out there and they'll both have to figure out how much bleach can cover the spots of DNA she'll leave all over the floor. Thinking to herself "This heffer won't go quietly either." Looking through her purse to find the right thing to use (Big folding hunting knife. 32caliber Derringer with long clip. Two pepper sprays and one gun stunner with three types of settings. Mini bat made of cherry oak with lead in the middle of it.) still listening how she was talking about taken over her sons life making him her personal cash cow. Elise went on talking about during their bonding period he'll need to think where he could get the insurance on himself and the house in case something happens to him. So she should get everything turned over to her and of course when they have children she'll be able to put them in the finest boarding school with the best education. Hutch starts looking at his drink and thinking maybe he spiked his own drink without knowing it, but then notice it was too quite in the kitchen where his mother was leaning on the door as it cracks open just enough for him to see her. That's when he told Elise maybe she better slow her roll there just a bit about getting married. They haven't even gone out on a serious date yet and he might not need someone to tell him what to do with his money or time spent at home. His mother comes out the kitchen saying "It's about time you came to our, I mean your senses baby and shut this gold digging schemer up!" Elise looks at her because she didn't catch what she said asking him "Is she still drinking and what did she say about me?" Mama Betty didn't hold her tongue and said "Sorry missy but you'll have to dig up another hard working man somewhere else this mine is closed." Elise wants to know what she's talking about digging somewhere else this mine is closed. Hutch went to say something but his mother cuts him off asking "Elise are you toasting or not and is he the chef" Elise thought his mother has had enough to drink and there was no reason for him to cook right now. Mama Betty looks at her for a moment then say something she could understand "Are you pregnant girl?" They look at her and Elise says "No! Whatever gave you that idea." Then Elise gets the idea since she already met his mother they can starts cranking out kid right away. Mama Betty thought to herself "DAMN! Should have keep my mouth shut sorry baby." Pulling him a side and saying "If you're going to hit that better put on two coats but the next time you want to date a phsyco do a back ground check first or check the expiration date on the back of her neck. There should be one there." He told his mother to take it down a bit and let him finish talking with his company so he could go upstairs to bed. Turning back to Elise saying "Excuse my mother she's had an exciting day and didn't get much sleep so she's going up to bed to rest now." Mama Betty said "Slept like a log today don't know what the hell he's talking about and I always could handle my drinking better than his father or uncles." Elise smiled and thought to herself "Nice to know where he got the drinking part from." Then said "Good night, Miss Betty hope you have sweet dreams." Mumbling low under her breath "Hoping it turns into a dirt nap old drunk." She goes back to looking around the room waiting for Hutch to come back down stairs. He was walking behind his mother making sure she went upstairs. When she heard what Elise just said. Mad about what she said Mama Betty turns around and starts arguing with him as he blocks her way to go back down stairs to get at Elise. She told him what she heard her saying "I'll give her ass a dirt nap and have a drink while doing it. You didn't hear what that little skinny ass gold digging scheming heffer said about me!" Hutch asked his mother to "Please go upstairs for him."

She looked at him "Alright but I better not hear you down there tappen that ass!" Hutch says "Ma!" She turns back around and continues to climb the stairs as Hutch comes back down to finish talking with Elise. Just as they sat back on the couch they heard from upstairs "If you're going to hit that away, just remember to aim for the stomach. I'd aim to squirt in the face, she won't be mad. Lord knows she could use the Vitamin E on those crow's feet she's got around her eyes. Tell her to smear evenly because I never saw a porn star with bad skin so she could take a double shot to the face if you ask me. Don't try to be no marks men here in this house, matter a fact I'm counting on you missing the hole completely. Tight ass as she is you can go up the Hershey high way that might loosen her up and don't be gentle." Hutch yells "Ma! Go to bed young lady!" She answers back "Alright! If it feels good pull it out quick but please be in missionary position, that way you could stand up quick and fire away. Just in case you need ideas I got charts. Remember she's got another hole not too far from that one either" Hutch yells "Ma would you please!" Her room door is heard slamming shut and he's turns to Elise saying "Sorry about that." She smiles at him "Your mother just loves her son and would be best understood if she didn't drink so much." Hutch was about to make a comment but Elise put her finger to his lips "Shhh I don't want to talk about your mother anymore." She looks at him as if she was about to kiss him when his mother is heard saying "I don't hear any noise down there, not that I'm listening but he's clean with no STD's so you can get a baloney wash from the young lady. Just take your time with her don't want her choking to death on that big piece of meat!" Hutch yells "MA! That's enough!" She continues "He's healthy and should give you a good mask when you brush quickly with that meat brush, just don't bite down or be afraid of the gush it's like Maxwell house good to the last drop. We don't have any mental health issues and don't need any even from you, and uncle Milbert was a fluke. They still can't prove any of that shit he did and we can get the doctors report plus court papers on it if necessary" Elise looks at him. He said "Long story." She stood up "On that note I got to go, I'll call you" Looking around at everything saying "I'll show you how to spend money the right way on decorations too." His mother runs back down stairs after hearing Elise say she's got to go. Asking "What's wrong she couldn't get the whole thing in her mouth. She got to work it slow, relaxing her jaws muscles. Chap stick would help it slide if it's tight!" Elise looks at her for moment about say something really vulgar but knows if she did that's his mother and didn't want to risk him getting mad at her. She tilts her head smiling to what his mother said, then asked him to walk her to the door. Saying "Good Night again Miss Betty. Nice seeing you." They start to the door and he turns back to see his mother about to walk behind them. Waving his hand she nodded and took a seat in the chair waiting. At the door on the outside Elise asked him "Is your mother going to be dropping by a lot, because I was thinking about changing the lock once I take over your house hold." Hutch looked at Elise explaining he likes her but don't she think she's really rushing things again with that talk and they haven't gotten to know any more about each other and what they both bring to a relationship. He told her he doesn't know what she does for a living or what she plans for the future. Other than getting married to him and having him work like a slave which he isn't going to be and don't even think about. She cuts him off by saying "If you think I'm going to put on a sweat suit and fall in the pool just so you can attend to my every whim then you're mistaken!" She continues to go about him not even inviting her to his pool party, asking him "What you did to me that night, didn't it mean anything to you. If you really want to be with me then you would show me that you do!" Not giving him a chance to answer she walks away gets in her vehicle drives off but has a smirk on her face looking at him in her rear view mirror.

Hutch felt bad about what she said to him going back in the house thinking about that night. Elise knew she had left him with something heavy and would string him along for a while. He walks in and listens for his mother to come at him with all sorts of questions but she's nowhere to be seen. He thinks to himself good he doesn't want to hear it anyways and goes upstairs, a while later he hears what sounds like his mother having a conversation on the phone about him. Thinking she was talking to one of the family or her friends getting close to the bedroom door that's slightly a jar. Hearing her say how she would have her ass beating the weave out that skinny heffers head one strand at a time if Hutch wasn't there. Opening the door about to say something to her about how she was talking he see that she was asleep with a display of her weapons in the dresser draw and talking about how she's not going to let that heffer mess up her sons life. Plotting his death to spend the money he's worked hard for. He smiled at his mother sleeping and backs out of the room closing the door behind him, it's about to close he felt five thumps on the door. Opening the door again to look at his mother still sleep about to close it again and hears another thump on the door, opening it quick to his mother still sleep saying "You gold digging skinny heffer get your ass out my site before I cut some more of that weave off" Opening the door wider looking at his mother sleep then looking at the back of the door seeing two throwing knifes, two throwing darts and two throwing stars stuck in the back of it, shaking his head thinking "Nice grouping she did" closing the door and going to bed.

The next day at work he was not like his normal self, as all the workers wanted to know was thing alright never seen him like that. He had something very heavy on his mind, thinking to himself about Elise and how she was the first woman he talked with in years. Maybe it's not her fault she acts that way because of all her pass boyfriends could have been jack asses. Not sure of how he's going to go about giving it another try with her, but thinks he's going to overlook however she acts and put an real effort in trying to get with her not sounding too convincing to himself. The day went on and before he got off work Mack called him to remind him it's the weekend and they have some other things planned for it. Mack hears how down Hutch sounds in his answer back to him and wants to know what's wrong because he doesn't sound right. He tells Mack "I'm alright, just not feeling something right now!" Mack told him "they'll be there at his house to plan what they're going to do and that will snap him out of what he's feeling right now!"

Later at his house Most of the G.D.M are there talking about what they want to do this week and notice Hutch still not himself and wants to know what's wrong? He tells them "Nothing I can't handle" and wants to know what they've come up with to do that weekend. The idea was to go Bowling and then to the strip club to end the day of drinking and fun. Hutch agreed with them it might be fun and they planned like usual to meet at his house and then head to the alley. At the alley they were drinking zombies and red devils and made it the name of the team verses each other and the winners get to pick which strip club they wanted to go to first. At the bowling alley Troy-H, 2Soon, Steel, Mack, Dave, D-train, Derrick (Dee), Dougie, Herb, Goodie, Doug, Tyrone, Tys/LIL-Rob, C-man, La-machine, Ron and Jazz with Hutch they were getting pretty buzzed, when Hutch and Mack heard a sound (OOH MARVEECE) that made Steel freeze in his tracks. About to throw the ball down the alley and turning to tell all of them "Stop playing like that." Mack looked at Hutch asking him "Did you hear that man?!" again it was heard ("oooh Marveece! Throw the ball baby!")

Steel turned around mad at Mack and Hutch saying "Go ahead with that man I'm not playing!" 2Soon told him "They did say anything fam, I was looking right at them. Why you mad at them it came from down there!" He points in the direction where came from but they couldn't see exactly who was making that noise, till standing up to throw her bowling ball making that sound again "Oooh Marveece I'm going to make a strike!" Steel also stand on deck facing the pins turns his eyes to the right slowly and then his head and saw 315lbs. Marveece 22 lanes down. Dressed in pink spandex black top with silver bracelets on both arms gold door knocker ear rings, black & blue with pink & yellow scarf wrapped around her braided hair coming out to one side, a sash tied on her waist the same side as his hair was coming out of the scarf going "Oooh Marveece!" Steel dropped the ball and dove from the wood deck for cover amongst the guys seated on the bench in back of the score chairs. Marveece was about to throw her ball and felt the back of her neck and shivered for a second turning left to see Steel standing there looking forward as people were throwing their balls down the lanes. Excited she closed her eyes for a second making a wish then taking a second look at where she seen Steel, thinking that man down there looks just like her Steel. When she took a good looks down that way again the man wasn't there as another man was picking up the ball. She turns back to his friends and "Oooh Marveece! I got Steel on my mind so much I'm starting to think every thin man is him girrrrl!"

Derrick wanted to know why Steel dove into them like that and what is he afraid for. Mack and Hutch looked at each other and busted out laughing holding each other up as they tried to explain what he was doing covering up in their jacket and coats. Mack explained everything to them about the supermarket as Hutch backed him up and all of the G.D.M.4.L turned to the right trying to get a good look at Marveece as he stood there looking down their way saying "I know he's here I can feel it somehow." The roar of laughter was loud coming from where the G.M.D.4.L were sitting having everyone look at them and Steel was pleading not to make it come down that way. The rest rooms were close to where they were and Marveece had to go to the bathroom. Walking their way wiggling as she walked making those bracelets clink swing his arms coming their way. Tyrone was the first to start the other up by making a comment about Marveece's bracelets stopping her asking "Where did you get those from because I wants some for my girl?!" Marveece stops walking to talk with Tyrone and tell him where she got them from saying "Oooh Marveece! It was a Steal of a deal he made to get them." Mack joins in by asking "Are they made of Steel or silver because they look like Steel!" Marveece says "Oooh Marveece! I know they're shiny but they aren't Steel they are silver!" Dave took his turn by asking "Where did you get that scarf it nice, because he knows that wasn't a Steal of a deal?" Marveece goes "Oooh Marveece! Thank you, it wasn't. I had a girl who sews make this one for me!" Jazz says "Ok we didn't mean to STEEL you away from where you were going, so we'll let you get back" Marveece looks at Mack and asked him "Don't I know you from somewhere?" Mack was standing by the coats and jacket Steel was hiding under about to say "Yeah" but a foot from under the coats Marveece didn't see kicks him making him say "Nah he don't think so." All the G.D.M.4.L laughs at how Mack moved knowing Steel hit him from under the coats and jackets. They let

Marveece continue on and talked about how they were going to get Steel out of there, Mack knows he got strength never used because he's both male and wants to be woman. In between the jokes they told about Steel having the strangest relationship with Marveece, not knowing if he was going to be the man or woman in it. Steel was getting up when Marveece came back out the bathroom and got jumped on by Herb and Goodie to hide him again.

Hutch was coming back with the tray of drinks for the guys when Marveece walking looking back at them bumps him and almost makes him spill the drinks. Hutch twisted and moved so they didn't spill over as Marveece turns to him and say "OooH Marveece sorry baby didn't see you." Looking at who it was, changing his voice turning his head quickly saying "That alright no harm done!" Then walks fast to get back over by the guys, Marveece walks on for second then stops thinking that man looks very familiar and turns to look at who he bumped into. Hutch gets to where his brothers are, La-machine said "Yo fam don't turn around because you're being crossed haired by it. Do you think shim would recognize you if it saw your face?" Now Marveece was looking at all of them together and they knew it as Mack said "Yo I think it's putting us in the memory card of her mind and trying to remember me and Hutch from the" Then he hears his words finished loudly "SUPERMARKET! Oooh Marveece. That's where I know you from!" Pointing at Mack and Mack turned looking back at Marveeve when he said that aloud. Mack looked at Hutch and Marveece saw who he was looking at and now saw Hutch too. Pointing at him then starts to calling her girls like Mr. Han calling his Hench men in to get Bruce Lee in Enter the dragon. "Davona, Shanuka, Bashita, They're here! Rashonna, Jamilla, Shimenda, Danellea, there are enough for all of us girls because these are friends of Stee-aals!" Magika, Maryarma, Lakisha, Traci, Mandasha, Desiree, Naringa, Kissanet, Bonisha and Peanut {why is there always a Peanut in every crowd of women} Then screaming over all the bowlers playing their games "There are enough baby daddy's here to last for years so come and get one girls." Goodie was by Jazz and said to him "Did you just hear that war cry? I'm not looking to be the baby daddy of something that looks like those things galloping this way man you better run!" Jazz said "I'm a grown ass man and I don't need to" Cutting his words short hearing the roar as he turns and saw the horde of big door knocker earrings and pasted hair dues on some heavy set, tall, big rounded women knocking over normal people in their way stampeding towards them.

He turns back to Goodie saying "I see what he was talking about!" Goodie looking at them then turns back to say something to Jazz and didn't see nothing but the big man's back as he turns the corner after going through the Exist door. Goodie said to the other "Jazz is the biggest out of all of us how could he move so fast?!" Then Jazz came back and said "Forgot my drink!" They all came back and toasted every man for himself. Good luck to those that get away because some of them look like they cheat and run on all fours! They all scatter in the bowling alley with so many places to hide like in the sports bar and buffet place, or pizza shop, burgher place, adult lounge, and game arcade. Finding somewhere to run to and hide leaving Steel at the bench. Marveece saw there was one man left but couldn't see Steel's face at first. Thinking it had to be him running over that way. Herb they didn't see at the counter was getting his shoes when one by one every Grand Drunken Master 4 Life passed him dropping their bowling shoes off saying "Get my shoe will ya." They ran for their lives being chased by one of Marveece friends, losing them for a moment they would make their way back to Herb to get their shoes and leave the building to get their vehicles. Steel was crouching down trying not to be seen with Marveece getting closer over to him, when he heard Herb yell "YO! Man yo better get out now or be got, so go man now!" Steel bolts and slides down the lane towards the pins but Marveece saw him and shouts "Oooh Marveece! Come here to me Steel!" He stood up and looked at Marveece standing by the score seats then saw the other being chased by some of the women. He turns to see the door to the back room where machines rack the bowling pins. Steel ran back four lane over hoping it was open so he could get away but the door was locked and he heard Marveece shouting "Rashonna, Shimenda, Bashita, Shanuka, and Naringa cover the Exists now" Steel looked at the Exists being blocked by the women but saw one he could get to and had to cross the lanes themselves and he took off across them towards it. Marveece looked at him running across the lanes, then looked at what he was running to and Whistles so loud stopping all the bowlers. Shouting to all of them "500$ to bring down that man!" Everyone looked at Marveece then went back to bowling their games. Marveece then yells "3500$ to knock him down!" Steel standing at lane 9 and knew he had another 35 lanes to cross and starts running dodging one ball then 2, 3, even 4 balls at one time being rolled at him. Managing to get to the last two lanes but one man decides he was going to stop Steel cashing in on him and stood there by the door as Steel came right up to him. The man says "I need the cash and going to get that money man so sorry!" Steel stopped at the man and told him "If you don't move you're going to suffer one of the worst beatings of your life and wish you were dead. When I get finished ripping flesh pieces off you and eat those pieces, rather than get caught by thing that wants me for her or it's boyfriend" The man looks back at Marveece coming their way "That wants you as a mate?" He drops his head and utters the words "Sorry dude no man should suffer." but another man says "I'm not and I'm going to get the cash I could use it now!"

Steel moved so fast beating that man so severely it made the first man cringe watching what he did to the man and still have time to get out the door. The second man lays there spitting out some of his teeth in pain and the first man said "Hope your medical insurance and dental covers a brother ass beating like that! To think that could have been me!" Marveece gets over to the man being helped up asking "How did he get away?" Pointing to the groaning man on the floor and didn't need any more explaining, as Marveece looked at the shape he was in "Damn! My future baby daddy can fight!" Then heard this thud as the first man drops the second on the floor and says "Poor guy no man should suffer a fate that." Marveece looked at the second man on the floor asking the first man "Well aren't you going to finish helping him because he looks in pain." The first man answers Marveece "I wasn't talking about him. I was taking bout the one being chased by you. This guy should have known better and to try and stop him" Then walks away having Marveece asking the second man "You need medical help shuga." Outside the exit 2 Soon was there with LIL-Rob and Steel as they push the container in front of the door so it couldn't be opened. Steel asked "How did they know he would come out this way?" 2Soon told him "Think you're the only one who had to make an quick Exist out a bowling alley across lanes." Steel wants to ask more about it and 2Soon told him "Fam Wes Craven would have ideas for months about that horde let's get out of here before one of those silver backs use her weight on all fours to move that container."

In the vehicles they all call each other making sure everyone got out safe and continue on with their plans as Goodie led the way having the rest follow him. Stopped at the bank and they all took out some extra cash then all met up at this strip club off Staten Island in Brooklyn somewhere by one of the expressways. Everyone paid their own cover charge as the walk in the place looking at all the women half naked either on the stage dancing with a pole or walking around giving lap dances. Some G.D.M.4.L heads to the bar to get drinks for the ones at tables. 2Soon bought the first round and C-man bought shots to go along with it, then coming back to the tables as the guys were looking at which woman they would throw money at or get a lap dance from. Derrick went to get another round of drinks and Goodie went to get the shots like C-man did. Hutch just finished his drink and went to the bathroom but on the way there he was seen by Janet right before he went in the men's room. He came back out and she watched him go over to the table and sit with a big group of men she recognized from his BBQ at his house. She walks over wondering why he wasn't interacting with the women there like his friends who either had a woman giving them and lap dance or danced in front of them wiggling her butt for them. Instead Hutch sat there looking into his drink or at the menu on the tables. She bumps him with her hips and he apologizes saying "My fault and didn't mean to bump you." She laughs "You didn't say that when you was hitting them before!" He doesn't look up not paying attention to her face asking "Excuse me I never touched you before!" She laughs again and told him "Well if you didn't touch me you sure did a good job because I couldn't walk right for a while after not that I'm complaining either!" Hutch does a double take looking real good at the woman standing next to him then realizes its Janet. He stands up and hugs her, then taking a better look at her saying "Wow no wonder I didn't recognize you looking so dimepeishous can I bite you?!" She laughs again "You're silly. What are you doing here?" He explains he came there with his brothers having a men's night out getting rid of work week stress like they always do for the weekend winding up some place new. She told him to turn and see Donna and Erikaa about to get on stage and do their thing. He's surprised that all three of them worked there.

She explained to him it's just to pay bill because going to school trying to get a career is hard enough and its work to them, she wants him to know they aren't like that as they sat talking. Donna saw it was Hutch Janet was talking with and she leaves the stage with Erikaa and go over to them as he hugs them both and they all sit and talk. The manager of the place notices the table with three of his best and fresh girls talking with one man and sends one of his guys over to tell them to get back on stage to work. Hutch didn't want that and told the man he wants them by him no matter what the cost and puts a few bills in front of all of them.

The man looks at Hutch saying "Long as they are making money for the club." That's when Hutch got an idea and asked him to "Get the manager." The guy told him "I'll be right back." and walks straight to Markola saying something in his ear. Donna asked Hutch "What are you doing calling the manager over. Don't mess with this guy Hutch Please?" Feeling tipsy he told her "I know what I'm doing trust me!" and winks at her. Smiling as Markola came over asking "What can I do for you mook!" Hutch stood up and said "I don't want any problem so out of respect for you and your place. I'm asking what would it take for me to keep talking with these women right here." Markola looks at his man and says "Wow a mook with manners. Let me see three of my best! You don't have that kind of money!" Hutch suggests if he bought the whole place three rounds of drinks including the women that are dancing. Donna, Janet and Erikaa looked at each other Donna said "That's ok big bear we'll get back up on stage and meet you later." Markola looked at Hutch thinking this mook's got a lot of nerve to say something like to him, but to be a smart about it he say to Hutch "How about you buy five round of whatever they are drinking including the dancer and myself." Janet looked at Hutch asking him "Please! Don't do this because we'll go back to work and see you after they get off." Hutch knew he was being a smart ass about it and looked at the girls and told Markola "If I'm going to do that then I want to take them out of there and any woman my brothers wanted too." Markola told Hutch "Then for that make it ten!" Hutch put his hand out to shake saying "Done!" Dougie saw Hutch shaking hand with a man and came over to ask "What's going on?"

Donna told him what Hutch agreed to do and Dougie pulls Hutch a side asking him "Are you crazy to buy that many drinks." He stops talking as this chocolate thick legged woman winks at him walking by and he says "I can have that one to go?" Hutch shook his head "Yes" Dougie pats his back going after that woman. Erikaa asked Hutch "Why'd you do that because it's going to cost you so much!" Hutch smiles at all of them saying "Their worth it and more, besides if I knew you did this I would find you better jobs some other place where you wouldn't have to take off your clothes to pay bills" Markola smug says "How about it mook! How you going to pay for it, we don't take food stamps here!" Hutch now pissed at what he said goes in his wallet and pulls out his Credit card handing it to Donna looking at Markola and said "Charge it for me baby! You do take credit cards here right!" Markola looked at him "Yeah we take Credit cards here hope you have enough on it, we're not a charity branch!" Not to be out done Hutch smirks "Each woman my brother wants to take with us, will take a two bottles of beer and a shot to go!" Markola being smart said "Done mook I'm a man of my word are you and won't try to cancel the charge!" Hutch smiled at him saying "Do it Sweetie." Donna took his card and went to the cashier with Markola. Tyrone and LIL-Rob came over asking "What's going on?" Janet explained this time to them what happened and what Hutch did for them. Dave gets mad "Man! See I told you we should never let him drink like that. He gets too generous with his cream

Tys!" Derrick saw the commotion and walks over to find out what's going on and once he learned what Hutch did he calls the G.D.M.4.L brothers over and let the rest know what's going on. They start to go in the pockets to pool their cash together for Hutch. He didn't take it saying "Bruhs I got this one this time I'll take the bite! Don't worry about it I should make it back up with over time." Explaining someone has to shut that wise ass mook calling fat cigar smoking mutha F#*^ker up. Donna and Erikaa was with Markola after he totaled up such a big bill with everything he and Hutch agreed to charge on the Credit card. Handing the cashier the card to swipe for that large amounted bill but to Markola's surprise he saw the read out show UNLIMITED FUNDS across the screen. He looks at Donna amazed at what he just saw and asked the cashier for the card. Donna quickly took the card from the cashiers hand before he could do anything and said "She's giving it back to its owner." Markola told her "Wait a minute he don't have to know he got back the wrong card, all I have to do is give him one of these stripper cards with some stronger drinks. Later he'll think he lost it!" Donna said "NO!" and starts to walk back to Hutch but Markola said "Alright I'll give you what you want just give me the card and let me handle him." Donna told Markola "Look at the size of him and know he works for a demolition company and his brothers are cops, security guards, EMTs, Sanitation workers. Movers and some in construction and a couple of them are legal aides, plus there's only one small one in that group think your few man could stop them once he knows you took his card" Markola said "How's he to know unless you tell him?" Erikaa clears her throat and said "We fooker we." Markola looked at them mad he could take it from her but watches as they both walk back with the receipt for Hutch to sign. After he signs it she hands the receipt to Markola who looks at her with "I'll get even with you" look on his face. Hutch smirks at Markola as he watches them get served their drinks with Donna, Erikaa and Janet kissing Hutch for what he did. All of the G.D.M.4.L picks a woman to go with them leaving the club and once outside Hutch feeling real good about what he did, screaming "That stupid ass shit head wanted to be a smart ass now look what it got him. Party at my house last one there cleans up the mess!" Everyone runs to their vehicle and drive off. Markola was standing outside looking at all the vehicles leave from the parking lot behind his building. Thinking he got to get that card from that mook but how.

Janet was riding with Hutch telling him "Our boss isn't going to like what you did and how you did it to him in front of everyone there and left his club with us like that." Hutch was feeling very invincible as he told Janet "it felt good to do that and just to see all of them." Then laughing listen to how he told her about what happened at the bowling alley with Steel and the horde with Marveece. That comment about feeling good seeing them made her wonder "What was wrong with things." For him to say that to her and before she could ask him anything about how was it going for him. His attention was on Donna driving alongside them getting passed by her on the expressway. Hutch pulls up to his house and parks on the grass close to his house so some of the cars could park in the drive way and other could be closer to his house on the street. Opening the door walking in the house with Janet and Erikaa followed by Donna after she parked her vehicle and the rest came in as Mama Betty was at the top stairs watching the parade of people waving hello to her. All the men saying "Hi Ma" and head down to the basement and other to the refrigerator then head down to the basement. Mama Betty could smell the alcohol coming from every one of them going by and knew she didn't want to see what else is going to happen there at Hutches house, so she head back upstairs and calls Cordell to come pick her up. Telling him "I'm not get in the way of his orgy about to go on in the house and might get mistaken for one of them women because they were drinking heavy."

Short time later Cordell is walking in the house hearing all that music coming from the basement then seeing an almost naked woman go by to the bathroom. Then watch her go to the Frig and get a bottle of wine and head back down stairs. Interested in seeing what's going on down stair in the basement he doesn't see his mother come up behind him and pop him in the head by her saying "Mind your business, that's not your party not yours now come on and lets leave him to his party." One of the women went upstairs to the bathroom to use it and found one of the silver capped cologne on the sink. After using the bathroom and wanting to spray some to cover what she did smelling the cologne liking what she smelled she kept the bottle and went down stair to see what it smelled like on a man.

Dancing around tipsy as she was getting all the man there to lift their shirts and spraying the cologne on them some heavier than others. When it came to spraying Hutch Janet took the spray and did him once and then Erikaa got to spritz him one time, not to be left out Donna got him twice liking the smell of that cologne. All the men were getting hot dancing the cologne was affecting the women as they were getting more touchy feely with the men. Wasn't long after they got sprayed couples starts disappearing to go off for some privacy, Erikaa took Hutch by the hand after getting told something by Janet and Donna. She said to him "We never thanked you for what you did for us." Hutch almost drunk says "It wasn't nothing I just didn't want to see you nice women in a place like that and I meant what I said if I could" Fingers to his lips shushing him as she pulls him along to his bed room where he sees Donna and Janet on his bed with most all their clothes off. The clicking of the lock on his door makes him turns to see Erikaa by it. With a gentle push to his back he moves to the bed, but then tells them all to "Stop!" Going his draw and taken out three pair of plastic vampire teeth and handing it to them holding out his arms lying on the bed saying "Now come draw some blood from big daddy!" At the foot of the bed he see three women standing there looking at each other then show their teeth to each other and then look at him before the light went out and he's heard saying "Damn those teeth are sharp, aaah who's got the cold hands that feels good!"

That morning Hutch wakes to see three bodies on his bed, he ease out of bed heading to the bathroom to take a shower and saw his body in the mirror passing it then stops and had to back up and get another look at himself in it. His body is covered in these little bite marks from the stomach to just under his eyes, front and back of his arms. He bends over looks down at his legs and their covered too as he starts scratching his head when he stood upright looking in the mirror and saw Janet and Erikaa standing behind him. Scared he jumps on the sink counter letting out "HAAY!" They look up at him and Janet said to Erikaa "Wow and he got hops too!" Hutch was climbing down going "Very funny I thought you all were still sleep?!" Erikaa said to him "For a big man you have NBA leaping ability when you get sacred!" Hutch answers her "I wasn't scared. It's that I didn't want to swing on you." Donna woke from the noise and heard them talking and puts in her teeth walking up behind him as he was talking to Janet and Erikaa about his reflex. When he turns and saw Donna with her teeth showing it scaring him again watching jump back stumbling backward till he fell in the tub with a big "Thump! Janet said "Good reflexes!" They help him out the tub so they could shower and get dressed. Hutch went down stairs and starts to cooking breakfast knowing some of them still there would be hungry since he the first one up. The smell of turkey bacon and sausages, eggs grits and toast has Zombies staggering the kitchen from the smells something so good cooking with coffee brewing too. It was Saturday and after everyone gotten something to eat they were trying to figure out what they all were going to do for the rest of the day and Derrick said "Since they're all here why not have a pool party BBQ?" The women said "They don't have any swim suits." The men said "Like that would be a problem!" C-man suggest why don't they go home or to the store and get some while the men stay here and clean up and some of the women could pick up more things for the party while they're out if they don't mind. Hutch asked Donna to the side and told her "Here take my Credit card and get whatever you need even if it's a new car or anything that you ladies might need!" Making a joke out of it adding "As long as you all come back with the beer and food, so get whatever you want. If you want to go home and change that'll be OK just come back to me!" She looked at him trying to figure out if he was serious or playing with her, but couldn't tell as she hugs and kisses him for the jester. Donna told all the ladies it would be a good idea for them to get their bathing suits and pick up the food and beer with liquor too. The guys agreed with her and said they would help Hutch clean up before they got back. When the all the women left out, Hutch starts to clean up for the party with the help of all the G.D.M.4.L which didn't take no time with all of them helping. Some went home to and got something to change into. Out doing some shopping for bathing suits at the mall Janet and Erikaa asked "How they were going to pay for new bathing suits and stuff?" Donna told them "Hutch gave her his Credit card to use and pick up whatever they wanted, he said he wouldn't mind." They looked at each other and went power shopping for things they needed at home and for school and while Janet and Erikaa were putting the bag in the vehicle. Donna did what Hutch told her to do since they're at the mall. She picked out new living room and bedroom furniture and TV's for each of their rooms to be delivered. Janet and Erikaa found her looking for some jewelry they all can get that would match the ring she wants to get for Hutch. Along with the man's bracelet that would look good on him too. Finding something they all agreed on then had it wrapped up as a present. Going back to their place first with all the new stuff they bought for themselves, when they arrived they were being watched by Markola's men he had go over to their place to keep an eye on them. They were walking in their building carrying bags of clothes and other things, so the men calls Markola and tells him they saw.

Mad at the report his men just gave him about Donna and the girls and what they had, Markola shouts "That bitch knew what she was doing keeping that card from me, when I could have had it. Now she's going to get him to give it to her and those two freaking friends of hers so they can spend my money!" He told his men to stay there and watch the place because he knows they're going out again and wants to know when they come back for the night so stay and watch.

Inside their apartment they change into their sexy new swim suits under their new outfits, then leave to go food and beer shopping for the BBQ pool party. When the women got back to Hutch's place with all the stuff only a few of the guys were there to help unload all the stuff from the van. With all the food in the kitchen Hutch and Dougie can prepare all the Shrimp, beef, chicken, turkey and fish with the right seasoning to be cooked on the BBQ grill. The girls helped chop up whatever Hutch needs to make a good vegetable and fruit salad. Janet asked "What about the Mack&Cheese can't have a good BBQ with no!" Hutch smiled saying "Been had that covered!" Showing her two big pans in the Frig already made with one cooking, "Whenever my mother comes into visit she makes Chyrelle's 10 cheese blend for me." Getting the meats out to the grill and ice on the beer and liquor. Dougie and Mack with 2Soon help Hutch set up the liquor and want him to make a punch like before since they all were going to be there. Donna asked him "You know how to make punches too?" 2Soon told her "Not only does he make a punch but it makes you do things not violent things but good and funny things too you can't remember." She looks at Hutch "Did anyone wake with hangover?" He answers "No! Never had anyone tell they did." She asked "So why not make the punch for this BBQ pool party?" Derrick told him "just don't make it as strong as the last time!" Curious Janet asked "What happened the last time he made that particular punch and what did you do?" Hutch told her "I had to work and they needed a party starter that time." Hutch told them "I could make a punch ever since I was a bartender 15yrs ago and know how to really mix so smooth you couldn't taste all the liquors in it." Explaining he mixed one of his many ones together for them, till this day some of them don't want to talk about some things but want to do it again. Then instead of going on with the rest of what happened he decides to make a punch and tell them all he's not responsible for what happens and don't blame him if some woman or women gets knocked up by the same man. The G.D.M.4.L agreed and Donna, Erikaa and Janet want to see it to believe it. At the party all the food was either done or still on the grill and everyone was told even if you eat this punch will still get to you quick so take it easy and drink safe. 2Soon held up these four big jugs that had corks to them and starts passing them around saying "You can't pour these contends in a glass it take the tradition out of it. Most of the of those that wanted to dance was in the basement doing so and other were either out on the back yard drinking, or eating, or talking with someone tipsy as hell. When one of the women there made a wild suggestion about the beach and how far is it. The meat cooking was taken off from the grill and covered up, short time after they all are in their vehicles heading to the beach which is only 10 minutes from Hutch's house.

While they all were at the beach Elise came over to his house to talk with him, getting out her vehicle she smells the BBQ and finds the door opens and food cooked with music still playing. She walks around the house and finds a lot of women's clothes in the bedrooms but when she got to his bedroom and saw more women's clothes she yells his name" HUTCH!"

At the beach the water is colder than his pool but no one is feeling that because of the punch in them, they are having such a good time at the beach. While Elise is walking around his house yelling she better not find him with some women. At the beach Hutch is being tackled by three women in the water laughing grabbing them up running around throwing them in the water like the others did to their women. Elise is sitting there eating plate of food thinking this is really good but she' still mad that he's not there and wonders what he's doing right now. They stay at the beach for a couple hours and then heads back to his house for more punch and food. Elise made two plates packed them up and starts to leave his house still wondering where did all of them go? On the ride back to his house Hutch Erikaa, Donna and Janet tell him how much fun they were having and can't believe they ran into someone like him and his brothers. Erikaa says "I don't ever want thing to change for us and love to stay together forever like this!" They all agree letting out how they feel about Hutch. Telling him they're so turned on right now and happy kissing him one by one. The vehicle pulls back up to his house and everyone jumps in the heated pool to wash the sand off them, some either get some more to eat or drink. Hutch realizes they were running out of ice and got dressed to go get some more and Erikaa and Janet said "They'll would go with him" and got dressed leaving with him. They left as Elise came driving back to his house and found all those vehicles parked either in the drive way or on the street by his house. She looks at all of them and gets even madder thinking they must have been hiding till she left. He doesn't want her to know he's with some of his brothers and women having another of their BBQ parties. Walking in the house really mad but thinking good thing she forgot her purse because she would have never known about this party. Going around the house looking to catch him in bed or kissing another woman getting madder and madder not finding what she wants. When she first got there 2Soon saw her walk in the house but she didn't see him. He avoided being seen by her but went to get Dougie because she knows both Milaya and Sonia and didn't want her to go back and tell them they were there with women half naked and drinking. They followed behind very careful as she moved through house looking for Hutch. Each room she looked into and found one of his brothers with some woman asking "Is Hutch in there?" Getting "Nope!" for answer she looked down in the basement cutting on the bright lights getting everyone there mad at her as she asked "Where's Hutch?" Hearing a voice "Hey you stupid ass! Turn down the lights and look up stairs for him!" She went to say something but got hit with a pillow form out of nowhere as another voice said "Hurry up!" She looks around to see who threw it but two more find her head knocking her off her feet, she gets up and goes to the switch turning down the lights again. Saying "If I catch who" Six more pillows hit her cutting off what she was about to say and a red dodge ball pops her in the head knocking her back against the wall by the stairs. She gets up again holds her head staggering back upstairs cussing about getting hit with a ball and if she finds out who did it she's going to kick their ass. 2Soon looks at Dougie saying "You couldn't find anything else to throw?" Dougie shrugged his shoulders "It worked didn't." They sneak upstairs to see where she was and saw her going up to the bedrooms. Elise heads right for Hutch's room first and opens the door to see the bed still made but then Donna came out his bathroom drying her hair in one of his shirts with her bikini on underneath. They look at each other and Elise asked "Is Hutch in there with you?!" Donna answers "No! He should be down stairs somewhere." Elise looks at her shaking her head and turns to head back down stairs. Mad she couldn't find Hutch but sees her purse on the table, she writes a note and sticks it on the Frig door and the leaves even madder before she got there. Dougie and 2Soon saw her leave and went upstairs. Donna was drying her hair as 2Soon and Dougie come in the room asking "What did that woman want?" She told them "Thought she was with one of the G.D.M.4.L women looking to talk to Hutch about something so I told her he's downstairs somewhere." They didn't ask anything more and went back downstairs because they had watched her leave the house very mad about something.

Shortly after Janet and Erikaa come back in the house carrying bags of ice and Hutch had three bags in his arms with two cases of beer. Upstairs Donna found the silver gold and black capped little bottle of cologne in the cabinet over the sink, smelling all of them and uses the silver capped one she really liked the smell of since it was on Hutch before. Drinking the punch getting very tipsy as she listens to the music come up from down stair, dancing around in his shirt and when Janet came into the room to let her know they were back. Smelling the cologne and seeing Donna dancing around like that she though wow some bodies really feeling that punch. Donna sprays Janet with the silver capped cologne asking her "Who does that remind you of?" Having her drink from the same cup of punch she was drinking from drink, as she sprays some more on Janet's body. Erikaa reaches the bedroom and smells the cologne saying "I know that smell from Hutch that time!" Donna sprays her body as well and hands her the big cup of punch to drink. Not knowing the effect of the alcohol with the direct inhaling of the cologne has a very intoxicating immediate reaction for them. When Hutch came up to his room after setting the ice up in the coolers and having a couple of cups of punch with the guys making sure everything was alright. Not seeing the ladies downstairs he walks into an ambush of vampire teethed very horny women that lock the door on him saying "You're not leaving!"

2Soon and Dougie heard Hutch came back from Dave who was drinking with him and they went looking for him. Not seeing him down stair they went up in his bedroom and got to the door. All they heard was growling and moaning and him saying "Who needs VAN HELSING!" Dougie was about to knock on the door but 2Soon stops him "Yo fam if you were in the moment, would you want a knocking on the door. Besides you got to be crazy disturbing a man scratching a 20 yr. itch. Remember Star Trek what Spock did after 7yrs not getting any!" With a very serious look on 2Soon's face, he says "Hutch is twice his sizes and black you do the math!" Dougie said "You right! He'll put a hurting on a world of Klingons and those space brothers are twice as strong as Vulkons! They go back down stair to find the ladies they were talking with.

Sunday morning Hutch is waking from the sun shining on his face and the room getting brighter. He lays there for moment then feels the soreness on his neck and feels something on his ear as he gets up and feels his body really sore. Walking pass his dresser and the mirror seeing a pair of plastic vampire teeth on his ear and again these little bite marks all over his body. Turning to look at his bed and sees three bodies sprawled out over it, he smiles shaking his head at the vampire teeth still on someone's behind. Taking the teeth off of not sure which one's butt it was and heading to the bathroom running the water in his tub Jacuzzi, filling it to the right height and temperature (hot). Turning on the water jets he slips in it with his tooth brush using it as he soaks in the water. Then a hand come from behind him grabbing the tooth brush swirling it in a glass of Listerine Janet kisses him and continues to brush her teeth. When she was finish she gets in the water laying on him. The tooth brush is done the same way by Donna as she kisses them good morning after using it too. When she was finished brushing her teeth she taps Janet on the shoulder and has her move as she got in the water to lying on Hutch for a while. Hearing more brushing going on as Erikaa used it and she kisses everyone good morning using then gets in to lying on Hutch as Donna moved over. Water jets sooths muscles and helps for a while as they just sit in the water relaxing. Hutch gets out first and tells them to stay in there as long as they like. Saying "I'm going down to see the damage the house suffered." A quick kiss to all of them he goes and gets dressed and heads down stairs looking at the living room seeing the sofa bed out and some bodies on it covered. Someone slept in a chair then he heads down to the basement to see the sofa bed out down there and the love seat filled with another person. Going back upstairs and looking in the back yard finding the grill still burning but nothing on it and some of the food still out but covered with foil. Floating in the pool were the inflatable toys and some unopened cans of beer, cups everywhere with some plates of food. Hutch starts cleaning up which helps him get loose from his stiffness. He hears Dougie say "I'm here fam I'll start on the other end." They talk about how the party was a good one and this time none of them wound up in another state calling for plane fair to get home. It doesn't take them no time to clean up the back yard and they go inside to start there but find Donna and Janet with Erikaa cleaning the kitchen and wrapping the food to put away. They kiss and hug Dougie good morning as he told them "I like you all for my brother, you all do him good. Never saw him happy like this before!" Hutch came back in the kitchen asking Dougie "What were you saying?" Dougie went "Nothing bruha! I just thank them for helping with the cleanup and they didn't have too because we could have done it" They all shook their heads agreeing with what he said. Hutch was about to say something else when his phone rang. It was his mother saying "This last day she's here she want to go to dinner with her boys and will be coming over there and hope she don't walk into a wild party still going on." Hutch told her the party was over and they're cleaning up so when she's ready she can come over. They all looked at him saying they have things they have to do as well. The girls said they have to get ready for tomorrows classes and Dougie said he'll wake the rest up and see if they need to be somewhere. Those still there either showered or took a plate home with them so they can help him get rid of most of that food that would take him weeks to eat by himself. The last one to leave was the girls and as he was out by the van with them talking about how nice it was spending time with them again. How it was so much fun being with them, then his phone rings again. This time it was Elise screaming at him "Where the hell have you been?!" The girls could hear her. He puts her on hold, feeling awkward about to say to them. Donna cuts him off and says "You should take your phone call and let them leave so you can talk." All of them feel like they didn't want to leave each other but he stand there watching them back out of his drive way and drive off. Knowing he wants to say to them stay with him. He looks at the phone taking a deep sigh and clicks over from hold hearing her yell "This isn't funny by keeping her on hold or was he trying to get rid of those women that was at his house from another one of the BBQ's parties he didn't invite her too!" Asking him "Don't you care about me, I got feeling too!" Sounding so pitiful wanting to know if he really wants to be with her making it seem he's playing with her feelings and she can't take that. He tries to calm her down and talk more with her but lets her know he's got to meet with his mother that night and they should get together after the dinner with his mother, because she's going back home down south. Happy to hear his mother is leaving she agreed because she knows it would give her a better chance to get to him if his mother wasn't around to influence him any further. Making him promise to her to get with her after his mother gone back, she wants him to give his word knowing he never breaks his word.

Later that evening: Hutch picked up his mother at his brother's house taken both of them to dinner at this place in Brooklyn where they serve the best red velvet cake for dessert in down town Brooklyn NY. At dinner Mama Betty was on Cordell and why he can't be more like his brother Hutch who works hard and keeps a steady job at one place not going from pillar to post not having all those babies. She turns on Hutch and attacks him too about not having a girlfriend for so long and then picking that psycho skinny gold digging heffer who look like she'll make children just to be her servants. That she would plot his murder right after they've been married one minute. Telling Hutch she might not have totally agreed with him having the three women like that but if that's the new age thing and he's happy she won't mind. She liked each one of them, not feeling they were about him for whatever they could get. Adding she thought he was turning funny and didn't want to tell her about it, thinking it would have broken her hopes of grand kids from him. She was already to make her call this visit to all her friends for every clean bubble butt, disease free with no kid that would put it on him in shifts. If they had to rape his ass to convert him back to liking women again, then she wouldn't mine it at all. She would give the one who turned him back a big cash bonus. Cordell looks at his mother "I confess I thought about going over to the other side for a period of time!" She looks at him "What time you going! It might do you good to be on the receiving part now shut up!" She went back and forth on both of them till the food came looking at how good the plates were then starts on Elise again. Telling him "Bet her skinny ass don't cook" just by looking at her and she could tell that heffer's an OOT (order out type). Hutch was more thankful to see the waitress for bring the food so they could eat. Hoping that would keep her from getting on them any further. Hutch had to use the bathroom and excuse himself going to find it walking to a waitress asking "Where's the rest room?" Pointed in the right direction he heads across the floor to it. In the same restaurant Marveece and Davona were sitting having dinner and looking at all he men in the place commenting on which one they would like to be a mate. Davona saw Hutch but points him out too late to Marveece as he disappeared into the rest room. Marveece didn't get a good look at who she was talking about before he went in the men's room but coming back out and again getting pointed out by Davona. He walks towards his table but this sound reaches his ears as he heard "Oooh Marveece!" That sound made him look around hoping he didn't hear that familiar sounded. He keeps walking back to the table but has a feeling of being watched after hearing what he thought he heard. Not sure where it came from or if what he thought was in there and couldn't happen at a worse time for him having his mother and brother with him. He stands at the table and takes one good quick look around before sitting back down. His mother asked him "What's wrong you looking around for someone to show up. Hope it's not that gold digging tramp!" Hutch told his mother "It's nothing" and they went back to eating and talking thinking about which dessert to have he then heard another "Oooh Marveece" a little bit louder that time. It was Marveece sitting with Davona telling her she knows that man from the supermarket where she met her Steel. He drove a blue expedition plus he's a friend of Steels but they didn't see Steel anywhere at his table but another man and an older woman. Davona made the comment "He's cute big and strong looking in that suit just my type" and likes what she sees and calls the waiter over. Hutch is trying to have a good time without letting on he's worried about Marveece showing up at their table, until this waiter came over with a bottle of wine. He told them it was from the lady and friend at the table as he points to them waving at Hutch and smiling. Mama Betty said to the waiter "Oh that's so nice where are they again?!" He points to Marveece and Davona waving and blowing kisses to Hutch. She quickly looks and said to the waiter "Who those two female?" Cordell asked "Which one is female again it's hard to tell!" His mother said "That's my point too and isn't that the same creature who came to the door and grabbed you.

Now it sits with another hell spawn from the depth of the black hole in the center of the earth." Then grabbing up her purse looking through it saying "I got my pepper spray, stun gun extra clips and why I keep forgetting my derringer when crime is not the only things I have to worry about now." Looking at Hutch saying "Baby I don't speak Matilda, but I'll give it a try to tell it you are not interested in mixing the human species with her kind. If that don't work then we can call animal control see if one of their Exhibit got took to dinner by an ugly trainer." Asking the waiters "Don't they have a policy in this place about letting in such creatures and their non-evolution cousins while people are eating or they just take money from any kind of species!" Hutch asked the waiter to ignore his mother and bring him and his brother another drink "Please." Davona puckered her lips kissing at him, giving him a big smile showing off her gold teeth surrounded by big gold out lined in black lips. Batting her eyes acting so coy as Marveece waves come to them. Hutch got an idea calling the waitress over to him and whispers something to her then told his brother and mother "They're going to leave" putting the keys to his vehicle on the table under a napkin for his brother to take and said "When I get up and they're going to watch me, you take ma and get my ride be in front ready when I come out!" taken the bottle of wine they sent over showing them he's pouring a glass then getting up walking over to the dessert cart looking at some of the dishes on it. Watching the waitress he spoke to brings him the check not to the table, nodding to Cordell to do what he told him. Watching them leave as the waitress came over to him thanking him for such a big tip. Marveece looked at the waitress giving him a hug nudging Davona saying "Tramp's trying to get your man" but then saw him pointing out some of the dishes on the cart and then to their table and go back to his own and finish eating his plate. The waitress came over with the car of dessert and told them "The gentlemen at the table has paid for any dessert you want" They looked at the cart and picked a couple and Marveece told the waitress "You can have which one we didn't want because we have to watch our girlish figures"

The waitress looked around and thought to herself "What girls are they watching?!" Hutch still at his table calls a waiter over and told him to let those two at the table know he'll be right over there soon as he washes his hands. Watching the waiter walk over to them and as they looked at the waiter, Hutch gets up heads toward the men's room which happens to be right by the front entrance. He looks back at the two sitting at their table as he stands by the men's room door then bolts to the entrance out to his vehicle waiting right by the front like he wanted. Marveece looked at Davona "Girl your man is getting a way let go!" They get up and run out of the place to try to catch Hutch or see where he went to. When they get to the front of the place they see him in the blue expedition on the passenger side hanging out of the window waving bye to them as the vehicle drives away. They run to get Davona's vehicle and fight over who's going to do the driving by the driver's door. Davona voice turned scary grabbing Marveece up walking him to the passenger side "Look I haven't had anything between these thighs that didn't run on batteries, so I'm not going to let a flesh and blood man get away because you want to drive, MOVE BI-OTCH!" Marveece eyes got wide and says meekly "OK!" Hutch still looking back thinking his brother is driving said "Do everything you could to lose them bruh, I don't want them to catch up to us." His mother answers him "Damn how do you drive this big ass thing." Hutch looks at the rear tinted window seeing Cordell in the back seat with his seat belt on waving to him. Pulling himself inside Hutch looks to sees his mother who could barely see over the steering wheel driving stretching her neck up holding her head up high as she could. The vehicle turns down one street as Hutch pleads with his mother to pull over but she says to him "Those things are not going to get their claws or whatever they use to feed themselves with on my son."

Making another turn which has Hutch screaming "OH GOD!" as they face cars coming at them from driving the wrong way on two lane street as his mother tries to remember which part of Brooklyn they are in running a red light with cars about to hit them. He pleads with her to pull over and let him drive but then screams again as she says "Think I've been in this part before." Racing down this alley with a truck on one side leaving a small space that looks like a mini coop wouldn't fit through the other side. She tells him "If you don't be quite with all that screaming I'll have an accident. I need to concentrate!" Hutch yells at her before they reach the truck "IT'S NOT GOING TO FIT STOP! STOP! STOP! IT'S NOT GONNA FIT!" Then closes his eyes and tightens up praying the crash won't kill them all but when there isn't one. He looks at his mother and then back at the small hole wondering how they went through it without touching anything with no scratches on either side with the mirrors intact on both sides of his vehicle. Never seeing the driver of the truck in it as he saw the vehicle coming down the alley behind him, he moved the truck before they can get to the open space and once through he moved back. Hutch looks back at his brother angry saying "How did she get behind the wheel, when I gave you the keys huh?!" He answers "You know your mother, she don't take no for answer from anybody" He manages to get his mother to pull over by telling her "If you crash my vehicle not only would I marry that thing, but have kids and drop them off at your house for the whole summer while we have more and name every girl after you!" The vehicle screeches to a halt and she looks at him with a tear in her eyes saying "That's the meanest thing you could ever say to me beside Cordell is having another steak stealer by the beast of a women who leaves foot chips on her couch!" He feels bad to have said that, but explains that's the only way to get her to stop the vehicle as he got out and switched seats with her just in time to see Marveece hanging out the passenger said of his vehicle yelling to Davona "There they are girl down there!" His mother yells "DAMN! She must have bloodhound in her family, would explain that big ass nose of hers. I'm not surprised she could sniff you out just by holding it up in the air, now move it or marry it!" Hutch didn't have to be told twice as he peels away using all eight cylinders of the v-8 engine and knows the arrear where they are very well. He tries to lose them but Davona uses her V-6 engine to its max keeping up with him. A couple time they get close to him within a block or two, being a garbage man and knowing the one way streets and hopes she don't have it in her to follow him. She does on some of the street till the gets to Prospect Park in Brooklyn and goes in there and she follows him but couldn't keep up on some of the grassy arrears and falls behind. They chase him all the way to Fort Green projects but he loses them through the down town one way dead end streets which he knows very well. Since the city changed some of the streets direction due to construction being done in that arrear. Making it back to Cordell's house on Staten Island so his mother could say good bye to his kids, because she was leaving the next day and she's staying with Hutch for the last night. The kids say their goodbye's to their grandmother and go back to bed. Hutch takes his mother back to his house and gets his things ready for work the next day. She reminds him of what he said to her about letting that things with the gold tooth marry him will haunt her in nightmares. Saying "If they should have a litter of ankle biters that she's got to drop fresh killed raw meat on the floor just to keep them from nibbling at her. So he better not get caught and has to marry it or she'll shoot off both her feet that way she can't visit and stab herself in the ears so when he decides to call she couldn't hear it. Making sure to pluck out her eyes so she can't see and be reminded of what he married hopefully before the hit man she hired does his job and she doesn't have to go through all that pain of ever having to see or know about it." He tells his mother she don't have to mutilate herself or call arranging a hit on herself because she's not going to let that happen but she still should've pulled over and let him drive sooner. She knows saying like your brother "I've had bad night mares about your brothers incarceration sentenced to a life of what the F*%% was I thinking. As the priest said "Be there anyone who object to this union and everyone turns looking at me with my friends after they saw the eight red dots on the back of her head. Damn! We should have shot it!" Hutch answers "Good thing Uncle Ernie and uncle Roy was there or I'd be visiting you all once a week behind bars" Thinking about it she replies "Yeah and he would be free, but then again I wouldn't have those beautiful gran-daughters" He smiles and agrees with her and talks with her a little bit longer. She saying how proud of him and his other brothers even Cordell for not having gotten into trouble, running from police winding up with records or anything like that. She smiles at him and knowing she did a good job with four boys with no man in her life, but always kept them reminded of the respect for a woman and how she can be the most important person in his life besides their children. How it took a woman to teach her own little men to grow into a real man of their own, being real men in this world not following anyone's group or ways knowing how a treat a woman and how they should act with her. Looking at how big and strong he's grown knowing some day when he does get with a woman, she'll know what kind of real no nonsense man he is. Not some coward that hides behind an excuse to put his hands on her, or man enough to face another man hand to hand without a gun in his. Able to use his head to defuse that situation and be able to go home with his head up or wonder why he needs to run out and get drunk not facing any problem they would have instead of meeting it with her together. (Hmm get the point!) She hugs her son smiling with a tear in her eye and before she went to bed saying "Here!" and gave him her stun gun saying "It'll go through the thick hide of that gold tooth behemoth just make sure it's on high" He smiled at his mother laughing a little as she also shows "Its clip ejects quick so you can get another round of needled off fast too!" Not arguing with her but taking it and watching her go upstairs thinking to himself "My mother, heaven help the man that ever crosses her!" The house is quite and Hutch is sitting in his chair thinking about what his mother said at dinner tonight and how she would like to see him with someone in his life. Not wanting to see him wind up with no woman or have the wrong one because he's not had the chance to give one a try and make it work. Thinking to himself he's going to give it a try with Elise since she was the first female he talked with and wants to be in relationship with him and maybe she'll come around to except him the way he is or he could really try and win her over with his just being himself. In his bedroom taking out the change from his pockets putting it in a bowl and his wallet he lays it on the dresser. He thought about giving his mother his Credit card since he made enough to buy that house. Knowing she wouldn't just take it only use it when she came to see the kids. Thinking she could really use it down there on herself or when she goes out with her girlfriends but again he knows she would say "Don't worry about her" and would give it back. Pulling out a Credit card from his wallet and going in the room while she was sleep and putting it in the wallet in her purse being really quite or she would hurt him from just sneaking up on her like that. Looking back from the doorway at his mother sleeping peacefully, smiling at her before closing the door then going to get some sleep so he could get ready for work the next day.

Earlier that night while Hutch was taking his mother and brother to dinner Markola was at his office talking about that mook and his Credit card. What he could do with something like that and things he could buy with a card like that and someone mook shouldn't have a card like that period. Trying to think of a way to get that card from him, Markola sits and brain storms with his goons trying to find a way Hutch would just give him the card without calling the police on him or his Uncle not finding out about it. Wanting to use it first till he's got everything he wants before he would have to hand it over. They thought about shooting him but that would be murder, one of his goons says "What about robbery they would go to his house and get it when he's not there." Markola says "It sounds good except for the part of him having the card on him at the times. They rob his house which would be considered a burglar for what Stu-nod!" They were thinking really hard on how to get the card from him without causing an incident which involves the police. Everything they came up with had an ending of the police being called. While they were still thinking about what to do there a big scuffle down stairs in the strip club, one of the men there ran out of cash and wanted to use his Credit card but not charge anything on it. The Stripper called the bouncer to get the man out of her face, when that news reached upstairs to Markola he got this very good idea about how he could get the card from that mook and he would need the girls to do it. Another goon asked "How is getting him laid by one of the girl going to get that from him. From the way those guys yammer are, the girl would be giving him her Credit card." Markola and the rest of his men looked at that one goon for moment and the whole room was silent then that same goon says "What?!" Looking at everyone in the room and saying "Oh come on man, you mean to tell me yous never thought about what if your body stuffer was thicker and longer?" Markola yells at him "Stu-nod what the freak!

Is this a commercial for dem viagro pills or sumpthin! How did we get from talking about a Credit card to a brother's yammer?" The men look at the one goon again he goes "What?!" Markola told them all to get out of his face for a while and let him think. They were leaving the office talking to the one that started everything. Markola calls the men who are watching the building asking "Where are the girls" The men tell Markola they saw the girls leave out a while ago and haven't come back yet, he wants them to call him soon as they see the girls come back to the building.

Late that evening Donna, Erikaa and Janet are walking to the building with the popcorn from the movies they have seen after parking one block away from the building, the men that was supposed to call Markola when they saw the girls come back to the building were asleep in their car.

Monday morning Hutch is up getting breakfast from his mother before she left to go back down south, he shows her what to do turning on the alarm system before she locks up and leaves asking her "Don't let Cordell go through my house because sticky fingers would walk away with anything he could hide from your site." She laughs at what he called his brother and assures him he'll be in her sight at all times. Kissing his mother bye and tells her she need to come to see them more since he works hard and could send her all the money she'll need to come up with. His mother said what she always says to him "No! Baby I'm fine you just worry about yourself." With a big hug and kiss to the cheek he leaves his mother and heads to work so he could be early like usual before any of the other drivers get there.

7am that morning Donna was getting a call from the good will people to pick up the donation of her stuff, she told them "Yes" come get it because other delivery men will be there at 10:30am. They want to know will she be ready for them, she told the delivery man she'll be ready so they can come. Everything Donna paid for at the mall over the weekend with Hutch's Credit card is being delivered like clockwork on schedule for Monday. The men Markola have watching the building see all these delivery trucks pull up after a good will truck came and took away a lot of stuff out of the building.

They report back to Markola what they see but not seeing the girls anywhere yet, he tells them to keep an eye out for them because if there are trucks picking up things and delivering new stuff it's got to be them and they're in there. Mad even more about the news he just got from the men watching the building and he calls his cousin Mario to let him know he might need him. Markola just wants him to keep things open for him in case he calls and don't want to hear Mario's busy. Mario tells him "I'll be waiting. I don't have anything planned yet!"

Hutch is sitting in his truck reading the paper and listening to the radio Morning show on FM, when he see the van pull up and the workers gets out but they don't look happy and he wonders what's wrong till he sees Moni gets out the front passenger seat of the van. He looks at Hutch walking right up to it and just stand there looking at him (with a you know I could kick your ass look on his face) so serious it makes Hutch put down his paper and get out his truck. Asking Moni "Why you looking at me like you want to hurt or kill me?" Moni yells at the men "You know what to do don't stand there waiting for me, get to the floor and start I'll be there soon as I straighten out this fookar here!"

Hutch looked at him never hearing him sound so harsh to the men before, curious as to how he's going to get with him as he goes to change his into his work clothes. Moni says "Where are you going I'm not done with you yet!" Hutch walks to the trucks other side changing his clothes answering Moni "Hey fool first of all I'm not your son or your child. If you don't change that type of tone with me, I'll be happy to put your broke up ass back in the hospital if you still feel your Dr Banner's alter ego." Moni just looks at Hutch then changes his mood asking him "Why every time you are around and leave people tend to want to beat me up?!" Hutch looked at him and says "Good taste? Or maybe they can tell what type of butt wipe you are!" Moni says seriously "Why is that?" Hutch asked "What makes you say that, I'm curious now?" Moni explains to him after he left the hospital, the women and some of the men there started to beat him up slapping him and even turning him over out of his bed, calling him shit colored man. It had to take some of the orderlies to stop these nurse and female doctors from slapping him. Telling Hutch it started with this candy stripper who came to his bedside and at first was so sweet to him but in minutes of her talking to him she said "I touched her and slapped me so hard" calling him all kinds of names that aren't in the dictionary. Hutch eyes went up asking "What did she say exactly?" He repeats her quoting "Something like his mother pushed out the good stuff of a man after he came out and other things like his looks were given to the sack left in her and something to do with one ball short stick" Hutch asked him "What did you do to make them so mad at you lying in bed." Moni said "I didn't do anything, all this happened shortly after you left me so I figure you paid them or talked to them to do those things to me!" Hutch answer "If I wanted you beat up I'd do it myself not get others to do it where's the fun in that and why waste good money on you?" Then adds "You were still getting your ass kicked in the hospital by the staff too?!" Moni said "They didn't use a staff on me but if they could have they would have use one to kill me." Hutch starts to explain what staff means but stops, just tells Moni he didn't send anyone to beat him up in the hospital. It would take a low life like him to kick a man when he's down and he not like him no matter what he thinks, that's a line Hutch don't cross. Moni understood he made another mistake about Hutch. They went to work not having much to say about that subject even though Moni still lets him know, they are still going to battle about him getting dusted in white and water poured on him. Hutch shook his head at Moni going over a list to use on him. The day went fast and the week came and went even faster, on that Friday Hutch gets a call from his mother asking him to go over to Cordell's house and get her other purse she left there and forgot to pack. Hutch wanted to know why she has two purses, she has trouble keeping up with all the stuff in her little one. His mother said "Boy go over after work get her purse before it uses my purse as a foot chip collector." After work Hutch pulls up to Cordell's house and see the brand new Tahoe with the sticker still in the window shaking his head alright his brother finally bought a new. Stopping his thought and thinking his brother never has any money so where did he get the cream to buy something like this from? Going to the door ringing the bell looking back at the Tahoe parked in the drive way then hearing a voice ask "Who is it?" when he answers "Uncle Hutch baby open the door" There was this scrambling sound and scream of a little girl "Uncle Hutch here to kill my daddy!" Then more scrambling around as he stood there wondering what's going on in there. Cheryl opens the door hugging her uncle and saying "My daddy's in the living room" Hutch walks in the living room and sees this big flat screen TV Cordell is watching as he drinks a beer and Bernise looks at Hutch saying "HI" eases her ass off the couch and goes upstairs. Cordell asked Hutch "What brings you over, want a beer?" Before he could answer he looks again at Cordell sitting on a new recliner chair and at the rest of the new furniture they have wondering how did he get all this. At first Cordell was playing dumb answering Hutch's question till he starts getting mad at Cordell and told him it was their mother she bought it and the vehicle too adding "You how she is and I can't say no to her even if she used your money to get me all this." Hutch took a deep breath and thought to himself "It had to be when he gave her the spare Credit card, how could she use all that money on you and beast without tell me." Then asked Cordell "What else did their mother buy, hoping it was not for him and Bernise Beowulf's big behemoth blind beast bounced from the Bronx Bombers Booted Back to Brooklyn!" He told Hutch she bought the kids' stuff from TV's for all the rooms and toys to I-pods, new phones, clothes for all of them plus shoes and coats, new frig and stove, washing Machine and dryer and yeah the Tahoe. Hutch looked at him an stood up and Corie looking down from the upstairs and starts screaming again "Uncle going to kill my daddy now mommy stop him." She comes down the stairs and runs over to Hutch jumping in his arms and hitting him "Stop don't kill her daddy." Hutch looks at her and holds her up and kisses her laughing at what she says hitting him in the chest asking "Where did you get the idea that I was going to anything to your daddy?" Corie says "Mommy! said to daddy if you found out grandma got this for us with your money, you would want to kill my daddy but not before she gets the life insurance papers ready to see how much we get for you killing my daddy, so please uncle Hutch don't kill my daddy I love him." They both look at each other then Coire and then together shout "BERNISE get down here!" She comes down stairs and Coire says "Grandma even bought her that Die-sheekna she warring uncle Hutch and other stuff too, you going to kill my mommy too?" Hutch looks at Cordell "Nope I'd be doing your daddy's dirty work and it's best to let him suffer for as long as he never pays me back for anything he ever borrowed." Bernise looks at her daughter really mad then said "Did you tell of the stuff you got too!" Hutch growls "Never mind the child." Holding Corie then giving her another kiss on the cheek saying to her "I'm not going to kill your daddy but your mommy going to get me a beer right!?" She shook her head "Yes" and goes in the kitchen. That when Cordell lean over to Hutch and says "If you want to kill her I'll help get rid of the lump!" Then yells "I want a beer too Lump!" The door to the kitchen opens and flying at his head is a can of beer but Hutch catches it before it could hit its mark. He looks at Hutch holding the can did she send one of the kids out with one to give you bruha then shouts "Where's mine since you gave him one I'd like a cold beer too!"

Hutch saw the door open again and this time four more can come flying out from the kitchen with some mumbling cuss words about helping get rid of the lump you M-Fer and other choice selected words are hardly heard from the kitchen. Cordell looks at the cans on the table and says "Wow she never moves that fast for me man. Guess it takes you to threaten it for her to really start moving fast huh!" Hutch say "Or get blamed for your murder" Looking at the kitchen door close and hears banging going on in there. Telling his brother he'll deal with their mother and now wants to know has he seen her purse she had him come for. Before leaving asking his brother "What if something really happened to you how are the kids going to be?" Cordell laughs "Don't worry about that!" as he walks Hutch out to his vehicle and tells him "What you didn't think I know about the beers to my head, I knew you were going to catch them and she did too. She knows better if she was to hit me I would leave her ass right there and who would pay the bills? Her not even, oh and you know your mother would take back that stuff and give it to me in my new place for the kids. That paper on me she got is a phony because my real policy says the kids get everything and she to pay them rent anytime they want it from her" Hutch laughs at what he did and wants to know are the kids going to be a caught in the middle of them? Cordell says "Nope! Their too smart for that anyways, the older ones are teaching the younger one anyways so I don't have to worry nor you either bruha!" Laughing about it again Hutch hands his brother some cash and says "It's the weekend take them out for pizza and movie and it needs some air too." Turning to get in his vehicle the cell rings, tapping his blue tooth to answer and hears a familiar voice. Before Hutch went to his brother's house the girls were arranging their apartment with the new stuff and cooking something to eat, half way done with organizing their closet from the clothes they had to put in there plus the dresser draws too. Sitting down on the couch watching their new big flat screen about to have a nice garden salad with baked fish they hear a knock on the door. Not expecting anyone they look at each other and wonder who could be at the door this time of day. Erikaa closest to the door goes over asking "Who is it?" The raspy voice says "Me! Your boss Markola, it smells good what are you cooking and aren't you going to invite me in for a taste?" They debate on should they let him in or not but he bang on the door and reminds them he's the land lord and could kick in the door all he'll have to do is replace it. Reminding them there won't be any trouble from the law, so they open the door and let him in but his two goons come in before he did. He looks around the place and says "I like what you did with it, all they need now is some paint and this place would be something" Donna asked him "What do you want and why you're here? They don't work this weekend, they have studies!" He walks in to the kitchen and looks at the salad and then opens the over to see the fish "Wow you girls can cook too, body and brains. See that's why I'm glad you know how to do things for yourself, not like the other girls I have to remind what to eat and not to take to ruin their bodies so they can make money at the club!" Janet says "Glad you approve of our diet and Exercise, now what are you doing here?" He walks to the couch and sits down patting it for Donna to come sit next to him, but she sits on the chair saying "I'll sit here thank you" getting comfortable on their couch he looks at Donna and tells her if she would have minded her business they would have everything they wanted and more. He would have given them anything to live like queens and even paid for their school and vehicles, all she had to do was let him have that card and that mook- err man would have never known the difference and they all could be happy. She answers "What about him and how could I live with myself knowing I cost a good man like that his Credit card and it ended up in your hands!" Markola gets angry "See you don't get it. Men like him don't deserve a Credit card like that, what would he do with it.

Buy some dancers a few things and help the homeless or do for all mankind!" Telling her it should be in the hand of a business man that knows how to take care of things and what people need and how to take care of them. Not some mook that had a good time with a dancer and her friends trying to win them over by getting small things like furniture and TV's. Saying this to make her feel better all he wants him to do is come down to the club and see the new girls that are going to be dancing there and if he likes them they he could be a regular at the club and get V.I.P treatment for being there that's all he wants. Donna told him they haven't heard from him since he came to the club and not sure when they would hear from him again. Janet and Erikaa shook their head agreeing to what Donna told Markola. He didn't believe them going they must have a number on him because he bought all this stuff for them, and no man buys something for a woman or women not expecting to come collect some type of payment for what he got them. If they have a number on this mook they better think about using it or things could get very different on how their living arrangements are going to be. Rent could go up dramatically and they would have so many days to move but not before there was so many home robberies having lost all this beautiful stuff to some crook that just wants to get their hand on it. "Bing!" The timer on the oven goes off and he looks at them going "A nice home cooked meal in place that is safe from crooks and they don't have to worry about their sleep being interrupted by an a-hole burglar and his buddies ransacking the place for drug money or getting very personal with anyone of them" as he looks at his goons standing there smiling at them shaking their heads sneering at all of them. Donna looks at Janet and them Erikaa as they nodded their heads with disappointed looks on their faces and

Donna asked him "What do you want me to say to get him down to the strip club?" With a big smile on his face Markola told her use whatever means you women have to get him to come down to the club tonight and see the new girls he's got to show him. Telling her sound convincing make sure he invites a couple of his guys with him that way it sounds more believable. Reassuring her once she makes the call he and his goons are going to leave but then Markola says "I want all of them there at the club not to dance just to be sure he shows up and had no warning of what's about too err get showed by the new girls he's got there to the club." Donna calls Hutch as Markola sits right next to her and listens to make sure she didn't say anything to tip him off. Hutch is about to get in his vehicle at his brother's house when Donna calls. She asked him what was he doing tonight because they haven't heard from him in a while, he explains been busy with the job working hard but apologizes for not getting in touch with them for a while then asking "How's Janet and Erikaa and what are they up to this evening?" Looking at Markola who's staring right at her she answers "Nothing but has an idea, how about him and a couple of his guys come down to the strip club because they have some new girls he would be interested in and could check out, Plus these girls are way better than me Janet and Erikaa put together. If you want to be treated like a king you need to come down there and I won't even take no for answer." Hutch could sense there was something wrong because why would she want him to see other girls, when they talked about him being happy with the three of them. He wants to be with them and no other woman or women could come into the picture and then he thought of why would she want to meet at the strip club wasn't that the place where her boss got chumped by him. It occurred to him what if the boss was right there with her and making her invite him down for a rematch or to get revenge for being embarrassed by him either way he better be on his Pea's and Queue's. Hutch tells her "Sure I'll come and bring a couple of my guys and it'll be nice to see you again too!" They hang up and Markola smiles at her "See that's all you have to do now get dressed because you all are coming with me as my guess and don't worry about dinner, so long as he show up you can leave to come back here and enjoy your fish." Telling her better wrap it up so it doesn't dry out or they could eat it there now. They all roll their eyes at him thinking the same thing "Not going to feed his sleazy ass with their food!" First they wrap the food and then get dressed to go with Markola down to the strip club. Hutch off the phone thinks about what Donna said, and how she sounded like it was phony but didn't want someone close to her know he caught on how she sounded. Calling Mack, Steel, Derrick, 2Soon, Jazz, Dave, Dougie and LiL Rob with Ron and La-Machine to meet him at his house because he wants to go back to that strip club on the invite of the pieces that were at his lab that weekend of the BBQ. Making a stop to the bank before going home and getting some cash so they all can have something to throw, Hutch pulls out his wallet and in the light gets his Credit card but see the top of the other ones the same color as the one in his hand. Trying to remember where they came from about to pull them out when someone come in the bank behind him, putting them back and continues doing what he came in there to do checking his account and seeing there's nothing been drawn out of his account. Puzzled thinking it took a lot to pay for the things at Cordell's house thinking his mother paid for it using her own money and didn't use his credit card. Thinking to himself good thing he gave her his other Credit card because now she could have money till he puts back all what she spent. Taking cash out his account so they can have he leave the bank to hurry home to meet his brothers and give them cash to spend at the club and take a shower so he don't have to smell like that day work anymore. The doorbell rings and Mack comes in the house because he knows the door would be open, Hutch would be expecting them to walk in. A short time later Jazz, Steel, La-Machine, Derrick, 2Soon, and Dougie walk in, Ron and Dave with LiL Rob arrive at the same time and come in to see the drinks on the bar and these white envelopes next to them. LIL Rob walks in saying "What's this it isn't Xmas or anyone B'day so what's with the envelopes bruha?" Hutch explains to them they need to go to the strip club and see friends there but to keep sharp because he might need them to put it down, Mack asked "Do we need heat" Steel says "Glock to rock drop 'em?" Dougie says "Come yall you know better than that your hand game not up got no one to blame but you" Derrick asked "Who's got the smell on and pass some here" they all sniff and then look at Hutch as he says "It's up I the bathroom but don't use it all because it's my favorite and there aint much" He watches as they all go up and get some then come back down ready for another drink before they head to the strip club with Hutch.

At the strip club watched by goons Erikaa and Janet are looking at each other sitting on the couch in Markola's office talking low to each other wondering what Hutch is going to do when he gets there and finds out it's some kind of trap for him to get his money and will he be mad at them for setting him up for it. Down in the club Donna and Markola are waiting at the bar for Hutch to come in, but then she see Roz one of the bad girls there which Markola gets to do some of the dirty work there for him come over to Markola as he talks to her and she just nods her head to everything he says to her. Roz is a very good looking woman and one of the best bodies in the place. Markola always wants to get with her but she knows better and also knows how to fight with the best of them, even seen her knock out a man like a professional boxer and he never laid a hand on her. All the women there either make friends with her or stay out of her way. She also has three other women with her, one she took under her wing but the good thing about Roz is she never lets Markola or any of his goons abuse or rape or grope disrespectfully even calling the name "BITCH" to any of the girls there she just won't have it.

Donna and Roz are cool to each other but one time Donna had to stand up to Roz about a shift she wanted and Donna didn't back down from her. That made Roz respect Donna in some way but there was always something everyone couldn't put their finger on about Roz and Donna as if they were big rivals. They even helped each other out with an opinion each one had and had words to each other that weren't nice but never engaged in anything that led to a confrontation because of the mutual respect. Roz's four girls did whatever she told them too and they did it with no hesitation or regrets. There was talk about Roz making them screw men but Donna never seen it nor talked about it, always shut it down as the other women gossip about it. Donna wasn't trying to starts gossip, guess that's why Roz also liked Donna and Janet and Erikaa they never followed the group in their petty catty jealous stuff other wants to get in to at the strip club. Hutch walk through the door spotted by Markola and Donna, he never sees them sitting in the shadow part of the bar. With him is the Grand Drunken Master warring their black and gold bomber Jackets. A loud mouth man looks at all of them and says "Look the singing group is here, so what church you all from" Jazz answers "From the greater get your ass out my face before I beat your ass down. Having you calling JESUS for help from messing with the wrong mother flower up in this piece Bi-OTCH! And my name is pastor "BUST YOUR ASS!" That's deacon "BEAT YOUR ASS DOWN!" Pointing to Mack and then showing him the rest going "They are the KEEP STOMPING YOUR ASS IN THE GROUND CHOUR IF YOU DON"T SHUT THE HELL UP! Along with THE WE BEAT YOUR DUMB ASS FIRST BAND!" The man looks at how big they are especially, Jazz with Hutch next to him with mean looks on their faces making the man think twice about saying anything else as he backs away quietly and going back to his seat way in the back. Donna waves to Hutch but he still doesn't see her until she gets up and goes over to him with Markola right behind her. He looks at Hutch smiling "Glad you made it, see you brought your crew too." Hutch noticed how nervous Donna looked and went to hug her quickly saying to her "I got it!" Backing away she smiled showing relief but puzzled at why he said it like that to her. Thinking he doesn't know what he's up against. Markola says "Hey mook err man that was a good thing you did last time buying drinks for the whole place, I never got a chance to thank you right and now here you are!" Hutch shook his head "Yeah? Here I am. Funny how I get invited back down here by one of the women I bought a drink for and to see you here to wow!" Markola told Donna to let the men talk for a minute and takes Hutch to table where he could tell him about these new girls he's got. Wanting him to see them in the private V.I.P. room in the back and walks Hutch back there giving nod at Roz as she were watching from the other side of the club with her girls. Donna saw the nod to Roz and she went over to her before she could go in the back asking "Could I talk to you for a hot second." Explaining to Roz she really likes that man Markola has in the back and she got this feeling Markola wants her to do something bad to him. Roz looks at Donna for a moment with a puzzle look on her face then answers "Look I know you and I never had any beef between us. I do like how you handle things here when shit gets stupid, keeping dumb shit down but I don't get what you are asking me to do?" Donna replied "I never asked you for anything and respect yours. All I want you to do is not do anything to that man because I want to be with him and Markola got mad because he chumped him buying drinks for the place to be with me." Donna really made it her case to Roz, agreeing they never clashed but agreed they both don't like Markola and his methods. When he has Roz do some of the things she doesn't want to and hardly gets a proper share of what she's done. Roz agreed with Donna and told her Hutch is good looking for a big man and looks like he's worth her doing a favor for, but it will cost Donna and she needs to get something good out of taking a risk going up against Markola for her.

Donna agreed to owe Roz a favor which shocked her, making her think this guy is really something for her to agree to that. Now she wants to see up close what's so special about this man and lets Donna know she won't do what Markola wants. Donna also explains this man is different from all the other sleaze bags that come in there wanting to hop on the first girl they see. Asking her "If you get alone with him then you'll see for yourself there's something about him that gets to a woman." Reminding Donna again she owes her for this and nods to her girls to follow her in the back where Markola is waiting for her to come so she could start dancing for him and Hutch. They sit as Roz has one of her girls start to dancing on the stage and she sat next to Markola as he talked to Hutch finding out more about him. Telling Hutch he's buying this time and asked him what is he drinking? Sending Roz to get the drinks, to keep Hutch distracted he wanted to know about his life and how he got started with trucks and did he go to school or college? Hutch gave him a short run down about his life, letting Markola know he graduated high school and got into trucking right away. Since he were into them in high school and after got into them fully but still took college course during the day and worked with trucks at night getting his masters in sociology, and psychiatry and physic plus chemistry but stopped doing engineering for a while. Markola looked at Hutch and went "Damn yous a freaking smart mook err man, but I don't get it why be a demolition garbage guy?" Hutch looking at Roz's girl says "It's because they not only let me blow up stuff but I get to drive a kool truck!" Markola looked at Hutch thinking he was really stupid for working on a garbage truck, that's why he was going to get that Credit card from him and he'll never see this coming. Roz is out at the bar making the drinks putting the Mickey in the one Hutch ordered but as she turns to leave from behind the bar she see Donna looking at her. She pauses for a moment looking back at her dropping her head down to look at the drinks in her hands and then back at Donna. It's clear She's got to go back with the drinks, she looks at Donna mouthing sorry and turns to walk back to the V.I.P. room where Markola smiles at her talking through his teeth "What took so long" when she comes in. Making a toast so he could get him to drink that spiked one down then ordering another two still saying "It's on me." Telling Roz to make it quick puzzled that the first two should have had him wobbling by now, but see him not even affected by them. Roz went to get the next round, he told Hutch he need to speak to Roz and make sure she has the other girls ready to come and show what they got too. Markola goes over to talk with Roz and Hutch's phone vibrated. He answers it while Markola is talking to Roz, trying to figure out how come this big mook isn't going down. Telling her she needs make them stronger just don't mix up the drink with his because their drinking the same thing. Each time Roz was sent to get the drinks, she would put less and less in Hutch's drink. She looked at Donna and gave a little nod to her before going in the back with the spiked drinks. Donna saw Roz mixing the drinks knowing the routine they do when a man gets to go in the back room. She's heard the rumors about them spiking the man's drink and doing things to him. She looks around the club and sees Derrick, Mack and Steel at a table in club and walks over to them. Talking to Derrick "Hi aren't you Hutch's brothers and don't you remember me. I'm Donna from the supermarket and was at the BBQ at his house." Derrick says "Yeah I remember you the other women that was there too!" Donna asked Derrick "Could you call

Hutch I needs to speak to him right away." He answers her "I don't have to call him because he's in here somewhere" Looking around to see if he could spot him. Donna concerned about him and didn't want to cause any unnecessary attention to him making Markola hurt him in some way just to get that card from him. She convinces Derrick she wanted to surprise Hutch. Seeing how Derrick never took his eyes off the dancer, she calls her over to them and says "Shelly this is a good friend of mine Derrick and Derrick this is shelly she'll stay with you for me, so now can you call Hutch" Derrick pulls out his cell saying "Speed dial number 3." Pressing it and handing her his cell. She stands by Derrick in case Markola came back out there and saw her using the cell knowing it would be to warn Hutch. When he answers she quickly told him not to drink the drinks Markola or Roz is bring in because they're spiked, that's how Markola gets women to take advantage of men in the V.I.P room. Hutch told her it's too late he downed about three of them already. He knows what he's got to do and told her stay around he's going to need her help, she told him alright she'll be there with Janet and Erikaa too. Markola told Roz to sit next to Hutch and make him feel really comfortable while one of her girls danced. Hutch went to make room and knocks over his drink on the table and Markola got mad but didn't want him to catch on to why he was mad about the drink being spilled. Telling Roz to clean up the spilled drink and he would get the drinks for everyone and went out the room but stood by the curtain to listen first at what's going in there. Hearing Roz making a comment on how big his hand and feet are. They laughed about that and Hutch thanked her for the compliment and she leans closer to him asking "I want to know why Donna doesn't want you harmed?" Hutch starts to feel the effect of the drink and says "It must be how I'm good with mine!" Roz felt that was arrogant of him to say that and asked "Why do you say that and in that way?

Hutch apologized to her saying "I didn't mean it in that way. I'm not like that but I try to be good at what I do!" Puzzled that he would even say that, but most men she comes across never apologized for anything to her and then explain themselves. To her it made think a little different about this big man, asked "Good? What are you good at?!" He told her "Take these off and I'll show you." Pointing to her shoes he, then took the hot wax and pours it on his hands. Markola heard him say that part standing by the curtain but not most of what they were talking about before. Thinking to himself "Freaking mook going to hit that" and he always wanted to sex Roz but if that's what it would take for him to get his hands on that card then he's willing to let this slide. Walking to the bar so he could mix a strong drink for Hutch, excited thinking about getting that card not noticing he was feeling the effects of the spiked drink Roz gave to him. Donna came over to him wanting to know what's going on back there. Markola asked her "What are you still doing here" and she told him his thugs are still up in his office with Janet and Erikaa and she wants them released. He told her hold on calling up stairs for his men to let them go saying "They're coming down and you all can get the hell out of my hair too!" Donna sees him wobbling a little bit but notices he doesn't notice himself doing that being in such a good mood. He continues to mix some drinks as Janet and Erikaa come down and saw Donna by the bar. They all hug as she asked them "Are you both alright" and took them to a table near the Grand Drunken Master 4 Life being entertained by the dancers they knew. Donna told them Hutch is there and she told him about the drinks Markola spiked for him but he drank about three of them. Janet looked very concerned and starts to get up and head back there but Donna stops her saying "Hutch told her for all of us to wait and stand by!" Janet wanted to know was he hurt or being held. Donna told her Roz and her girls are back there with them, explaining she had a talk with Roz and owes Roz a favor for looking out for him. Erikaa looked at her and asked "Are you crazy owing Roz a favor!?" Janet said "It's for Hutch! I'd owed her a favor for him too and whatever the favor I'll pay it with you!" Erikaa said "Well that make three who owe her then!" As they all held hands looking at each other Janet said "I need a drink calling the waitress over to get them a drink while they were waiting. Hutch was in the V.I.P room with Roz and she was moaning so loud and making noises behind the curtain from what Hutch was doing to her.

When Markola came back to the room just outside the room, he didn't go in because he heard Roz saying "Oh shit! It's so freaky big (gasping) you sure it won't split me. How can you fit it all in there! Ssss right there Oh shit! I never had it like that before damn that feels so good don't stop give me it harder. Wow you are hitting the spot dam oh ffreeak what are you doing to me!" Markola listening thinking they're in the room having sex hearing Roz said all that to Hutch. He heard him say "Like that huh! Well I'm going to do this move that would crack your back loudly and you might call my name." She answers "No man ever could get me like this." Sounding out of breath and when Hutch did that move on her. On other side of the curtain Markola heard her moan then heard something cracking as she went "Oh shhhhhhit! How can you keep going I'm shaking already, you're not human F*&k!" She shakes telling him "Wait let me catch my breath wow, how did you get it all in there like that wow!" Markola really upset hearing what she walking back to the bar to make Hutch's drink really strong. He also calls to some of his men to do something when he's ready. Hutch looks at Roz and told her "See all you really needed was a good foot cracking massage with a nice back rub and cracking. You are on your feet for a long time plus in those shoes. I know after all that attention now you feel like a whole new person" She was smiling and told him "That's not all what came while you had your hands on me like that" then blushes. He asked her "What did Markola want from me and why have you here?" She told Hutch "He wants me to pick your pocket and take your wallet, so I can get your Credit card and give it to him so he could run a big bill like the other men I've done before!" He then asked her "Could you get his wallet and give it to me" She asked "Why?" He smiled at her "If you do that I'll show you what I can do with some baby oil to your calf muscles" She got weak in the knees standing there looking at him and had to sit back down to catch her breath, she thought about it and shuddered telling Hutch "I'll get it for you." Markola walks back in the room with a big cough like he was clearing his throat and saw Hutch sitting there and Roz with her hair a messy and thought "How could she give that mook a quickly like that" as he walks towards them. Roz up already bumps him picking his pocket getting his wallet without anyone even seeing her do it. Markola trying to keep his kool sat by Hutch and told him "Here my man you're going to like this one it came from a bottle that I was aging myself" Hutch wobbling a little takes the glass about to sip some hitting his lip and letting the glass slip out of his hand dropping the glass catching it but spilling most on the table, Markola looks at him mad he didn't drink any saying "It's no problem bro, I'll be happy to get more but be careful with this next one it's very expensive stuff you are spilling." Thinking it must be working on him, now if he can get him to drink another one. With a big grin on his face and tipsy himself, happy about Hutch feeling the effects from the drink spiked. Markola forgets himself as he told Roz "Bitch! Get the wallet while I'm out getting another drink for this stupid mook! I'll take my time!" Looking at Markola mad he called her that name for the first time in front of someone. Guessing he called her that name behind her back but never to her face like that, she waits till he left the room and hands Hutch his wallet going "That mother fluker got some nerve." Hutch looks through his wallet and find a credit card the same color as his, looking at the card but somehow has to change the indentured name from Markola to something else like it quickly too. Looking at Roz trying to think of something he sees what he could do. With a strange look on his face he motions for her to come close to him. She gets coy and wants to know "Why" but he smiles looking at her licking his lips rubbing his hand together and wants her closer. She move close and he wants her even closer till she stands right in front of him sitting there with her hips right at his face as he looks up at her. Asking says "You mind?"

Parting her legs moving his hand on her thigh as she closed her eyes leaning her head back thinking he was going to, but instead moved his hand down it to that switch blade in her boot she keeps on the inside of her leg. Feeling his hand on her boot she looks down then sees him working on the card thinking to herself "Damn! But shudders at the thought of him" She asked "What are you doing?" Hutch using the switch blade point changing the name Markola to a name he thought of close to it. (Meepbo) Altering the k and o to look like the letter p and l-a resembling letter b adding the letter o on the end. Handing Roz the wallet and asking her "Can you put back his wallet and not let him feel it?" Still mad from him calling her a "B" she says "I can shove a dick in his ass and he'll never know it till he sat down!" Hutch looked at Roz and he shuddered "Remind me not to get on your bad side, ouch!" Then taking the rest of his drink pouring it in Markola's glass then sitting back down as Roz waits for Markola to come in. He finally comes in the room with a tray of drinks and again Roz bumps into him putting back his wallet in his jacket and takes the tray from his hands saying "I got it before you knocks over anymore of the drinks" He leans into her asking "Is it working on him?" She looks at him sneers saying in a seductive way "Oh yeah he worked it!" Looking at the expression on Markola's face she quickly changes her answer "Yeah it's working on him the drink Is working." Markola looks at Roz and says "You look a little taller lose for some reason." She coughs and take the tray over to Hutch handing him a drink saying "Here your drink and could she get him anything else?" He goes "Yeah a red bull and big glass of ginger ale please!" She gets up to get what he wanted looking at Markola and gave a slight nod and mouthing to him "I got it!" As she was leaving out of the room, sending up to the small stage another of her girls to dance for them while she's out. Markola thinking now all he's got to do is get Hutch drunk enough so if he ever comes back there saying he lost his Credit card. Markola can easily say Hutch never even pulled out his wallet to pay for anything because everything was on him. Out at the bar Roz was getting his red bull and ginger ale. Donna saw her at the bar and walks over there with Janet and Erikaa asking "Is everything alright back there?" She looks at them "Damn! Is he always like that? If he is, are there any more of him around!" Donna said "Told you he would grow on you, to answer your other question (she smiles pointing) look over there. See all those guys in black and gold jackets they are his brothers." Roz looked over at all the men in those jackets and saw how big and tall they were, getting lap dances giving the girls money. Liking a couple of them already, she turns back to Donna saying "All of them came with him, wow!" She told Donna what he was doing and what he did to her to using his hands. Cracking her back so good that she wants to know, does he do that to them all the time? Donna looks at her smiling about his strong hands so gentle to be such a big man with that much power in those fingers saying "Look at them." Pointing to Janet and Erikaa smiling too about what he does to them. Explaining that's not why they want him out of there, they know Markola would do something to him and being a good man like he is they don't want anything to happen to him. They don't want him to have to do anything either to have to be in serious trouble behind it to save himself from such A-hole like Markola. Roz looked over at the G.D.M.4.L saying "Since I've helped you, could you put in a good word to help me get one of those G.D.M.4.L" Donna asked "Which one?" Roz point to LIL-Rob saying "The one that looks like the boxer (Tyson)" Donna replied "Then we're even Ok you got it!" Asking her "What is the red bull and ginger ale for?" Roz told her Hutch wanted it she doesn't know why he asked for these two things to drink in a bar. Donna thought back Hutch was talking to them mixing drinks at his BBQ and told her he used to be a bar tender Mix-a-lo-gist. Knowing how to counter any mickey or spiked drink with just red bull and ginger ale, having to drink both down really fast and beer after that's how it clears you up.

She was smiling as Janet shook her from her thoughts asking "Why are you smiling at a time like this?" She told them to let Roz get back there with those drinks and they walk back to the table. She reminds them of what Hutch told them at his BBQ. Roz walks back in the room with what he orders and give it to him. Markola pulls her over to the side and wants that card from her, she gives it to him and he looks at it without really looking at it carefully. Putting it in his pocket then telling Roz to get her girl and leave but send in the one girl he asked for. Roz knew it was going to be something, every time he has that one white girl come in the room. She always claims a man touched her in the wrong way and Markola has his thugs throw the man out. She goes to get Cindy and told her Markola wants her to dance. Markola wanted to do a couple of bottoms up toasts, what he didn't see was Hutch switched his drink with the red bull and ginger ale in a couple of the glasses while he was over there talking to Roz. When the new girl came in the room and starts to dancing Markola told him to look at her because she's his finest dancer. She wants Hutch to keep his eyes on her as Markola spiked the drinks even more. Markola wants another bottoms up toast then makes an excuse for him to leave but his other manager will show him a good time, he's to take care of business some other place. Leaving out the room giving a winking to the dancer, she sees there were still two more drinks in front of him and knows she got to get him to drink them. She asked "Want a lap dance baby?" Giving Markola time enough while he's out the room before she went into her act. Markola walks out from the V.I.P section and held his hand up to some men sitting at the table and they nodded back to him. Roz came over to Donna and told her Cindy is in the room dancing for him now, she knows his thugs are going to go in there ruffing Hutch up and throw him out she's seen it before. Janet said "Not this one!" Looking at both Donna and Erikaa nodding before they split up and head over to each G.D.M.4.L and told them their brother's about to get jumped so get ready for a fight. Four men at the table wave after Markola waves to them, they nod to another four men sitting at another table waiting for a signal to head in the back to ruff up and throw out Hutch. Dancing for a few minutes Cindy came down to Hutch and starts give him a lap dance, then gets up and says "You didn't have to touch me that way." Hutch looked at her and says "I didn't even put my hands on you." She takes the drink and tries throwing it his face but missed as he moved out the way, seeing him that she runs out the room going to the manager with her strap to her top broke hanging off to show something happened. (Snapping it herself before she got there) Going to the manager and tells him aloud "The guy in the back got ruff with me and tried to pull off my top" loud enough for others to hear her all upset about it. That was the signal for the manager first to go in the back with two men. The acting Manager confronts Hutch about being ruff with one of his dancers but Hutch denies ever doing it. The manager explains he's in charge of the safety of the girls, even if he were back here with the boss that's no reason to get ruff with one of the girls and need to be taught a lesson right now. Hutch gets up fast feeling woozy thinking that sneaky ass spiked the drinks again when he was looking at the girl, that's why she wanted him to keep his attention so Markola spiked the red bull or ginger ale. The guy come at Hutch to get him but gets knocked down but the second one gets in a punch send

Hutch back over the table. They get to swing and Hutch knows he's going to get hit because the drink is making him a bit slow, he manages to gets hit by the second guy accidently with a good hard right knocking him back through the curtain. Cindy screams which is the signal for all the other men to go back there and get him. Both table of men rush to the back which made everyone in the place look at them rushing back there, Donna looks at Erika and Janet worried but saw four men backing up from being pushed by Hutch.

Then one jumps on and held him as another hits him. Janet, Erikaa and Donna stood up when they saw that but heard 2Soon yell "Yo man! That's Hutch!" All the G.D.M.4.L turns and saw him getting hit before he kicks the man back and flips the other off his back. Two of Markola's goons tackled him from behind into some table about to throw a punch but gets his arm locked with another arm in mid stride. He looks at Tys/LiL-Rob saying "What the F!" Never getting to chance to finish his word getting punched out by Tys, then he helps Hutch up but they get tackled by two other men. All the goons of Markola are jumping on them and never see the wave of black jackets coming at them turning it into a full brawl with the black jacket beating all the men down. Cindy looks at the fight going on, so she turns to run out but see Donna standing in her way "POW!" She gets punched out by Janet as she stood over her saying "You started this BITCH!" The fighting didn't last that long, Hutch sitting in a chair very woozy from moving around with that stuff effecting his system. Donna says "Why did you come here?" He answers "Could tell in your voice something wrong, but you see I'm not stupid didn't come alone!" Janet says "Let's get you out of here before they call the cops and we all need some help to get us out of there!" Donna takes his keys asking him "Where did you park?" He's helped out by Erikaa and Janet. 2Soon asked "What's this all about fam?" He told him "Remember they came there and they all left with girls, well the owner was mad I made him look stupid so he wanted to get even with me." Tys said "They better get out of there before one of them wake up and get their heat. I'm not in the mood to be leaking and have to go get them pulled out of me right about now" Roz was standing by him and Donna said "Oh Tys this my girl Roz!

She gave us the heads up!" Roz smiles at him and he looks at her saying "I like the leather look you got on tough!" She smiles saying "Like the way you stopped that punch kool." Taking his arm feeling it, looking at Donna wide eyed walking away they get to talking. Some of the girls came over to Donna asking "What they're going to do now, the place is wrecked and they can't make any money for this night." Hutch trying to focus his eyes and counts the women standing there by Donna and says "You need dates with cash to spend?" He whistles and the rest of the G.D.M.4.L standing around him as he said "These ladies need to make money for the night" and they watch his brothers pull out the wallets of the men out cold on the floor taking all of their cash. Holding up the bills they took as he says "Pick one and parties at my house, B.Y.O.B ladies." Some of the customers there looking at them leaving and one says "What about us we want to come party too!" One man says "I got just as much as they got" and held up a big not of cash. Roz looked at her girls and told them "Take him and only ones with big cash to my place and get paid." Another man says "Can I go too?" Holding up a knot just as big as the other man's got. Roz looked at him and told her girls "Only the ones with phat paper girls." The place was empty except the men and one woman out cold on the floor as the phone rings and there is no one there to answer it.

At Hutch's house Donna with Janet and Erikaa are looking the swelling of Hutch's face as the rest talk about what they did to a man who got in the fight. Roz even told Janet nice punch she hit Cindy with and didn't know she had a hand game like that. Hutch told them they can't go back there anymore and don't think about trying to go to another club either he's pretty sure they all are connected any ways once Markola put the word out. Donna told him not to worry they have their studies to do any ways since they're just about finishing with the college course they're taking. He went to stand again but got caught by Erikaa and Janet as they told him he needs to get that stuff out of his system. He told them to get the club soda out the Frig and bring it to him.

All the other went down stairs with the women from the strip club, Donna asked Roz "What about you? Are you going back there anytime soon?" Roz looked at Donna and then at Tys and says "When I do be keeping my ears and eyes open, because you're going to need one on the inside to keep my new man heads up on things." LIL-Rob slaps Roz on her ass (Pow!) saying "Come we going down stair with the others" She turns to Donna "He wants to take charge, he just don't know I like to fight too!" Donna says "Ding Ding watch that upper cut!"

Later back at the strip club some of the men start to wake up and see all the damage to the place as they wake others up and Cindy too holding her jaw. Markola came in the place looking around shouting "WHAT THE FLOCK HAPPENED HERE! All yous guys were to do is get that freaking mook out of my club!" The manager said "They were but he had some help with him" Markola shouts "Yous guy couldn't take the mook and his boys and throw them out. You had to bust the joint up!" Again the manager speaks "They could really fight! I think some of them were boxers and how was I to know he would bring the champ with the rest of them!" Markola says "The champ was here too?" Yelling for them to clean this mess up while he goes to think about things, Mario his cousin says "Wow he had the champ with them, you got to admit the guys were no match for him and with other boxers too!" Markola shook his head "You right didn't think that mook would bring ringers with him, but I got something that will make all this go away!" He tells Mario they have a place to go tomorrow and all this week he'll take him through Manhattan like they never been before.

At Hutch's house he was in the bathroom drinking gobs of the club soda and then throwing it back up getting what he could of those mickeys off his stomach, then brushing his teeth using mouth wash and getting in the Jacuzzi laying back with his eyes closed. Feeling a body get next to him and then another on his other side and finally one in between his legs laying her head on his chest. A voice says "You did use mouth wash I hope with all that throwing up we heard right?" Hutch says "Kiss me and find out its minty clean." Water sloshes Janet says "Hey hay! What's this poking me in my back!" Erikaa says "What about the others down stairs?" Hutch says "They know where the rooms are in my house and how to close a door when they leave!"

Saturday Morning Hutch wakes first seeing three bodies in his bed again smiling at them sprawled all over it snoring like they had a hard day's work at the lumber yard. He shakes his head as it rings and he goes to the bathroom, looking at his face a little bruised. Then showering again before going down stairs to see who's there. Seeing no one in the living room, he goes to the kitchen and starts breakfast. First drinking some more club soda to have on his stomach and start cooking with turkey bacon and sausage grits and eggs putting on coffee too. The smell of breakfast bring those out from the rooms and down to eat, Derrick and his date, LIL-Rob and Roz, Steel and his date, Mack and his date come down to eat and from the basement came, Dave and his date with la-Machine and his date, when everything was almost done. Hutch asked "Where's the others?" Mack told him they left when everyone started pairing off and you didn't come back down stairs but we see why. Donna with Erika and Janet came down in his stuff, one had on his sweatshirt swallowing her body, another has on his dress shirt like a dress and the last one had on his PJ's baggy as she walks on the pant legs. Mack says "See that stuff he gave you wore off and you wore them out from the looks of them.

Damn! Herc you need to be easy with that untold usage of yours" All the guys laughed knowing what he meant and the women looked at them wondering why he said that to him that way, but Janet, Erikaa and Donna knew smiling then laughing too.

Markola is calling Mario and they are going shopping in the Diamond district first thing, getting watches and rings for them and them making a stop at this custom tailor suit place for a few.

Hutch is sitting with everyone thinking about what they're going to do and like usual when they want to take it easy they BBQ and have a party at his house. That night Elise calls him wanting to know what he's been up to and she hears the noise in the back ground so she yells at him "What the hell is going on another BBQ?" He walks away from everyone trying to explain he needed this one because of the time he's had and wanted to be with friends and family. Elise wasn't happy about that and reminds him they were going to make a go of things together, he has to let her know what he's been up to then asked him "Was there any women at his BBQ?" He told her "Yes but their friend and" She cuts him off screaming "I don't care who they are! You were supposed to let me know when you have another of these BBQ's. I think their trying to come between us and you just let them, so how are we to be together when they always show up and you forgot about me." Hutch sighs "Your right! This is the final time and I'll call you tomorrow then we can talk" Hanging up the phone and walking back to the BBQ not seeing Donna who was sitting in his vehicle and heard everything he said with Elise on the phone. She walks in after he did and talks with Janet and Erikaa about them getting in the way of him and Elise getting together. Even though she feels that woman is trying to manipulate him because he's too nice of a man. Later after everyone was ready to leave and he drove them home. Donna has a talk with Hutch again and tells him they are really going to be busy with their studies and wouldn't have time to see him, besides they have to find jobs to take the place of them dancing. He understood but told them if they need him they can call and he'll come running, just because they have job that doesn't mean they can't meet up and do things. Donna reminds him he's going to be with Elise and she's not going to like him around them. He hugs each one of them and Janet told him "You better not forget us and we'll be here if you need us too." They stand there and watch him drive away and walk in the building. He looks back in his mirror and sees them walk in the building feeling like he should turn around and tell them he really should be with them instead of trying to give her a chance which seems not be in the cards for them.

End of that month which seems like it was longer to him since he finally got with Elise now for the last three weeks and they were dating and going out with her phony acting friends. These were the type of people who wore name brands clothes and acted like they were more than their clothes they wore and every time they went out they had to drink expensive wines and champagne standing around talking about meaning less things that don't happen in the real world. It's morning when he pulls up to the building parking his truck waiting for the work crew to come, he starts to eating his food listening to the radio before changing into his work clothes. The van pulls up and the workers gets out and don't seem to be in a happy mood because of Moni getting on them even before they got to work. He looks at Hutch with a dirty look and walks into the building. Hutch knows he's going to try something to get him for some of the things done to Moni, but every time he tried the prank back fires on him anyway. Hutch gets a call from Elise and she wants to go out to another place to eat that she heard from a friend of hers that likes gourmet food prepared in front of them.

The place is very expensive but good, telling him it's a fancy place and he needs to wear a suit and tie with his good shoes. He asked her "What about me cooking for you?" She laughs at him "You're not a gourmet chef like this place they're going to." He says "You use to like the time I cooked for you." She told him "No! I was being polite you should know better than that by now. I just didn't want to hurt your effort in trying by letting you see me dump that food in the garbage, but it was sweet not gourmet style right?" Later Hutch and Elise were at this place along with Elise's friends. She was admiring her girlfriend's jewelry and told them Hutch was going to get her the same kind of Diamond with a few more carrots. She needs the right type of stone to put on her hands and he looks at her after told them that. Elise went on about the vehicle she were driving and told them Hutch has plans to get the new Mercedes for her their anniversary and again Hutch looks at her. Wondering why she's telling these people all that stuff about what he's going to do and never discussing it with him in private. They were about to eat and she calls the waiter over to order some more champagne and Hutch looks at her asking "Didn't you have enough." Elise looks at him and says "It wasn't so long ago you were ordering stuff for your friends she didn't complain about you paying for it so why cry about it now!" Then telling him "If you want to be with me and better class of people you better get used to it and stop with the complaints because it's unmanly of you and she doesn't like it and not going to stand for it!" At the same place were Janet and Erikaa they were double dating and the guys wanted to take them to this place figuring it would impress them, they saw Hutch but he couldn't see them because of where they were seated. They watched as Elise kept trying to be little him by saying things a little loud like "Why you can't pay for this and if she wants to drink champagne why can't you get it for me." Going on how he would pick up the bill for his friends so why can't he pick up the bill for hers and soon to be his friends too because she's got plans for his butt. Hutch tried to be nice and excuse himself from the table but Elise had just a little too much champagne and shows it by yelling at him "You're not going anywhere and especially not back to those low class friends of his to complain about me!" Everyone in the place heard that as he looks at her and says to her friends "Guess she's had enough huh?" Staggering behind him as he paid the check and asked the valet for his vehicle, he helps her in and drives off. Janet looks at Erikaa as their dates talk about Hutch saying "What a loser he is for taking that crap from her any man with a back bone would have kicked that drunken bimboe to the curb after the second bottle went dry." They laugh about it a little too much for Janet and Erikaa as they told their dates they want to leave and the dates over. Janet's date says to her "You act like you know that loser!" Erikaa told him "He could kick your ass if you were to say that to his face!" Erikaa date says "Then you do know him." They get up and say never mind we'll catch a cab home and leave out the restaurant. Outside they hail a cab and gets in as their date stand there looking at them as the cabby drove away.

Hutch makes it back to his place in no time because he was mad but didn't want to show it, he opens the door after cutting off the alarm system and head to the frig to get a beer and shot from the bar. Elise came in drunk looking for him and found him in the kitchen eating turkey sandwich with a beer and shot, she says "See you can't teach some people to be upper class, they're just not worth it." Hutch looks at her and says "You need to sleep it off and we'll talk in the morning!" He goes to the living room and turns on the TV to the watch some wrestling.

Donna was home looking at Wrestling when Erikaa and Janet came in there and says to her "Guess who they've seen and looks like he was so miserable on his date with a certain woman who got drunk and showed her ass at this four star place." Donna cuts down the TV and her eyes got wide wanting to know more about who they were talking about. Her mouth opens "NAH! Really?!" very interested in what happened and they starts to tell Donna everything they saw and heard but them the door is being pounded on which makes then stop and wonder who could be knocking at this time of night. Janet looks through the peep hole and saw Markola's face trying to look back in the hole saying "I know you're in there because he heard the TV" and he pounds again on the door. Janet went back to Donna and Erikaa telling them who it was, but then goes to her room and for some reason takes her phone and throws it in her boot. Erikaa open the door and Markola comes in their place and he' not in a good mood saying to them "I wants to know where that mook friend Hutch of theirs is?" Donna asked "Why! they haven't seen him in over a month and don't know where he is!" He told them if they don't know then there must be a way they can call him again and asked them for their cell phones. He rants about thinking he had got his card from that mook but he pulled a fast one on him and gave Markola his own Credit card. He ran up such an bill on it they took his Credit card and cut it up right in front of him and all his guess at this place in Brooklyn where some of his very important friend and him were having a great dinner till the bill came. He didn't like what happened and have to go in his pocket and dig up what cash he had and leave his watches and rings for collateral. He wants that mook to bring that card to him or he won't see one of you ever again looking at Donna.

Over at Hutch house outside Marveece and Davona had just pulled up on his street to watch his house hoping to catch him or Steel coming out so they could grab one or the other. Hutch watching TV in the living room saw the lights outside and then how they cut off. He got up and went upstairs to one of the bedroom that faces the street in his house and saw Marveece's vehicle and two people moving in it. Thinking "They are going to stake out my house for Steel wow" going back down stairs to finish watching TV while Elise slept off the champagne she drank. He knew he was going to have it out with her this time because she went too far at the restaurant in front of those people like that.

Markola in the living room talking to Donna, Erikaa and Janet about the bill for all the things he bought that month on his on what he thought was Hutch's Credit card, from Diamonds to rings and expensive dinner flowers and other thing for his house and cousins loft. Showing them the shoes and coat he was wearing, mad that he got played for a fool by Hutch again. Donna told him "She don't know where Hutch is and wasn't about to look him up for Markola". He told her "You're going to call to make sure none of your other friends don't get hurt" and one of his the man grabs Erikaa and the other guy grabs Janet. Donna told him "Alright!" After hearing Janet and Erikaa scream in pain being held like that and she looks at her cell and finds Hutch's number and calls. Hutch was sitting there looking at this picture of the couch seeing Janet sitting between his legs and Erikaa on the side, Donna on the other and they were laughing about something. His phone rings its Donna asking "How you been long time no hear from?" Before he could answer her it gets taken by Markola says "Hey mook! Guess who the hell this is, you freaking think your slick huh bro giving me my own card freaking mook!" Hutch says "Why don't you let the girls go and we can talk about it!" Markola said "I would let them go if you bring down your Credit card to their house and gave it to me without calling the cops or reporting it gone to the authorities." Hutch wants to speak to one of them, and gets Janet on the phone as Markola kept him from talking to Donna. Hutch asked her a couple question like how many Markola got with him and are they alright? Thinking he needs to get help down there fast, but that's too many numbers he has to call. Writing a note with their address on it at first thinking to leave it here and call his brothers to find it as he goes down there, but then waiting for them to get there would be too long and thinking he needs monster help now. Then it accrued to him what about just two monster and told Janet "Listen real careful when help arrives say that Steel's little sister stays there" but if they asked where is she "Tell them she spending the night over her cousins house in the Bronx" Janet asked "Why say that?" Hutch told her "Just so they won't throw you out the window for Steel not being there or his sister." She went

"OK" and he told her hand the phone back to Markola which she does. Hutch told him he'll bring the card just don't hurt the girls. Markola told him if he thinks about calling The Champ or any of those boxer friends of his that he'll let them go off the Brooklyn Bridge on his way to Manhattan to go eat dinner and get some more men yelling "To come find you mook." Hutch told him no he'll be right there and it won't take long that way he'll know he didn't call any police or his brothers "Alright!" Markola agrees but asked Hutch "Where do you live or just how far away are you so I could time you." Turning the tables on him by saying "Why don't you take the girls to your house and I'll bring the card there" When Markola repeated back what Hutch said to him over the phone, Mario says "That's a good idea that way they can see if he had the police or his boys with him" Markola yells at him "STU-NOD! Then he'd know where I lived and could come back there with the police or his boys you stupid mother flockin IDIOT!" Markola says to Hutch "See what I got to put up with" Hutch says "Let me guess he's your first cousin right?!" There was silence on the phone for a moment as Markola thought how come this mook is smarter than his own flesh and blood. Markola tells Hutch to bring the card there and he'll make it easy for the both of them, if he sees one cop car stop by or gets there with his boys. The girls go with him and he can pick up the pieces. Hutch said "I'll be there as fast as I can with the card just don't hurt them" and hangs up and went to change his clothes into something more street looking and casual. He goes in to the basement and gets his helmet then goes to find his Halloween costume he wore last year dressing up like a dread lock and get the dreadlock wig putting it on under his helmet and then getting on his ninja bike and coasting it down the path way to the street in back of his house. Thinking to himself he knew this back alley way path would come in handy one day that's why he liked this house. Getting to the street costing a good ways down away from his house where major traffic is and starts his bike up, thinking how and what he' going to do when he rides next to Marveece's vehicle sitting out by his house. Not lift the visor and let them even see his eyes and remember to keep his voice disguised or they would know it's him for sure.

In the vehicle Marveece and Davona call themselves taking turns watching Hutch's house to see if he or Steel came there but they both were in a dead sleep snoring like they were two big Vikings after a meal. One laying her head on the other's shoulder when Hutch rode up on his bike knocking on the window waking them up. They wake to see this man on a motorcycle with dreads coming from under his helmet on banging on the window waking them up motioning for them to roll down the window, they look at him as he spoke in Jamaican accent "YO me taut you be Steel and he gal. Cause iz lil sista she be aving trouble wit sum mon an ee boiyz at er ome deer. Me noe Steel be doin any ting fur me protek-in iz lil sista."

Marveece now fully awake says "What! My future baby sister in-law is having trouble with some men at her house and Steel would do anything for you because you was to protect her? Hutch says "Ya-mon!" Marveece let out an "Oooh Marveece! I could get in good with my Sta-eel baby sister and she could bring him to me, so I can have a piece of Steel broke off in meh" Marveece told the bike ride (who was Hutch) that they'll come with him and they can help Steel's baby sister at her home. Hutch says "Me don noe if you kan take dees mon deer dey big large dem goon mon." Marveece told the Jamaican bike rider "Look I'll be able to handle any man for my Steel, so we'll follow you to my future baby sister house now go!" Hutch says "We ride den." Hutch knew from being chased by Davona and Maveece before that she didn't have no trouble in keeping up with him as she sped through the streets fast to get to the building where Markola and his men are holding the girls in their apartment. On the way there he was thinking on how he was going to get them to go up there without having to go up with them, if he did he knew he would have to take off his helmet but had to think of a way not to go up with them. Close to the building Hutch pulls over and says to them "Yo mon woman and boti boy! Me gon take you to de front of dis place but dere be dees mon dere in front mite try and stop yu. Steel lil sista she be in dis place apartment she be in iz tird floor numba leven S four. Steel cause Ee like dem numba see!" They look at Hutch and asked "What did you say?!" Hutch goes "You no understand meh? Bumble clod take yor bodti up to numba 11-S mon, she be in dere and let no mon stop yuh or Steel never wan see yuh gen nah mean!" They asked the bike rider (Hutch) "What are you going to do if they go in the front?" He answers "Meh gon do (ghost eyed woman politician) cum min hard in da-bak-mon olding me nine ready for shot some mon who cum bak tru dere and den me cum up to dey front see" They look at him and don't say a word but look and he says using his hands to illustrate what he says at the same time "Me gon cum to dey bak holden me tool (gun), so if a mon cum dere. Me gon put sum shot in ee body." Marveece looks at Davona and says "We don't need you to have a gun in this situation better let us handle the front just cover our backs so no one sneaks up on us OK" Hutch slip and says "Alright! Er ya-mon!" He takes them right up to the front and watch as they get out and some of Markola's asked "Where you two think you're going?" Marveece told the one man "Oooh Marveece to save his baby daddy little future sister in law now move!" The man asked which apartment she lives in and after Marveece told him the same number apartment Markola was in he said "You ugly ass bitches aren't going anywhere now beat it!" Marveece looked at Davona and put her hand on her chest and gasp at what he said to them, then laughed and hi fived Davona saying "We got your ugly ass bitches shit!" A third man came out from the big Lincoln car he was sitting in and up behind Marveece and Davona asking the one they were talking to "Hey what with the dog show, this building allow pets!" Marveece said to Davona "No he didn't with that missing hole on his head looking like friar tuck." Before the men could say another word it was over just as fast as Marveece and Davona are walking through the front door of the building and men are laid out on the sidewalk outside the building. Marveece walks up the flight of stairs and see these two men standing down the hallway in front of the door to the apartment Markola has the girls in. Davona took the elevator and got off close to them. One man says "Hope you two things don't want to come in here. It's busy and you have to go back to the zoo with the other beasts!" Marveece said "Girl everybody wants to be a comedian today, well here's something that sounds funny to me!" There is this sound of men getting their ass beat outside the door in this hallway. The men about to pull their weapons out but is stopped by Marveece and Davona as they beat the men hard making them cry out in pain before going unconscious.

Inside the apartment the sound of fighting was heard faintly right before Marveece knocks on the door. Hutch is one floor down coming inside after he saw the men outside the building laid out, they had a bunch of plastic ties in a bag in the car they drove up in. He used them on the men putting them in the trunk of the car before coming in with the rest of the plastic ties in his pants waist belt. Hearing all that beating wincing himself as he heard the men sound like women getting their ass beat and then the knocking sound on the door by Marveece. Markola told him man to go see if that's the mook with his card because they got there faster than what he thought he would and only cops responses that fast. The man looks through the peep hole and jumps back at the close fish eyed sight of Marveece right at the hole. He goes to Markola "There's this thing at the door and it aint no cop or that mook it's hideous looking boss. I might have to see someone after this, I can' get it out of my head help me." Markola walks over to the door and takes a look through the peep hole and sees Davona up close fish eye view and he scream "AHH! What freaking night mare is this? The walking dead looks better than what I just saw!" Again Marveece knocks on the door and says "I know you're in there. OOOH Marveece Open up I want to see my sister in-law." Markola gets mad and says "Which one of you never told me you hand monster in your family history" They all point and look at each other. Markola says "One of you have to get rid of that thing and its pet. Hope it's trained not to bite I don't like the shots for rabies" Erikaa goes the door and opens it up, Marveece says "Oooh Marveece where's my little sister in-law." Erikaa asked "Can I help you? Who are you here to see again?" Marveece says "Oooh Marveece I know you got company baby they don't bother me. I just want to see my girl." She walks right in and Markola's man says "This aint no woman and if it is DAMN! She's an Ugly bitch." Marveece looked him up and down saying "OOOH Marveece! Let me tell you this fooka. I'm no, oh what the hell DAVONA!" The man says "Was that you're war cry?" Marveece says "Oooh Marveece you're about to do the cry whimpster." He didn't see Davona in back of him till he turns to be met by her fist knocking him down and dragging him out the apartment sounding like a woman screaming then get beat till knocked out. Markola said "So he sicked his monsters on me." Marveece said "Who you calling a monster you little fat ugly leprechaun!" Snatching him up as he yells for Marveece to let him go. Davona said "I don't like you or your men talking about my girl like that." Markola said to Marveece "If you don't put me down I'll blow your brains out and" cutting his words then asked "Do regular bullets work on you or do they have to be sliver like for your kind." The girls cover their faces so they don't see what happens to Markola when Marveece growled at him. The sounds he made had them flinching hearing him gasp and whine then whimper and finally go "Mommy please!" Janet phone rang and she uncovers her face to go get it to hear who it was Hutch, telling her let Marveece and her partner know Steel's little sister snuck out the back way when they came in and she's with her brother at his house. Tell her you just talked to her and she's going to stay with him for a while. Janet says "You got some explaining to do man." He answers "I know but right now let's just get the things out of your place so I can take care of Markola and his goons." Marveece was told everything Janet was told to say by Hutch. Sounding disappointed she didn't get a chance to see what Steel's sister looks like asking "Are you all going to be alright with these thugs laying around here?" Janet says "I'm going to let Steels sister know you save us and if she was here she would be great full too I'm sure of it. I will tell her if you hadn't come along we would not be here now." Marveece gets all flustered about to cry at how Janet said she was going to talk about her saving them and Davona says "She just one big softy." Erikaa says "We're going to call the cops and have them hauled away to jail." As Marveece and Davona was about to leave they looked at each other and asked "Who did their hair?" Going if they ever want it done right with their nails and feet, here giving all of them her personal cards saying "That way you don't have to wait in line just show that card and you get to have the very next open spot at my salon ok girls." Watching them leave and outside the building they were wondering where that stupid Jamaican went to hoping he didn't stop for work saying "I know they're wanting to work all the jobs they could find like the cook, the baker, the salesmen, the waiter, and host, the valet, even the towel man in bathrooms at some places and he was supposed to back us up" They didn't even see his bike and went looking for it. Hutch finally came in the building up to their apartment, not before using the plastic ties on all Markola's men he saw out cold in the hallways and ones in their apartment. Using them on Markola too after getting all of them tied up Donna asked Hutch "What was that all about?" He explained he needed some muscle faster than his brothers could get there and wanted to surprise Markola and his men. When they were outside his house looking for Steel, he thought about using them as muscle getting the job done and it worked. Donna asked "What to do with them, it not like we could throw them away." That gives him an idea and told Janet he'll need her to drive the car. She asked "What car!?" He told her "Markola's car of course." All she has to do is follow him and wait by his bike as he does the rest. He loads all the men plus Markola into the big Lincoln using the trunk and back seats propping them up as if they were looking out the window. Janet followed him to this spot in Brooklyn under the BROOKLYN Bridge where he knows this garbage barge always pulls close at the end of this dead end of the street. Having Janet get out of the car she just followed him in and handing her the spare helmet saying to her "Here put this on, so no one could see you but open the visor so you could see clearly out of it." Asking her to stand by his bike, he gets in the car with his helmet on and drove the car down to the top of the dead end street stopping. That garbage barge on the river at the end of the street three blocks straight ahead as he has the car pointed in that direction. Janet watches him wait for all the green lights revving the engine, when all three turned green. He floors the gas pedal wheels smoke as he heads that way with all that weight in the vehicle, heading straight for the end of the street. Using her cell phone saying to herself "We're going to enjoy seeing this over and over again. It's exciting to know a real stuntman who I know I'm falling in love with wow! This shit is crazy!" Hutch went roaring by and waves to her not realizing she was recording it and WHOOM! They went up and landed in the garbage barge right where Hutch wanted it to, but as he starts to get out he looks at the man starting to wake. Punching them all back out again and took everything valuable out their pockets from watches rings and wallets Credit cards, but not keeping the wallets or ID"s just took all the cash they had and guns as well. Not forgetting the ones in the trunks too. Markola is starting to wake as Hutch with his helmet on saw him stir while he's taking his stuff. When he got to his wallet Markola yells "Who the fock are you!? Do you know who I am you focking Mook!" Hutch says in a Jamaican accent "Ya-mon! You dis piece of sheet dat gowon be tro away, an me don wann be hav to lick sum shot at yu hed. But I–n-I wil so heer meh mon. Yu bes leav my mon Utch a lon four meh hav to cum bak an see ya neh mean!" Markola looks at him and yells "I don't understand one focking word yous said you freaking rosti freaking mook!" Hutch said "K let me say dis bad mon heer meh now? Don't you mess wit me mon Utch or" Holding a knife to his throat "You don't know what me look like, but me no you and what you will look like heer meh now bad fat mon. Bad boy pull up. Bui-yaka Bui-yaka Bui-yaka Yu Bum-Ble Clod!" Then he head butts him hard knocking Markola out again not letting him say a thing just as the other men woke. Janet watches the car rocking as they all get knocked out again. Hutch left the knife in Markola jacket in case he had to use it to use their hands so they wouldn't drown not wanting that on his conscious in case the barge starts to sink. Leaving men to drown like that was not his style so he covers the car with this big trap where the car can't be seen by any one. Placing some of the garbage bags and stuff around it then climbing to where he could jump off the barge back on land carrying a bag of loot he took from Markola and his men. Tossing their guns in the river going back to Janet standing there waiting for him. She is so turned on about everything she told him how excites she was from watching him do that and take off her helmet kissing so passionately, he got excited as well as they got on the bike. She holds him tight excited about that too and on the way back while the bike was in motion she climbs around front of him, laying her back on the bike's tank wrapping her leg around him holding on to the handle bar above her head. Cars saw how she was laying on the bike and blew their horns approving what they saw as he rode along with her like that. Some of the local bikers for the boroughs (Shaolin Riders) riding along saw Hutch and Janet like that they were doing wheelies showing their approval of the way he was riding with her. Hutch pops his on wheelie with her still laying like that other bikers revved their engines making a lot of popping noise and beeping their horns showing they like what he did too. Shortly after Hutch and Janet are pulling back up to the building where he parks the bike not far from the front entrance and they went in. Janet still excited about what they did and shows Erikaa and Donna what Hutch did with Markola's car with him in it. He told them it looks like they won't be bothering you for a long time if they get back and if they do he'll be looking for him and his Jamaican friend that head butted the mess out of him. They are safe plus he knows about Marveece and his partner that would beat them down with no problem. Erikaa asked him "What are you going to do now?" He told her there's some unfinished business he got to deal with and they told him they know about what happened at the restaurant. Janet and Erikaa were there and heard everything, how she went on about trying to be little you in front of her friends. Hutch you're too good of man for that we just didn't want to say anything at first. Hutch looks at them "I miss you all too, that's why I'm going back there to do something I should have never started." Donna said "If you're going to do what I think you're going to do, try and be tactful because you're dealing with some ones feelings." Janet said "Yeah, his! You should have heard how she didn't want him to even call his brothers, now that's not right!" Donna went "In that you case kick the tramp to the curb. Do you want some help, not letting you talk with your brothers. Family is who you are Hutch. You're all about family so go and get yours back and we'll be here for you." Hutch didn't know but Elise was up when he got the call from Donna wanting him to come there, listening at the top of the stairs to just part of that conversation not knowing it was Markola making him come there. She walked down to the living room really mad after he left and saw the address on the note pad he left on the table. She wrote down the address and apartment number still tipsy, now madder he was seeing another woman and left her there to go see her. Elise's mind was twisting thing in her head about him, even went back to him and Becka having sex laughing about she'll never find out about them. She hears her own voice telling her how he played her for a fool, because that's what men do to women. This man had the money to play her for even a bigger fool when she knows he should pay for everything he did to her, making her look like a fool not wanting to buy her friends food and drinks but would give a lowly waitress an big ass tip. Saying she was doing her job and was worth it. Then she hears the laughter of women and Hutch all around her saying "Elise is stupid! She'll never know and his mother going that skanky gold digging money grubbing skank better not have her hands in my son's money."

Elise screamed for them to shut up and gets up and got dressed leaving his house before he could get back there, but had in her mind she was going to fix them all for doing this to her.

Hutch leaving the building puts on his helmet walking to his bike but didn't see Marveece and Davona turn the corner to see him getting on his bike to leave. Marveece says to Davona "There he is that no show up till everything is over dumb jerk ass man." They head his way when he pulls off and stops at the corner of the block but as the light turned green a car cuts him off making him almost fall with the bike, he take off his helmet and screams at the car "YOU ass wipe! Watch where you're going and who the hell taught you how to drive butt head! Right signal means turns right not left signal means right you MORON!" Shouting "I should" Stopping mid word after hearing "OOOH Marveece there's your man Davona! He's the Jamaican on the bike get him girl!" Hutch turns to see them speeding up to him and he gets on his bike and takes off faster than they can get there. "Shit!" He was thinking should have known better than that to let some meathead make me take off my helmet, forgot about them even being around and what are they still doing here. Thinking "Duh! They're looking for Steel and that Marveece is like a blood hound pit bull lockjaw once on your scent she never giving up shoot! He speeds down the street with them hot on his trail like they were cops after a suspect. He shoot down short blocks making quick turns and even running some red light to lose them, they stay with him because there is no traffic out that time of night and it's easy for Davona to keep up and with no cops around. They even go down the one way streets after him, thinking of a good way to lose them as he flies down another two blocks toward these warehouse buildings. Making a left turn down the one way street finding a way to get on the side walk close to the building facing the opposite direction he just came down, thinking quick he stops and lays down his bike on the ground. When he saw Davona's car turn the corner heading down that one way he picked his bike up and starts to push towards the corner looking back making sure they didn't see him. Just as she gets to the corner he is met by Davona herself as she grabs the handle bars of the bike surprising him "Where do you think you're going huh?!" Hutch looks at her smiling at him with those big gold lips and teeth puckering up to kiss him. He pulls down his visor to protect his face. She told him "Think you're the first man to ever run from me. I know all the secret a man would do in trying to hide thinking he would get away, so don't try no fake accent with me and answer my question where do you think you're going huh?" Hutch had to think fast and come up with something or he was going to really be in trouble with this man huntress. The first thing he thought about was how she looks like she takes care in how she looks, so he asked her "Did you use to strip. You have the build for it?" That made her blush and starts acting coy with him, so Hutch put the kick stand down and got off the bike and told her "Let me see that bang body you got" and starts making the sound of Snoop Dogg and Pharelle's song "Drop it like it's hot" click and clucking his tongue rapping the words "Drop it like it's hot!" She lets go of the bike and starts moving to the rhythm a little at first and he encourages her even more "Come on girl show me what you got! Drop it like it's hot, Drop it like it's hot!" She then smiles and starts dancing for him and Hutch changes songs "You a big fine thang girl, back that thang up, show me what you got, back that thang up!" She starts to backing it up and dropping it like it's hot for him. Now really getting into it and he says "I can't see what you're doing girl, we need more light something like a spot light not something overhead from the street lamp pole" Davona said "Use the light on your bike baby!" He kept raping and starts the bike up not getting off and shines it on her clapping his hands really getting into what he was rapping and revving the bikes engine getting louder and louder as he rev's the bike engine in rhythm with what he was saying "Go head girl, back that thang up! (Varoom) Drop it like it's hot! Drop it like it's hot! (Varoom) woman come show me what you're working with (Varoom), shake it fast, watch yourself, show me working with (Varoom), Drop it like it's hot (Varoom) shake it fast (Varoom) show me what you're working wit (Varoom) and he pulls off right pass her as she was backing it up and drooped it, but didn't get up quick enough but gave him room to jet right by her and keep going. Just as Marveece had come around the corner stopping watching her dancing for him till he went by her too then getting out the car asking her "Wasn't that him going up the wrong way on a one way, what happened?" Davona told her to just get in her car backing up fast smiling from being fool by him but liked how he had her entertained for a moment telling Marveece "This one has brains, he know how to think fast on his feet, I'll give him that! Fine ass red bone mother Fer" Marveece say "Watch your mouth." Davona says "But I'm talking about red bone!" Marveece says "I can dig it!" They look at each other and laugh then finish the rest of the Shaft verse using the red bone instead of John Shaft name.

Hutch is long gone from them and heads home fast as he could, hopes they wouldn't be there when he gets there. Coming up the street he stops his bike and looks for her car, then pulls into his drive way and rides his bike to the back of the house parking it by the path that leads to the alley way. He goes in the house and locks the door and sits in his chair in the dark for a moment thinking how lucky he was to get away from her. Then realizing he's not in the house by himself and goes upstairs to check on Elise but finding her not here. Checking the whole house and looking outside to see that her vehicle isn't there, he calls her to find out where did she go and when did she leave? She answers her phone as she was looking at the building from the address she wrote down from his note pad. Telling him she's decided to go home because she didn't feel right and wanted to check out something for herself about a hunch she's been having. Puzzled that she would just up and go like that he wanted to talk to her because they need to have a nice sit down. Thinking it has to do with this building and the woman in there he'd snuck off to see behind her back, she got really mad but didn't let on she was fuming over it and told him she didn't want to talk right now. She wasn't feeling up to it and would call him later so they can talk. He agreed and wished her well as a pair of light came through his window and he told her he was going to bed, she told him "You do that" thinking he had to be tired from having sex in a hurry like that and hung up.

Davona and Marveece was wondering if he made it home already and got out to knock on his door. Barking like a dog and talking like a woman saying "I'm the house sitter and Mr. house owner wouldn't be back for a couple of days" Marveece looks at Davona "He's got a dog girl and an house keeper you're going be living large. All you go to do is put it on him right and clink clink! He'll get that ring for you." They told the door they'll be back when he comes back and be prepared to greet the new woman of the house. Hutch slips and says in his regular voice "AH hell no you aint!" Marveece looks at the door and says "What did you say?" Hutch clears his throat and says meekly like a Mexican woman "Sorry I go back to my country when he come back bye bye!" Marveece looks at the door and tries to see in the peep hole but can't see anything and walks away with Davona.

The next day Markola woke up by the noise of his men in the trunk of his car bumping around trying to get someone's attention so they can get out.

The birds making noise flying over and around the barge plus the dinging of the floating buoys passed by the garbage barge as it floats pushed on the river. He opens his eyes slowly with the feeling like he were going up and down as he looks to see where he was and feels that big speed knot on his head from the head butt he received from the guy in the helmet. There are two men in the front seat and one next to him, they were still out and he looks at his hands and feet feeling them still in the plastic ties' that was put on him to keep his hands bound up like they would do to someone. Markola head is throbbing and has dry blood on it as he looks at himself in the rear view mirror from the back seat. He nudges the man next to him saying "Wake your dumb ass up, Stu-nod. You're snoring and drooling on the seat!" He kicks the seat in front of him waking the man in that seat up and wanting to know is his hand tied too. He told Markola "Yep!" Shakes his partner to wake him up also, now fully awake everyone is trying to see if they could get their hands lose.

The man next to Markola told him to hold still because he sees the knife, the one Hutch left in Markola's front jacket pocket. Taking it out and cutting Markola lose first so he can get cut lose to the others in the car then opening the trunk to cut the ones in there loose as well. They look up and see that their under a blue tarp and get from under it to find they are a float on a garbage barge floating down a river and see that it's being pushed by a tug. Markola told one of his men to go talk to the captain and stop this thing so they can get off. The man gets to the tug and up to talk to the captain, he lets the man know his tug don't stop because he's got a schedule to keep and time was money for him. Going back and relaying the message to Markola and figure out what he wanted to do. Markola went to talk with the captain and he repeated what he said to his man the first time. Markola smug in his attitude told the captain he's got money and went for his wallet but it wasn't there, so he asked his man to give him some cash and he didn't have a wallet either. Markola looked at his wrist and hands to see that his watch and rings were gone too, asked all the men to check for their wallets and valuables. None of them had anything, thinking he could threaten the captain but their guns were gone too. The captain told him when and where he was going ashore but until then him and his men could work for their passage and he's keeping the car to compensate for the meals he's got to feed all of them, but they have to sleep in their car because he's got no room on the tug for them.

Early that next morning the tug is letting Markola and his men get off and told them where the nearest diner is so he could use the phone, walking with his men two miles to some diner in Delaware mad about what happened and how they wound up here with no money or nothing. They make it to the diner and he's get to use the phone making a collect call to his house hoping his girl is there to pick up and he could have her wire him some cash to eat and get out of there because he didn't want his Uncle to find out what happened to him and his men he would never live down the humiliation. The phone rings for a few times and Ginger (his girl) is there yelling for someone to picks up the phone when no one did she answer it asking "who is this?" Markola Yells in to the phone "You stupid

BimBo! You don't know my voice! Stu-nods I'm surrounded by freaking Stu-nods/ Ba-fun gool" (Idiot/Mother-Fookers) he told her "I want you to send me some cash so I could get back there." Asking her how much cash she's got on her to send? His blood pressure went up ten points hearing her say to him 2$ and another 6$ in one of the purses in the closet. Gripping the phone a to choke it trying not to have a heart attack gritting his teeth talking to her "How come you only got that much money on you?" She told him "You never gives me more than 50 buck saying, I'm not going to waste your money on stupid stuff, Stupid!" Taking a deep breath and exhaling using the receiver hitting himself in the head with it, calming down he asked her "Do you know the phone number to my Uncles place." Changes his mind remembering he doesn't want his uncle to know about what happened and how he got there. Markola told Ginger to go in his bedroom behind the picture of him sitting in the chair with his suit on and a cigar in his mouth looking cool. Go behind it and there is a safe and the combination is 10-9-8. (She pauses and think to herself now didn't some idiot have a similar combination in space somewhere?) Then listening to him tell her which way to turn to the tumbler to get the number right so she could open the safe and take out only 5,000$ and send it to him there at the diner ending with "You stupid Bimbo" and hangs up the phone. She said "O-k!" Doing what he wanted opening the safe looking at all that money, as if a light bulb went off and played a movie of him calling her all kinds of "Bimbo's, Dumb C-word, Tramp, B's, Stu-nods, flock head" and the most insulting thing he ever told her was "Just suck my thing you bubble lip B. First wipe that lip stick off!" She looks at all that money and went to the closet grabs a small travel bag opening it and putting all the money in that safe in it, then going down stairs getting the mustard, ketchup with the squirt mayo and went to work on each of his pictures in the house. Going back down stairs and getting a bottle of champagne popping it and drinking from the bottle like she was celebrating winning the number. She looks at all the money in that travel bag and thought careful about what she was going to do next, because she knows he'll come looking for her so leaving out two stacks of cash out she's going to spend. Going to find every picture she took with him and ripping her image out of it and putting it in a plastic bag going out to the BBQ grill lighting it on fire. Getting dressed putting on two sets of clothes and carrying an extra pair of shoes to change as well. She took another bigger bag and put the smaller travel bag with the cash and all jewelry in the house in it, then took all her wigs laying them out on the bed even all the blond ones she's got. Thinking he's never seen her natural dark brunette hair so she kept on the blond one knowing she's going to take it off at some point when she changes her clothes. Ready to go she goes and finds all the keys to the car he's got there and spear ones too plus the house keys and calling a cab to drop her at the subway station she wants to let off in Brooklyn.

When the cabby came she had all the doors locked with keys broke off in them waiting outside the house at the curb letting everyone get a good look at her and what she was wearing as she got in the cab with her big bag. Telling the cabby to drop her at a subway station far from his house and tipping the driver nicely before she goes down to catch her train, once there she lets the train with people leave the station as she waits for another one. Quickly changing out of her top layer of clothes putting her clothes in the garbage just as the another train came into the station, she got on and travel from Brooklyn to Manhattan and the second stop in that borough she got off the train and went to the street to hail a cab. Telling the cabby head to the nearest bus station where she bought a ticket down south and gave her big suitcase with clothes to a homeless person with some cash if they took the bag which they did happily and the cash too. When the bus came she got on putting the smaller travel bag next to her then putting in her ear phones of the I-pod she had closing her eyes as the bus pulls off.

Late that evening Markola is sitting in the back of a Moving truck trailer with his men being bumped around and hit with the boxes on their way back to New York. The Bus Ginger is on happens to pass the truck going the other way as she looks at the tractor trailer thinking to herself "How pretty it looks with all those lights on it" not knowing in back of that same trailer is Markola and his men. He is thinking to himself how stupid of him to even think she was capable of sending him the cash she's probably shopping getting some shoe or something stupid broad! Her brain went numb seeing that much cash, thinking he'll back slap her ass for being so dumb and not sending him the money. It's very late and Markola and his men finally get to his house, he's so mad he starts yelling before he even gets to the house "You stupid Bitch! I'm going to kill your ass if you went shopping! How could not send the f-ing cash for me to come home!" He gets to the front door and knocks on it yelling for her to open the door but there is no answer so he rings the bell, then he pounds on the door but there is no answer still. He talks softly to her "Ok sweet heart I'm not that mad any more if you just open the door we can talk about your mistake and see how it won't happen again!" Still no answer and he starts back to pounding on the door for her to open it up, then telling one of his men to kick the thing open. Watching one by one try to kick and then ram the door open but he realizes those door he had put in were meant to stop bullets even a hand held battering ram would do little to open it. Sitting down and telling the men to go find a way in and come get him when they get it open. They walk around the sides and back trying every door they saw even the basement door, but one man tried the side door to the kitchen and found it open. Going inside and starts to the front to open the front door for Markola but he sees the food and as starving as he was he makes a sandwich. Another man at the back door saw him and taps on the door for him to open it and he too heads for the food. One by one all Markola men find the sliding back door open and see the others eating in the kitchen and join them, Markola is sitting out front for a long while and he starts wondering how long does it take for them to get inside his house even if they had to break the glass door in back. He gets up and walks around the side and sees the light on and then heads to the back where he finds the sliding glass door open. Going inside and sees in the kitchen all his men eating sandwiches or plates of food they heated up. He takes the sandwich right of the nearest man to him hands and starts to eating it, trying to yell at them calling them all kinds of name not nice but all they hear is mumbled and muffled words through him chewing and breathing heavy. They shake their heads as to agreeing to him not knowing what he's really trying to shout at them. The loud muffles stops and nothing but chewing and heavy breathing is heard beside scrapping of forks on plates and loud slurps and sips along with the occasional "Umm." One man heads in to the living room and comes back to the kitchen trying to say something with food in his mouth but they can't understand him saying "Boss come here and look at this!" He goes to see what it is and drops his food after seeing his picture with mustard and ketchup on it and then sees the others. He goes upstairs looking at the others on the way up to his bedroom where he yells loudly "YOU BITCH! I'M GOING TO FREAKING KILL YOUR BLOND BIMBO ASS! YOU'RE FOCKING DEAD YOU HEAR ME!" Looking at the safe cleaned out his pictures all messed up and her wigs on the bed with pictures of them tore up. He sits there and looks at the safe thinking how could he been so stupid to think that broad was dumb like that, how was he going to explain it to his uncle how all that money got took by a woman he gave the combination too. Unless he had it replaced and thought about that card but it was his wallet that got took by that helmet mook along with his other stuff. Getting on the phone and calling around to find his cousin Mario and hoping to get in touch with him. Glad he's got his answering machine on but have flash backs at what he had to do to get change for the phone down in Delaware at that diner. He leaves messages for Mario to get to his house because they have to see some broads about a mook a on bike that took something from him but knew he couldn't tell him what happened about the Ginger taking the money from the safe. Going back down stairs telling his men go home and get rest they're going to need it and get their gun and other ID"s. Then going back upstairs to take a shower and get some sleep for tomorrow.

Early in the morning Hutch at the garage ready for work and hearing it from Meepbo about how they were supposed to be out of the building two weeks ago. He told Hutch they're going to be doing long hours this week to make up for time work needed to get out of the building. Meepbo being the greedy man that he is answered the request orders for doing more floors but left the order on his desk as he was talking to Hutch about them being behind and having to stay longer hours to make up the work. Meepbo went to get his coffee and left Hutch in his office where he saw the forms for more floors done in that building. Hutch got mad at Meepbo trying to make them work longer and hard for nothing where he would collect for more work without paying them for the work done. Meepbo came back to the office and he told Hutch he might have him come back to sign for his renewal of health benefits and insurance. Hutch asked him "Could I sign at the end of the day" and Meepbo told him if he wants then Hutch thought about it and changed his mind. Thinking of how sneaky Meepbo is and he knows the mail girl come there before the end of the day so he said call him and he'll come back to sign them.

Also that morning Elise didn't go to work and decides to go confront the woman she thought was seeing Hutch and he's been sneaking around on her with. She was in her vehicle talking with herself to make sure how she was going to tell this woman off, if she thinks she just to take her man without a fight then she's got another thing coming. Standing outside in front of the building now looking up trying to see if she would live in the front part of the building, where just in case there might have to be a brick thrown through the window to send a better message case the talking didn't get through to her. Then Markola and Mario pulled and gets out their car talking loud about this mook he called Hutch and how he was going to fix all three of them broads he was seeing. Elise heard him say Hutch's name and she stops him and asked him "Did he know Hutch?" Markola looked at Elise "Yeah I know that mook" and asked her "Was you seeing him too, because it's bad enough he came to the strip club and bought them drinks just to see them women that use to work for me, now he's seeing another in this building." Asking her "Was he going to buy your new furniture and things too." She told Markola she don't live in that rat trap of a building, she's got better taste than that. She's even madder wanting to know more about those three stripping B's he's been seeing and buying thing for because he's her fiancée and was trying to get end their relationship. She now knows he was seeing not one but three stripping BITCHES! Markola looks at Mario then Elise "Guess you're not seeing him anymore then huh?" Elise was really mad going on about fixing his ass but first she wanted to get her hands on those women that think they're going to steal him away from her and starts heading in the building. Markola got an idea and stops her saying "I want to fix that mook Uh Hutch too" and asked her could they talk about it somewhere else instead of in front of the building and suggest there is a nice breakfast place not far from here that serves a very good breakfast they can talk over. She told him "OK!" but she wasn't leaving her vehicle around there and he told her "Why don't you drive me and my cousin will follow in my car" and they head to the restaurant. Walking in the place they sit in the one of the divider booths in the middle of the diner facing the window from those at the counter. Sitting in the middle on the right hand side facing towards the entrance as Elise had her back to it. At the table Elise wants to know from Markola how long Hutch's been seeing these strippers and what else did he do for them. Showing him how upset she was after he told they were strippers in that building and some of the things Hutch did for them. Markola starts feeding her more stories about things he did that weren't true but he knew that would upset her even more.

Telling her Hutch would come to his strip club and have sex with other strippers and get them things too, but those three were his favorites because he did the most for them. Watching her facial expression as he went on about Hutch and the three of them, how he would spend money on them till she was all worked up enough for him to ask "How would you like to get even with him in such a way it would make him regret it?" She looked at him and asked "like what?" He told her all she has to do is get his Credit card and bring it to him. Puzzled by his question she asked "What's his Credit card got to do with fixing him and his cheating on me with those stripper bitches?" Markola says to her "With that kind of money he's got" She cut him off by saying "I know he's got a little money and a big house but to take his Credit card unless he showed you a little more than he showed me!" Markola looks at Mario and thought she don't know about the Credit card and it's Unlimited Funds ability so he told her "Yeah he's got 100 Grand more on his card because our machines showed it when he used it for the strippers to get them drinks and screw with them in the back V.I.P section of the club." Mario looks at Markola asking "Where's the V.I.P section that let you screw in the back of the club?" Markola kicked him hard. Mario got the message in pain quick "Oh that V.I.P. section yeah I've seen him back there with even two women at one time that had V.D or was it herpes I couldn't tell" Markola looks at her face after Mario said that and went "Hope you didn't get very intamid with that guy or you could have something you don't know you have!" She says "Hell no and it's a good thing too, I could have something that he gave me and could take me out of here the nerve of that bastard!" Markola knew he struck a nerve with her saying that and smiled before asking her again to get his Credit card for him and even sweeten it by saying "I'll give you some cash for your trouble too!" That way she could buy something to flaunt it in front of him to brag about her not being with him anymore when he sees her. Elise wanted to get her hands on them and asked Markola of the three which is Hutch's favorite because that Bitch she wants to see her face to face to let her know "I beat her and she can't have what I have".

On the other side one booth down from them were Janet and Erikaa, they were having breakfast there because none of them felt like cooking that morning and Janet said she would treat for it. Donna stayed home she didn't feel like leaving the house and let the two of them go but wanted a sandwich brought back for her. When Mario made that comment about Hutch and strippers having diseases, she wanted to jump over straight at him about it. Erikaa told her not to or she would give them away being there, so they just listened to Markola and Mario plot with Elise to get Hutch's Credit card. When the waitress came with Donna's sandwich, Janet wanted the check and told Erikaa "When they leave just don't turn around and keep walking till they get outside to the vehicle." Janet paid the check said softly "Erikaa go to the vehicle, I'll be right there" As Erikaa was leaving Markola looked at her walk out of the diner and saw Janet looking back at him but turned quickly back to the cashier. He looked at the person at the cashier catching a glimpse thinking she looks familiar but didn't get a good look at her then watched her leave the diner. Not giving it another thought he gets back to talking to Elise into getting Hutch's Credit card for him before she really finds out how much it's really worth. Elise was concentrated on getting her hands on one of the women that he favors. Markola calls his men told them to meet him at the building where the girls live, he doesn't want them to leave before he gets there with someone that wants to see them. Then he says "After you see them, then will she try and get the Credit card from Hutch for him?" She agreed just as long as she gets to see the one he really likes so she can brag in her face about it.

Janet and Erikaa get back to their apartment upset about something talking to each other as Donna asked them "Where's my sandwich?" Janet put the sandwich on the table telling her what she and Erikaa just heard about Elise-a-Bitch. The woman who Hutch wanted to get with is planning with Markola to get Hutch's Credit card from him. Donna told them to slow down asking them "You've seen Markola. He's back in town already?" Janet says "Yeah, he's with Elise-a-bitch! Hutch would be dating, but wouldn't know about her ass being with Markola and their planning against him." Janet and Erikaa told Donna everything they heard them talking about at the diner, then got out of there before he saw them. He even had his cowardly cousin Mario with him and the three of them were in the booth on the other side one down from their booth in the middle of the diner. Donna told them they better call Hutch and let him know Markola is back with his cowardly cousin Mario Lamehola, who uses a gun to fight a real man with. He can't fight with his hands being the bitch man that he is. They don't want Hutch walking into danger of getting hurt and his Credit card taken from him if their all working together. The slamming of car doors is heard as his men arrive at the building and have three other cars as back up. Two of them have men and the third one has two heavy set former professional wrestling women Container Crusher Kathy and former world wrestling champion Silver back breaker Beatrice. In case Marveece and Davona shows up again. The men need pro help with those two beastly women so they thought to have some of their own on hand as they wait for Markola to get there.

Hutch is at working doing his normal throwing in heavy things in the back of the truck and letting it crush the things up and having people watch as the biggest pieces of office furniture is being crushed by the truck making the loud "Crunch & Boom!" He doesn't hear his phone rings from the noise as Donna calls hoping to get him and let him know about Markola and Elise-the-bitch! Markola pulls up to the building in Elise's vehicle and told her give him a few minutes with these broads. He wants to keep Elise as surprise thinking if he got a chance to blind fold them first, just to keep the edge on their mook boyfriend Hutch. Then he's not going to know she's in on it because they saw her face, Elise agreed with that idea but don't want to be kept out too long and as long as she gets a look at Hutch's favorite.

Erikaa was looking out the window and saw all the men down stairs and runs to get Donna and Janet to show them. Janet saw Markola get out of Elise's vehicle with her and he stands there talking to her then she gets back in the vehicle, at the window Janet looks at Donna "Now you see what we were saying!" Donna went to calling Hutch again hoping he answers the phone that time but kept calling back when she got the voice mail so leaving a message about as they knocked on the door makes her look at Janet and Erikaa with concern on her face. They didn't panic hearing the bang as its gets kicked open and this huge man walks in looking at them. Markola walks in right behind him and two more men behind him, they see the women standing there Janet with a bat and Erikaa with a lamp in her hands and Donna with her hands on her hips. Markola looks at them wanting to know why all the violence. He explains didn't come there to get into a big ole fight with them or for them wind up hurt, because if they really think they could take on his muscle then let him get a chair and have the front row seat to this ten second bout. Laughing "That's how long it would take for them to hurt you women because they have no problem smashing women like men too." Donna thinks about it knowing she's got to be smart and wants to know what did he want? He looks at her and asked "Where's the mook and his monsters" because he wants another round and this time the outcome will not be him in a car on a garbage barge floating down the river, instead it'll be him at dinner with a big smile on his face laughing about what he got for the mook. Having them sit on their couch after dropping the weapons and told Donna she needs to call the mook now and waits for her to dial the number.

Hutch is standing by the back of the truck and his cell ringing, he answers and it is Meepbo asking him to get back to the office so he could sign the papers for his insurance. He told Meepbo to "Let your watch dog know I got to leave before I have to stuff him in one of the containers for leaving the job." Meepbo laughs at what Hutch called Moni and asked "Where's the little brown nose loud mouth?" Hutch told Meepbo "I'm impressed you finally called your pet lick ass the name he is and is that on his ownership papers you have in the office" Going in the building and in the elevator up to the floor to find Moni but in the elevator the signal for Hutch's phone doesn't go through as Donna was calling him. In the apartment Markola is waiting for Donna to get Hutch on his cell and down in her vehicle Elise feels she waited long enough and starts up to the apartment. When she gets to the door she argues with the man outside making him come in there to get Markola about her wanting to come in. Markola told his men to tie them up and blindfold them too as he goes the door and him and Elise have a little argument about her and how she was supposed to wait for him to send for her. She wanted to see which one Hutch had a favorite thing for and walks in with Markola to see three women on the couch blindfolded and tied up. She asked him "Point out which one it is" and Markola points to Janet and then changes to point to Donna saying "This one because at the club she was so protective of him and all she had to do was walk away." Donna asked "Who's there! Who are you talking to Markola?" Elise said "Me Bitch! You can't see who I am and you better be thankful you can't just know this if you think you're going to take what's mine you get another thing coming." She rears back to slap Donna and Markola stops her mid swing telling her "She hasn't made contact yet and don't need to" Then changes his mind and says "Maybe that's what is needed to make a point go ahead but you only get one." Standing aside and lets Elise slap Donna(Whap!) Erikaa stood up and yells "YOU BITCH!" Elise turns (Whap!) hitting Erikaa too. Janet sat there for a moment being still sizing up where Elise was standing then explodes off the couch charging Elise knocking her down, falling on her using her hands swing at Elise hitting her once in the face before one of the men grabs Janet off her. Elise gets up holding her eye as she looks at Janet being held by the man and he lets her pick a shot at Janet and then another one. Donna doing what Janet did and listened sizing up where everyone stood in the room and everything moves as movie in slow motion, as she jump up just as Elise was about to hit Janet again but Elise gets foot slapped kicked in the face knocking her back and across the coffee table to the floor as Markola yells "WHAT THE FOCK!!!" Then tells the men to tie their feet before they decide to kick him and he has to shoot one of them Bitches. Janet smiles knowing Donna did something to Elise because she could hear Markola picking her up off the floor. The men quickly tie all three of their feet and Elise is holding the same side of her face where Janet slapped her the first time, but now her Jaw and lips starts to swell from Donna kicking her that way. The man watched Donna get attacked by Elise and has no way of defending herself from the vicious way Elise gets to pick her shots hitting the mark each time in the face and body. Janet and Erikaa cry out for her to "Stop!" Knowing their friend can't help but hear her taking what is dished out to her by Elise as Markola watches. Janet yells "How you going to get your card if she can't talk." Those words make him go to stop Elise but that final punch thrown makes the blindfold come off and Donna gets a good look at Elise face to face. Markola pulls her off Donna "See what you did now, she knows what you look like!" Elise said "So take her with you there's still two more that could talk, they have mouths for other things like talking too don't you think." Markola told the men to take a sheet off the bed and cover her so no one see what's under it when they leave, then turns to Janet and Erikaa and told them "You need to get in touch with that mook Hutch if you want to see her again. Better not have the police involved or they will find what's left of her somewhere if they find something." Elise is still mad about her face and knows she's going to have to hide what happened as they all leave and the men carry Donna out like kidnapped person over one of their shoulders and put in the trunk of his car and drove off. Janet and Erikaa left behind in the apartment gets their hands and feet free, Erikaa gets ice for Janet's face as she calls to try and get in touch with Hutch again. He is sitting in Meepbo's office listening to him talk about how he needs to get his hands on his favorite cologne but don't know who sells it, the stuff he found it in the bathroom in the garage and since he's used it on himself he's been having the best sex he's had in years with his wife Toni pointing to the sliver capped bottle on his desk. Hutch looks at the little sliver capped bottle of cologne Meepbo put in front of him on the desk about to say that was his bottle of cologne when his cell phone rings. Answering it to hear Janet upset crying about Donna and how Markola came there with Elise. They took Donna and want your Credit card and no cop involved or we won't find Donna alive but in pieces somewhere if they let us find her at all. Hutch told her to slow down because she was talking so fast he could barely understood her, so he talks to her where she was calm enough to tell him everything that happened at the apartment. How Markola took Donna, he told them he's on his way soon as he's done with his boss and this paper work, but Meepbo over heard him and said better get to signing these papers for his insurance before you go running off. Asking "What was you about to say the cologne was what and where should he look for more."

Hutch mind is racing about Markola taking Donna thinking of what his next move is going to be, as he drowns out Meepbo talking about the cologne. Thinking about how Markola wants his Credit card but looks at the little bottle of cologne on Meepbo's desk thinking what he said about "Having the best sex of his life" because of that cologne. He sees his wallet under some papers on the desk and remembers he marked up Markola's credit card with Meepbo's name the last time. While Meepbo said "He's got to use the bathroom" Hutch takes his wallet and the cologne bottle off his desk. Meepbo came out the bathroom and Hutch told him "I'm going to work on that cologne problem for you if I can get go take care of something that just came up." Meepbo said "I overheard you having trouble so take as much time as you needs and don't forget my cologne." Hutch looked at Meepbo "Thanks I won't" Leaving out his office Hutch took his own vehicle over the building where Janet and Erikaa are waiting for him. Wasn't long Hutch is looking at the door kicked open and goes in there calling Janet and Erikaa's name to find them in the living room crying. Janet and Erikaa hold him tight as they cry aloud feeling bad about Donna and safe that he's there now. Hutch just holds them, comforting them, letting them get it out of their system for a moment, feeling and hearing him tell them it's going to be Ok. He gets a looks at Janet and wants to know who did that to her seeing her lips swollen and cheek red. Janet told him "I got my shot in too so don't feel bad it'll heal. Donna got her shot in real good from the way she cried out hitting the floor after Donna got hers in, but they let her get at Donna for a bit too" Erikaa told him "Elise-the Bitch! She was here with Markola. She got to Donna bad because she could hear her getting her good until Janet said something" Janet added "They heard them at this diner they were having breakfast at talking about you and how they can get their hands on your Credit card."

Hutch (thought because he bought some drinks at the strip club this guy's got a hard on for my Credit card and wants to run up the bill more wow.) told them he's can't figure out how Elise got involved with Markola. Wondering if she ever work at the strip club before they got there or during the time they worked there. Janet and Erikaa told him they never seen her there and they've worked there for two years, then Hutch says "We can figure out more things later" and told them got get their stuff together because they're going to stay at his house and "Don't worry there will be no kicking open my door" They grab something for Donna too "She's going to need clothes when I get her back!" Going to the hardware store buying some pad locks, speaker wire and rubber gloves a screw gun with screws and long nails, foils and cans of spray oil and lighter fluid they watch Hutch rig an anti-thief system on their windows and doors. If any one came in there through the windows they would have a hot oily time putting themselves out after being shocked by the wires running across the entrances. Janet and Erikaa helped him set everything up in their apartment before they left out and they asked him "Did you study under MacGyver or Mr. Tee from how fast you set up everything" He laughs and says "Both of them but it come from years of on the job training Italians not to bother my truck long story." On his way to his house he kept thinking about Donna and how to get her from Markola as quick as possible but then remembers he's got Meepbo's wallet. He thought if he gives him Meepbo's card and Meepbo reports it stolen then the cops would get Markola but then how is he going to get Donna back. They get to Hutch's house and he shows them the alarm system where it is on the wall and how to turn it on and off. Helping them get settled in his place and then made a couple call to some of his brothers to come over, he calls Mack, Derrick, 2Soon, C-man, Dave, Ron, Jazz, La-Machine, Tyrone, Tys, Byron, Herb, Dougie, and Goodie with Steel. When some of the GDM.4.L get to Hutch's house and he fills them in on this Markola so they could let the others know but he needs some good ideas about how to handling this without the cops till he gets back Donna. Mack asked him "Where's the girls." Hutch told him they're up in his bedroom resting. Dave had to let Hutch know it was his spending when he gets really drunk "You get too generous with your cash big bruh and a lot of time we can't stop your big ass!" 2Soon looks at Hutch and says "Dave's right! From now on we decided to take your wallet whenever we go out drinking fam it's for you own good." Hutch looked at all of them and said "Fine but which one is going to take it when I get drunk and catch a beat ass. We'll we have to figure out something about this Markola ass wipe first!" They starts thinking about things and what to do when Hutch says "I think better with a drink!" They all looked at each other and agreed Hutch is right they do think better with a few drinks in them. The more they drank the better an idea they would come up with, till they had a good few thoughts but the main thing was to get Markola and make sure he doesn't come back any more. Erikaa and Janet hear all this laughing coming from down stairs and Erikaa went down. Janet not wanting anyone to see her face but knew she was amongst friends came down anyways. Erikaa gets down first and they all say "Hello" to her but rush over to Janet when she came down asking "What happened to her?" She told them who did it and how they got to Donna too. They all promised with Hutch they're going to get Donna back unharmed and let her get even with Elise one on one showing her about the hand game giving Janet a few pointers on boxing.

A short time later they all were pretty tipsy and left Hutch with Janet and Erikaa, saying they had to get up and go to work too but will come there right after to check like Hutch wanted. Janet and Erikaa walk his brothers out and came back to the living room to see Hutch in deep thought sitting in his chair.

He was blaming himself for Donna being grabbed and how he should have had them come to his place after doing that to Markola. He didn't think they would get back so fast and come right after them instead of him. Janet tries to comfort him with Erikaa's help, both sits on either side of the chair leaning on him Janet says "You had no idea this would happen. How could you know what a meat head like that would do after being sent sailing off on a garbage Barge." Sitting there they try making him feel better but he's still trying to come up with just the right plan and thinking about some of things his brothers came up with saying to them "Hope Donna knows I'm going to get her back." Then told Janet and Erikaa they would be staying at Goodies' house if what they say is true about Elise. Reminding them she knows where he lives too and could easily tell Markola that information, they could come there and he doesn't want the Janet or Erikaa there if things get nasty. Having them caught in the cross fire of things getting handled, they understood and told him if Donna was there she would agree they didn't want to cause him all this trouble. Hutch walks over to Janet and holds her tight and looks her in the eyes "All of you are worth this and more." He stretches his hands out for Erikaa and she comes over to him and he holds both of them to let them feel his warmth for them like he never wants to let them go. They feel the big man's caring for them in that hug he gives, they feel him take a big deep breath exhaling in a growl like a big bear in frustration and they hold him tight as both women let the tears roll down their faces. He watches them go upstairs and told them he'll be up in a while so they can get comfortable but as they fell asleep, Hutch was down stairs thinking really hard about what he was going to do. Then going up stairs thinking a nice hot shower would clear his thoughts and he takes one. After the shower he was looking at his dresser draw and the little bottles of cologne lined up on it and remembers what Meepbo was saying about the silver capped one and thought he needs to check out what Meepbo was talking about as he looks at the three types of capped cologne up there.

The next day he gets up making sure Janet and Erikaa are up and ready when Goodie gets there to take them to his place before he goes to work. Taking the three colored capped colognes with him to try and find out more about them other than the smell of the colognes. At the sandwich shop getting breakfast turkey bacon eggs and turkey sausage before work Hutch was looking at the sliver capped cologne when Gerard came over to him and asked "How was things going because ever since he gave him one of the colognes things for him couldn't be better" Hutch asked Gerard "When you sprays that cologne on you what happen" being curious Gerard smiled explaining "My gal becomes very aggressive but seductive for me and we have the wildest sex plus it give my thing a wider longer feel she always tells me. I feel bigger and thicker each time to her." He went on about how when he sweats she got very horny and they go at it like two high school teens very under sexed. With that information trying to keep him from giving every sexual detail about each position they achieved listening to Gerard for as long as he could without blushing. Thanking him for sharing his experiences like that. Hutch leaves to get to the building before the work crew got there. Sitting there listening to the radio but thinking about the little bottle next to him, watching the van pull up in front of him letting out the work crew and Moni gets out last.

The day goes normal with Hutch working up a good sweat from the heat on this bright sunny hot day thinking how was he going to test the cologne and on who. He wanted to see it work for himself so his first subject was the security guard and the sliver capped one. Having a conversation with him about the day, how nice and bright it was.

That got him to move out his seat towards the door to see and Hutch sprays a nice cloud of mist for him to walk into on the way back to his seat. Apologizing explaining he was going to walk into the mist himself that's how he puts cologne on to keep the funk off him. The guard told him it smells good and he don't mind but says

"Sorry you used it on me." Hutch told him he'll just have to use soap from the bathroom and heads to the restroom. Going in there for a couple second and coming back out Hutch watches as women coming into the building see the guard there sweating but sniffing as they came in and head right over to him. Giving him compliments about his looks and how they never noticed him before and some even gave him their numbers and a kiss too. Seeing how that one works now he starts wondering who he going to test the black capped one on, it doesn't take long for him to find his next tester. This thin man was getting yelled at by his large woman walking with four others, she didn't care who heard her calling him names humiliating him in public like that as they came down the street. Seeing the man sweating from carrying all their stuff as Hutch walks right up to him spraying him good, asking "Do you want to buy some cologne?" The man says "No thanks but it smells alright." Hutch watched as the man gets yelled at by the woman and told to walk in front of her like some child on punishment. The cologne she smelled as she walked by starts having an effect on her right away as she yelled at him and he turned around and looking at her mad. Her eyebrows raised and eyes got wide as he told her "Enough! I'm not some child of yours, I'm your man!" The woman's friends went next to her telling her how was she going to take that from him but they too caught a whiff and smelled the cologne blowing up wind at them and stopped suggesting to their friend. He told them "You need to be quite and mind your business nagging cows!" Noticing the look of fear in their faces he told him "You need to be carrying some of your own stuff." They rush over to get the bags they had him carrying and took them from him saying "Sorry for being so rude to him before." Hutch watched and came over to the man and said "Since you smell different they listen don't they?" He gave the man the little black capped bottle and told him use it every once in a while and bet your life would be a whole lot better. He agreed since Hutch sprayed him with that cologne his woman and her friends did starts acting as if he were the big man and took the bottle of cologne from him saying "I will use it in good health and maybe now I could get some the way I wanted this time without having to put on that bib getting it all wet from" Hutch stops him from saying any more

"Hey bruh that's good you the man again but I don't need to have mental picture of that in my head." Turning and walking back up the block now knowing what the black capped bottle does and then looking at the gold capped bottle wondering but then it hits him. When he used it on the flowers that time he went to see Moni in the hospital that's why he got his ass beat again, also guessing Moni used it on himself and that's what caused the riot at the Two Potator.

The rest of the day Moni was his normal annoying self to Hutch every time he would look around there was Moni watching from the door way and up in the window, down the block and across the street at lunch time. Hutch was thinking of a good prank to pull on Moni when the idea came to him why not get him hook up with Marveece's friend and use the sliver capped cologne to do it. When a break came Hutch approached Moni and told him "Stop trying to think hard of a way to get me. Let's have a truce by letting me hook you up with one of my girls." Moni looked at Hutch and didn't say anything thinking about what he said and asked him "What does she look like?" Hutch told him "She is a rare fine, only one of her kind I hope." Moni asked "Was she packing?" Hutch went "Oh yeah! She's packing all over, in fact she's what I call thick thickness not fat but grotested er robusted kind you like."

Moni wanted to know what's the catch and "Is she pretty?" Hutch said "Hell yeah, she's pretty to another gorilla uh all my fellas!" He talks to Moni about her body finding out Moni wants a woman with meat on her but not fat. Hutch convinces him to go on the date and even pick his own place to eat at. Moni wanted to eat at this place in Manhattan close to the Greenwich Village that was popular with people because of the food and drinks served there. Hutch asked him to give him some time to get in touch with her and he would set the time and night they would meet. Moni told him "If this was another trick you would regret it!" Hutch responds "No way! It's not a trick and I won't let you down, because you two have to meet, I'll see to that!" The rest of the work day Moni didn't bother Hutch but then he saw some men way down the block from him stop and pointing. He looked carefully and saw more men standing and pointing at something wondering what it could be until he saw Kameisha coming that way. She is the only thing that would have men doing that, so he ducks out of sight as all the men was looking at her dressed in something sexy and tight coming up that way. She walks to where his truck was parked in front of the building and looks around for him but doesn't see him. Looking around at all the men who work with him, she walks very sultry over to one of the workers and stands right in front of him. He faints not before pointing at another one, She looks at him pointing and says "Don't you move!" Walking over to him as he stands there swallowing nervously. She asked him "Do you know the driver to the truck right there?" He smiles answering "Si" She then asked him "Where is he?" The worker spoke Mexican "Yo no K say senior Rita!" She looked at him "Como say Yama truck driver?" He shrugged shoulders saying "Sorry no!" She looked at him for a moment sucked her teeth and exhaled before going in her purse and looking for something. She pulls out some photos and shows the worker whose jaw dropped open and eyes got wide then spoke proper English to her every question after seeing what she showed him. He told her "Hutch was around there a minute ago but I didn't see where he went" She asked "You know anything at all about Hutch?" Then showed the worker again what she pulled out of her purse. He licked his lips blinking at it. Saying "I'll find out his full name, mailing address, home phone number, license plate number to what kind of car he drives, social security number, what time he goes to bed and had for dinner, and even what kind of toilet paper one ply or two he uses even if I have to beat it out of someone to get it" She smiled and told him "Good when you get that I'll make sure you get to meet this! Until then look at one more time." Giving him another quick look at the photo again, snatching it away putting it back in her purse then walking back down the block. Every man around watched her hips sway walking down the block and turns the corner, the other workers rush over to him asking "What did she show to make him want to go after Hutch like that?" He told them "She had a picture of this healthy toned body beautiful dark haired Mexican woman. Saying she's one of many friends of her that she would have do things to me I'd like to meet and remember having it done for the rest of my life." He describes the picture of her doing a side to side split naked on her back oiled up eating a pickle in way that would have a man drool pointing her finger to somewhere any man would want to be in now. Hutch came back around and the workers all went back to work in the building except one who starts asking Hutch all kind of questions about his life and what he likes to eat. He didn't answers any questions but asked him "What did she promise you?" The man tries to play dumb but Hutch told him "She did the same thing to another worker last time." Hutch told him the workers name pointing him out. He drops his head in shame as Hutch told him "She could be very persuasive can't she?" Not mad at what he tried to get and letting the man go back in the building without giving him any information so they can finish up for that day.

On the way home Hutch saw what looked like Marveece and followed him to this gas station where he looked around to see if her friend was with her and then approached Marveece while she was getting gas. "Excuse me. Can I talk with you for moment" Marveece looked at Hutch and starts to tell him go away she don't want to buy anything or give money but doing a double take look at him lets out a loud "Ooooh Marveece your Steel's friend aren't you. I don't forget a face and is he with you?" Hutch said "Nope! That's why I want to talk to you." Marveece looked at Hutch "Oooh Marveece, Then we have nothing to talk about good night baby." Hutch says "Ok guess you don't want to see Steel then." Marveece Lets out a big "OOOH Marveece! Wait a minute you. Why be so hostile to me and keep me from getting my piece of Sta-eel!" Asking "What do you want from me?" Listening to Hutch say "I want you to call off her girlfriend, what's her name anyways?" Marveece goes "Oooh Marveece. You want to know my friends name but don't want to meet her why?" Hutch says "She's not my type alright!" Marveece says "Yeah we saw your skinny ass woman's type!" Hutch laughs and told him "She's not my type either, pysco with those hidden issues don't think so!" Telling Marveece she would be happy with a man that would appreciate her for who she is and what they could be together, but in order for that to work they have to meet at this place in Manhattan. Marveece asked "What's in it for me?" Hutch said "I would bring Steel if you could get your girlfriend to meet my friend Moni" Marveece explained

Davona's like a pit bull lock jaw, once she gets her teeth locked on a man it's hard for her to see another man. Hutch made a comment about not having his shots and don't look forward to having to take any so they talked some more with Marveece agreeing long as Steel would be there, they set a meet time agreeing on it. Marveece said to call him and Hutch convinces Marveece to give up his number. She pulls out one of his business card and writes on the back of it after kissing it saying "Give it to my baby Steel say it's from his future coming!" Hutch looks at the front which reads "Marveece's Marvelous Magical Miracle Makeovers Manicures Making Many Men, Movie Moguls and Multi-Millionaires Move Mad Money on Your Modern Matrimonies. Hutch looks at the card hard about to say something but Marveece says "Believe me I bring out the best of any women hair and looks that comes to see me. When they leave and always bring back ten friends or more, to see me because I do wonders for women." Hutch told Marveece just have his girl there and he'll show up with Steel and his man that he knows would be the perfect match for his girl. Marveece was happy about going to see Steel he gets on the phone after Hutch walks away and arranges the meet in Manhattan that night. At the same time Hutch was calling Moni telling him about the meeting that night and to get ready adding "This woman likes a man that smells like he just got out of the shower." Hoping he doesn't use that Gold capped cologne on himself but asked him to bring it with him because he needs some for a date he's got. Moni excited about the date didn't question why Hutch wanted the cologne back and told him he would be there and needed to know what time should he show up? Hutch told him to take a shower now and he'll call him when he gets home. Racing home thinking about how he was going to make everything work, now that he knows about those colognes and what they do. Calling Janet and Erikaa making sure they are alright letting them know if they need anything just tell Goodie and he'll get it for them. Janet said "I know you are working on getting Donna back I can hear it in your voice baby." Hutch answers her "Wow you know me like that already huh!" Erikaa also says in a sultry way "We all feel you like that big Bear!" Hutch smiled then said "I got more reasons not to let you two down then!" Janet ends the conversation with "Work your thing baby and bring her back to us!" Hutch hangs up and gets more focused than ever on what he has to do starting with getting Marveece's girl off his back as he pulls up to this drive way and gets out of his vehicle and goes in the house. Dave and Tys with Jazz Happen to drop by Hutch's house with their dates for the night after he got all cleaned up wanting to know what he was going to do that night. Hutch wanted to experiment with the colognes to see what kind of effects they would have if he mixed them but couldn't tell his brothers what he was going to do to them. Telling them he had to meet with someone in a little bit but wanted to know what kind of smell should he use and one by one took his brother up to the bathroom starting with Tys having him close his eyes explaining it's like a smell test. With Tys eyes using closed the combo of the just one spritz of the Black and three spritz of the Sliver capped cologne on him and having his go back to his date. Jazz comes up and using the combo of one spritz of the Gold capped and three spritz of the Silver capped and having him go back down to his date, then Dave came up last and he used the one spritz of the of both Black and Gold with three spritz of the Silver capped cologne letting go back down to his date. Before Hutch came down stairs he turns up the heat in the house to make them sweat more and see what happens. Making sure he didn't get any of the cologne of him as he sprayed each one with the stuff, Hutch comes down and has one more drink with them hoping it makes them sweat faster to see the effects of what he did. Each of their dates sitting close smelling the cologne on each of his brothers and it didn't take long to see the effects, on Tys date she told him she was feeling afraid of him reminding her of something dangerous but feeling so excited an horny for him. Then POW! They heard a slap as Jazz's date hit him and told him she just wants to have the most angriest sex with him now and wants to go. Dave's date was mad she didn't act out like the other women but didn't tell him she was afraid and so horny about it at the same time whispering in his ear they need to do something kinky, they all told Hutch something came up and would catch up with him later. Hutch laughed watching them all leave knowing what he did to them with the cologne and would make it up to them later, looking at the time grabbing the Black and Silver cologne then going to get on his bike to go meet Moni at the place in Manhattan before Marveece and his girl could showed up. Moni shows up first wearing what Hutch told him to wear a pair of dark blue pants with black socks and shoes light pink shirt with white tie and dark blue jacket to match his pants. Looking at Moni and calling him playa then going over the things he should say to the woman when they meet. Asking to follow him in the bathroom telling him he changed his mind about the cologne to open his shirt so he could use some cologne on Moni. He said to Hutch "I brung the cologne like you wanted." Hutch took it quickly out his hand and told him to spray this one Silver capped bottle 6 times on himself, then fix his clothes and use it two more times again. Making sure he stood out of the way not to get any on himself as Moni used the cologne. He wanted to know the difference they both smell good but Hutch explains this is his lucky cologne and wants Moni to have good luck saying "This is to make up for all your bad thing happening."

Marveece and Davona came in the place and saw Hutch sitting there with Moni waving for them to come over to the table, making room so Davona could sit next to Moni and Marveece next to her with Hutch on the end in the booth. Marveece wanted to know right away where's Steel how come he wasn't there yet? Hutch explained Steel was on the way but running late so be patience. Davona was looking at Hutch but kept smelling the cologne Moni had on then turn to look at him for moment watching him smile at her then she turned back to look at Hutch. The waitress came to the table for drink orders, Moni and Davona made the order for the same drink at the same time, Davona looks at Moni "Oh so you do speak and good choice on the Apple Martini with the beer chaser."

He looks at her and says "Sometimes I use a Bourbon and soda chaser too!" She looked at him and went "Me too! Nice to see a man that don't drink light beer" commenting about the light beer Hutch ordered. He looked at her and didn't say anything to that comment hoping to stall even longer to let the cologne effects work on her so she would like Moni even more, then out of the blue he says "The way you drink like a man, you could use some light beer too!" Moni says to him "Because she likes to drink that way doesn't make her a man." Hutch says "Big as she is who could tell if she was a man or woman!" Moni looked at her and then Hutch and told him to take that back before he do something to him and stood up as if he was going to attack. Hutch says "Whoa no need to get violet Moni I'll apologize for my comment!" Davona looked at Moni and told him "Thanks for having my back." Moni said "He should know and likes it when a woman drinks what she wants." She like what said and they starts talking more as Hutch took that cue to asked Marveece "Outside to have a word for a moment." Getting up walking out first using the black capped cologne on himself as he walks in front of her to let her get a good whiff of it. Outside he stands up wind of Marveece thinking it should work right now so he told him Steel wasn't coming. Marveece went "Oooh Marveece I thought we had a deal. I was supposed to bring my girl and you were to bring Steel and your other friend." Then grabbing up Hutch with both hands his voice got really deep "Look here red bone mutha footer! I want my Steel and he better be coming or some body's going to get hurt feel meh!" Then he threw Hutch into a new stand guy and they both went into the news stand on the side walk. The news stand guy says "Wow what a lady! Dam she got balls to throw a big man like you around" She heard what the news guy said to Hutch and yelled "Hey you LIL shit colored man careful what you say about this women my dick could be bigger than yours." Hutch looked at him and then turns to see Marveece charging at the both of them, pulling the news guy over to his spot just as she leaped in the air and tackling the news guy like a linebacker busting the through news stand. Hutch looked as she dragged the man out of the street before a car ran them over, about to walk away from them he slips on some of the candy on the ground and Marveece had a chance to get over to him grabbing him up again. He takes the cologne sprayed it in Marveece's face as Hutch thought to distract Marveece and she says "What the?" Coughing then she starts to show the effects of being sprayed close. Seeing how Marveece was acting Hutch took full advantage of it yelling at her "Let me go before I" and she puts him down quick looking scared of him as he said "Steel's going to know how you were treating his friend." Marveece got very apologetic begging him not to let Steel know what happened. The news guy said "Wow you really are the man. With just your words you caused the woman in her to come out, screaming like that. Teach me how to be the man!" Marveece turns looking at him "Hey shit colored just because he's the man that doesn't mean your ass can't get flushed by me!" Hutch looks at the new guy after he said that then gets cocky with Marveece agreeing Steel shouldn't know about this suggesting Marveece to go back inside and wait for Steel. He'll try to forget all about what happened, Marveece still afraid shook her head "OK" and went back inside. Hutch took off running down the block to his bike and rode off. The news guy standing there watching it all says "Wow he aint the man at all but a BI-OTCH running away like that. Look at this mess I have to clean up after a change my shorts damn big scary women had me shard my short growling at me like that!" Inside Moni and Davona were really getting to know each other and didn't pay any attention to Marveece who sat down by them talking about how she almost blew it with Steel and didn't want to make his friend that mad at him in such a way he would tell Steel.

Then looking over at Moni and Davona again telling them they need to get a room with all that their doing and Davona says "Thanks girl I know you would understand!"

Hutch is on his way home when he remembers something Janet and Erikaa said about Elise and how she's in on it with Markola, but he couldn't see how she got mixed up with him at all. Then he gets a call it's her and she wants to come over to go have dinner talk about what's going on between them. Hutch asked "When?" She asked him "You home now?!" He told her "No! But will call her when he gets there!" She agreed and hung up, now he starts thinking how to catch her in the act if she really is down with him and it comes to him when couple in a car takes his pictures on the bike as they drove along. Hutch is arriving at his house and going inside to fine the hide away camera in the fakes books he bought as a joke, setting it up in his bedroom to get ready for Elise when she comes over and goes up there.

Davona and Moni pull up to her apartment building where a lot of people are out in front on the steps sitting and some sit on cars parked in front talking and playing music, she gets out of her vehicle giggling like a school girl which has everyone stop talking and music stops playing to see her laughing like they never saw before. They watch as Moni gets out of the vehicle and walk arm in arm with Davona into the building telling her "Next time he drives because his woman should be chauffeured like a Queen!" They wait till they go in the building and everyone busted out laughing but stop as she stuck her head back out the door having everyone get really quite from her mean mugging them, then shout "Mind your dam business and not one word I better hear!" Slamming the door going back in she never hears them snickering and laughing a softly one man says "I never seen a real life walking dildo before and didn't know they come in that color!" Everyone busted out laughing from that joke and moved from in front looking up at her window watching for the light to come, because it's where her apartment was one of those that are in front of the building. It was a good while since they went in the building together and many of the people had gone in for the night, inside Davona and Moni were kissing and acting like a couple in heat as Davona told Moni "What I'm going to do with your little ass" Moni looked at her getting underdressed "I'm a little man that carries a BIG stick mama!" She saw what he had to show her and surprised at how much he had, her wide eyes looking at him as she could hear BARRY WHITE'S deep voice go "YEEESSSS BABY Shoo you right!" The biggest grin on her face shows him she's pleased at what she sees, everything was quieting down for the night till out of Davona's apartment window hearing her yell out "Yes Moni right there baby you hitting my spot!" was heard louder and louder. Lights came on in apartments in the front of the building and on the side of the building as people open their window to hear what was going on as "YES MONI" Was heard louder and louder and faster and faster, then cats stop digging in the garbage cans poking their heads up to hear. Rats come up from the sewer grades in the gutters to hear, dogs starts barking in houses and out on the streets. Light turned red for blocks and blocks in all direction from the building and some distance there was a roaring fire in a building that died down as the water pressure from the hoses the firemen were using when low and everyone could hear Davona going "YES MONI YES!" At her building everything went quite for moment then rumbling and shaking came first her windows explodes out as a loud voice says "OOH SSSHHIIOTT MONI YYEEEESSSSS!!" Miles above the city it could be heard as the lights went green and the animals duck for cover cats pulling the lids on top of the cans they ducked into, all dogs stopped barking going under beds covering their heads or in closets closing the doors behind them, jumping in tubs and covered their ears where ever they were. Rats scattered back down the sewer and the blazing building fire roared bigger as the hoses of the firemen took four extra men to hold them steady from the pressure going up. For miles around that echo could be heard as people still outside heard it like a call of some kind and they would look to see where it was coming from but only heard the echo. Back at her building it stopped shaking and trembling as people were standing outside thinking it was a real earth quake till this old woman on the first floor looks out her window at all the people standing there in front. She asked them "What are they doing standing out there like that?" One woman answers "There was a big earth quake and you should get out of the building before it come down on you old woman!" The old woman laughs "That wasn't an earth quake but the earth moved for the Beast of Brooklyn upstairs, I hear she finally got a man and he made her cum so hard you see I'm smoking a cigarette!" Then another window on the first floor opens up and the old man smoking a cigar stuck his head out and says "Yeah it was a good nut hard enough to give me a woody again" The old woman looked at the man and said "Is that right! Well you don't want to waste it now do you?!" Winking at him motioning with her head to come over, he got wide eyed "Hell no be there in moment and I'm bring champagne!" She turns back to the people looking at her and told them "Look at my age forget that fore play stuff, foreplay for me is if they have one and still able to walk on their own without Oxygen tank following them or young enough to like older ones" A woman voice says "Go head mama get your thing on" Old woman replied "On? Off, hell I got manuals and velvet posters still on the wall with all the Zodiac sign positions."

Hutch had everything set up in his bedroom with Meepbo's wallet in place of his as Elise rang the bell and came in. Hutch just got out of the shower and changed his clothes when she came to the house. Telling her to have a seat and wants to know what she wants to talk about so late in the evening at this time, she asked him where was they going to eat because she a little hungry. He told her there was a place not far that serves some nice Porte Rican food because he knows the waitress there from one of his brothers, she got mad at hearing him refer something from his brothers and asked him "Do you have any more of that drink you gave me that night" Hutch told her "I'd have to make it if you wants a drink like that" and goes to make it as she told him she needs to use the bathroom and head upstairs. Hutch was making the drink and Elise was in his bedroom looking through his pants and found a wallet and looks through it finding a black Credit card and taking some of the cash as well before heading to the bathroom and flushing the toilet then going back down stairs. Hutch was still making the drink when she came to him and said "I change my mind, I don't want to go out but stay there instead" He went "OK but what you want to order Chinese or Spanish?" She told him you choose, so he ordered Chinese. After he made the order and handed her the drink he wanted to know what she wanted to talk about. She got right to the point "I didn't like the way you treated my friends but you treat your friends better and spend money on them without blinking an eye" Hutch looked at her as if she had two heads going "Are you serious? What part of "MY" friends don't you get in this equation I work hard for that money, spending it on what or who I spend it on shouldn't be any ones business but mine!" Elise gets real mad "So you're saying since I was your woman I wouldn't have a say so to whom you spend our money on, when I wanted to spend it on some of "MY" friends you have a problem with that!" Again Hutch looked at her trying to figure out if she hit her head or is on something as he sniffs around her trying to detect an funny odor of anything "I didn't see you out there driving a single truck I worked on or throwing any wet or dry bags of garbage right next to me. How could you say ours!

When it's clearly mine the bank statements are in my name not ours!" That statement sent her into a rage going on how men always say they want to share their world but not their cash, always want sex and even to have a woman call her friend over to join in and then leave her for that friend. Hutch looked at her and knew she really had some issues she needed to resolve with a professional. Explaining to her they haven't had sex nor has he told her about calling in another psycho for them to have therapy sex with or for him to get chopped up by both traumatized women who got hurt by a-hole man. He advised her when women chose to be with a bad boy not a man and not take the time to get to know that boy and all his childish shit. Waiting too long get out of that bad relationship until it way too late, so a woman can't blame a good man for all the dumb ass men she chose in her life. Her back was to him but he could have sworn her head spun around looking at him as her hair looked like it was being blown from the wind in back of her, and face turned white as her eyes went black like her lips with her fangs growing and forked tongue long flicking about in and out of her mouth. She told him "If you think I got issues then why did you have me drop my guard down and feel like I was going to be the next and only woman in your life and there would be no other huh?" Hutch starts to question himself about having sex with her (Thinking did they have sex or not?) now he's getting confused. She didn't want to hear any else from him but said "Mutha footers like you are going to pay for playing with a woman's emotions like that and the bitches that think they can take what's mine are going to get it too, especially those stripper bitches!" Hutch asked "What did you say?" The doorbell rings and it's the delivery man from the Chinese place with their order and Elise said "I got it!" Tipping the man a fifty bill and then saying to Hutch "See how easy this was for me that you didn't even have to come out of your pocket to pay for something we could have been paying for" Hutch looked at her not knowing what to say after she did that and starts feeling like maybe he made a mistake with her. Then asked her to "Repeat what you said a minute ago about the stripper?" She looks at him and starts to put on her coat saying "Suddenly I lost my appetite." Knowing she came there to do what she wanted to do but before she left told him "Since you got yours I'm going to get mine and what's owned to me and won't feel anything on how it's done." He thought he never got a chance to get to talk about Markola and her involvement with him, but then again it was best thinking it could have made things worse for Donna. He closes the door and starts to fix his plate of food sitting down to turn on the TV. It hits him to go upstairs and check the hidden camera in the bedroom and when he does he gets such a surprise, to see Elise come in his bedroom and starts checking his draws and then finally getting the wallet he left out and going through it finding the Credit card and even taking cash too. He plays it over a couple times in disbelief how could she do that to him and then making sense of what she said. Thinking now he knows she's in on it and won't have no problem dealing with her like the others, thinking whatever happens to her she can catch it too. Going back down stairs to finish his food and go to bed and rest for the next day still having Donna on his mind knowing Janet and Erikaa are still worried about her too.

Early that morning Hutch was up going over to Goodies to let Janet and Erikaa know and leave them the tape of what he saw in his bedroom so they could watch it. Then getting to the garage early enough to take Meepbo's wallet and stomp on it in the watery gutter in the street in front of the building and leave it there. When Meepbo came to the garage he was still talking about where he could have left his wallet, Hutch starts to spit in the street and says "Hey Meepbo look here!" He comes over and sees his wallet in the street "Ah man, I must have dropped it outside yesterday and someone found it but good thing they didn't take none of my Credit cards or ID's" Hutch told him to check to be sure and he did finding just one gone, advising him to report it stolen after 24hrs that way they can shut it down immediately and won't charge you none of what that person charged on it. Meepbo liked that idea and told him he would do that then asking Hutch did he ever found out about the other thing he said he would look into, not thinking about it at the time Hutch went and gave Meepbo the cologne he used on Jazz that night. Meepbo asked him "Where did you found it" Hutch quickly said "Around at some small hole in the wall store" Getting in his truck and takes off to head to the building but stopping to get his food he ran in to Gerard his good friend. Gerard was thanking him because not only was he going steady with the woman from the office but she had a couple of female friends that didn't mind joining in with them on some weekends. It's like they just took to him for some reason and now he's happier than he's ever been thanks to Hutch saying they have to get together for night out dancing or something. Hutch say "sure when the time is right no problem" hugging his friend and left to go to his truck.

At the building he was waiting for the work crew to show up and when they did, he saw something he never thought he see Moni smiling walking around like he just had some up-tang. The work crew gets out of the van laughing and joking about Moni's good mood how he's bragging about his woman. Hutch was sitting behind the wheel of his truck looking at them laughing and walking and waving to him as they went in the building. He was looking at them going into the building and didn't see Moni as he stood right at his door "Boom- Boom- Boom!" On the door he knocks hard making Hutch turn slow to see him standing there and say "Get out the truck now!" Hutch thought not now Moni I don't want to hear about how she messed up your life, or what time you had to get out of the hospital again. Looking at Moni standing there by his window Hutch rolls down the window and told Moni to get out of the street before he get hits by a car and blame him for it. Moni told him he'll be waiting for him on the side walk. He walks up to Moni just to get it over with and let him get it off his chest, but hears Moni tell him how he not only knocked boots. Waxing it and polished even stretched it a bit to fit him right and can't wait to get off so he could put the creamy filling in his big chocolate bunny. Hutch looks at Moni and tells him "Thanks you just threw me off for Easter candy with that mental picture of you and her both naked calling her Chocolate, please don't insult my favorite candy anymore." Moni thanks Hutch for bring them together and told him there will be temporary cease fire from him but don't think that's it makes up for all those time he done thing to him but lets him know that he does owe Hutch one and only one. Hutch told Moni "If you two decides to breed, I don't want a puppy or cub or whatever life form you two mutated DNA to make a new species that would have the Alien close his mouth signing his threat at people or have the Predator hang up his hunting gear and sign with PETA to go fly fishing with the catch and release clause to his contract." He walks to his truck and changes into his work gear as Moni went in the building and they began to do their jobs. Hutch got loaded before lunch and pulls off to beat the crowd because there was three other trucks there waiting. On his way to dump the truck waiting to the light to turn green he sees Elise go by and she was talking on her cell. He decides to follow her to the Westside of Manhattan where she parked her vehicle and got out looking as if she were waiting for someone to show up. He saw a big group of City Sanitation Workers in their orange vest and coveralls like his cleaning the sidewalks but then saw a big Lincoln car pull a few cars in front of Elise's vehicle and Markola got out with some of his men walking back towards Elise. Hutch got out of his truck and put on the top half of his coveralls and then a vest and cap to cover his face, grabbing a broom and long handle collector he starts to sweep the street like the working moving close enough to hear Markola and Elise talking. She was telling Markola that she got the card from Hutch and Markola asked her "Do you have it on you now!" She laughed "I'm not so stupid to have you take it from me and not get something for my troubles. We agreed you would give me something for it!" Markola says "Ah you remember that huh, Ok let's say somewhere in the neighborhood of 75 thou!" Elise went "That's a poor neighborhood, how about I use it to move myself because taken a man Credit card isn't lady like!" Markola mumbles "You're no lady but a phsyco lady!" She looks at him "Excuse me?" He thought about it and knew he couldn't take the chance of her finding out about the card and what it really cable of or she would never give it to him in the first place, so he said "how about 225 thou move!" She smiled at him "Now that's a good neighborhood I could live in!" He again asked for the card and told her he'd send the money with one of his guys. She laughed again at him shaking her head saying "How about on the Staten Island Ferry about 4:30 pm during rush hour where there is a lot of people and just you and I can get what we both want, so don't bring your goon squad or I throw it in the water!"

He thought she's no dummy but he wants that card and agreed to meet her with the cash at the time she said, asking her "What about Donna?" She turns coldly saying "What about her, Bitch don't mean anything to me and she could disappear for all I care!" Markola told her the rats down in that dark warehouse by the Brooklyn Bridge would make short work of her once his guys spread more feed down around her. They won't tell what's feed and flesh by the time someone find her they would have to use her teeth to identify her. Elise went "Better have your guys knock out and take her teeth so they don't." Markola looked at her "Wow you sure are cold and heartless remind me never cross you in any way." She wanted him to know before she left not to be late or she'll use the thing and throw what she don't need away since she went this far in taking it. One of the men says "They should have grabbed her and searched her for the card." Markola looked at him and says "It's always the wiry one you have to watch out for, when you don't think they'll fight back they kick your ass good Stu-nod! Now let's get out of here before someone sees me talking to that crazy pysco chic." Hutch bumps into one of the men "Sorry" as he held his head down not looking at the man in the face but kept on sweeping the ground till they all left. He goes back to his truck but some people are there taking pictures of it, when they see he's the driver they want pictures of him with it. Since he took off the top half of his coveralls they want him posing showing his big guns posing with them. After a few good picture they lets him leave so he could get out of there and go get Donna before those men showed up with that feed at the ware house. It wasn't long after leaving from over by the Westside of Manhattan hearing Markola and Elise talking about their meeting on the ferry, Hutch was kicking in the door to the warehouse he thought Donna would be tied up in the basement. Finding the stairs that leads to the basement and going down there using his pen light because that's all he had, he bumps and knocks into things that little light didn't show him as he walks around looking for Donna somewhere tied and gagged in the dark.

Markola was in the car and calling his guys to bring that feed to the warehouse and spread it around her and knock out and take her teeth so when they find her they couldn't identify her right way, then call him when they finish and leave.

Donna is opening her eyes again trying to adjust them to the darkness and saw what looked like a light moving back and forth, thinking it must be more of Markola's men coming there to either feed her or make fun of her using the bathroom in that smelly back room they let her use. Watching the light move around and then hearing his voice that sounds good to her as he bumps into things going "Ah Shit! Donna I know you're down here somewhere, say something or make a noise so I can find where you are girl!" Hutch hears a low moan "Uuumph" He listens to hear which way it was coming from and heads in that direction, passing a barrel of ball bearing and some other barrels of things till he sees another part of the basement and heads in part. Still bumping and banging into things calling Donna's name out. She sees the light getting closer and closer and now hearing Hutch's voice but she still can't call out anything because of the gag in her mouth but manages to muffle something that sounds like "Over here Hutch!" Only thing he hears is muffles sounds she makes but it helps him come towards her anyway.

Outside the building a car pulls up behind the truck, the men look at each other wondering where the garbage man is and if he was taken a break of trying to pick up some trash from the building. Either way they better see where he is because if he comes across her tied up in there they would have a problem. They walk to the front of the truck and see there's no one in the driver's seat looking over to the door of the warehouse and see it's been kicked in, pulling their guns out knowing they have to find him and hope he's not with the woman down in the basement. If he is they would have to get rid of him too so there won't be a problem with the boss. Hutch sees Donna in the dark tied to a beam with her hands around it gagged crying as he came over to her and starts to undo the ropes on her hands, he tells her "Baby I'm so sorry they did this to you but they're pay for this I swear!" She falls into his arms tired from standing up most all that time from being there in the dark not knowing what was crawling on her, he could feel and hear she was exhausted by the way she was breathing when he caught her. Letting her get some of that relief from being tied up in the dark emotion out of her system as she cries in his arms, but it's cut short as they see the beam of a flashlight and hear men talking as they came down the stairs. Asking her "Can you walk?" She said "OK." He told her keep close to him taking her by the hand leading her back the way he came down there so they wouldn't be seen by the men. Getting close to the stairs he came down right by the barrel of ball bearings and what smelled like oil of some kind, he heard the men reach the spot where Donna was tied up because they shouted "Where the hell is she! Somebody untied her, they must still be down here find them!" Hutch knew it wouldn't take them long to find them with those flashlight they have, he told her to wait there and stay out sight but don't make any noise as he went into the darkness. Donna was staying low when something ran across her foot. She didn't scream but gasped loud enough for one man to get an idea where she was. The man starts heading that way shining his light to see where she was but gets jumped by Hutch hiding in the dark targeting the light the man was holding. Going after the other one and during the fight both light gets busted making it hard for them to see each other. With both men down Hutch calls to Donna again and goes over to get and take her out of there, one of the men wakes and hears them waking around in the dark and starts shooting waking the other man with the loud shots. Hiding behind some the stuff down in the dark, Hutch remembered the barrel of ball bearings he passed and goes over to them. Knocking them over spilling them out on the floor, the men shoot at anything making noise in the dark. The small ball bearings all over the floor making it hard for them to even move, they stand quite listening for anything they think is Hutch and Donna moving in the dark. Hutch gets Donna to focus on the dim light coming from the top of the stairs as they crouch down in the dark. Telling her he's going to get their attention on him so she could get up the stairs and get to his truck parked right outside.

Concerned he might get shot she didn't want to take that chance, he tells her it's the only way of them getting out. He told her stay there and when the shooting starts focus on the stairs nothing else and head towards them, the flash from the guns should give her enough light to see and be able to get there with no problem. She kisses him and told him "You better behind me when I get to that truck or I'm coming back for you!" He says "I made a promise not to let two other ladies down either so you won't, now get ready!" Hutch uses that little pen light to move far away from her knowing when they start to shoot at him the light will give her the way to the stairs. He starts moving around with the light held high enough for them to see it moving and they starts shooting in his direction. After the second shot Donna starts walking towards the stairs and reaches them, one of the men sees her during the flash of the gun going off in the dark and starts shooting at her. She squeals from the bullets ricocheting at her and the flash of the guns gives her enough light to run up the stairs fast as she yells "Hutch they were supposed to shoot at you not me!" Hutch knocks over some more barrels containing more ball bearings. The whole basement floor is covered with them as the men stand there. He moves towards the stairs as they reload and saw these gallons of liquid soap on a shelf. Grabbing six gallons (three in each hand) opening them pouring them out behind him as he reaches the stair, while they're shooting at him but fail to hit him. He runs up the stairs pouring the soap out all over the steps going up getting away. One man starts to run after Hutch but slips on the ball bearing and both his feet come out from under him, causing him to fall backwards hitting his head on the floor knocking him out. The second man was about to move when his cell rings, he slips a little but keep his footing as he answers the phone. Markola wants to know did they put the feed down and knock out her teeth like he told them. The man starts to say something to him but loses his footing from moving a bit and starts slipping and sliding trying to talk on the cell. Both his feet come out from under him like the first, he too going up falling backwards tossing the cell in the air as he hits the floor hard on his back and head together. Right before he loses conscience the cell pops him in the head then everything goes black for him. Markola calls for him to answer him, as he lays there a rat comes to the phone sniffing it hearing Markola's shouting for someone to answer him and the rat steps on the button cutting it off.

Outside of the warehouse Hutch is starting up his truck with Donna in the passenger seat, he tells her to hold on as he backs up pass the car that was behind him. Thinking about it he pulls behind the car and pushes it into the river at the end of the dead end street, smiling at Donna saying "Now we can leave." All she does was shake her head at him and smile "You're so silly!" He reaches in his little cooler handing her a water to drink as then shifts gears rolling up his tinted windows and heads over to Goodies house. Hutch calls Meepbo to let him know he's going to be a little late getting back to the building so call off his watch dog Moni. Meepbo told him long as he gets back there it's Ok with him since he found that little bottle of cologne wanting to know the name of the shop he got it from so he can get more of it. Hutch is knocking on the door at Goodies apartment a voice asked "Who is it?" He says "It's me Janet open up baby. I got something to show you." The door opens up as Janet eyes got wide and teary from the sight of Donna standing there. Her eyes all watered up as well look at each other for a second and hug crying, Erikaa came to the door and saw Hutch and Donna being hugged by Janet as they cried. She rushed right over to them hugging Donna and Janet crying just as hard them happy to have her friend back safe. Hutch swells and shakes his head holding back his own tears trying not to let them see him feeling the moment too.

He thinks to himself never again will anyone get to someone he cares about in order to get to him. Janet comes over to him and hugs him tight saying "Thanks big bear! You know I love you for that!" She starts crying again in his arms holding him tight then Erikaa and Donna came over to him doing the same. Hutch told them "I'm not going to ever let any of you go now better get used to being with me." They all agreed it's alright with them. Janet went to set up Donna's shower and Erikaa went to make something for her to eat. Hutch had to go back to work and told them he will be back to take them back to his house after he gets off work.

Back at the warehouse Markola is calling the cell phone again getting no answer but gets hung up on each time he calls. Rats are all over the two men laying there out cold on the floor and a rat stands on the cell phone still on. A pizza shop phone rings and the man takes an order of sixteen pies, fourteen with extra cheese and one with beef toppings and the last one peppers and onions, he gave the total $298.75 and told the caller he got the address from the cells location. One hour later the delivery man is knocking on the warehouse door saying "Pizza delivery!" 4 one hundred dollar bills are slid under the door at his feet. Waiting at the door he looks down and saw them "Ok guess I'll leave them right here!" Walking back to his car he never sees the door open and the pies being pulled in one at a time real fast till none are left out at the door. He turns back because he forgot to leave the menu at the door and saw the pies gone so he slips the menu under the door and 20 dollars more come back out at his feet again. He takes the money saying "Thanks my name, Tommy! just call and I'll be bring what you need" and he walks back to his car scratching his head but happy about the big tip he just got.

On the Staten Island Ferry Markola with two of his men are standing on the back of the boat as Elise came walking on the gang way to board the boat before it closes up to pull away from the dock. She saw them looking down at her and heads to the upper deck towards the back where they stand looking at the city. She walks up to him shaking her head going "Why's it always the want to be tough men, has to have two men with him when they're told to come alone?" Markola points to the other side of the boat and says "We can go over there and talk, if that will make you feel better!" They head over there as the men watch them sit and talk. He wants to know did she bring it. She told him you first since you have two men with you and was told to come here alone. He bows his head and snaps his fingers as one of the men walk over to him with a small bag and hands it to Markola. He looks at her "You're not having second thought about this now are you? Keep in mind what he put you through with those women!" Saying that to her hoping to egg her on not to have second thoughts just in case and get what he wants from her as the sit here on the boat looking at Manhattan. To his surprise she told him "If I had second thoughts about giving you his Credit card, then I wouldn't be here looking at this cash that you have for me or have taken it in the first place!" He opens the bag and shows her the cash and says "Now if you please!" She looks at the cash smiled at it with a big grin to see such amount at one time in front of her, then reached in her bra and pulls out the black credit card which had him smile at that. They make the exchange a bag of cash for Hutch's black Credit card as the boat continues on to Staten Island. When it reaches the dock to Staten Island people starts to get off the boat. Elsie took her bag of cash with her off the boat into the ladies room to look at all that cash again she's got from Markola. Walking off the boat not far Lou Markola's man after he got a nod from Markola which meant to go and get back his cash from Elise in the bathroom, where no one could see him take it from her in there.

While in the Ladies room Elise had looked at the cash satisfied about how it looks to her she goes over to the sink and starts fixing her hair, in the mirror she see him walk in as he locks the door behind him. The look on her face turns very serious as he stood there and then said "You know what this is, so why not make it easy on both of us and give me the bag back!" She rolls her eyes at him in the mirror and take the bag pushes it in the corner of the counter top. Turning to face him knowing she's got to fight with this big man to keep her money. Dropping her head and taking a deep breath but when she lifts her head to show him what he's in for, she has changed teeth grew long sharp, eyes red & black nails grew too. From on the outside of the ladies room there was no noise for a moment after he walks in but as the face off erupts there's a sounds like big cats having a fight and a woman screaming for her life like a banshee. No one outside knew it's the man screaming like that, clearly out matched in claws and fearousity. She slams then banged him around into things finding that untapped women's strength. He tries to put up a good fight, but she's too strong, wild and mad about what he's there for making him screaming like a white girl in the most horrifying scary movie of all times about to die. People standing by the outside door commenting about what sounded to then like the biggest cat fight between two women as one screamed for her life hearing all the crash and banging going inside. He manages to get in the stall holding the door with his feet closed with shredded clothes all over him and clumps of hair missing from his head. Thinking she must have left but looks up and sees her climbing over the top like a big cat and jumps in to the stall on him and begins to go wild on him scratching and clawing him up. All that banging and booming sounding like a big angry cat growling and then a scream for the final time, then there was silence nothing for a moment but the sound of water running. The door opens up to the ladies room and Elise comes out to a crowd of women looking at her with her hair messed up. There's a little thin line of blood from the corner of her mouth. She walks on one shoe heel broken holding her purse and bag trying to look normal, brushing her hair out of her face getting back on the boat to Manhattan. Markola wondered what was taking Lou that long so he sent Salvatore to find him which didn't take him long to find Lou. Goodie an E.M.T in the arrear got a call there was a man in need of transport to the hospital after a domestic fight with a woman. They were wheeling him out from the ladies on a gurney as Goodie said "Domestic fight hell! She thought like a man and Kicked his ass like a bigger man could, DAMN!" The other attendant said "This man caught NEH-FUBAR!" Goodie asked "What's Chinese got to do with the shape he's busted up in?" Second attendant explains (neh-fubar) "Not Ever Healing, F- Up beyond Any Recuperation! He's gonna be scared of women for the rest of his life" Goodie said "Looks like the work of a pissed Sista that would explain the NEH (Not Ever Healing) part, seeing the hair and shredded clothes those aren't lee press on nails she used. That Sista was in rage this bad case of FUBAR means 2 things happened, he was caught cheating or tried to take her money!" Salvatore looked at Lou with both his eyes blacken bloody nose and lips bleeding with scratches all over his face, hair missing in big spots and clothes shredded looking like he was just attacked by a big wild animal. Salvatore just cringes at the sight of how messed up his friend was wondering what kind of wild thing did this to him, (flash to something that looked like Elise fighting with Lou) he hurry's back to Markola and explaining what kind of condition Lou was in. Trying not to tear up about it as Markola slaps him telling him to get it together, but paused in fear after hearing his name growled loud from what sounds like a monster woman's voice. They look to see Elise walking towards them on one shoe heel broke going up and down (clip clop, clip clop) pushing the hair a side that keeps falling in her face. Her lip stick smeared across her mouth and the corner has a line of blood going down to her chin.

Big Salvatore standing next to Markola eases in back of him as she came closer with such a serious look on her face calling his name out "MARKOLA! You little wanna be scar face bitch ass punk, sending a man to beat on a woman!" Markola turns to tell big Salvatore to get her but didn't see him on his right nor left but behind him looking surprised as Markola told him to get her. Big Salvatore shook his head and backs away some more as she came closer to them. Markola looks at her and he backs away with big Sal and told her "Look you got to understand, it's just business nothing personal!" She growled at him "Come here, I'll show you what's personal and take care of business with your ass now!" They move all over the boat with Elsie in pursuit. Markola asked her "What can I do and make it up to you." That makes her think about it and sat down plus she was a bit tired from the fight and chasing them all over the boat. Telling him she was going to let him know, she took his front door key so he could get the other two that was staying at his house. Markola asked her "How did you know the other two was there?" She told him when she came over to his house, while he was making her a drink. She walks upstairs and saw female clothes there in his bedroom and in other rooms too. While she had the chance, she took the door keys because she was going to come back there and bust him red handed with them there. Markola looks at her and took off his watch then asked big Salvatore for his and all the cash he had on him. Wanting to exchange them for the key and then promised her more, after he gets a chance to make something off the card. She gave it to him and told him "Don't make me come after you because I will." Telling him as an added bonus she'll set it up by calling to make sure they're at him house for his men to get them too. Only when she gets her cash so those two other bitches don't know his guy are coming there to get them. "Wow!" Markola said "You really are a cold hearted "Ba." About to call her "Bitch!" then looking at the expression on her face saying "Brilliant!" She told him "The faster I get the cash the faster I get to make that call." The ferry docks back on the Manhattan side and she walks off the boat to her vehicle as people are looking at her walking with one heel broke going up and down as if she was just in a fight. Markola looks at big Sal and wanted to know why he didn't just shoot her. Big Sal explained it would have only made her even madder, plus the way she did Lou and how he's going to need GOD for what she did to him going "I didn't want the same or worst boss!" Markola said "Stu-nod! She's just a woman one lousy woman!" Big Sal said "Yeah tell that to Lou, you didn't see him in that condition!" They leave the boat talking about it and Markola threaten to tell his mother about being a coward.

Hutch is back at work thinking about Markola and what can he do to really get this idiot off his back about him and the girls. When Moni came over to him and says "Good thing you have a boss that like you and lets you get away with things. I would have you cleaning my car or even fired you for coming back this late in the afternoon!" That had Hutch thinking did Markola have a boss or who did he have to answer too. If he could get to talk to him about Markola's dumb ass not noticing he was talking aloud instead of thinking about it, with Moni standing right next to him. Moni says "You're talking about Markola Muspulo right the gangster!" Hutch "Yeah it's about him?!" Moni laughs "Come on man you're so smart you're stupid, do you not know about this type of man!" Then he realizes he knows something Hutch needs to know and starts his normal thing "If I tell you, what are you going to give me for it?!" Hutch looks at him "This coming from the man that says he owe me one and would never forget about bring him and his chocolate silver back tree swinger together?" Moni's drops his head "You are right my friend, how could I be so foolish about it.

Now let me tell you what you don't know is, Mr.Narkita is his uncle who he has to answer to on anything he does!" Hutch looked at Moni asking "How do you know this?!" Moni says "My Mountain of sweetness, she works with Marveece in her main salon in which she has 30 salons City wide. There isn't anything Marveece can't find out or know because we did more than bump uglies there in all that darkness with my vision of woman hoodness." Hutch replied under his breath "Only way she can be seen with a man is in complete darkness with a hood on. To think of what you two uglies did don't need to be visualized and kept out of every neighborhood period." Moni still talking "We talked about things in between and after, do you not know about the cuddling time" Hutch told him one day he's got to enlighten him but right now he got to find a way to set up a met with Mr. Narkita. Moni told him "That is easy to all he's got to do is talk to his love mump and have Marveece tell her when you can see him" Hutch asked "Moni not to use my name when he talks to his girl because he don't want to seem like a man that couldn't do it on his own in front of his girls." Moni smiles saying "I completely understand the lack of manhood you are Hutch. It would stay a secret with me of your bitchness!" Hutch took the insult wanting him to set up that meeting and knew if Moni was going to do it he would have to let him have the upper hand for the moment.

Later after work Hutch was at Goodies place with the girls telling them of his plan to see Mr. Narkita to get rid of Markola. Explaining if he's going to do anything to Markola gets him off his back Hutch doesn't want no retaliation now that he knows Mr. Narkita is his uncle. He also called the rest of the G.D.M.4.L to meet him at his house tomorrow because he's bring the girls there then tell them of his plan when he comes up with one. Hutch stayed there at Goodies place with the girls telling them about Marveece and her friend has 40 hair salons in the city, Goodie stayed at Hutch's house with his dates laughing about the man he picked up from the ferry and who beat his ass. Hutch cell rang and Moni told him the meet is set up for the day after tomorrow and he needs to bring a Tribute for the consultation with him or there would be no meeting. Hutch asked "What kind of Tribute he needs to bring?!" Moni says "1500$" Hutch got loud "WHAT!? For that much I could have him hit myself by a couple of thugs that would dust half a neighborhood for the cream!" Moni says "I didn't set the price and if you want this man off your back go see the uncle and I'll see you tomorrow at work"

That morning Hutch had a talk with Meepbo and told him he needs some time off to take care of a family issue, at first Meepbo wouldn't go for it telling Hutch he's his best worker and needs him there. Hutch explained if he didn't take the time off now then he would have to quit and Meepbo didn't want that but asked "How much time do you need 1 month or 2?" Hutch told him nope just two weeks and he needs one of them right now starting tomorrow and the other when he gets ready. Meepbo had no choice but to give Hutch what he wants and also wanted him back there soon as everything is over with. That day went by quick Hutch didn't tell Moni about him taking some time off to deal with Markola, at the end of the day Moni wanted to know what he was going to do. Hutch says "You'll hear about it"

That next Morning Hutch is dressed nice and casual as he goes to the bank and gets the Tribute for the meeting then going to China Town's Little Italy restaurant next to the Italian bakery. Hutch knocks on the door one time like he was supposed to. The door opens up and this huge man come out and asked him "Are you the 8:15 am." Hutch looked at him and shook his head "Yes" all the while thinking he would have some trouble if he were to fight his mass of human.

The man searches him for weapons and takes the Tribute. He walks in front of the man who opened the door looking over his shoulder hoping he don't trip and fall on him thinking of how big he is. They walk into this room only to see five more massive suit wearing men looking at him with such serious looks on their faces. First thing Hutch thought if he was to fight with them, he knew it would result in him badly hurt. Even if he used kill shot blows to their bodies, because Hutch is 6'3" 278lbs. These Mansters are 6' 7" and 6' 8" weighing in the neighborhood of four pounds and better. He's told to wait there by a table with three of them as one goes in the back, then comes out just to stand there looking at Hutch again. Two more huge men come out and stand by a table that has only one chairs on opposite sides of each other. Some waiters came out carrying trays of food and placed the food down on the table in front of the two chairs and the same done at the other tables surround that table. Hutch wondered who all that food was for looking at pile of silver dollar pancakes, steak and eggs, turkey bacon and sausages plus cups of what look like espresso. They remain standing till this gentle old man came out and took his seat at the table with the two chairs. He told Hutch "Please have a seat" looking at the one opposite of him. Smiling as Hutch sat down then he says "I don't like to eat alone before discussing business." Hutch couldn't resist saying something "Eat alone, one of them equal four people. With this crowd you have, that looks like a small army. I wonder if you get to eat at all" Mr. Narkita looked at the men and laughs at Hutch's comment but the men didn't crack a smile but looked more intense at him. Mr. Narkita held up his hand and they eased up on their looking at Hutch that way. He told Hutch "Please eat! I don't like to talk any business on an empty stomach and want my guess to feel like home." Hutch took up his fork and knife which made all the men stand up. He looked around at them and put it down and told Mr. Narkita "Please! I insist after you age before youth" that made the men sit back down as Mr. Narkita picked up his fork and knife. Hutch bowed his head and starts saying grace over the food which had Narkita smile at Hutch and join him, snapping his finger the rest did as well. Waiting for Mr. Narkita to take his bite and then join him. Hutch turns at the sound of forks scrapping the plates, breathing heavy, chewing and slurping and sipping out of cups (scrape, glump, chew, smack, slurp, sips, Ump, ahh!) Mr. Narkita looked at Hutch who was watching his men eating asking him "Is the food not good, why aren't you eating?!" That made the men stop even with food in their mouths and look at Hutch, as he said "I can't keep up with the rhythm and pace their going at!" MR. Narkita looks at his men and laughs again saying "Eat at your own pace I do!" Hutch starts to eat and the men went back to devouring their food. Hutch knew he had to finish his food before Narita even if he didn't have half of what he had on his plate, but his men had three time of what Hutch did and was almost done. Finishing before Mr. Narkita, Hutch is feeling full as he see the waiter roll a cart out to take away all those empty plates from the tables. Then come back out with some cannolies and cups of espresso setting down three of them in front of Hutch with the cup. Hutch looks around seeing each other table and each man has a plate of eight cannolies and espresso in front of them. Mr. Narkita says to Hutch "Now over breakfast treats we can talk, if that's ok with you." Hutch was about to say something when the waiter came and put a bill right down in front of him and he looked at the bill for $328.72 cents. Saying it out loud having the men stand up again, he turns looking at all of them and pulls out his wallet asking "Was twenties Ok, because I put the big bills in the Tribute!" He counts out 17 twenties and hands it to the waiter but the waiter didn't move looking back at Hutch. He said to the waiter "What!" looking at his hand stuck out as the waiter clears his throat. Hutch says "Oh you wait for a tip?!"

Hutch laughs and looks at Mr. Narkita with a very serious look who isn't smiling and the men are starting to stand up again. Hutch clears his throat and pulls out a twenty and puts it in his hand but the waiters hand doesn't move. One by one the men stand up as Hutch turns looking at all of them so he puts three twenties in the waiters hand which had him smile and say "Why thank you for such a nice tip!" The men sit back down as Hutch says "I see you guys don't need to exercise at the gym just invite people to breakfast and see how much they pay and tip, then you guys would get all the exercise you need huh!" Taking the small cup drinking fast as Mr. Narkita looks at Hutch wondering when he was going to cough from drinking that cup of espresso like that so fast. When he didn't Mr. Narkita ordered a bigger cup for Hutch saying "Good! I see you're a strong man now here try this one!" He adds four spoon of sugar to the cup and watches as Hutch drinks half of it then coughs a little and eats the cannolies to kill the taste of such strong coffee. Mr. Narkita smile at him then asked "What brings you here? Tell me it was not to insult my men because I hate to see them violent." Hutch starts explaining about Markola and what he did to him and his girl Donna. How he keep threating him about his Credit card wanting to run it up and have him pay for it." Mr. Narkita couldn't believe Markola would dirty his hands in such mess and told Hutch he would look into it. Hutch wanted to know if he does something to Markola would he have to face him about it!? Mr. Narkita told Hutch "No! He's all for protecting ones family and valuables, especially if you didn't do anything wrong against his Nephew. Why is he attacking you for no other reason than to get money from you I don't understand?!" Hutch explained he works driving a garbage truck for long hours and all he did was buy drink for the whole club one night to impress 3 women. Mr. Narkita knows about the garbage business and knows how hard the men work at it, telling Hutch he respect what he does and that's no reason for his nephew to be trying to extort him for money. He knows garbage men make good money but work hard for it day and night. Telling Hutch he'll have someone look into and see what he can do, but if he has to defend himself please don't kill his nephew for stupidity. Then he nods his head at the man who let Hutch in as he walk over to him and shows the envelope Hutch had on him. Standing up and telling Hutch to finish his treats and except this gift from him for bring this matter to his attention. Hutch rose with the men as Mr. Narkita left the room and Hutch hurried and finish the cup in front of him and the rest of the last cannoli as the waiter came over to him asking "Was there going to be anything else?!" Hutch said "Nope" and the waiter laid another bill in front of him it showed a bill for $127. 45cents for the cannolies and espresso they had. Hutch looked at the bill saying again "What?! You want me to pay for that too!?" The men still sitting at the table after Narkita left with his two men starts to get up. Hutch heard the chairs move turning to see them now standing up looking at him. Cussing under his breath about the cost he pulls out more cash and hands it to the waiter standing there. Again he saw that hand as Hutch looks at it blinking his eyes at the waiter looking up and down to his hand and then to his face. The waiter clears his throat and there's this sound of a lot of knuckles cracking. Hutch looking around at all the big men taking a breath shaking his head mad about paying again going into his pocket pulling out his wallet cussing some more. Hutch paid the bill and gave the waiter 40$ tip and told him "I'm going to put you down as a dependent with what I'm pay you or do you work for commission on the meal they serve here. Good thing I didn't come for dinner or I might have to take out a small loan and mortgage my house just to get though the first course. Then sell my ride to get desserts." Waiter smiles again saying to him "Thank you for such a generous tip." Snapping is finger and another one brings out a bakers box wrapped and tied putting it down in front of Hutch. Looking at the box asking "What's this going to cost because all I've got is gas and toll left after breakfast here at this place." The waiter told him there was no charge it was a gift from Mr. Narkita. Hutch looks at the box as the waiter asked "Did you want to order something else?" Hutch looked at him with a F-U look and turns to see all the men gone saying "Wow they're silent when they move out. Thought I would hear the shuffling of buffalo hoofs when they moved, it's scary big men like that move so quite!" Hutch took the box and was out the door so fast in his vehicle on his way to Goodies' place as the sugar rush and espresso kicks in while he was driving. Playing music loud when (M.J.J who's Bad!) came on and he starts feeling the music. Hutch is at Goodies apartment building running up all four teen flights and knocking on the door like police telling the girls "it's him." They open the door and he rushes in and sits down only to get up talking fast while walking around saying how the meeting went he just had with Narkita. Telling them how his men were eating and what he paid for the breakfast. The girl didn't know what to do because they never seen him like this. Erikaa asked "What did you have to eat at the meeting?!" He described breakfast and what they eat after for a treat." Janet told Donna and Erikaa "He's on a serious sugar and caffeine rush." Erikaa asked "What can they do about it?!" Janet told Donna "Get the blow up bed out of the bedroom and for Erikaa to help her get his clothes off" Erikaa looks at Janet "I know we're not going to do what I think you have in mind to do to him?!" Janet asked her "You have a better way to calm down a big man with a hard on that would rival any dildo you got plus in a sugar rush mode." She shook her head "NO" as they took him to get into the shower first to cool him down a little.

At Hutch's house Mack is talking to Goodie about Hutch and wondering what time he was going to get there so they can talk about his plan saying "It's not like he doing anything that serious or getting dirty."

(Flash over to Goodie place) Hutch is in the shower getting rubbed down by Janet and then led to the living room where Donna and Erikaa give him a massage taking turns then went to shower off. While they were in the shower he was being handled by Jane but it wasn't enough till Erikaa came out and helped at the same time then switched off to Donna when she came in. At Hutch's house Mack told Goodie he was hungry and wondered what Hutch was eating or bring there. (At the apartment) Donna is blinking she can't believe such a feeling he was giving her holding his head while he was under her as she was looking at Janet who was getting the ride of her life, then switch off with Erikaa who got the same thing as they all rotated on the big man so energized.

2Soon got there early that morning too asking "Where was Hutch! He wanted me here early when he got done after his meeting!" saying "Hope they didn't try and flip him because you know he won't go for it" (over at Goodies apartment) Hutch is holding Janet upside down in his tight grip as she shakes wildly.

Mack said "I just hope they didn't try any tricks on him to make him flip out but you know he could take on two at one time. (Back at Goodies place) Hutch has Donna on his shoulders holding her up with his mouth full while behind Erikaa bent over on all fours in front of him.

Tys arrived asking "What's going on. I got a call from Hutch last night to be here after some meet this morning with some man's uncle. Hope he doesn't be to tire to talk when he gets back there. (Flash over to Goodies place) Erikaa is asking Janet "Will he ever get tire and ware down?"

As they sit on the couch breathing heavy while he's with Donna, getting up looking at Erikaa smiling Janet says "Soon I hope it's like he trying to catch up on what he missed all those years of not having any but I'm not complaining!"

Jazz and Steel came in the door followed by Dave, La-Machine, Derrick, Ron, and Dougie they had coffee and doughnuts, Herb's already in the kitchen "Where the hell is the coffee so I can make more I looked all over the kitchen there's none." 2Soon answered "Yo fam you know Hutch don't drink coffee it sends him into hyper drive and if he ever drank espresso look out he's a big over grown energizer battery." Mack went "That's right! He only uses it when he's really want to get a good work out on the weights because it kicks up his energy so high. Imagine him with a woman wow she would be half dead by now." (Flash over to Goodies place.) All three women are laid out tired as Hutch told them they need to get to his house to meet with his brothers. They shower and all put on jean shorts that fit so well showing the shape of their asses, Janet had on sleeveless top drop neckline back out. Erikaa had on sports top which showed her belly out and Donna had on tank top knotted in front showing her belly as they left out with Hutch. Most of the G.D.M.4.L couldn't stay any longer because they had their job shifts to get to so 2Soon, Mac and Dougie with Steel had later shifts and stayed till Hutch showed up with the girls. Janet is the first one through the door as they guys looked at her with a strange look on their faces that had her looking back at them wondering why they're staring at her in that way as she went upstairs.

Erikaa is next to come in and again the G.D.M.4.L looked at her with strange looks on their faces as she says "HI" to them and head in the kitchen. Donna came in and saw the guys in the living room staring at her as she said "HI" and like Erikaa she head to the kitchen with no one saying a word but heads turning to watch her every move having her look back at them wondering what's wrong with them like they never saw a woman in a tank top before. Hutch came in looking all fresh and energized and they looked at each other and then him again as he asked "What he's been up to?" 2Soon says "We can tell what you been doing fam. Hell C.S.I could tell what you've been doing without dusting from the print you left." Mack laughs and went "Don't try and deny the crime, we have all seen the walking evidence, all we need is you're GUILTY plea!" Hutch looked at them wondering what was they talking about when Donna and Erikaa are heard in the kitchen going "Hutch what did you do to them?" Now with their shades off they see the hand prints he left on their bodies. They came out of the kitchen looking at him as they passed and went right upstairs then Janet is heard saying "What the Hell!" They're upstairs comparing hand prints then starts to laughing realizing that's what the guys were looking at. Hutch and the guys watch as the ladies had run upstairs then they all turn looking at Hutch as shrugged his shoulders and couldn't say a word about what they all just seen. Tyrone talking to Tys "What did I tell ya, he would need to release some of that and it took three. Look at him, he isn't tried or nothing wow!" Mack walks over to Hutch "That my boy!" The others start clapping. Steel says something they all couldn't make out and turn to look at Mack who interprets what he said "Go head boy! You the man! Mack is right didn't know you had it in you like that my brother." Herb looks at Mack asking "He said all that? All I got out of that was Mack!" The rest of them agreed with Herb they didn't know what the hell Steel said and Hutch added "Told ya we need that manual to change the speech setting on him to BLACK ENGLISH or brother man." They all laughed some more. Hutch asked "Where's the others?" 2Soon told him about their shifts and Hutch wanted them to help him come up with a way to handle this Markola once and for all and he don't have to worry about him ever again. They start thinking of ways as his cell rings. It's Meepbo and he's begging Hutch to come in because two of his other drivers can't make it for work. It's their late day shift and Hutch usually works late on that day for them. Because he was taken time off, he didn't come in that morning and the other workers got mad and didn't come in so they wouldn't have to work late it. Hutch didn't want to leave Meepbo hanging like that even though he's dealing with this situation and it's only for that evening he agreed to come in but told Meepbo "It will cost him." Meepbo reply's "Put it on my account and charge me for it." Hutch asked his brother to give him a minute and went upstairs to talk with his ladies and let them know he's got to go in for that evening but his brothers will be there and the others will come to watch till he gets back. Showing them something about his house with his bedroom closet, there's this hatch door in the closet that has a small concealed door that allows him to go from his closet in that other bedrooms closet next to his. Telling them he always plays with his nieces and nephews whenever they chase him in there, he uses it to avoid getting caught by them so showing how it works he says it might come in handy one day. Kissing them all he goes back down stairs and having a talk with the G.D.M.4.L letting them stay there till they have to go in for their own shifts. Hutch gets dressed and heads to work thinking about his Credit card after he said that to Meepbo, hoping he calls the bank to stop any charges from being put on his card and report it stolen like Hutch wanted.

Markola was still shopping after getting a lot of new suits and shoes with ties to match then head to the jewelry store where he wanted to see about some new watches, but as he was about to purchase one and use that card. The salesmen told him that card was declined and cut off by the bank which made Markola very mad thinking Hutch doubled crossed him again and cut it off. Thinking what he was going to do to him for that. The guy Markola sent to deliver the cash he owed to Elise and he relays the message she was going to make the call so he could get the other two ladies at that mooks house at 8:30 pm that evening. Markola went good and told him to get three other guys and be there at that time so they can get those broads for him, but then asked "Did you hear from Giovanni or Marcello, because they were to do something at this warehouse in Brooklyn for me. I never heard from them yet." The guy says "I'll look into it boss."

Down south at Hutch's mother home town: Mama Betty had found the Credit card Hutch wanted her to have he hid in her suitcase knowing she would use it, he didn't know it was the Unlimited Credit Card. Since she came back from her visit with him up in New York and knowing what she has is that Unlimited Funds Credit card thanks to Cheryl showing her at the mall. Her son wouldn't mind her using it to help out some of the people that he grew up with and live there with in that town. She started with her house first having it remodeled bigger with more rooms added on plus a pool because she always wanted one and with the room on her property to do so she had it put in. She also went one by one to some of her old friends that owned their own businesses which needed help, starting with MR. Allen Grocery Store. She helped him remodel and stock it up his with all the things he needed. MR. Pearson Roller Skating Rink followed by Evelyn and Sandy's dress shop. Wally Gee's Brass rail bar along with three other bars Tommy's joint, Big Man's Water Hole and Meryl and Lip's old time lounge. Using the Credit card she has to help Darleen and Freda's bakery get better supplies along with remodeling the place also and Lenny's BBQ ribs and chicken shack, plus Sherri and Terri's club The Savoy FAM, Bunny Nelson clothing store, Punkin and Fran's Ice Cream shop, with Tuckers auto Body Repairs. Rey Cousin's Bowling Alley, MR. Means Record shop, and the Outlaws soft ball club house and field. She had Bernadine's Diner remodeled and restocked where she knew they would have to have a place to eat while working also helping out Doris, Dolly and Donnie's café where they planned on getting the construction company from the towns own Mikey Nelson Construction Company along with John Hornez Plumbing and Robbie and King-C Electric wiring and light Co. She had all people she needed to contact because the whole town had skilled workers and fill of labors from out of work man to high school seniors looking to learn a skill and trade to use in their future. Thinking the best she way to pay her son back by getting part ownership of all the businesses she helped with the Credit card. She then bought a vehicle just like the one Hutch has for his baby brother Larry, since he was finishing with law school and sent him up there to visit his brother as a surprise. With all that going on down there she couldn't come up there with Larry, she told him to keep it to himself because she was hoping to surprise Hutch when everything was finished. To have him come down there and see it all that she did. Larry told her he would before leaving with the direction to get to Cordell house.

Back up in New York Hutch was at work telling Moni thanks for the hook up with that meeting because he knows that his uncle would do something or stay out of the way just as long as he don't hurt him too badly. Not to let Moni off the hook Hutch came across these big five gallon plastic bottles of trap grease they were throwing out from the lunch kitchen in the building and got an idea on a prank for Moni.

Elise was looking at the money she got from Markola and saw what time it was, so she calls Sonia and has a talk with her about Hutch. Sonia said she wanted to talk to her too about Hutch and that she learned about him. She told Elise while she was over his house with Dougie, his brother Codrell came there with his kids and the oldest girl was talking to her friends on the phone about her Uncle Hutch. How he's got more money in the bank like he's a humble millionaire and keeps money and doesn't want to spend it on himself but uses it for the rest of the family and friends. That made Elise really mad now wondering why Markola wanted his Credit card so badly all that time and gave her that small sum compared to what she could have if she had it. Thinking that's why he was quick to send those guys with the money to get his key from her. Feeling like she was played again by a man, she calmed herself and continues with her plan by whining she caught him with not one but three women. Sounding so hurt by it and telling her she needs her help in busting that no good ass cheating man who would do something like that to her. Sonia feeling mad about what Elise told her convinced what Hutch did to her friend, said she would help and wanted to know what she needed to do. Elise explained Sonia needs her to act like Hutch sister and call his house to get them to open the door saying she wants to talk with them. She needs to have a nice talk with those women that don't know or do know he's cheating on her. Sonia said that's a good idea and wants to be there for support, Elise said "It's something I need to do on my own."

Hutch was telling the workers to keep Moni inside while he sets up everything with the gallon bottles of grease so as Moni comes out there he could spring the prank on him. Taking the bottles and placing them in the truck where the blade of the truck when it's crushing the garbage would squeeze the gallons of grease causing it to spray whoever is by the back of the truck. Hutch knew this would remind Moni their war is still on but the grease is so smelly, he would have to go to the van to change is clothes and there another prank set up with two fire extinguishers that wouldn't activate when he first opens the door. He would be expecting something a second time as he would get sprayed with them and then placing the water balloons again on the top of the back of the van. Having some left over horse shit he keeps in the body in the truck, setting up again to blowout the trap when he opens the door to get something to go after Hutch with. The truck is nearly full and Moni came down to check plus to get Hutch away from his truck so she could rig a blow up raft like Hutch did to his van and get him before he goes to dump. Moni thinks he really is going to get Hutch good with this raft he found, rigging it to wire where he could pull it on after Hutch gets in his truck. Hutch stood by his truck and told Moni "Almost full." Setting the blade saying "I got to use the bathroom." Moni told him take his time and he'll watch the truck for him. Hutch didn't go to the bathroom but up to the second floor to look out the window watching Moni set up his raft and wire in Hutch's truck. Laughing on how simple Moni rigged it up, when Hutch came back out looking at the stuff to be crushed. He told Moni he needs a drink of water and was going to get one from his truck. Moni went to the wire and grabbed it up holding it behind his back as Hutch stop short before reaching the passenger side door. Looking back at Moni standing there trying to be cool about what he's got behind his back. Hutch knelt down to tie his boot string and reaches for the wire thinking he never learns using the knife that's on the side of his boot he cuts the wire and goes to the truck door opening it getting his water out of his truck. Hutch came back and said he'll go to the dump now and leave that stuff for tomorrow but Moni told him he can't leave that stuff out there like that. He told Hutch move "I'll throw the stuff in myself you don't even know how to crush things up in the back of the garbage truck right." Moni told him watch a master work his magic. Hutch told him "Better keep an eye on what's being crushed so it doesn't break that blade in back." Moni starts the blade and moves right in back of the truck right in the line of fire as the blade crushes everything in the back of the garbage truck then "BOOM!" A wave of oil came out to cover Moni as he screams "What the FLOCK!" He turns to run after he's covered with oil and fall to the ground still covered in it. Going to the van mad covered in oil saying "I knew your ass was up to something!" He stops before opening the van back doors standing to the side then opening one side real fast and seeing nothing happens he opens the other one and gets sprayed by the extinguisher covering him in Co2 again. Mad about that he stands there and three water balloons falls on top of his head breaking one by one while he stand there pointing at Hutch asking "Is that all you got?" Taking off his wet pants and shirt right there in the street behind the van going to get something to dry off with and then his clothes to changing into. He opens his lock door looking at Hutch and waits with his arms open for a few moment nothing happens, he says "Thought you were good" POW! He gets splattered with Horse shit standing there motionless using the hose to clean up after getting covered with it. Mad he gets in the front of the van slamming the door close and looks over at this paper bag that grows big into a blow up boat again filling the front of the van pinning him against the door. He says softly "I hate that man, I do really. I hate him so much right now!" Moni crushed up against the door as people looking at him after he said that abut Hutch and closes his eye as the boat explodes and turns into white powder filling the front of the van. Hutch told the workers better get the hose as he crushes what's left out in the back of the garbage truck and pulls off to go dump the truck as Moni got of the van coughing white powder trying to scream Hutch's name.

At Hutch's house 2Soon let the girls know he had to run home for a bit and would be back not to worry the others should be there in a short while, having them close and lock the door after he left. They all walked around his house looking at everything thinking they never got a chance to look at his whole place and now would be a good chance to get to know it. 8pm after seeing all they could see the ladies were in the kitchen making something to eat for the movie they were going to watch on his big 86" flat screen TV. The phone rings Erikaa thought it was Hutch calling them and she picks up answering it to her a female saying she works with Hutch "He was in a bad accident and she needs to let his neighbor know so he could call the other family members because they would know what to do." Hearing Erikaa getting very emotional while on the phone Donna asked "What's wrong?" She turns to Donna repeating what she was just told by the caller. Outside Hutch's house a car pulls up with the lights out and four men get out being quite as they walk to the front door and wait there. Inside Donna told Janet and Erikaa to go over to the neighbor's house and she'll go try to find a number to contact anyone of his brothers and goes upstairs to Hutch's bedroom. Janet and Erikaa went to the front door to open it and they get rushed by the men that stood right outside of it. Screaming "Let go of me" loud enough for Donna to hear while she was upstairs looking for a number to call somebody for Hutch. Two men that grabbed Janet and Erikaa held them and told the others to go look in the house for anyone else before they leave so they can't call the cops on them. Two men walk through and search the down stairs first as Janet and Erikaa are told to be quite taken back in the living room. Donna heard Janet's cry and went to the bedroom door closing it, then she looked for her cell phone but it was down stairs and they were starting to come upstairs. Thinking about where she was going to hide as they reached the top of the stairs looking at all the bedroom doors open but one to the master bedroom, they start walking towards it as Donna heard them coming and went to the closet remembering what Hutch showed her as they walk in the bedroom. Inside the closet she just closed the trap door as they stood by the closet door thinking they have someone trapped in the closet, pulling the door open and looking in it to see the closet empty they leave the door open and walk out. Donna is in the other bedroom next to his Hutch's and heard the men coming in there after they came out of his bedroom, she went back through the trap door and back into Hutch's closet and stayed there because she guessed they wouldn't think come back in there again.

2Soon had to turn around and go back to Hutch's house because he forgot his cell and when he got there he saw some car that he didn't know in the driveway. Trying to think of whose car it was but didn't look familiar to him. Sitting in his vehicle just looking at the car he sees the lights of Mack's bike coming down the street. Turning around and heading him off Mack telling him there's some car at Hutch's but he didn't see who got out. Mack says "They might be those guys Hutch wanted us to watch out for to keep the girls safe fam!" Mack calls Hutch but getting no answers, he calls the other GDM4L to see where they are. Goodie, Steel, Dougie, Derrick, Tys, Jazz, and C-man said they were about five minutes from the house. Mack told them to meet him and 2Soon down the block away from Hutch's and hurry the girls might be in danger explaining about the car that's in front g Hutch's house they don't know.

Inside the house the two men are looking around upstairs making a comment at how good his house looks and what good taste he has even for a mook and taking note for some decorating ideas about their own homes. The head man calls them from down stairs "Did yous two find anyone up there or not for crying out loud. You're not taking a tour or yous?" One man answers "They don't see anyone else up here guess them two must be here alone!" The lead man shouts "Good now get your butt back down here so they can leave this mooks house!"

They come back down stairs and tell the head man this mooks got a tub big enough for four people in his bathroom and a multi head shower too. The lead man shouts "Are you finished with the mook's grand home tour. One of you pulls the car up and the other signal when it's clear to bring these two broads out the house." They look at him walking to the front door still making comments about his Frig and how the Island sink has a hand beer dispenser along with one multi head for the kids with 8 kinds of juices on it.

Outside and down the block the rest of the GDM4L showed up and then quickly planned on how they were going to handle things as they walk up to the house to surprise whoever is in the house with the ladies. Mack was by their car parked in the dark arrear of Hutch's driveway, when he saw the front door open and two men talk as one walks out to the car. Mack comes up behind surprising him and sticks his gun in the man's face saying "Open your mouth." When the man did he shoves the barrel in saying "You scream a warning and I pull the trigger. Shake your head yes if you understand!" The man shook his head as Mack took the keys then asked "Was there a signal for the all clear?" The man looks at him as Derrick says to Mack "Man you watch too much TV!" Mack tilts his head pulling the hammer back to his gun and the man shook his head "Yes" telling him about it when Mack took the gun out his mouth as Mack points it right as his privates. Telling Mack "Whistle twice and tap the hood lightly twice for an all clear." The man looks at Tys coming up to him from the dark bushes and says "Aren't you?!" Tys says "Nah but I hit just as hard like him!" Punching knocking the man out not letting him hit the ground but putting him in the trunk of the car after duct taping his hand and feet then ducking back in the bushes as Mack gives the signal all clear. Sitting at the wheel of the car thinking "Hope this work" since he didn't pull the car out from the dark part of the driveway. The second man told the leader everything's good and clear so the lead man says "Now take this broad out to the car." Talking about Janet and walks to the front door with her seeing their man in the front seat of the car waiting for them. The man with Janet walks to the car right pass Mack sitting behind the wheel and he puts her in the backseat but before he could get in 2Soon snatches him into the dark bushes where he and Derrick beat the man unconscious. Then Goodie opens the back door and held out his hand saying "Come on girl Hutch sent us." She recognizes Goodie and gets out of the car and goes in the bushed with him, she starts to tell him about Erikaa and Donna still in the house. He told her they know so stay by him and keep quite till they handle these guys. Mack gave another clear signal for another of them to come out. The lead man told his guy with Erikaa to head on out and he'll be right there soon as he calls Markola and tells him their own their way with these boards. The man with Erikaa heads out to the car and he too walks right pass Mack sitting behind the steering wheel, putting Erikaa in the back seat but this time he takes a second look at the figure behind the wheel asking "Everything alright?!" Mack shook his head and gave a scratchy voice "Yeah." He looks at him for a moment thinking that's not one of them but still gets in the back seat anyways. He doesn't see Erikaa there just Tys/LiL-Rob sitting there looking at him with a mean face as Mack cut on the interior light for a few second so he could see LIL-Rob face. The man ask "Who are you?" LIL-Rob doesn't say a word but stare at him for a few moments. The man says "Shit! You know who you look like?" LiL-Rob says nothing but lean closer to the man and Mack turns around saying "Yeah we get that a lot!" He looks at Mack turning back to LIL-Rob seeing a fist before everything went black. He's dragged out of the car into the bushes where Janet and Erikaa are safe with the rest of the GDM4L.

The Lead man hears the all clear and sends out the third man to tell the others to get ready when he comes out. The third man never makes it to the car as Derrick and 2Soon tackle him in the dark bushes because he was walking slowly up to Mack sitting behind the wheel. They told Mack to give the all clear again and get the last one out and he does. The lead man comes out of the house still talking on the cell with Markola. He goes to get in the front seat and a figure sitting there points to get in the back so he gets in the back still talking with Markola and never notices there wasn't anyone in the back till he hangs up with Markola. Looking at the back two figures in the front seats wondering where are the women. The door open and someone get in on his left so he moves over, then the door on the other side opens as someone gotten in on his right side. He moves over to let that person in too sitting between two men now. He looks left and then right wondering who they are these men. There is not a word said as all the men sit there quite in the car for a few moments, then the lead man looking at 2Soon on his right asking "Who are you?" 2Soon points to Derrick in the front seat "I'm his brother." Then turning to his left asking "Who are you?" Lil-Rob points to Mack behind the wheel "I'm his brother." Tapping Derrick on shoulder "Who are you?" Derrick turns and points to LIL-Rob "I'm his brother." Before he could ask Mack who he was, Mack turns and points to 2Soon "I'm his brother." Looking at the man and he says "You're all brothers in her but not me." Mack reaching back there opening his jacket getting the man's gun from his side saying "You won't need this right now. Though you wish you had it, but you still couldn't use it." Pulling out the clip and emptying the chamber and handing it back to him. Outside the car the rest of the GDM4L with Janet and Erikaa watch as Goodie says "This aint gonna be pretty ladies better not look!" The Whole car is rocking back and forth as four figures beat up the middle one in the dark part of the drive way. Four doors of the car open up at the same time and four figures step out with one dragging a man with him to join the other three taped up and out cold from getting beat or punched out. Inside the house Donna is thinking Janet and Erikaa were taken by those men calling Hutch from the house phone, he answers hearing the fear in her voice tell what has happened to Janet and Erikaa. Telling her to go down stairs describing where the alarm system box was and telling her to punch in the code to get the police there and stay there till he gets there because he's on his way. She does what he told her too but just as she was punching in the code she heard Janet's voice at the door knocking on it. "Donna! It's Ok you can open the door." Janet knew they didn't find her in the house and thought they should get back in so they can call Hutch and let him now about the men that tried to take them. Donna looks out the window and saw Erikaa talking with Derrick and Mack, then she saw 2Soon with the rest of the GDM4L tying up the other men and dragging them to the front of the house. She opens the door so they could come in saying "I didn't know what to think calling Hutch and telling him you two were just kidnapped by Markola's men." She explained that Hutch told her to call the police by punching in his code on the alarm system and waits for him and them to come there. Mack said "All they are going to do is waits for bail and come back here again with their boss." Ron gets there asking "What did I miss." 2Soon explained what happened and about the fact they're going to jail but like Mack said would be getting out and coming back there with the boss. Ron smiled says "You know what would Hutch do about making a statement for them not to be coming back at him again." Explaining they don't have much time asking for help with the guys putting all the men but one in their car and he needs one of them to follow him. Goodie, Dougie and LIL-Rob followed him as he drove away with the men in their own car. Leaving Steel and the rest of them there for when Hutch arrives with the cops to his house. Far from Hutch's house is a school doing some project work in the playground arrear and have this big blue tarp covering the monkey bars they just put in. Ron pulls up to the school and gets out walking over to Douige and laughing saying "I've got a good idea these guys won't ever come back again." Going in the trunk seeing the plastic ties they had and were going to use on the ladies with other things in the trunk of the car. Ron took everything he could find then asking Goodie for a hand with the men dragging them under the blue tarp.

At Hutch's house the police get there and Derrick talks to them since he's one of them and tells them how this man came there armed to the teeth with all those hand guns he shows them saying "He wanted to kidnap these women and hold them for ransom." He didn't count on him and his brothers being around stopping his plan. Hutch is pulling up in the garbage truck 25 minutes later runs towards the house knocking three cops down trying to stop him from getting in his house to see if the girls are alright. Mack says to the girls "See told you he'd come here in hulk mode." Then says "Let me talk to him, I know how to calm him down. Hutch no Smash. Ladies safe, house clean, bad man go to jail errah" flexing a pose at him. 2Soon busted out laughing like the other saying "Son you stupid"

Hutch looks at Mack and took a deep breath asking "Where's the rest?" Steel answered by saying "Ron said something about how you make sure guys don't want to come back at you ever again. He knows what to do with them taking the rest of them somewhere followed by Goodie, Dougie with Tys/LIL-Rob." Hutch starts laughing and says "Hope they took some pictures, I always do." Everyone stopped and looked at him as he goes "What?! It works they never come back or they would have to explain a picture on how I got them to pose like that in a very uncomfortable position." Herb told Hutch "Your sick man but I'm glad you're my brother and don't ever take my picture without my consent!" Janet tugged on Hutch "Could I see the pictures!" He told her "After the police leaves he's got a few of them guys in the scrap book too" That made all the GDM4L, even Erikaa and Donna look at him again wondering what else did Hutch do for him to even start making a scrap book like that. The police took the man into custody with the recommendation of Derrick to charge him with assault with attempted Murder, attempt kidnapping, weapons charges, burglary being ugly with no brains on all accounts, breaking and entering the Honey Comb Hideout adding to their paper work. As they were leaving Ron, Goodie, Dougie and LIL-Rob came back to the house laughing so much at what Ron and Dougie did at the school yard under the blue tarp with those men. Ron told Hutch "I texted all the pictures to your phone I took of them you'll like them all. Hutch took the cell and hooked it up to his computer and took the pictures Ron and Dougie sent took to him of the guys on the monkey bars and how they posed them and what little they had on. They try and figure out how these guys knew that the girls were there. That's when Donna gets on Hutch about not leaving his emergency numbers to his family with a neighbor instead of in the house. All of the GDM4L look at her thinking whatever gave her the idea that he gave his emergency numbers to the family to a neighbor? Explaining the call she got about him, what was said to her by that woman with the winey nasal voice sounding like she comes from the projects. How she knew Hutch and the GDM4L, 2Soon looked at Dougie both said a name (Sonia) at how Donna said the woman's voice sounds like. They came over to Hutch asking him not to get mad but they think they know the woman. "Sonia!" 2Soon's girl and she's a friend of Elise's remember they all met at the bar at the same time that night after work. Sounds like she put Sonia up to this but couldn't understand why would Sonia help her harm Hutch's ladies when she don't even know them. Donna said "Friends stick together like you brothers do all the time having the others back."

2Soon couldn't believe it and calls Sonia to find out but when she hears how the girls would have been taken away and killed, she breaks down crying saying "I would never want to see anyone dead much less be a part of them being killed on account of me." She explains Elise told her Hutch was cheating on her and she wanted to help bust him for it but she sees now her friend used her and to almost get them killed that wasn't right of her. 2Soon went to Hutch after he talked with her about everything because he knew she did have it in her to be that vicious toward someone she never met before. Hutch sat there thinking he's got to get back at this Markola for just thinking he could violate his house like that and fix Elise for helping him too. Trying to think of a good way to pay him back when he heard Ron telling Steel "Way he left those men stripped of their dignity they won't be coming back again." Hutch was mad that they had the nerve to come to his house like that and wants to get this man badly for that feeling violated. He needs to get this straighten out with him once and for all before things gets to the point of someone getting seriously hurt. Still trying to figure out how he got Elise to be on his side. Thinking whatever he did to her, in order for her to turn on him and from her mind being out of touch with reality. Now all he's got to do is get away to contact this guy so they can talk. Looking at the girls and being mad that they were attacked in his house like that, it hits him where did it all start at the strip club. He got the idea to leave a message at the strip club for Markola to meet him in a public place. Asking 2Soon, Steel, Dave, Mack, Dougie and La-Machine to go this strip club and find the manager there, have him get hold of Markola anyway he can so they can talk. Reminding them find the manager there to give that message to Markola, not to bring back any more female out of the club. Dave wants to know why they can't because he did it and that's not right for Hutch to be so selfish. He looked at Dave and told him

"I didn't says not to make any new friends just don't pull them out of there till everything is over and done with this asshole Markola." Thinking of a place to have his meeting so it doesn't get dangerous for any of his brothers who's going to back him up then the Seaport came to mind. It's close to one police Plaza and he wouldn't think of doing anything stupid with all the cops around on the seaport anyways. Derrick said "Thanks for reminding him, he's got to find a place where his buddy from the department is going to hold their bachelor party. They left it up to him to find a place and get the entertainment for that night, sorry fam I can't go with yall." Hutch about to say something when he looks at Derrick and turns to look at Janet, Erikaa and Donna smiling at them then says "I go that covered for you Dee" and points to the ladies and walks over to them asking them do they know of some ladies that wouldn't mind dancing for the police at a bachelor party. Answering Hutch "If they didn't know Derrick they would do it themselves because cop and secret service men are the biggest tippers, next to congressmen!" Then telling Derrick "See problem solved so you could be there at the seaport now with the rest of us" The ladies told Hutch they better get to making some calls because once it gets out they know of a bachelor cop party there's going to all kinds of their friends calling to get booked for it. They went upstairs out the way to make their calls and let the men plan out what they're going to do knowing Hutch would fill them in later. Planning out everything with his brothers on how they're going to be at the South Street Seaport pier7 before Markola's men get there and try to get the jump on him when they have that meeting there. Hutch said "We're going to need all G.D.M.4.L so conference calling the remaining G.D.M.4.L Drea, D-train, Troy, Jeff Kinslow and Doug." Telling them they need to be at the seaport on Thursday before 1pm because that's when he setting the met time with that asshole, and know his men would be there way before he ever gets there. Then finishing telling them about the plan to let this man know he's not going take what he did, showing him there will be action to answer his attacks. The rest of the night they all talked about actions just in case and Hutch told them all to use their best Judgment on anything they have to do long as they don't draw blood unless they have too. Letting them know if there's a mark or two that's left behind on any of them by all means have at it and do take trophies too. Hutch stayed there as all his brothers left to get rest for the next day. He told the girls he like to see any one come in there now that he's home and ready for anything. Janet looked at Hutch all swelled up like he was ready to fight now, asking "Are you sure you're ready for anything?" They all start up stairs leaving an article of clothing behind on the stairs as they walked up. Hutch was already feeling the drinks he had, but when he heard a voice say "The waters hot now!" He goes over to the bar and makes a quick boiler maker with Gin, Drambuie, E&J brandy, Vodka and Guinness stout beer. (READERS how's your stomach feeling) That next morning at this school parents were dropping off their kids and some were staying around having the normal conversation like they always do. Some kids were running around screaming and playing going in and out from under the blue tarp. At first the parents weren't paying any attention to the kids because they always play in the morning before going into the building. This time the kids were saying things that caught some of their parent's attention "Wow does your daddy look like that without clothes on." Another kid asked "Why is that man's face in the other man's butt like my dog? Are all men part dog and say Hi like dogs do?" One kid says "I saw my mommy tie a man up like that but she beat him with this belt and he liked it! I heard my uncle say he likes plays S F M games, but he says my aunty too soft on him that's why he plays with mommy's sister aunty Carol she hits hard!" The parents saw all the kids run under the tarp and come out screaming "Their awake and moving!" One of the parents went under the tarp and came out with a look on her face and went to the other parents. They kept the kids away as the principal was alerted and calls security and then the police. Some of the parents were upset that this could happen at their Elementary school. Some people even took pictures to have of the men in those positions on the monkey bars, watching the men try to free themselves with all that clicking of the cameras going on. When the police came they went under the tarp and some came out laughing so hard they called for more cops and even tipped off the news crew to show up.

That evening 2Soon and the rest of the G.D.M.4.L went to the strip club in Brooklyn to go deliver the message for Hutch. They were crossing the street one block away from the club on third ave under the expressway and got spotted by Elise driving home from work. She recognized 2Soon and Dougie from that night she first met them with Hutch at the bar that night. She parks her car quickly thinking Hutch can't be far if they're around and waits to see where they are going. Watching them go into the strip club and then go in after them thinking Hutch must be in there already. She's thinking "I would love to catch him with another stripper if that's what he prefers over me."

Hutch is home cooking with the girls and getting ready to watch a movie and the news came on about some men being a modern day art master piece at the local Elementary school. That gave Hutch the idea to call his brothers because should be there by now. Janet told Hutch to call his brothers and let them know not to drink anything served in the V.I.P back room, because Markola always has his girls drug the drinks so they can take advantage of the men that way. He calls 2Soon and gave him the heads up and asked "How things are going" He answers "They didn't see any of the managers yet but the place is kind of crowded."

Erikaa reminds Hutch to let 2Soon start flashing big cash like a big spender that would get the managers attention. Hutch told 2Soon to use whatever he's got to get the managers attention and for the others to do the same, he'll give it back to them so they don't lose anything. 2Soon replied "Alright Fam." Going over to the others and told them what Hutch said. Somehow they were hoping Hutch would have said that and went to the bank before they came there anyways. Using the cash to get the stripper they want to come over to them as they threw money at her. The Managers sees them spending a lot of cash and wants to know if they were interested in going to the V.I.P room where they could have some special strippers do their dances and lap dances as long as the cash is there. 2Soon told the man there are more of us and he said "Not a problem bring them." Elise came in to the club looking around and saw 2Soon and a couple others going into the back with the managers. Thinking Hutch must be back there with them, now all she's got to do is get back there and bust him. Walking in to the back where the dancers are and getting some of their clothes to put on to blend in. She changes into an outfit and comes back out only to be handed a tray of drinks and told to follow the other girls into the back V.I.P room. The girls came back there and the guys wanted the waitress to sit with them for second. Elise didn't want to take the chance of Dougie or 2Soon recognizing her, so she got up on stage with the other girls and starts dancing moving all stiff. La-Machine went up to Elise and gave her one of the spiked drinks and told her "If you want a tip, then drink it down." She didn't want to get noticed so she drank it and La-machine had another one to hand her saying "That drink was just one here have another one." He then pulls out a couple bills and stuffs it in her bra as she stood there looking shocked that he would do that to her, forgetting that she was in a strip club for a moment. It occurred to her where she was when another lady came up to her and said "If you don't want it I'll do it then!" La-Machine didn't want the other lady because he liked picking on the stiff dancing one. He got her to drink four more and that's when they told her to dance with the other ladies. All the strippers back there was getting rocked off their own drinks because 2Soon told all the GDM4L the heads up about the drinks thanks to Erikaa letting Hutch know about it. Things start getting wild because the ladies were really getting loose and acting out. The manager wanted to know how come the guys aren't out cold from the drinks. He went back there but the girls were doing things that had them really cheering at what they were on the stage to each other. Elise was the main one really getting the most cheers from her getting frisky with some lady. What Elise didn't know was the woman she was dancing with was a bi-sexual exhibitionist that liked her and that's why they were going at it. The drinks being drugged Elise didn't seem to mind preforming in front of them that way with her. Steel had got in between the both of them and they took him over to the dark both. 2Soon wanted to see the head manager because something wasn't right back there. The junior manager told him "Wait there" and went to get him. The club manager came there and 2Soon asked him "Do you have direct contact with Markola?" He asked "Why?" 2Soon grabs him up and told him "Here's a message from my brother Hutch, Markola knows who he is. Tell him to be at pier 7 Manhattan the South Street Seaport and come alone so they can talk. The seafood place inside be there at 1:30pm." Making sure he got the message right then throwing him back out front, his men saw him flying out from the back and they came running. A small brawl began in the back but quickly got quite down because all his men got their ass beat and knocked out by the GDM4L. 2Soon was doing a head count and saw that Steel was missing and went to get him and found him and the two women in another part of the V.I.P section. Turning the lights up to tell him they need to leave but saw the face of one woman engaging the other woman with Steel behind. 2Soon looked at Steel

"Come on man we have to. Oh shoot do you know who that is eating?" Getting a good look at the woman's face when she raised her head up from between the other woman's leg as the light got bright. Telling Steel they need to get out right now because he's not going to believe what he was doing. They leave before the men could wake and more came to help them. On the way back to (the Shoal) Staten Island 2Soon let Steel know that was Elise Hutch's ex he was boning from the back while she was muff diving. Steel says "Yeah she was doing a better job than me from the sound the other lady was making!" They start laughing about what happened and made more jokes about her, that she would act so high class around them. Not knowing she was a street level fisher-man who really likes raw fresh Sushi or Susie if that was her name and can't wait to tell Hutch of the technique.

Elise is waking up and looks around to see that she is not in her bed or her bedroom, thinking she's still dreaming turning her head back and forth to see she is in somebodies bedroom laying there. Taking a big yawn closing her mouth quick at the sight of a body walk pass the room without any clothes on, blinking she didn't see that until the person walks pass the room again. It's not a dream as the woman walks in still naked and looks at her saying "Ah good, you're awake. Hungry?" Elise just looks at the woman as she starts to get dressed and says "Things got so intense with us. I didn't get your name. I'm Barbra" Elise looks at her sitting on the side of the bed next to her half dress answering softly "Elise! I'm Elise!" Barbra gets up and finished getting dressed explaining she don't do things like one night stands that often. Last night it seems Elise had a lot to get off her chest, the way she were talking about some guy name Hutch and you're going to hit this the way he should have even tried to hit it. Elise looked at Barbra with her face turning so red when Barbra told her "I never had a woman that was so aggressive and hell bent on making herself and me reach a height which rubbed us both bald." Saying "The pain of having hair pulled out at the same time feeling pleasure like that WOW!" Elise looked under the covers and saw she didn't have any clothes on and feeling sore now that she mentioned it, asking "How did we get here to your place?" Barbra explained after Elise starts dancing on the back room stage, they went with a customer in another room where they started getting really down and wild. When she touched Elise a spot that made her moan things took off so did their clothes. One of the man's friends came in and they had to go because of the fighting, after that the manager came in and caught us in the midst of doing an act without any customer there. He told us to take that elsewhere but not before offering to join in which she told him go to hell. Then you grabbed up two more drinks downing them quick looking at him and saying "Go to hell you troll." Barbra said "I could tell you weren't in any shape to drive, I got you to give me the keys to your vehicle and brought you here to my place. You were talking about some dumb ass man Hutch, spending his money on his friends and brothers but not his woman or any of her friends." She hands Elise a towel and wash cloth and points to the bathroom and said "We'll talk more after you shower and eats breakfast." Getting up heading to the bathroom Elise is reminded of what she done because of the soreness when she walks. Looking down seeing hair gone from spot on her body she rolls her eye shaking her head. Clean and dressed Elise and Barbra sit at the table as Elise listens to more about what she did that night and what she talked to Barbra about. She gets walked to her vehicle given an open invitation to come back any time before Elise went home.

Larry is waking up in the motel room and takes his shower afterwards looking at what he's going to wear thinking about what he wants to eat saying to himself "It's a little hard driving alone that far from home but it'll be nice to see my brothers again" and with the news he's a graduate from law school. He gets in the vehicle wondering if he has enough clothes and which brother's house will he staying at till he gets his own place.

Hutch is woke down stairs sitting in his chair watching TV when Janet comes down stairs kisses him good morning "Glad you're one who brushes and use mouth wash when you first wake up!" Then sits in his lap and lays back on him. He chuckled "That's why there are four places for tooth brushes in the bathroom next to that big jug of mouth wash!" Giving her a good squeeze, and holds her in his arms. She wanted to know does he regret meet them at the supermarket, because of all the things that has happened since they came into his life or was his life always this much excitement never a dull moment. He laughs about to say something when Donna and Erikaa are heard from the stairs "Wait till we get there, we want to hear this too." They come down and like Janet they kiss him and each other good morning. He tells them they should cook breakfast because this is going to make him hungry and he wants to see what they come up with together. Going to the kitchen he starts with "Yes" to Janet's question his life has had it never dull moments. He's very glad now that he's got all three of them to share it with and in time they'll get used to all the craziness. Letting them know his other name the GDM4L calls him (MADDNESS!) because of all the wild and crazy things somehow only happens to him. Derrick calls reminding Hutch of all his policemen friends about having the party at his house. Hutch told Derrick just make sure they park the patrol unit cars down the street out of the way and not in other peoples drive ways because he got to live there too, for him to be there at the seaport because he's leaving in a few to go there.

At the Seaport Hutch is sitting at the table in the restaurant telling the waiter he's got one more persons coming so he'll have a shot of E&J and bud light. The waiter came back with the drinks and he saw Markola walking in with two of his men right behind him. He takes a seat at the table with Hutch and starts to tell him about the message he left him at his club, how there's going to be damages billed to him even hospital bills too. Hutch Laughs and downs his shot chasing it with the beer then answers him with "My house violation was a priceless move too!" Markola looks at him and wants to know why they're here in the first place? Hutch looks at him and says "Wait here's something I learned recently let's eat and be civilized like grown men do and talk over a good meal first." Markola thought either he's been to see his uncle or he really is under estimating this guy. He agrees to take Hutch up on his offer and calls the waiter over so they can get some food. The waiter asked "What did they want to drink?" Markola saying "I'll have red wine" and Hutch orders E&J double no ice either, that makes Markola nod his head at Hutch. They get the drinks and Hutch looks at his men and asked Markola "Were they going to eat too or wait for the scraps off the tables" Both men look at Hutch when he said that about them and sneered at him. Hutch looks at them telling Markola "Your mutts don't look happy better feed those things they might turn on ya." The food came with the waiter putting a big steak and lobster with boiled shrimp on the side in front of Hutch. Markola says "Wow you going eat all that. I rather clothed you than feed you?" Then the waiter puts a lobster and sausages with pasta in front of Markola. Hutch says "Huh on diet I see." They start eating and Hutch is finished way before Markola is even done with half his food as he makes a comment about how mooks can put away some food. Hutch comes back with your people aren't no picky eater either and I've seen them at their morning carnage.

Markola wants to know why Hutch cut off his card, when he was told not to causing an embarrassing scene for him at a place. Some of his friends now look at him like he's having financial trouble and want certain cash advances back from him seeing how there was a certain food bill that couldn't be covered at that time. Hutch looks at him and says "Should have paid cash it works for me." Markola leans forward on the table "What if your girl Donna pays for your arrogance or those two other one you seem to like so much mook huh!" Hutch looks at him thinking "He doesn't know they're all with me now" and taunts Markola by saying "Go ahead and kill them see if I care, but first you might want to get that feed out of the basement where all those rat are. If you can't do that then check the paper about a certain school and look at the face of the men on the monkey bars." Markola called one of men over telling him to go call and check on the guy with the girls and see if they have them and where's the other meat heads that were supposed to be dropping feed in the warehouse in Brooklyn. Both men get up and leave out to go make the calls. Hutch wanted to know why is he do such a thing and all about his Credit card. Saying to Markola "Is my six figures worth all this trouble because I worked hard all my life for that money and bled for some of it too, but to keep coming after me about my account is going to make me fight you with everything I got till one of us aint here anymore." Markola looks at Hutch and wonders why he never said anything about his Unlimited Credit card that he wants from him. Unless he does know he even got it. Thinking it must be some other card not the one with his name on it this mook has and still don't know he's got a card like that. Making Markola want to take it from Hutch more than ever before he finds out about the Credit card he's got. Markola is trying to figure how Hutch doesn't know he's got something like that in his possession unless he came across it and never looked at it just putting it in his wallet till that night at his club. Thinking he must still have it on him and in his wallet right now but he's got to wait till his men comes back to make his move. Hutch was sizing up his men and how he was going to get out of there without having to do a lot of damage to the place before his men came back there. He saw this waiter use a pan and some liquid he pours in it to making the flames go up, that's when Hutch got an idea and not too soon as the men came back to Markola leaning to hear saying something only he could hear. Markola looks at Hutch who now knows he must have found out the ladies are not where he thought they would be as the men went back to the table and sat there waiting for Markola. He lean forward and take another fork full of food chewing it and then a drink from his glass wiping his mouth smiling at Hutch pointing at him "Wow you are one smart mook! You have the girl don't you." Hutch smiles "Yep! I put them somewhere you can't find them either!" Two more of Markola men came in the place and stood by the front door as Markola looks at Hutch asking "Since you're good at getting them out of places without me seeing. How you going to get out of here without me seeing you hurt!" He smirks at Hutch leaning back in his chair. Hutch asked "So what do you want from me then?" Markola just says "Give me your wallet and you can walk out here and never hear from me again." Hutch looked at him because he said that same thing before and here they are sitting here having the same conversation. Being the wise answering man he is Hutch says "What! Leave me with the check not being able to pay for it no thanks. We split the bill or going Dutch seeing as how I'm the only man here and you are drinking wine!" Markola looks at him puzzled at what he said, as one of his men says to him "I think that mook just call you a BI-OTCH?" Markola looks at him for second and then at Hutch, who was laughing at Markola because his man got it right away but he didn't. Markola looks at Hutch about to say something when Hutch calls the waiter over and orders a drink, asking the waiter for the check and "A triple E&J no ice with double shot of Rey & nephew plus three shot of Drambuie also no ice all in the same glass." Looking at Markola going "If I'm going to get my ass beat might as well feel no pain." The waiter said "Hell you could pull teeth and not feel it drinking all that mixed!" The waiter asked Markola "Do you want a comatose drink as well?" Markola shook his head "Just bring the check!" When the drink came Hutch swirled the drink around in one glass and took a swig feeling the drink out in his mouth as Markola cringed at him doing that. Hutch said "When I come out the bathroom we can get on with it." Markola smirks going "Got to drain the lizard huh?" Hutch laughs at him "You guys have Gecko's but I have a dragon to worry about!" Take a big gulp of the drink he ordered heading towards the bathroom. Markola calls his man over to him and didn't see Hutch take a book of matches from another table as he walks to the bathroom. Two men came in the bathroom and saw Hutch with his back to them at the urinal, then he turn quickly spraying that drink in his mouth and lighting a match shooting fire on them like a dragon. They come running out of the bathroom all ablaze as people see that and starts running out of the place. Markola looks to see his men on fire and signals his other men to help them as Hutch use the distraction to get out the front door. Markola saw him leaving out yelling for his men to put them out and go after that mook, then starts to go after him too but the waiter says "Whoa little man who's paying for the check?" Markola cusses "Dam mook got me again" he pulls out a wad of cash and hands it to the waiter. Hutch is walking along the store fronts followed by two men, he ducks into the radio shack where Mack is standing and gave him a nod watching him go by. Mack sees the two men come in after Hutch did and he took out the stunner testing it to make sure it works but it doesn't. He opens it up to check the batteries.

The men are walking around the store and split up to cover either side in case Hutch tries to get out. One man see him and walks toward Hutch slow so he doesn't cause a scene in the place and security has to be called where he would have to explain. Mack goes to the counter buying a pack of batteries paying for them and trying to open the back of the stunner as he walking passed one of the men. The man sees Mack with the stunner and says "Hey let me see that. You know I just bought my wife one of these" He takes and opens the back for Mack and puts the batteries in and hands it back to him. Looking at Mack asking "Is that for your wife?" Mack smiled at him and zaps the man right there saying "Think I will get my girl one of these." Then takes a cord and hog ties the man with people looking at them as Mack shows the people he had a gun "He was going to rob the place." People applauded what he did. That noise made the other man look to see his partner tied up but when he turns back he's greeted by a fist that knocks him out. Hutch drags him over to the other one where Mack says "Here's his partner good thing I got a partner too" and people applauded again as Hutch looks at Mack who's shrugging his shoulder and told him "Get out of here I got this." Hutch leaves spotted by Markola as he told his men to "Get that mook right there" and they go after Hutch. He ducks into a beauty and body shop and walks pass Dougie and D-train as they gave Hutch a nod then continues at act like they were buying something when the men came in. The place is one big open room and the men split up to come at him from either side as Hutch stood there smelling the candles. The sale woman came over to one of the men asking "Could I help you" but the man was rude telling her

"Get out my face and go somewhere." Hutch calls her over and asked her "Do she have any green apple that's his mother's favorite." The sales girl smiled "Yes over here." They walk to the other side of the store with the men right behind them. Hutch asked her "Did she make a lot on sales this week" When she starts to answer the men are jumped from behind by Dougie and D-train.

The thumping and bumping is quick as Hutch kept her from turning around but when she did and saw the men on the floor out cold with Douige and D-train standing over them. Hutch says "They shouldn't have been rude to you, I hate that don't you?" Hutch goes in their pockets taking out their wallets, giving the woman all their cash saying "Here that should make up for this week and their rudeness." She smiled at him and took the money and said "Here" she gave Hutch the bag of bath oil, body lotion, foot cream, body oil and gel wash plus facial cream in the green apple scent for doing that. Dougie and D-train said they helped too and would like something. She smiled at them asking "What flavor do they like. Hutch told D-train to make sure he throws out the garbage after he leaves and meet on the third deck. Watching Hutch leave first then Dougie, D-train say to the sale woman " I'll be right back as they drag the two men out the back door to the back garbage room, when they came back she told him "Your friends left his stuff" D-train says "That's my brother and don't worry I'll make sure he gets the stuff." She said "How when you're going to be trying this bath oil with me tonight." They get to talking and he helps sell some stuff with her while in the store. Hutch is walking on the second level of the pier when Markola see him wondering how do he keep getting around and not being caught by his men. Now with more men by his side Markola sent three men after Hutch walking up on that second level. They hurry up to the second level hoping not to lose sight of him and see him go into this clothing store with a lot of mannequins standing displaying clothes. Hutch sees Dave and La-machine with Jazz and nods to them. This store has part room divider walls where the mannequins could stand displaying the clothes and Hutch walks around in there. The men split up like to cover more ground and catch him quicker but as one man thought he had Hutch it was a dummy. Another man stood right behind Hutch and told him to turn around he wants to see his face, when Hutch did he was smiling at the man and he wants to know what Hutch was smiling at. Hutch points in back of him to La-Machine standing there looking at him. The man says "It's a dummy" La-Machine taps him waiting as he turns punching the man out saying to him "Who's the dummy now Bi-otch!" Another of the men saw what happened and went to sneak up on Hutch and La-Machine, thinking he'll get the drop on them as he moves closer behind them. Dave was watching him and moves right where the man was going to sneak up on them and stands still, the man bumps into Dave who goes "Ow!" The man says "Sorry" turning quickly to look at Dave then turns back to see where Hutch and La-Machine were still there tying up his partner. The man thought about it for a second and then turns back to see a mannequin standing there then turns to see Dave face to face say to him "Going to sneak up on my brothers huh" "POW" Dave's punched the man so hard knocking him out and watch slide over to La-Machine and Hutch. They tying that man up too after he slid over when the clicking sound of a gun hammer is heard and tells them to get their hands up. They stand there looking at the wave moving the clothes in back of the man with the gun, he turns seeing nothing quickly turning back to see they are standing wide apart. He turns back for another quick look just as Jazz comes out from under the clothes and tackling the man as they heard a small meekly "oh shit" before he's hit. Dave caught the gun that came out of his hands and Jazz got up off the man after knocking him out with that tackle. The salesmen came over to see them with the men on the floor asking "What's going on here?" Dave answers "They need to have better gear on if they're going to hang with us but they wouldn't hold still for the fitting can you help?" The sales men looked at the men out cold on the floor "Why are they tied like that?" La-Machine says "They wanted to grab everything at one time and just like kids we had to say no pick one thing and they wouldn't so we improvised" Jazz asked the salesmen "Do you work on commission?" He answered "Yes but things were slow!"

Jazz said "Not today their buying! We all need new gear but starts with us first and then we'll get to them do you have a dressing room where they can wait in?" Jazz, Hutch, Dave and La-machine take the men in the back dressing. Hutch takes their wallets and all the cash out and gives it to the salesmen saying "Here take care of them and keep the rest." He walks out of the store and heads towards the other side of the pier of shops but is seen by Markola again. Telling his last four men to "Get that mook, before he gets away" pointing out Hutch as he looks down at Markola yelling about him. Two men take one side and the other two take the other side, they go up to get after Hutch who sees them and takes the elevator up to the third floor. Now on the third floor he looks at them on the stairs to come up after him. Markola is waiting for the elevator to come back down to the ground level with three more men so he could get on and come after Hutch too. The four men are up there on the third level closing in from both sides to catch Hutch and behind two of the men on the right is 2Soon and on the other side left Ron is behind those two. Hutch sees that he'll be Ok and walks into the men's room as all four men go in after him. Mack sees Ron as he was looking over the rail trying to find the others to let them know where they are. He calls Ron on the cell and hears him say "Third floor bathroom fam Hutch is there with four of them." Mack says "On my way!" Hutch is at the urinal taking a leak when two of the men come in there and stand behind him talking softly, then charge at him as he pees on that man making him stop dead in his tracks going "What the FLOCK!" The other man says "You're going to pay for that" and charges at Hutch. They are fighting with Hutch getting the best of both men in there and the noise carried out to the other men rushes in now to help the other two. Mack is getting to the third floor and sees La-Machine, jazz and Dave. He lets them know Hutch is in the bathroom with four of them so they should get there fast. 2Soon and Ron stand by the door hearing the fighting going on in there as Ron says "Wait for Mack fam, he's on his way now!" Seconds after he said that here comes Mack, Dave, La-machine and Jazz, they all go in the bathroom to see Hutch being held by two men while being hit by other two. One man boldly says "The bathroom is closed" Opening his jacket showing the gun on his side. 2Soon laughs "Fam You good with this!" Hutch says "Yeah just waiting for you!" Using the two men holding him he kicks the man with the gun close to him right in to 2Soon punch and the brawl begins. The fighting doesn't take long with all the men being knocked out and their guns taken from them. Dave holds Hutch's face asking him "You alright big bruha." Hutch chumps his teeth twice saying "They didn't knock any out but thinking I'm going to leave them a message why not to mess with us and draw blood." Herb and Goodie get up on the third level and saw Jazz standing by the men's room, they went over and Dave came out the bathroom saying "Let's keep people out for a minute while Hutch and the others do their thing to these guys." Herb looks at Dave "Is Hutch in there with 2Soon, Ron, and Mack?" La-machine says "Yep!" Herb says "Them brothers need help man if they're in there doing to those men what I think they're doing. Who started that shit any ways?" Dave says "Hutch did! He got the idea from the brother you know. He turns to Herb with a crazy looking face smiling RENTA COPS! I HATE RENTA COPS TOO!" They come out of the bathroom laughing so hard Mack told Hutch "Yeah man we got all the pictures we need for U-tube!" Herb goes in and sees the men and comes out asking "How do you get their hands tied like that?" trying not to laugh but still does "You still need help Hutch badly!" They leave from the men's room and Hutch head outside to the level that faces the water and Brooklyn side of the pier. Markola and his men saw Hutch walking outside and take another exit to head him off. Outside Markola shouts to Hutch "Don't know how you made it this far mook! Now you got nowhere to go unless you want to swim and I don't think mooks float too well!"

Standing there with three men Hutch turns to show his face now starting to swell from the punches he took in the bathroom. Markola says "Well, well well guess you didn't have it that easy after all huh mook!" Two more of Markola got lose and happens to come up there to find Hutch facing Markola and his three men. One of them walks over to Markola about to tell him Hutch is not alone but gets told to be quite by Markola as he gloats. The three men in the clothing store are woken up and cut lose by security when a man found them in the dressing room, they find Markola up on the third floor facing Hutch too. Again one of them try's to tell him that Hutch is not alone but he gets told to be quite as Markola stand there thinking about the Credit card he's going to get from Hutch. The last two are the first two to be knocked out in the radio shack and they make their way up on the third level outside and see Hutch standing there facing Markola. One of them walks over to him and Markola looks at him wondering why he's being bothered by his own men. Hutch saw his brothers coming up behind Markola and all his men there. Laughing he says "You know I didn't want to take it there but you just did want to leave me alone did you?" Then adding "Let's skip the big speech part where you go "You and what army? Just turn the hell around and look in back of you ok." Markola turns around to see the GDM4L standing there with serious looks on their faces and he shouts to his men "Where did all these mooks come from?" One of his men says "That's what we've been trying to tell you, he didn't come alone either" Markola is about to say something to his men but gets tackled by Hutch and the GDM4L got into the fight too.

On the first level in a thrift store lots of people are shopping when they heard what sound like a man screaming as he went by the window and made a big splash in the water below. Then they went back to shopping when another man goes by the window and the big splash is seen by the people in the store. People in the store stop and look at the window thinking they might see another man go by and they do. Now the store is crowded with people who heard about men going by the window splashing in the water from other people in the Pier shopping. The store crowds looks at the window and another man goes by as they cheer him after he splashes into the river. Another man goes by and some people even starts holding hold rated numbers on the splashing the men made. The manager of the store quickly shows a sale on big number cards and sells a lot of them in the store as another man goes by and people hold up what they think his splash was. When another man goes by and splashes people in the store hold up 8 and some hold up 9 cards. The fighting is almost done as they throw two men that time over the side. Hutch looks at the remaining four men plus Markola. He asked his men "Was it worth for them following him to the river and getting thrown in." None of the men say anything as yet another one gets thrown in and then there was three. The last three look at

Markola and shake their heads and Hutch points to another one to get thrown in. Hutch said to the remaining two "If you think about coming after me or any of my family. I'm going to bring it to yours just like you would (holding their I.D's up so they see what he's got) I suggest you pass on the message when you guys get dried off" Then pointing to another one and watches as he get thrown in and this time they could hear a muffled cheer coming from down below. Hutch walks over to the last man asking him "Can you swim?" He said "Nope!" Hutch looks at his brothers and says "Now a good time to learn." They throw him up and over making a good splash and having the people below cheer loud. Hutch looks at Markola and they all said "This one's yours fam" and watch as Hutch said to Markola "Where you going to go unless you can swim and I do believe shit can float watch this!"

Picking up Markola over his head showing him how strong he is and tossing him up high first and over the rail. People in the store hear this man screaming "I'll get you mook for this!" Hitting the water making a little splash and everyone showed 1 or zero booing that one guessing that was the last one they leave out the store. Security came up there where the guys were being thrown off and wants to talk to Hutch. Derrick shows his badge along with Dave and Goodie and told them it was a college prank and should charge the guys in the water for everything. They wanted to be thrown in and paid for it. Hutch and his brothers laughed at how they threw the men over the rail and Derrick reminds everyone about the party it starts at 8pm. Hutch told Derrick he got that covered and calls his girls who told him everything is set so come home. He told all the GDM4L what time to be there and don't be late or they might miss out on a woman or two. They all told him see him there and went to their vehicles. The police boat is fishing out of the river Markola and his men as they told them they were robbed and thrown in the river, the guys are still up in the pier shopping mall. The security had a different story for the police and they charges Markola and his men with miner offense. At Markola's house he was there with most of the men that got thrown in the river, when his cousin Mario calls him asking him "What's he's been up to" Markola told him to "Get some of his men and come to his house, they need to talk about a certain mook and how he's going to get even with his mook ass." One of the men that were tied to the money bars came to Markola's house wanting to get even with Hutch and what he did to him. They all look at him and told about being thrown in the river by that mook. The man who got tied up says "I know where this mook lives and he might be there with the rest of his mook brothers partying about what they did" Loading their shot guns and hand guns wanting to get even. Markola told them he's waiting for his cousin and his men to come there so they can have enough to get that mook and the rest of them too. The man from the monkey bars said "What if I takes some of the men here and goes there to wait and watch the place till they and the other men get there" Markola thought about it and agreed it would be a good idea but told him not to do anything till they get there.

Larry is driving the Turn pike in New Jersey getting closer to New York and thinking about how he was going to surprise Hutch. Looking at the city from that distance how breath taken it looks to him as he gets closer and closer and the buildings seem to grow the closer her gets.

Mario and his men are at Markola's and he was telling him how that mook threw him in the river and stole all their wallets and he wants it back at any cost. Mario told him anything for his cousin because their family and he would do the same for him.

Most all the officers from the police station, court system, prison guards, and certified department of justice who were invited are at Hutch's house as he hosts the party getting the guys ready for their entertainment. Keeping Janet, Donna and Erikaa close to him making sure they all know these three are off limits to everyone but having them call their friends out as all the men cheer at the sight of women looking so good to them. The party is in full swing with the music playing and the men dancing and talking to some of the strippers there and telling Derrick he and his brothers throw a very good party. Hutch house has such a high basement ceiling they were able to hook up a few poles so the ladies can do their thing on a couple of them.

The man from the monkey bars with some of the other men are listening to the party going on getting madder by the minute talking to each other "Listen to them celebrate about having me tide to the monkey bars and you guys thrown in the river!" He gets them all worked up as he talks on about what he's going to do to them and make them feel so sorry about ever seeing his face. Markola is in Mario's vehicle with two of his men that stayed there with him, they are talking about what to do once they get to Hutch's house. What he's going got do to Hutch and make him feel just like he did when they threw him in that cold river water.

Larry is getting close to Hutch's house when he calls Cordell to let him know he's about to drop in on Hutch's place, but Cordell told Larry not to go to Hutch's house to come to his first and gave him directions to get there.

One cop outside Hutch's house in his car with one of the strippers was talking to her when he sees these men with guns sneaking up on the house. He gets on his cell and calls a couple of his guys in the house and they warn everyone else about the men about to come in there with guns. Having some of the officers leave out the back way from the basement to come around to the front that way they would have the men covered from both side as the men came in the house. The man from the monkey bars had convince the other men not to wait for Markola and get theirs before he came out there and he could have what's left of the mooks when their finished. They open the front door and hear the music still playing and decide to move into position coming in the house waiting by the basement door having and countdown to when they burst in the basement. Outside some of the cops circle the ground and sees the one man they had by the car and they sneak up on him and surround him as he smokes his cigarette. Looking at all the guns stuck in his face that came out of nowhere surprising him, he puts up his hands. Inside the house the men count down to one and they rush in down the stairs but stops just at the bottom of the stairs looking at all those cops and even the strippers too pointing their guns at them with serious looks on their faces. Then hear from behind them the clicking noise of more guns being cocked back loaded ready to fire makes them put their hands up handing over their shot guns and frisked for other weapons. One of the men says to the man from the monkey bars "Least in the river I had a choice to swim to the other side or float away. Damn the river doesn't seem bad right now!" Ron came over to the men "Hey I know these guys!" Calling Hutch over to look at them too and they told some of the cops these are the guys that tried to kidnap his girls and had a big fight with them at the Seaport and that one was one of the men tied to the monkey bars, all the men in handcuffs point him out real quick. Trying to figure out what to do to these men Hutch said "What about a human centipede and we'll have them wait outside for the wagon to pick them up after some good pictures to add to the others. One of the men says "Shoot me now Please" Hutch and Ron said "They want to try something new yet old and got the camera. Hutch said "This would be much easier if they're out cold first" the police agreed It's his house they came in so handle his business. Hutch called Tys for some work, after taking pictures with everyone there and how those men are in that double conga line naked in a sixty nine position. Hutch told them as they were being taken away if he ever sees any of them again the internet will get those pictures all of them. See if you can explain that to your bosses and community. They swear they wouldn't see him ever again just don't send those picture because they have families.

Markola is getting close to Hutch's house when he sees what looks like Hutch's vehicle driving not far in front of them. Telling Mario to follow that mooks vehicle they don't have to go to his house to get his wallet from him. Thinking he'll wait till he stops and they can catch him because he doesn't even know he's being followed. Larry is following the direction Cordell gave him to the letter and pulls up in front of his house and gets out going in the house after parking. Markola riding next to Mario following the vehicle they thought to be Hutch's turns the corner to see a figure go in this house and another men look out as if he was looking for anyone that followed the person there to the house before closing the door behind them. Markola looks at Mario and says "Remember that house because the mooks in there with his wallets and he wants it back." They circle the block to come around again parking down from the house to plan what they're going to do once inside. Larry is greeted by all the kids "Uncle Larry!" They hug and kiss him hello except for Bernise who stays on the couch and waves "hi" to him. He looks at all the girls and says "I have something for your gals" going in his bag and pulls out these envelopes with their names on it. They're so excited to see what's in the white envelopes like they really didn't know he had cash in them. He gave them their envelopes one by one they kissed and thanked their uncle Larry saying "Your just like Uncle Hutch but smaller." Jordell come over to him and says "What about me unck. You forgot about me and Coire Uncle Larry!" He looks at Jordell and says "How can I forget the little man of the house!" Going in his bag and bring out the latest play station 2 set up and 8 newest games to play with, and for Corie he told her he's going to take her to pick out what she wants and gives her the latest girl things to play with. Cordell is asking "Hungry what you want for dinner." Bernise looked over at them and says "Hope it's something that gets there in 30minutes or less and can be delivered because I aint cooking till I'm ready!" Larry told her not to bother his mother taught him how to cook and went into the kitchen with Cordell to make dinner for everyone. Bernise lying on the couch says "What the hell happened to teaching Cordell to do that, if your mother taught you how to cook!" Jordell was up in his room hooking up the play station2 when he heard noises coming from outside below his window that sounded like men telling each other to be quite. He looks out his window and saw the men in suits looking in the house with guns in their hands surrounding the house going to the back. He knew Corie was in the other room playing with her dolls and went in there and took her to his room telling her "They're going to be robbed by the men in bad ugly clothes with guns so they need to hide." He dumps out his big toy chest of toys that's big enough for both of them to hide in now that it's empty. Telling his sister to stay there and went to Kita's room and got the phone and calls 911 as he looks for his toy recorder that has two speeds instant play back to it, then gets his B.B gun that looks just like a real shot gun for protection. The operator comes on and asked "What's the emergency?" Jordell answers "My family is about to be robbed by the ugly men in bad suits, they have guns going to kill us all please come there!" The operator hears how young his voice is and tells him "Little boy this in no toy and could get you in serious trouble for playing on the phone like this!" Jordell says "I know I'm a little boy! My family is about to get robbed and I'm not playing so send the cops now" The operator says "Listen little boy where are your parents?" Jordell says "This is what happens when family hooks up family with a job instead of hiring outside the stupid DNA pool!" The operator gets mad at what he said going "Where's your parents because they aren't going to like the way you're playing on the phone" Jordell says "When my parents are killed because some high school drop out with an online GED didn't believe a little boys cry for help. You're going to asks yourself were your mommy and daddy a king and Queen that was brother and sister who shouldn't have had a child like you that's a butt wipe fool!"

The operator was furious at that remark about to say something else until she heard screaming in the back ground. Markola and Mario with the men burst into Cordell house knocking down the door scaring the girls. Markola is heard saying "Shut them up because he'll have to kill them all and go upstairs to check to see if anyone is up there calling the police." Jordell says "See were going to die you stupid drop out B-I" His word are cut short because Markola pulls the phone line out as the men search the house. Jordell quickly jumps into the toy chest and told Corie to be quite as the men ran upstairs checking the house. When they shouted all clear up here and walks back down stairs, Jordell was about to get out the toy chest and Corie cries "Don't go I'm scared!" He says to Corie "I'm scared too but he got to save the family and Uncle Larry too so stay here where it's safe. I'll try and figure out a way and see if he can call uncle Hutch for help OK."

The operator was thinking should she tell her supervisor or not, because of what that brat said to her. She forgot all the 911 calls cut off goes across the supervisor screen for alert and she listens to some of them. When the supervisor heard what Jordell said to the operator she was laughing till she heard the screaming in the back ground and listens very carefully to hear men crashing thing and the girls screaming. The supervisor hears Markola's voice says "He will kill all of them if they don't shut up and be quite then searches the house for others." The supervisor come over to the operator and asked her why she did call that in. The operator says "It sounds like some little boy playing on the phone and they don't have time for that!" The supervisor says "Do you know what a phone being cut off sounds like and that sounded like the line was cut because I'm sure that little boy knows how to call someone a stupid drop out bitch after how he said what he said to you." She told the operator S.O.P (Standard Operating Procedure) to call back the number standing right next to her and heard how it was a busy signal. The supervisor shouts out they have a line cut and need those that aren't doing anything to help out because whole family's life is at stake and they're being killed as she speaks because the line was pulled out the wall. All available operators work on where the call came from and others called the police saying "There's a family being killed in progress it's a 911 emergency 187 in progress all available units!"

Markola had everyone sit in the living room then asked "Where Hutch is?" Cheryl said "My uncle Hutch isn't here. I wish he were, because you would be so sorry you ever came here!" Mario looks at Cordell sitting and then at Larry, saying Markola "These guys aint him?" Markola says "He was driving that vehicle outside don't tell me he's not here!" Larry said "That's my vehicle outside, because my mother bought it for me down south. I know it looks like Hutch's but it's my ride!" Markola went "Alright, where's the girls? If you don't know where Hutch is, I know he came there for the girls. They have to be here." Mario suggest they beat the men in front of the woman and they would tell where Hutch is hiding or where he gone to. Markola looks at the young girls by their daddy and Larry, thinking about it and know it would be wrong to do such things right in front of them and told his cousin to give him a minute about that will ya. Mario didn't mind holding the family while one of them called Hutch to get him to get over there. Thinking Markola could get his card from him when he got there, so he suggest that Markola tell one of them to call Hutch and make him get over there to give him what he wants. Bernise just lying on the couch wants Cordell to do anything that would get those men out of there bickering at him.

Larry was trying to calm down the girls from being so scared of the men standing over them looking scary. Mario getting more and more excited about doing some damage in there to leave a message for Hutch. The men looked at him waiting for him to give them the go ahead look. They had the things to tie them up with in their hands wanting to know which one to start with as they wait for Hutch to show up. Markola looked at the girls crying, Bernise and Cordell were going at it plus Mario wasn't making thing any better wanting to hurt the kids so he went up on the stairs to the first landing to get everyone's attention. Trying to get an idea on what his next move was going to be. He yells at them "Be quite" so he could think about things and in back of him the lights upstairs were turned out, everyone down stairs looked in his direction right pass him. Their facial expressions gave him reason to pause asking "What's wrong?" They all saw slowly sticking out from the darken upstairs this long black barrel of what looks like a shot gun coming from darken out part from upstairs behind him. Jordell had Corie in his toy chest safe and staying there till it's over, he had puts her Barbie dolls in with her leaving the top cracked for air and light saying "If you're going to play make sure it's quite OK!" she shook her head "OK" He leaves out the room feeling he's got to protect his family somehow. Taking with him to use his two speed voice changer tape recorder and his BB gun which look like a real shot gun. The water pistol which could pass for a life like Glock nine plus the man Halloween mask. Before pulling his Halloween mask down over his face cutting off the lights. Markola turns to face that long barrel sticking out at him and hears a man's deep voice say to him "Hey ass wipe move and there's grey matter all over everyone down stairs!" Markola looks but can't see anyone's face up in that darkness. He's told to turn around and put his hands in his pockets but Markola starts to say "Hey listen maybe we can" his words are cut short, with Pop, Pop, Pop! Getting hit hard on top of the head with the gun barrel and told again "Turn around and tell your men to stop and get on their knees NOW!" One man close to Markola looks at him thinking he could sneak up on the person upstairs and grab the barrel of the gun. He didn't see was Cheryl looking at the spot up behind Markola pointing out the man trying to sneak up behind him. Jordell in the darkness with his BB gun see Cheryl pointing out the man trying to sneak up on his barrel. He sees the man moving in the china cabinet glass saying to Markola "Stop that man where he is now, fooka!" POPPING Markola in the head as the voice told the man "Look up!" to see the barrel of hand gun is pointed right at his head. Thinking its real gun from the way it looks he stops right where he was and hears to what the voice says "Since you want to be Mr. Sneaking man lay face down on your stomach didn't let this butt wipe guy stand on your back NOW!" Markola again about to say something when BOINK, BOINK, BOINK! Hard poked to the back of his head, the hall way echoes by what sounds like a shell being loaded in the chamber of the shot gun "Clack Clock!" the voice spoke again "When I want your mouth to open, I'll stick a gun in it!" Markola told his man to hold still as he gets on the man's back lying on his stomach. Another of the men watching says "Wow he really sounded gangsta." The voice speaks again "Now tell your men to get on their knees or the next sound you will hear is in heaven after your splattered all over them" Mario stand next to Cordell asked "What kind of father are you to have such a pysco upstairs with weapons like that, while your family in the living room?" Bernise looked at Cordell then Mario "Oh that's not the first time he's had company over I didn't know about. Did you invite another one of them over again" Mario looks at Cordell and back at Bernise saying "It's not the first time he's done this?!" Mario looks at him with discuss on his face when Markola get hit again BOINK, BOINK! BOINK! BOINK! BOINK! Tell your man to stop talking to my friend there or he could get it too. Markola repeats the message then ask "Can I say something without getting poked in the head, it hurts" The voice says "It better be good" or "BOINK!" poking him in the back of the head hard again "You know what's coming." Markola says "Look it's a mistake we came here to talk to Hutch and invite him for a men's night out that's all. They were excited about the idea that's why they made a mistake and knocked hard on the doors." BOINK, BOINK, BOINK, BOINK! The voice speaks "You must think I'm stupid ass wipe. What school you went to so I don't send my kids there to learn how to be dumb ass wipes stupid to like you. I heard you outside the house before you came in. BOINK, BOINK, BOINK! Your voice carries meat head!" There a silence for a moment then the voice says "Oh sorry I didn't mean to do that!" POP! POP! POP! And one more POP! Hitting Markola hard on top of his head hard with the gun barrel making sounds like that saying "There I'm not poking you Ok, I stopped is that better!" Wincing from the pain on top of his head Markola stands there with tears forming in his eyes. Cordell see that the person upstairs got thing in hand and decides to get up saying "I'm going to get another beer if you don't mind." The voice spoke "If you don't sit your narrow ass down! You won't have one to use to sit with." Cordell sits down and shakes his can and tries to get that last drop of beer out the can he's holding not saying another word looking around. One of Mario's men says "We can take that guy, because he's not going to shoot with his friend family right here." Jordell took one of his loud Poppers and throws them down the hall echoing the loud POW! "Now who wants to be the first to leak red!" The men point at the man that did the talking moving away from him keeping their hands back on their heads. Mario's says "Hey stu-nod you want him to starts shooting that's my cousin who get hit first you want to explain that to my Uncle Narkita!" The men shake their heads no. The voice goes "Since you butt wipes have guns too and we don't anyone to feel frogish, girls take all their guns and put them behind the lazy fat women lying on the couch with the big butt!" Bernise says "Who in the hell you calling" her words are cut too with what sounds like a hammer of a gun being clicked back and she asked "Should I sit up or just continue to lay here while they put the guns behind me." With all their guns taken and the men on their knees, Mario smartly asked "Now what?" The voice spoke "What you want with my unk er man Hutch for because that's my boy!" They didn't pay to close attention to way he said it, but Markola answers him by explaining they just want to talk to him and see if they can get this misunderstanding straighten out. The voice spoke "Ok let's see who I'm dealing with. Girls take all their wallets and put them on the table next to your father. That way when I come down there I can see their faces" The girls do as they're told putting all the wallets from the men on the table asking "Can they leave and let the adults deal with this." The voice says "If they don't sit back down there they won't be able to leave from anywhere ever!" Markola says "You should let the girls go." The voice says "They can go when I'm done" POP! POP! POP! BOINK! BOINK! BOINK! BOINK!" Hard shots to Markola's head to make his point and told "Now shut that pie hole and turn around for a second" When Markola turns around the barrel of the gun is shoved in his mouth hard knocking out a tooth. Markola stand there really in pain bleeding as the voice says to him "Yo mofo! Want a hole in the back of that fat head like the front that keeps opening up!" Markola shook his head "No" The voice says "Then take your wallet out and throw it up here to let me see who you are, so when I look you in the eye. I can call your punk ass name right!" Markola does what he's told tossing it in the dark upstairs. Jordell caught the wallet and takes all the cash out of it because he saw his father doing the same to the others wallets on the tables when no one was watching him but Jordell from up on the stairs. Then throwing the wallet back down to the floor and telling Kita to take it and put it with the others. She does what she's told and goes back to sit down with sisters.

Meanwhile the supervisor of the 911 operators was telling that one operator to keep calling back the number she didn't want to report and hope that the little boy was joking, because if not it would be her job if anything happens to his family. She calls getting busy signal saying no one is answering at that address. The supervisor told her to cut into the line and explain to the person she cut into that she was checking because of the little boys call from there. She tries but again gets a busy signal and now knows that wasn't some little boys playing on the phone. The supervisor takes over and uses her computer to get the phone number and address where it came from and call the police letting them know there's a family in danger assaults in progress with murders being committed and intruders still on premises. The SWAT team and police and other emergency vehicles race over to the address plus a news van which heard the call and wants to get the scoop on the story, thinking there would be multiple murders there making a good story. It wasn't long before the block at both ends are blocked off and the SWAT team uses their probe machine to see where the suspects are in the house without alerting them to their out there. Markola saw the lights and thought to himself great now the police are here and they would have to explain how they busted in on this family. Jordell saw the lights too and thought his Uncle Hutch can't be far behind. Corie came out of the room over to him asking "What's going on and she's tied and wants mommy." Markola heard her but then heard Jordell say "We're getting help the police are here too." Markola says "Hey man you got kids up there with you? How much of a freaking coward are you, bet you were going to use them as shields too huh!" Jordell dips down a little and everyone looking at the dark part at the top of the stair case saw a man's face with a five o clock shadow fade. They all gasp at the sight of the man's face. Markola said "What?" Mario said "We saw that creep and he's tough looking man." Everyone just look at Cordell again and Mario said "What kind of friends you got that would hold your kids hostage like that, even as shield if he had too." Bernise says "It's not the first time he invited one of his friends over and not tell us he's got company." Mario looks at her "Oh bitch shut up you said that before." Cordell smiles, Mario asked "You still going to be friends with this freaking Stu-nod!" The voice yells "Shut up!" Markola says "He's not the one holding kids Hostage up in the dark like some coward!" BOINK, BOINK, BOINK, BOINK! There's a Pause then one more BOINK! Followed by 3 POP! POP! POP! The voice "You got something to say toothless dumb wise ass, or you want to suck on the barrel again of the gun I'm holding!" Really in pain now Markola shouts "I'm going to kill you but first take that gun and shoot you till the shell are gone and then get more, oh I want you dead so bad!" That was all the SWAT team needed to hear and from the condition of the front and back door they didn't have any trouble with getting in. They rush in yelling FREEZE! Everyone to get their hands up and do not move!" Puzzled by what they saw with the men on their knees, hands behind their heads that way. Markola standing on the first landing with his hands in pants pockets with what looks like a gun barrel to the back of his head. He asked them to "Get this guy to lower his weapon." All the police in there with SWAT have their guns pointed at the dark spot behind Markola asking "Whoever is up there well take him to jail, now throw out the weapon and come down with your hands were they can see them!" They put all the men in hand cuff and wait for the person upstairs to comply with what they asked saying "They don't want a shoot out here!" Larry says "There's kid up there with that guy and they should be careful!" everyone agreed that they heard little kids up there with the man. The captain asked "Send the kids down because they don't want them hurt and they have nothing to do with this." There is no answer for a moment as Jordell tell Corie she's got to go down and take this with her giving her his water gun pistol.

Telling her "I know they shoot black men with or without a gun and young boys too, so I'm going out in a blaze of glory" Coire asked "Who's glory and why you going out blazing with her. Come blazing with me down stairs!" Jordell says "Wait" and uses the voice recorder again "Ok One time, storm troopers, B.M.K(black men killers) Heart stoppers Mayor Lackeys, Blue Serpermises 5-0's Joy killers. I'm sending my uh, the little girl down now so nobody shoot her or there will be hell to pay by a greater force then me!" The sergeant say "Ok wise ass send down the little girl and come out after she's down, but first throw out all your weapons." They watch as Corie comes down with his water pistol saying "Don't shoot my brother he save me." The police looked at each other puzzled and asked Larry "Is there a little boy up there too?" He told them "Yeah my nephew Jordell is up there!" Pleading with them not to get that guy mad or do anything that would get him hurt. The police shout for the man to let the boy go and come down with his hand up as they point their weapons up at the top of the stairs waiting for some kind of response. Jordell says in his normal voice "Ok. I'm coming down just tell my Uncle Hutch I went out in a blaze of glory making him proud of me." The SWAT team and police and everyone here including Markola and Mario with their men watch as this little boy carrying what looks like a shot gun and some kind of box with him as he walks down the stairs. The police and SWAT tell each other to hold their fire in fear of hitting the little boy. Jordell gets down stairs and the police take the BB gun and asked him "Son where's the man that was up there with you." While another radio's to keep an eye on the back of the house for the man to try and get away back there. Jordell tells them "I was the only one up there handling those men like that, because my mommy was on the couch and she wear the pants in this family. Plus my uncle Hutch wasn't here either because I know they wouldn't stand a chance against him." Bernise says "That's right baby I wear the" Then it hits her, if it was him up there then who called her those names. She looks at Jordell puzzled as he smiled back at her so innocent looking. The police went up there to search and found no one, coming back down eight members of SWAT and four policemen after searching the whole entire house asked Jordell "How did the man get away and it's OK. You could tell us because the man's not going to get you." Jordell looks back at everyone looking at him and shows them there was no man upstairs but him and with his recorder, using it saying in that voice "Shut your pie hole or I'll shut it for you ass wipe!" All the men I cuffs say that's the voice they heard coming from upstairs, then everyone starts staring at Markola who's head starts to knot up in many places from being hit all those time with the shot gun barrel. He was bleeding from the mouth with his lip swelling from having that gun barrel shoved in it so hard knocking out his tooth. The EMT treating him gives him gauze pads to help stop the bleeding and asked for some ice pack for those knots swelling on is head. There was not a sound as everything starts to sink in to everyone there and this big burst of laughter coming from all the SWAT team first and some police men standing around looking at the weapons they are holding. Larry wants to know "What's so funny" and one cop told him "That's not a real shot gun but a BB gun and the glock is a water pistol" Mario's men turned slow looking at him, wanting to go beat the hell out of him after hearing what the weapons really were. The police stops all the men from going after him as Mario said "I'll pay for your bail to make it up to you guys I swear!" Then it got out fast that this little boy held ten men at bay and even had them on their knees disarmed till the police came there, after they burst into his house knocking down the door and threating to kill this family. He used a two speed voice recorder play back and a water pistol with Winchester BB gun on them. Out smarting ten men and even knocked out the leaders tooth with the BB gun by shoving it in his mouth.

Repeating that quote he said "If he wants another hole in the back of his head like the one that keeps opening in front then he'll shut up." All the cops at the scene laugh about what happened as they take the guns from the couch and wallets from the table in front of Cordell, as they were putting the men in the wagon one of the cops says "Hope you guy got your bail money ready for this one." One of the answers he's not worry because he got plenty money in his wallet and would be able to make that and then some." The cop shows him one of the wallets asking him "Which one is yours?" The man motions that blue one there with the print and the cop looks in it to see it's empty, asking "Where's the money?" The man says "I've been robbed and one of them in there must have done it" That make the cops laugh even harder and go tell the others what the guy said. That had bigger roar of laughter, because all the cops and SWAT team were trying to figure out how the kid done it. He held them prisoner with BB gun and water pistol, then knocking their boss's tooth out and now robbing them too. One cop says to everyone "Wait they're forgetting the most important thing" and walk over to Jordell asking him "How old are you son?" Jordell says "I'm 7 years old!" Not one cop was standing after Jordell said his age, fall out laughing repeating 7 years old?!" One cop ask "Wasn't you scared!" Jordell says "Yeah and no." Another cop asked "How did you come up with the idea to do this?" Jordell says "This aint no home alone McCauley Caulkin movie, where I got a team of people ready to fix things up for me so actor can play like they got hurt. I had to handle my B-I the hood way, using what's available to me and streets smarts my Uncle Hutch gave me, Shaolin hill ooh building big up nah mean!" After the police and news crew leave the house Cordell and Larry with the girls clean up. Putting up temporary doors till they replace the ones that got kicked in the next morning when the store opens. Larry sits and talks with Bernise about things and how they are going in the house.

Up in the girl's room they were happy when everyone left, taking the envelopes out from in the back of their pants that Larry gave them, seeing the cash in each envelope they were jumping up and down excited about going to the mall and spending it. At the same time Cordell was up in his bedroom counting the cash he took out of the wallets from the table, Jordell walks in on him and sees all the cash he's got laid out. Looking at his son asking Jordell "What do you want son?" Jordell says "I saw you from upstairs taking the cash out the wallets and now you can't break a man off a piece?" Holding out his hand waiting and looking at his father to put something in it. Cordell told him "Here" and gave him five dollars. Jordell looks at the five then says "You can do better than that with all that cream on the bed." Cordell took back the five and gave him a 20$ and told him to go on. Jordell says "What if mom found out about all the paper you got then what?" Cordell knew he didn't want Bernise to find out about it so he looks at Jordell and thinking he would out smart his son and told him "ok take what you want and I won't take it back either" thinking his son would only take a few big bills then says "You won't tell your mother anything about this right!" To his amazement he watched Jordell take a stack of 20 and 50$ dollar bills that equals to 1280$ and asked him "What are you going to do with all that?" Jordell looks at his father and says "College fund dad college fund!" Cordell looks at the cash on the bed and then looks at his son and says "Well put me down for another 2500$" and gave him a stack of hundreds and told him "Go hide it but don't tell your mother." Cordell counts up the loot quick because he knows if Jordell knew he had money Bernise wasn't far behind him. Minus what Jordell got from him the counts was 18,475$ so quickly counting out another 4 thousand dollars leaving out five hundred in twenties on the bed.

Cordell goes his daughters room and knocks on the door, the girls know it's their father because their mother don't knock she tries to come in but they learned to keep their door lock. Cheryl's opening the door to see Cordell standing there and hands them each a thousand Dollars and told them to "Hide it and not say a word to shredder their mother or she'll take." They each kiss thanking him for that and close and lock the door back. Bernise was down stair talking with Larry and noticed Cordell wasn't in his chair his drinking beer like he always do. She told Larry "Excuse me" and bolts off the couch so fast to hurry upstairs to their bedroom, where she sees Cordell counting cash on the bed. Standing there in the door way just looking at him with a mean face till he hands her two hundred dollars saying "What!? It fell out one of the wallets on the floor so I didn't see any harm besides they did break into our house right?" There is not a word coming from Bernise as she stuff the cash in her bra and turns to heads back down but walking pass the girls room, she hears laughter and them talking about something behind the door. She tries to go in but the door is locked. Twisting the knob back and forth but it won't open for her. Bernise gets mad saying "Open this door and how come it's always locked?" Cheryl says "Coming" as they all hide their cash then she opens the door. Bernise looks at all her daughters and wants to know why they're so happy. They let Cheryl do the talking because she knows what to tell their mother to get her off their backs and go away. Cheryl just explains they're happy those men left because they were scared and now that Uncle Larry's there it means they're going to get to show him things about the city. Bernise ask "About the door being locked all the time?" Cheryl says "Come on ma, Jordell always coming into our room at the wrong time when we are changing clothes and little boys shouldn't see his sisters without clothes on." She told them she'll talk to their father to have that talk with him about that and closes the door leaving the room going back down stairs to the couch again. Coming back to the couch as Larry asked "Was everything alright, by the way you took off upstairs never seen you move so fast." She looks at him and put her feet back up on the couch and turns the channel of the TV. At the police precinct Markola was telling Mario he thinks he's got a way out of there so don't call for any bails bond men because most of them know their Uncle Narkita and word would get around about them getting arrested. When it came for him to make that phone call he calls Elise remembering her number and asking her to come get him bail him out from a misunderstanding. She smiled while holding the phone because she knew if he wanted her to get him out she would asked him to let her hold that card for a while so she can really get some of things she wanted to get from it. The she gets on him about not telling her about the card in the first place. Markola said "You can hold the card just as long as she get him out before his Uncle does, then he would have to give him that Credit card." She wants to know what she's got to do to move quickly and he tell her what to do and where to go.

At the restaurant in Little Italy the Boss's right hand man (Vincent) walks in to the place and he's laughing a little to himself about something he heard about. He tells one of the men there who passes the news to the others and this roar of laughter comes from where they are, the right hand man comes over to Mr. Narkita and tells him about Makola. How he got arrested for busting in a house holding a family hostage and got lumped up by a seven year old with a BB gun and water pistol, then claims he was robbed by the same 7yr old at his house. Mr. Narkita looks at his right hand man and busted out laughing the other men follow having a good laugh on Markola mishap. The right hand man gave every detail and the photos of Markola he got from one of his policemen they have known for years, letting the men have a good laugh and making comments about him. Mr. Narkita told the right hand man to keep an eye on him then busted out laughing again thinking about a seven year old doing that to him.

Elise is paying the money to the bails men to get out Markola and Mario and waits to see them because she knows Markola has that Credit card on him and she's not going to wait for him to send it to her when she can pick it up right there. Standing there seeing them come out the precinct she leans on her vehicles hood as they walk up to her and she looks at Markola wondering what the hell did they do to him in the jail by the lumps on is head and busted lip. Markola looks at her saying "Thanks they really needed to get out of there fast!" Elise looks at him "I didn't do it to hear your thanks now where is that card?" Markola looks at her thinking she's not wasting no time and he pulls out his wallet and takes out the Credit card he got from her before, he gives it to her and then asked for a ride because they don't have any cash on them adding "It's a long story."

The next day after helping Cordell fix the door Larry calls Hutch and told him he's been at Cordell's house for a couple days and wants to come see him and tell him what has happened since he came to Cordell's house. Hutch told Larry to stay there till the weekend then he can come over and meet his others brothers the G.D.M.4.L and he'll give the girls the heads up he's coming. Larry told him their mother still thought he would be with that pysco skinny woman but Hutch answers that by saying "I'm with three pieces that are Diamonds but you'll get a chance to meet them" That weekend the BBQ pool party Hutch threw for Larry graduating law school and coming up there and meeting the rest of his family. The party had everyone there and even some of Erikaa, Donna, and Janet's friends over for the GDM4L that didn't bring anyone. The party started early that afternoon with a big lunch for everyone there and the BBQ pool party for later because most of the others had shifts they had to finish before they were off for that weekend. Things were running low so Hutch said he was going to the supermarket to get more things so they don't run out and Donna wants to ride with him while Erikaa and Janet played hostess and keep things going.

Markola and Mario were eating at this Chinese Place talking about if they ever ran into that mook they would get even for everything, feeling it's his fault for all that's happened to them. Now to be the laughing stocks in the family, Mario said "I should go by that house and whack that guy for putting those lumps on your head and knocking out his tooth." Markola looks at him asking "What you're going to whack a 7 year old are you really Stu-nod lunk head. It's a 7 year old like that would really impress everyone we whacked him." Mario says nothing but continues to eat his food thinking about what Markola just said looking at him. Hutch and Donna had funny in the supermarket talking and getting everything they'll need for BBQ. Getting a call that everyone is there waiting for them to get back, and he told them to start and they'll be there in a bit. They went to his vehicle pushing the cart of food loading it in the back of his ride. They were spotted by Markola and Mario that were sitting in the Chinese Place in that small plaza and they came up behind them with Mario grabbing Donna first. Hutch saw him with her and then heard Markola's voice "Hey mook. Since I really have your attention now, guess you can hand over that Credit card of yours and he won't snap her neck." Hutch gets mad saying "You just won't give that a rest with the Credit card thing" and he takes his wallet out and throws it to the ground front of his vehicle. Looking at Markola saying "Not even trying anything on you so go get that dam thing and let us go."

Looking at him walk towards the front and then looking the way Mario has Donna around the neck knowing if she just drop he would be caught off guard and then he can react. Markola said "Hold her there till I get that wallet and what's in it" He pulls out his gun pointing at her and smiled at Hutch saying "Not so smart now are you mook?" Hutch said "How could you hold a gun on a pregnant woman like that, she might faint with her foot swings" She picked up on what he said and drops straight down out of Mario's grip on her. Mario took his eyes off Hutch long enough for him to spin kick him knocking him back and down. Helping Donna up and rushing to the front where Markola just bent down to get the wallet and heard something and looks up to see Hutch coming at him with such a clothes line that spun him in air for a loop before hitting the ground hard. Still holding on to the wallet as Hutch takes it out of his hand and goes to get in his vehicle hearing Markola groan in pain for Mario as he lays there. Hutch told Donna to hold on as he takes off out the parking lot but she looks back and saw then get a car and come after them. She told Hutch their not far behind as the back window shatters from the bullet shot into it. Hutch told her to get down as he sped down the street running lights to get away from the bullets coming from the car chasing them. Mario is shooting at them with his big gun making loud bangs and Markola hits him as he hung out the window shouting at him "It's bad enough we're chasing them but do you have to draw attention by using your big gun with all that noise?" Mario came back in and looks at Markola for a few seconds holding his and then reaching in his pants and pulling out a smaller gun then going in the glove compartment of the vehicle screwing on the silencer. Now looking at Markola as he does it then hold it up to his face saying "Better!" Markola told him "You better check that before I do!" Then realizing Mario is holding the guns staring at him thinking about shoot him as he looks at Markola with such a serious look on his face. Markola told him "Never mind just stop that Mook." Mario leans back out the window and starts shooting again as Markola tried to get close to Hutch as he dodges by turning corners and heading down one way streets. Hutch knows he doesn't have the speed and agility of that smaller car with the bullets going into the back of his vehicle each time they get close enough for Mario to get a clear shot at him. The more he turned down a block and floored the gas pedal to get away they would somehow catch up quick and then he would have to maneuver down a few more twist and turns to get some distance from them. He could tell Markola wasn't use to driving like that, so when he noticed the sign for the park he remembers the hill that every four wheeler loves to take because they test their vehicles climbing ability on it and that smaller car wouldn't have the power to keep up. Doing his best to keep up with Hutch as he dodges down street turning corners and racing down stretches of long ways buy the water. Hutch lead them through some streets where he loose Markola for a few moments but as Markola and Mario keep looking the see Hutch a couple blocks away and begin the chase again. Having him that far in back of him Hutch head towards the hill and seeing in his mirror where the car has trouble pulling such a steep hill. Hutch gets out and taunts them for a second then making sure they see where he's going he lead them to the park where his 4 wheels has the advantage. Donna asked him "How come they just didn't go back to the house where everyone is" Hutch didn't want to get anyone else involved or hurt behind these two and kept thinking they should have ran into a cop car by now, but then realizes the Staten Island police men especially the one from the 120 precinct would rather stop and search a young black man from the project than stop a car being shot at by two white men in suits (go figure). Once in the park Hutch switches he ride to 4 wheel drive and leads them to the grass arrear of the park. On the way there Mario was shooting at the back of Hutch's vehicle and a bullet came through hitting a can of tomato sauce bursting it at the same time Donna decides to get in the back seat another can flew up hitting Donna on the head from all the bouncing the vehicle was doing. The big can knock her out and Hutch thought she was hit calling her name but she didn't move. Now he went on the offensive ramming their car as Mario took out his big gun and starts using that one too. Like jousting knights they come at each other and Hutch would throw cans and other items he could get his hands on as they passed each other by. Smashing their windshield in with food cans and then messing up their view with condiments about to toss a can of beer at them but having second thoughts he drinks the beer.

Then hearing Donna moan and he asked "You alright! I thought you was hit" She answer "No but her head hurts" Telling her "Keep your head down or you won't have one" as the vehicle continue jousting at each other. Hutch asked her to pass him anything she would get her hands on. She handed him a big melon and again he drove right at them and used to melon bop Mario in the head as he rode on the door shooting over the hood across at Hutch passing by. Hutch had this pineapple and when he threw it managing to hit Markola in the head but it left him exposed and he was hit in the top part of his chest by Mario, it changed Hutch thinking real quick. He didn't want Donna to know he's been hit and told her to buckle up back there because he going to do something that should end this. Pulling away from them he goes to a part of the park where the hills are and having a good lead on them he uses the vehicles four wheels to go over and down a set of stairs then around a bush and down another set of them. Hearing the noise in back of him like a car coming down the stairs, Hutch goes to another set of stairs and this time back tracking enough making it look like he took those stairs down too as he backs into the bushes and waits. Markola and Mario come to the stair following the tracks he left and thought here's another set they have to go down stopping just at the top of the stairs looking to see which way he went. Hearing an engine revving from behind before they're bump hard and feeling the car being pushed over the set of steep stairs by Hutch behind them. Mario shoots as their being pushed by Hutch using all the horse power in his vehicle he had as they went down the first set of stairs but the second is where Markola tried to get a way turning the wheel. That made them turn and Hutch Tee-Boned their car making it roll over as he still pushed from going that set of stairs. Watching them roll down the stairs he follows them and even pushes them more down all the stairs to the bottom where they are out cold from being thrown around like that in the small car. Hutch sees them not moving and trapped by the metal of the car's hood then he slumps over his steering wheel as Donna asked him "You alright?" She saw the blood as she pulled him back off the steering wheel and screams his name "Oh GOD Hutch! what did you do!?" Her hands starts shaking as she tries to stop the bleeding, telling him to hang on as she looks for her cell through all that mess in the vehicle.

Near by the horse policemen patrolling the arrear heard the shots and rode their horses to where they heard Donna screaming for help. They look at each other and then see the wrecked vehicles and race over to her, she explains what happened and how she needs to get him to a hospital. They call it in and a short time later the ambulance is trying to stabilize Hutch to take him to the hospital. The EMT on the radio to the hospital "Their patient lost a lot of blood and now his heart stopped!" Helpless she watched as the EMT went into action when that happened to him. Calling his partner back there they work on Hutch to get his heart started again. They don't give up working hard and fast telling him to hang on screaming at him "COME ON MAN DON'T GIVE UP HERE!" Donna watching them franticly working on him trying to keep him from going under as she feeling so helpless crying for Hutch not to die on her.

Looking at them as they shock him once then again, Donna cries for Hutch "Please don't give up on me I can't lose you. We can't lose you. Baby PLEASE! Don't go." She cries in her hands saying Janet and Erikaa name and how all three of them love him so much, his heart starts beating again and they stabilize him as Donna cries holding his hand in the back of the ambulance. The one E.M.T says "Burn it man get him there I don't know how long he's going to last back here we need ER!" Police escort them there. At the Hospital they get him out the ambulance and the EMT says His heart stopped again and got to working on him as they rolled him in with a nurse on top of him pumping his chest as Donna cried for not to die.

Everyone at Hutch house was wondering where he was with the rest of the food and stuff, Janet looked at Erikaa and told her she feels something isn't right. He should have been back here with Donna too and as she was about to call, everyone starts going to the living room where the news came on. It had a breaking news story about a car chase that ended up with one man shot and the woman he's with on their way to the hospital. The two others pinned in their car, it showed the vehicle that was Hutch's and Mack said "That looks like Hutch's ride!" everyone was looking at the flat screen as the new told of the two vehicles the smaller one chasing and shooting at the larger one with the one male shot and female with bruise the police reports. They agreed to get over there because if that was Hutch and Donna they need to be there for their support, just hoping that wasn't Hutch as everyone starts getting their coat and jackets. There was a knock on the door and these police men standing there with bags of groceries saying "They know him from the bachelor party and he'd told them to bring this stuff to his house before they took him away in the ambulance." Dave looks at everyone "That's your brother always concerned about everyone else except himself" Erikaa looks at Janet with tears in her eyes and 2Soon told them he would take them to the hospital, everyone there left to go to the hospital. They get there and Erikaa and Janet find Donna in the waiting room of the hospital all alone in the back crying hard with blood all over her clothes. She looks up with tears still flowing out of her eyes as Janet calls her name runs over to hug her asking "You alright and where's Hutch?" Trying hard but can't stop crying she get the words out to tell them his heart stopped and they don't know if he was going to make it because he lost so much blood then she cries even harder as Erikaa held her. Janet can't believe what she just heard and it stuns her as she backs away from Donna and Erikaa with tear in her eyes saying nothing just shaking. Mack came over to her because of the way she was shaking asking "Janet you alright shorty?" She just shakes, Dougie had tears in his eye as he and Mack stood by her saying "Watch her be for a moment bruh" and then she looks at everyone as in disbelief letting out this blood curdling scream "EERRRAHH! OH GOD! PLEASE DON'T LET HIM DIE!" dropping on her knees crying and shaking hysterically. That moment is when it all sunk into all GDM4L and Larry who just came up there, he might not make it and they would have to face the fact he could die. Donna and Erikaa went to Janet to comfort her as she cried hard "He can't die, I won't let him die, I love that man. He's not going to leave us like that, he promised us that he wouldn't go anywhere without our permission. Well I'm not giving it, your hear me Hutch I'm not giving it!" Everyone in the room felt the word she said, some throwing their heads back taking deep breaths trying not to let the tears come out and other just held another one. The whole waiting arrear was crying about him some silently and other not ready to hear that about him feeling the same way Janet did. They all start Praying for him trying to hold themselves together not believing their brother is laying there dying like that. Mack is held by Dougie as he cry's why he always have to take on everything himself why didn't he come get us!?"

Derrick shaking his head as the tears flow out eyes says "He always was stubborn like that never letting you know how much pain or trouble he's in." Steel mad and crying says something loud and fast and everyone just shook their head agreeing to whatever he said. Trying to be brave as they could hear Hutch's voice "Would someone interpret what Steel said" Then doctor James Samples came out asking for the family of the man they just brought looking at the whole room move at him. He backs up and asking "Are you all his family and Janet said "I'm his wife" Donna said "me too" Erikaa said "I'm the third one." They all showed rings on their fingers as Donna said "He's got the other one to match ours!" Doc J. Samples says "That would explain why this big man is still here." Even though he explained his heart did stop three times but they got enough blood and fluids in him to keep it beating but he keeps trying to take the I.V out his arm but they know he's not conscious. Derrick says "He been doing that since I was little because he hates needles even scared of them!" Everyone turned at looked at Derrick and 2Soon said "Wow fam glad you don't know my weakness or everybody would be using spiders to get to me" Mack went to plant and broke off a piece that looks like a spider and put it on 2Soons shoulder and a showed him as he knocked over a couple of old ladies and some kids trying to get away from it. Mack said "Yep, now we know his who's next?!" The girls asked "Could we see him" and Doc. Samples says "He out of surgery now in the recovery room but you all can't crowd in there so I recommend shift. Wow I could use a drink after all that." He looks at the GDM4L standing there in front of him and Dougie asked "What would you like to drink?" Doc Sample joking says "If you got some vodka I could use a shot right now." Everyone move out the way of 2Soon as he walks over to the Doc. Samples and pull out a bottle of Grey Goose and a shot glass from his jacket. He smiles at 2Soon and says "Good thing I didn't say Hennessey!" Tyrone pulls out that bottle from his jacket and shows him, then they all pull out a different bottle that could stock a bar right then and there. He looks at them and Jazz said “We’re GRAND DRUNKEN MASTERS 4 LIFE we always come prepared, now go get some nurses”. The girls walk in the recovery room where Hutch is lying in bed with that patch on his chest, they all kiss him still with tears in their eyes, but it was Janet’s tear that fell on his face that made him stir. He opens his eye slowly to see them right there by his bed side and he smiles at them saying “Hope you brung mouth wash and chap stick, I know this dragon is drying my lips from my breath kicking like that” They laugh and tell him to stop being silly, they let him know his brothers are there and he wants to know are they mad at him? Erikaa says “Yes! We all are how come you always tell us family and friends come first but do you have to take the brunt of everything it’s not fair. We almost lost you and we don’t ever want to have that happen to none us.” He looks at her and held out his hand for her to take his and squeeze her hand enough to let her know he feels what she said. Janet says “What are we going to do with your hard headed ass you!” Hutch coughs first and chuckle “You all can just move in with me that way you can keep me on the straight and remind me of family.” Donna looks at him “How can you ask that of us with everything going on. Is there a dull moment in your life, it seems you’re always getting into something either car chases or being shot at now? How’s a woman now three supposed to put up with that huh you tell me? Janet said “I’m in” Erikaa said “I’m in too” Donna looked at them asking Hutch “Are you ready for this, can you live with three women who will have their mood swing and moment they don’t want to be around you. Having their own lives and wants to do their own things and grow in our own way.” Hutch looks at her “Guess you would want another man and not me huh.” Donna looks at him “Are you CRAZY! you know how hard it was finding your ass! I aint going nowhere!” Janet said “Guess that means yes! You have three women to deal with forever.”

Hutch said “I can live with that can you all?” A kiss from each one in the mouth dragon or not told how they feel. They send in the brother set by set glad to see him moving and talking, but excited about the news he's going to live with all three women. Steel said "Maybe he should get shot in the chest too." Everyone understood him and looked at him standing there. Mack shrugged his shoulders saying "Go figure want me to get my heat."

On the other side of the hospital in the prison ward were Markola and Mario and Markola is waking up with a very bad head ache looking at his wrist seeing hand cuffs on it, looking over at Mario sleeping peacefully in bed. Markola grabs his bed pan and flings it over the bed and hits Mario in the head waking him up BRANG! "Hey Stu-nod you couldn't shoot the tires out to slow that mook down you had to keep shooting into the freaking ride!" Mario woke trying to get out of his hand cuffs wondering what happened and who hit him. Markola told him they're in cuffs in the hospital ward waiting to be taken to jail. Telling Mario they better get ready to hear it because he knows they're uncle is going to hear about this one and this time he can't call that crazy broad to get them out thinking what she'll do when she find out that card is worthless.

At the restaurant Mr. Narkita is notified about Markola and Mario and how they're facing attempted murder charges on the same man that came there and told him about what Markola was trying to do him and how he wanted to know if they would get involved if he took action against him. Telling his right hand man (Vito) to handle that situation because he's very disappointed at Markola and having that gun toting Mario with him to be caught in this mess.

The right hand man says "I'll handle it and do the best for everyone" but asked "What about the mook that came there to talk to him about Markola?" Taking a deep breath and looking at his right hand man telling him to negotiate with him the best way you know how. Vito shakes his head "ok" and leaves.

3 weeks Later and Hutch is getting out of the hospital feeling good because his girls took turns in shifts coming to the hospital after their classes. He wanted them to keep up with the college and not fall behind to fail any course. They would stay with him even as his brothers came by to see how he was doing. Dave and La-Machine with Erikaa picked him up from the hospital and took him home

to the surprise welcome home party they all planned for him. As Hutch was having his welcome home party. Markola was greeted at the court for his and Mario's hearing on charges for the thing they did to Hutch and his property. The right hand man told Markola he was getting out but Mario had to stand trial because they found his finger prints on all the weapons, going through the proceeding Markola was fined and released but Mario got five years for attempted murder and weapons charges on him. The right hand man told him if he behaves himself they would get him out after two year or so but he got to watch his behind in there. He'll see what he could do about any problem he might come across in there, hugging Markola telling him to "Get that mook for me and don't let up!" They watch as Mario is lead away in cuff and Markola is walking free with the right hand man of Mr. Narkita. He asked "What's the deal with this mook you're trying so hard to get, it better be good. I got time for the long story" as they drive to Markola's house.

Two days after the party they all were at the supermarket shopping for supplies having a conversation about Markola always trying to get his Credit card because he's got all that money in his account. Janet asked "Why don't you stop pretending with us, you know we want to be with you no matter how much you have. We'll always want to be with you and we hope you know that?" Hutch smiled at her answering "I don't know where I would be without any of you since we crossed paths, it look like we're meant to be together." Donna says "I can understand why Hutch has so many brothers, with all that money you got. It would be easy to take care of all of them instead of making them go for their own careers" He was lost in the conversation again because they were talking to him like he was some kind of rich millionaire and keeping it for them. He remembers Erikaa trying to show him something about his Credit card at the supermarket before he was shot by Mario. When they got to the cashier to ring up everything they bought. Janet kissed him saying "We'll be with you not matter what." Erikaa says "Money comes and goes but people who love you stay forever." Donna finished with "If you had all the money you needed in the world what would you do?" He smiled at them and says "First I would never let any of you go out my life and we'd be happy together forever." They watch he gave his Credit card to the cashier for her to swipe to pay for the thing they had, she swiped the Credit card as Hutch was looking at them. They rushed him turning his head telling him to look showing him the read out at the register. The ready out across the screen showed Unlimited Funds and he looked at them as Janet said "That's why Markola been hunting you like a just released horny convict after a young man walking around the street with his pants half down showing his ass tempting him advertising to come hit that." (LOOKING AT YOU THE READER Janet saying (fashion statement my ass {t.t.n.t.r} for those of you in) (denial "THAT'S THE NEW TENDER RONI!" young men with their pants half way down their ass watch!)

Hutch looks at them with a stun look "That's why he's been so relentless at coming at me!" In that instant it comes together for him, why they kept saying something about spending to him. Then Elise's comments about him spending money tipping the waitresses and how they would react to him. It all rushed to him like a fast track playing in his head the bills, the waitresses, the bank not showing any with drawls in his account. Elise mad about his spending, Markola keeps wanting his Credit card and the girls talking about they don't care about how much he's got they love him for who he is. Hutch comes back from where he was from Erikaa and Donna calling his name, he looks at them and says "Wait a minute let him see that card!" Looking for the cashier who decides to walk away with it after seeing the read out too, but Janet's hand is grabbing enough of that blond hair from behind as she was walking "Hold on bitch you're not going on break out with my man's Credit card!" Erikaa and Donna with Hutch looks as Janet walks back to them with pulling the cashier saying "She didn't want to leave without giving you the receipt or card back right!" The cashier says "What card?!" Hutch looked at her and Donna told him to stand back as the three of them surrounded her. Erikaa cracks her and neck. Donna cracks her neck and back. Janet took her fingers using them to puncture three holes in that Watermelon and snatch out that piece. Then Janet showed the cashier a sidekick holding her leg in the air saying "Yall stand back I got this!" The cashier eyes got wide "Oh that card! I was going to clear it with her manager." After they get the card from the cashier and Donna sunk her head in the watermelon and took their groceries to the vehicle. On the way home Hutch was looking at the Credit card thinking where did he get this card from with such unlimited spending on it. Telling his girls "Do they know what people would do to get their hands on this thing" They just look at him and he goes "Oh yeah right!"

He slams on the break having them look at him like he crazy, he give them a concerned look and then take off again. They want to know what's wrong and why is he driving like a mad man, there's no one chasing them anymore. He pulls into the drive way and without saying word to them he runs in the house and they look at each other and wonder what's wrong and run in after him, calling his name asking again "what's wrong?" He calls for them to come up to the bedroom where he was sitting in his chair with concern look on his face. They want to know what's got him looking like that because they're not liking the way he's acting but then he shows them another card that looks like the one they showed him. He sat back in the chair taken a deep breath looking at each one of them. They look at the second card he shows the and wonders what's going on because they thought there was just that one and now to see the second one they look at him. He exhales and saying to them "Get ready for this, there's another one!" Looking at them as they now sat on the bed looking back at him wondering what's going on. Donna asked "A third one. What do you mean a third one?" He now remembers the Credit card that he thought was nothing but a joke and explains where he got them from. Janet walks over picking one of the cards up looking at it while he talks about the cards. Janet curious about the card looking at it reads the card and see where it says "This card is untraceable like others put back after using." Learning there are more cards then reading "If lost call this number" Janet see the number on the back. Before she could say anything Hutch is telling them he gave one to his mother because like them she was asking him these crazy question about did he make honest money and how do he make his money. If he was doing anything illegal that she should know about. Donna's cell phone rings and she answers it to hear her Roz from the strip club thanking her because "They haven't seen Markola for a while, it's like he's out of town or something and things at the club have been running smoothly" They talk for a little bit more and hang up. She told Hutch what Roz said about the strip club and he told her "I need to call my mother to see is things alright and try to explain that I need that card back." He calls but there is no answer which is strange to him. She never fails to answer the phone always thinking somebody would call her with news explaining she's very nosey. Erikaa reminds him how he used to talk about the town where his mother lived, how everybody there knew something about someone else because the place is just big enough to be a small city. Hutch laughs saying "She's right" and he calls another person he knows from town wanting to see if they know where his mother was, but that person didn't answer either. He calls good friends he's known for a long time down there the brothers Nelson, Mikey, Ricky, Bunny but when they don't answer he starts to thinking what in the world could keep all these people from answering their phones. Laughing that he's being silly working himself up all for nothing, their probably at work or something because it's not like she's in any danger from the card. Who would know that she's got such a card like that in the first place, he stops talking to them and looks at them like he was trying to remember something. Janet looks at him "Hutch what is it, you have that look on your face again!" He looks at them explaining "The only way to get to me is through you ladies and if I were someone that knew about this card. How would I get to someone like me if I knew the girls were with me somewhere, I would go after his family like his mother" Donna looks at Hutch with concern on her face now and when she looks at Janet, she too caught thought Donna was having. Then she looks at Erikaa who looks back and forth at the both of them then like a light going off she got it and looks at Hutch. He looks puzzled at them for having such looks on their faces but looking at Donna and it hits him, when she talking on the phone to Roz about Markola not being there. He's the only other person that knows about the card and Roz did say "It's like he's been out of town."

Thinking Markola could have found out about his mother just to get to him through his family. How it's easy for anyone to know who one's family is and where they live by looking up. He looks at them wondering since Markola went into his brothers Cordell house like that and he's been gone for a while and nobody is answering the phone down there. Plus it if he could see for himself what's really going on there and if they need his help but he's not going alone this time he's calling his brothers. Janet asked him "What about the Credit cards are you going to tell all your brothers about them?!" Hutch looks at her and kissing her so passionately and having her sit back down then walking over to Erikaa doing the same thing to her then Donna as well leaving them wondering what was that for. He looks at them all "HELL to the NO!" "Remember all the trouble I had when I didn't know about it, now can you imagine all the trouble of 22 brothers that know they could have anything and the flood of ideas that would come in at all times of the nights and where they would call from. What would you do if you had a Credit card with unlimited spending ability that is untraceable with all those brothers?" They agree with him as he said "It doesn't mean I won't take care of them, but right now it's best said I hit the number which is a lot better" Donna asked "What if your mother found out about it what do you think she'll do?" Hutch looks at her answering "She'll most likely buy some food and sit with her girlfriends talking about remember when or who's doing what in the town, then play cards maybe even have a sip of shine and bake something for later"

Hutch's mother(Betty) talking with Mable and Margret about calling their other close friends Lira, Rose, Mildred, Phyllis, Sherylann, Eddy, Sheila, Enid, and Ruby and short time later they all are sitting in Mama Betty's house. Mable is the shortest of the group next to Mama Betty, Lira, Enid, Sheila, and Phyllis. Mable the lightest one there in her 70's looks like she still in her 40's along with Margret 6' 1" the tallest in her 70's, next to her is Eddy 5' 10" almost as tall same age, under Mama Betty. Sitting across from Mable at the table is Sheila and just made her 70's not too long ago plus the same height as Lira both 5' 4" standing behind her is Sheryl Ann 5' 6" who's in her Mid-60's but still looks like she in her thirty's along with both Mildred 5' 7" and Ruby 5' 7" they all have maintained their shapes from working most of their lives. Men always stop and get their ages wrong from living such healthy lives but especially Lira the oldest and Mama Betty's dearest friend. Lira who's in her 80's but looks like a slightly thicker Angela Bassett not by much and has the legs when she wears shorts men always look at her legs first followed by her butt and then the rest. They don't get disappointed with what they see in her but don't know she likes both men and women. Mama Betty is telling them what she's got planned for all of them, it's a trip to New York where they can see some things up there and go shopping. The ladies looked at her wondering where they was going to get the money for such a trip, when Mama Betty told them her son is paying for everything because they all were like mother to him anyways. They all practically raised him too. Telling them now he wants to show his appreciation and she doesn't want to go back up there alone. Margret said "Why not she don't have any one to look after anymore it would be exciting." Mildred asked "Where are they going stay and what would they see." While Ruby said "Since her husband left her for a younger woman and their daughters all grown, why not are there strip club up there?" Lira said "Honey there are strip club, strip joints hell make a man strip for ya, message polar even naked Cowboys singing on the corner up there I can't wait to go again" They looked at Lira and she just replied "Another time another place girls!" Phyllis and Sherylann got the refreshment and they all planned out where to go on that weekend coming and surprise Hutch.

While at the beauty salon they saw this white woman come in and wants to change her hair style knowing she wouldn't be recognized there in a black beauty shop. The salon owner wants to know what kind of style would she like and she told them anything to make her look different. They make her feel comfortable and the women get to talking and even starts to pass around the home made shine one of the women brings in to share with the others while having her hair done. Having a few drinks and getting her hair changed the white women starts talking about how her ex-boyfriend use to treat her, calling her all kinds of names putting her down and even not giving her money to spend on herself. The women there told her she should take him for everything he's got and never look back. She told them she did and was feeling guilty about it but after talking with them and listening to them, she doesn't feel bad about it anymore. Mama Betty listen to her and how she really don't have any family to run to so Mama Betty said if she sticks around she'll introduce her to one of her sons and they got to talking even more that day as their hair was done and they all went to get something to eat.

Hutch was planning with the girls and some of his brothers to go down there in full force needing the help of all GRAND DRUNKEN MASTERS 4 LIFE to come with him. If Markola is down there with his men and since Larry just came up there, he would stay there and watch Hutch's house with their older brother Cordell. Hutch made arrangements with the car rental place to get some vehicles to get down there, first wanted all the GDM4L to drop off their Credit cards at his house with some information he needed from them. He and the girls went to the bank since Erikaa was studying to be an accountant she would know all about what he wanted done to all the Credit card even the girls card too. Showing the girls what he's done to the cards to set them all up for life, but not tell them GDM4L yet having them think he needed them for the rental purposes for the vehicles. They thought it was sweet of him to do that for all of them but they wanted to make it clear to Hutch they're not here for his money.

Hutch knew and understood that be said what if something happens to him or the cards they will be able to take care of themselves just in case. Then quickly changed the subject asking them "Which one can drive the best" Because that's the one who will take the first shift driving when they leave.

The Next Morning Mama Betty and her friends are at her house eating breakfast while she made travel arrangement for the van to pick them up for the airport after they ate and pack some things to take. She also told her new found friend her son would take care of her down there since she was from New York and didn't want to go back there. The woman said she would be in good hand with him and see her when they came back.

Hutch was waiting for the rest of the GDM4L to show up and gave them back their Credits card and had some of them go with him in his brothers Larry's vehicle to pick up the rental vehicles. Coming back to his house to pick up the rest of the GDM4L, Hutch told Larry to "Stay at my house but don't let Cordell get you into any trouble while there" before they left that afternoon for Hutch's mother home town.

Thursday that same afternoon in New York City Hutch's mother and her friends were arriving at J.F.K airport and taken to a hotel by the limo service. Outside the Hotel in Manhattan Mama Betty bumps into a of all people Elise doing some shopping thinking about all the things she was going to get with the Credit card Markola gave her to get out of jail.

When she saw Mama Betty and her friends getting out the limo van which brung them from the airport she calls her name out as they were walking into the hotel which made her stop and look at who was calling her name like that. Mama Betty sees Elise waving to her walking towards her asking "What was she doing there?" Mama Betty told her my son gave them a nice weekend vacation on him with his Credit card and she was going to show his aunts some of the city but since Elise was there how about she show them all the sight and where to go. Elise agreed to then it dawns on her what Mama Betty said, wondering what card of Hutch's he gave her. If Markola had his Credit card taking out the card looking at it and going into hotel behind them up to the front desk clerk asking "Could they check her boyfriend's card for her" The clerk check it and told her "it's worthless there's nothing on his card because it's had been canceled" Mama Betty walking back to the front desk heard what the clerk said to Elise. She told her since she didn't have enough to stay there and she was going to show them around the city anyways why not stay there on her for the weekend and she'll cover everything that she needs. Elise agreed and saw her pullout the same kind of Credit card she said Hutch gave her and keeping it to herself but mad that Markola gave her a worthless card just to get out of jail. Thinking she got played again by a man and now more than ever wants to get even with men, starting with Hutch since he's got the money to make her happy and she was going to get that Credit card from his mother since she's staying with her. Not long after they all checked in Mama Betty want to go shopping and get some new things for her and her friends. Elise told her "They can walk to a lot of the store because it's in walking distance from the hotel they're staying at" They all the set out with Elise to go shopping.

At Hutch's house Larry watched Hutch and his girl with the GDM4L leave out, he gets on the phone and calls Cordell to see what he was doing because he let Hutch take his ride and didn't have one to get around the city. Cordell told Larry he'll be right over and they can start with a drink and take thing from there, asking him "Ever had Meyer's Rum?"

They haven't left New York State yet an Hutch is already drinking his fifth energy drink saying "I wants to be really pumped up when I get there." Asking Erikaa to hand him one of them cannoli's eating it fast then smashing the gas pedal so they can go faster. Janet and Donna looked at Erikaa both saying quietly to her "Please don't give him no another cannoli, remember what happened when he came over to the apartment to get them after the meeting. What we had to do to calm his ass down" Janet says "He had so much energy they all were wiped out just trying to keep up with him, and now he's driving already mad about his mother." Erikaa looks at Hutch eyes in the rear view mirror and see how wild eyed he looks when he looks back at her asking "You alright back there?" She answers softly "Yes" Out of the window one by one goes the cannoli's till there's none left. 2Soon is behind Hutch's vehicle and he's driving with Mack riding shot gun and they are looking at each other every time a cannoli came out the window hitting the ground. Mack asked 2Soon "Is Hutch smuggling something should know about with all those things being thrown out the window like they're being chased by the cops and have to get rid of all the evidence." When they saw another one hitting the ground breaking open showing the cream inside and piece hits the windshield sticking to it right in front of Mack. He reaches out and grabs it looking at the cookie shell then at 2Soon sniffing it then tasting it saying "It's one of them cannoli's Hutch had him pick up for him at the bakery and those things are good" 2Soon knew the girls must be trying to keep Hutch from getting hyped on sugar as he laughs and tells Mack what he's thinking.

Cordell is at Hutch's house with Larry and they are drinking and talking about good ole times and Cordell suggest that he calls a couple of friends over to keep them company like a small party and promises Hutch won't even know they had a couple of girls at his house. Few minutes later there's a knock on the door and four women are standing at the door looking hot and sexy in their clothes asking for Cordell. He comes to the door and told Larry these are friend of his and invites them in but they told Cordell they were at a party and didn't want to leave a few of their friends cold so they told them about his the party he's having and they wanted to come. Cordell told two of the women this is my little brother Larry and he just came to New York show him and good time while he's here. The woman with big boobs comes over to Larry sticking her chest in his face asking "You're his little brother huh, your cute where you from?" She leads him back in the house and Cordell lets the rest of the people in. Some people coming in had their own music wanting to play it on the stereo system and put in the mixed CD"s they had. Then heading over to the bar Hutch has in the living room. Larry was sandwiched between two big chested women keeping him from noticing all the extra people in the house at first handing him a drink and them dancing with him. After a while he sees there are a lot of people dancing in the living room and then goes in the kitchen and sees more in there cooking and even more in the pool swimming and hot tub. Larry looks for Cordell and finds him in one of the bed room with two women, he shouts at Cordell "A FEW FRIENDS BRUH?!" Telling him about all the people in the house, Cordell calms him down explaining their not going to tear up the place these are responsible people and if he was worried about Hutch's bedroom don't because he locked the door and put a sign on it "busy getting busy don't hate" The two women Larry was with came in the room and found him with Cordell and the other two women "There you are we looked all over for you, come back and have a good time with us Larry." They pull him out of the room and take him back down stairs to the rest of the party.

Back in Manhattan Mama Betty and her friend with Elise now has been to a few stores and heads back to the hotel to change wanting to go have some seafood for dinner. Elise told Mama Betty about CITY ISLAND where a lot of people go for good seafood when they come to NEW YORK city. She agreed to go and they made arrangement with the hotel for a limo service with a vehicle big enough to take them all there and after they got dressed they head to CITY ISLAND. Finding one of the popular places out there, they're seated inside and starts ordering drinks but the drinks they ordered each woman would have an extra something to add to it. Elsie watched as they would put these small corked bottles of shine on the table and even add them to their drinks. Elise asked "What's in the bottles?" They all seem to have one except her. Mama Betty told her it's puts a better kick to their drinks and gave her a shot to drink by itself. Elise looks at the clear water liquid and from the cheering on by Lira, Margret, Ruby, Mable and Mildred as she downs the shot. Surprised it was so smooth saying "It wasn't that bad." Mama Betty gave her a bigger glass and told her they need to eat before they get to really having fun, but Elise thought if she got Mama Betty drunk enough then she would be careless with that Credit card and that would give her a chance to get her hands on it. Insisting that Mama Betty toast with her Elise pours two big glasses of the shine they have and hands the other to Mama Betty saying since she was here in NY they all can get loose with this girls night out. Then ordering more drinks for the table but in her attempt to get Mama Betty to drink more she never notices Mama Betty eating pieces of the fresh bread with garlic butter on it they had on the table. When the food came Elise heard Lira say "After we eating we want to go to see the black strippers, the Chocolate Chip and Dales" and all the women agreed.

Elise didn't eat that much because she was too busy planning in her mind on how to get that card from Mama Betty and not paying attention to how much shine in her drinks she was drinking. The check came Elsie saw Mama Betty pulls the Credit card out of her bra and hand it to the waiter saying "You did such a good job she's showed him where she signed for him to get a 100$ tip for dealing with all of them." Elise mumbling "Now I see where Hutch gets that tipping the hired help good from" Mama Betty said to everyone "We need leave something for the bus boy for cleaning the tables" and everyone elected Elise to leave the bus boy something which she did and handed him two dollars. She looks at them saying "What he's just the bus boy, they get paid to get the dishes." Mama Betty and the rest went into their purses and came up with a nice tip for him too. He thanked all the older women but looked at Elise and mouthing words to her 'You freaking cheap ass!" Then he walks away heading to the kitchen with his tub of dishes. Mama Betty said "I need to stop a couple places first" When they did she had them picking up a snap shot camera's and camcorders for video for some of them, then to the bank where she got cash for all of them to spend at the strip club. They reach the place where the black male strippers "The Chocolate Chip and Dales" were performing and paid the cover charge to get in. Mama Betty handed out a nice stack of cash to her friends and a few bills to Elise because she didn't want her son to know she had her at the strip club handing out his money to strippers. They get there and the door man looks at all these older women asking "Are you ladies ready for what's inside" Lira felt him up and held on to him then put a couple of bill in his pants, going "I could teach some of them a trick or two and hope they are ready for me" All the women agreed with her watching the door man blush and he made sure they got a table so they could all be close to each other. When the music starts Lira was right up front cheering the first dancer on stage waving her bills to come over to her sticking bills on his oily skin.

In the vehicles on their way down south Hutch was talking to Donna as Janet and Erikaa caught some sleep, he was telling her he blames himself for getting his mother into this mess and should have known better. Trying to think how they're treating his mother and aunts down there.

At the strip club Mama Betty and her friend were given drinks by the men in tight shorts with no shirts flexing at them telling them their going to be treated like Queen tonight, sending more strippers to come over to their table dancing in front of them. Having them give lap dances by picking them up holding them in front on their thighs.

Back in the vehicle Hutch was telling Donna he just hopes his mother could hold on till he gets there because he knows she's a strong woman guessing how strong he can't say, but hoping she just don't give up no matter what. Inside the strip club being held up by this big armed dancer sitting on his lap with her arms around his neck Mama Betty was saying "I can hold on baby all day baby give me what you got!" The stripper answer "I've never drop a women yet and I've had some very big women on those thighs of mine" She looks down at his chest and then his legs again and said "Well giddy up man I'll put you back wet after a good riding."

In the vehicle Hutch was saying "My mother is not the type to scream out, she would hold it in and take all they can give her." Back at the strip club Mama Betty was screaming "DAMN MAN YOU GOT A GRIP ON YOU! HOT DAM! I DON'T WANT TO LET GO, OH YEAH! I CAN TAKE ALL YOU GOT NOW GIVE IT MAN!"

Donna asked "What about your aunts would they give up easy or be like your mother and take it" Hutch looks at Donna saying "Aunty Lira might, aunt Mable is very strong, aunt Margret she's a fighter, aunt Mildred is just as strong as Mable, Aunt Sheila is tough wouldn't crack. Adding aunt Ruby and Enid are stubborn Jamaican women." Saying his "Aunt Sheryl-Ann, and aunt Eddy are the skinniest of the group like Lira and not even his aunt Phyllis the biggest but toughest too." Going over in his mind and telling Donna just imagine those frail old women being treated like they were rag dolls or something that any man could pick up with one hand and do what he wanted to them and they have to take it.

Back at the strip club all the women are having a ball, Mable & Margret and Mildred have the strippers holding them on their thighs being cheered on by other women as the other strippers either dance in front of or picked them up letting them grinding on them. Elise watches and drinks more and more of the shine they have there. Margret was taken pictures of some of them with the strippers and saw Lira on the other side of the stage with this big muscular dark skinned dancer name Chocolate Power. Looking through the lens of the camera, she saw Lira riding Chocolate Power like a cowgirl riding a bull, taking a couple pictures of them. Then noticed each time she looked through the camera Lira was wearing less and less clothes till she was riding the man in her bra with no panties. He was saying "Wow you look good for your age Ma!" Holding on to his neck with one hand and reaching down with her other hand and have his eyes get wide from her grabbing hold inside the jock strap as she said "I'm about to plug in and you're going have a power outage" She holds him in her hands then they back seem to disappeared for a while. Margret saw them and yells "Go head Lira! Don't whip too bad and he better be just as thick when you bring him back girl" Taking pictures as he carries Lira behind those curtains. Mama Betty was being lifted up like a Queen by some of the dancers there after buying drink for every one there and putting a nice wad of bills in each of the four strippers holding up Gee strings. Elise was sitting at the table sulking not having any fun as Mama Betty came over to her asking "What's wrong? You're allowed to have fun even if you do date my son with all this meat swinging around!" Elise sits there wanting to grab her and get that card, but instead thinks of other way to get the card. Then an idea came to her while drinking with Mama Betty when the waiter came over to her for payment of the drink she bought. Elise watches her pull that Credit card out of her purse this time and hand it to the waiter saying to him don't forget his tip too. That made Elise roll her eyes shaking her head each time she hears Mama Betty said that, getting mad about tipping people she feels is just their job anyway. Quickly acting on her idea to get the card, Elise says "We need another toast and more drinks, so I'll go tell the waiter what we want." Mama Betty told her "Knock yourself out. We still have lots of shine left." Elise explains she wants another mixed drink to have a good toast and went to find the waiter with the plan to tell him she's there to get the drinks and take her Credit card back to her. Thinking she'll tell him she'll give it back to Mama Betty. Finding it hard to get through all the screaming women either dancing with a stripper or cheering their friends on for what they're doing with the stripper. Elise sees the waiter and stops him saying "I want to get another drink" and he could give her back the Credit card to take back to Mama Betty she's with. Mad that he told her he already gave it back to her and their drinks are on the table. Elise cussing at him and gave him such a look as he wonders what he did wrong to get a look like from a woman especially in there. Getting back to the table and seeing the drinks and Mama Betty waiting for her with two strippers by her side saying "Let her get that drink in first boys." Elise try not to let her anger show and put on a smiling face taking the drink which she don't know has lots of shine in it and downs it like she was drinking water. Mama Betty said "Not the best of them could down all that much like that. Girl you got to take it easy with this stuff. It's known to make people have the regrets the next morning from doing the Vegas thing and it should have stayed there!" Elise rolls her eyes at what Mama Betty said. A few minutes later after Mama Betty told the strippers to loosen her up they are on the stage with Elise and she is showing everyone in there how to handle two men at one time. Mildred walks over to Mama Betty asking "Isn't that the miss thing that you said acted so classy at your son's house?" Ruby next to them says "Classy what's classy about what she's doing in front of everyone like that?" Margret still taking picture gets yelled at by Mildred wanting to know why she's filming that kind of stuff they sell in the porno shop. Margret answered "Those are people that get paid for it, but she's supposed to be our nephew's girlfriend! Well I think he would like to see what a Assy giving it up both ways woman does when he's around. The way she's doing things with both of them she could show Lira a few move Whoa!" They watch as Elsie gets held upside down and swung like a pendulum back and forth from one man to the other catching his thing in her mouth. Lira came out for the back just as Elise was done and got cheers from a lot of the women there, asking "What's was that all about" Margret shows her in the camcorder and Lira said "Wow she's got talent!" They looked at Lira as Phyllis told her she would think that being just as wild as you are. The announcer came up on stage and gets the women all amped up to see Chocolate Power is next but as he calls his name there is no answer from him. One of the strippers came out to tell him something and he says "Chocolate Power will be coming to the stage later he's having a nap back stage, so who drain the Power man?" Mama Betty and her friends look at Lira as she fixes her hair taking a drink saying "What? He'll be fine after a recharge. He's still young enough to bounce back quickly I hope" A stripper come over to Lira and hands her a piece of paper saying "It's from Chocolate Power." He stand by the curtain waving at her holding a big can of red bull and muscle milk. The paper has his real name and information on it. Mama Betty says "Like the others huh." Margret said "Damn my bad yall! I forgot to tell her not to twist that man out." They laugh at the paper knowing it's going on the pile of papers she already has, even though she never calls them saying "I like being single and want to stay that way." While all the women were having fun getting the stripper they wanted and getting cheered on by some of the women in there. This group of eight young women got mad at Mama Betty and her friends for the having the money to get the good strippers attention. The Leader of the young women comes over to Mama Betty and starts with her by telling Mama Betty she got no right to be in there with these young men strip dancing. She should be at home baking cookie for her grandchildren. Mama Betty looked at the young woman and told her she got more right to be in there than her young ass do. Another young woman came over griping Mama Betty is hogging the good strippers from everyone, should be saving retirement money for knitting something. Then saying "Why don't you go buy a pet to keep you company before you drop dead. Besides what do you remember about sex and wouldn't know what to do with a man like them." Margret and Mildred and Ruby saw these young women standing around Mama Betty and they looked like they were having words so they came to stand by her to see what the problem was. The first young woman says "Oh look it's the golden girls the ghetto version, FLORIDA, ESTER, FLORENCE and MS JEFFERSON." Mama Betty told the young "If you can't afford the men you want, then you need to spend more money on those weave and eat some more to have a body these men might want to come over to." Another young woman said "These men don't want some old bitches like you that suck down Geritol wearing depends diapers to stop the leaks because you can't help yourself anymore so go home!"

Lira heard that standing next to Mama Betty about to jump at the young woman, when Mama Betty told her "hold up Lira I got this! Look you fake hair wearing bean pole crack head, looking like you just got your half payment child support check cashed. Because you don't have a real job except sweeping the park in those green suit before going home to a bottle of rock gut beer that you can afford when your serving more men than Mickey Dee's in a week! I was trying to be nice about it, but since it seems the men on the corner where you live. Got tired of seeing each other coming in as another were going out of not only your home but your ass and that hole between your legs called the HOLLAND TUNNEL! So you decide to come here and ruin my good time. Or was it the just release inmate you don't turn on because he rather still see that big fat ashy man he loves better than you he left back behind bars, GOD knows he made the right choice by the way" Before Mama Betty could say another word four other young women stood by their friend and said "You old dry up hole bitches!"

Hutch was looking around with a mean face then starts breathing heavy getting grouchy with everyone and says to Janet, Erikaa and Donna "I feel like I'm about to get into a big fight somewhere right now!"

(Finishing Mama Bettys sentence) "You couldn't get a man looking like that even if a lifer on death row with conjugal visits had a choice of the needle or screwing you. He'd have his arm strapped up choosing the needle knowing he went out not having to screw something like you" The young women calls some more of her friends over and Lira goes "Bitch you aint showed nothing" Then shouts out "25208 OLD DOWN AND DIRTY DIRTY HOLLA BACK UP IN THIS PIECE HEARD MEH!" All of Mama Betty friends stood by her in the face off, but it was Lira that said "First I'm beat your asses like you stole something. Second I'm going to beat your asses because you are something STUPID!" Going in her purse finding and tossing the young woman a pack of aspirin. She looks at what Lira tossed her asking "What am I going to do with this?" Lira smiled and Punches the young woman back over the table, then went after her. Which gave Mama Betty and the rest of them reason to attack.

The announcer shout out ladies please stop. Mama Betty with young woman in a head lock come over to him and gave him a few bills and he said "Well they did start it." Mildred boxed and knocked out the young woman as she wind milled swung at her, another young woman had a bottle about to hit Enid with it but she took the bottle from her and back slapped her then pimp slapped her followed by the old one two knockout punch. Sheryl-Ann just D.D.T the young woman followed by body slam and knockout punch. Phyllis clothes line the young woman and upper cut knocking her out. Ruby gut punched the young woman and bull dogged her to the ground followed by a choke slam through a table. Mable speared the young woman then picked her up and power slammed her to the ground, while Rose foot slapped the young woman then gave her sweet chin music kick knocking her out cold quickly. Margret just punched the young woman straight knocking her out, Sheila grab the young woman giving her a stunner and leg drop picking her up to body slam her out. Eddy went the SUGAR RAY LEANORD and hit this young woman so fast with a flurry of punched she had no choice but to be knocked out. Lira surprised the young woman she was fighting with ending it by back flip kicking her out cold. Mama Betty did a Chinese style of snake fist and elephant punches followed by the rock bottom and peoples elbow to the loud mouth young woman who started everything. The young women out matched, under weighed and out powered get their butt beat good by Mama Betty and her friends. Most of the other women in the place cheered them on each time the put another young woman on the pile of them in the middle of the floor.

The younger women with long extensions braids and weaves with tight dresses on couldn't handle the older bigger healthy stronger casual dressed fueled by shine experience women from the south. When the bouncers got there they see all the young women beat up on the floor picking up themselves or their friends. The bouncers that were talking to Lira watch her says "If they're still hooking up later then get rid of the garbage." Pointing to all the young women beat up on the floor. They shook their head "Yes" and told all those young women they have to go helping some get to their feet and out the door. Mama Betty says to Lira "Four of the men shook their head at you, do you know them?" Lira smiled at Mama Betty "I still know how to turn more than one out in a few seconds, where other would take minutes or hours." Mama Betty hi-fives Lira "Girl you so crazy! Now let's get back to having fun Dee Jay turn it up in here!" Lira stood at the door with the bouncers as the young women stumble and fall outside the club after getting their asses beat from the older women inside. Lira says "Next time you Y.D.M.F.S.B's and that's no hit record but you (Young Dumb Mo-Fo Stupid Bitches) won't worry about what an experience woman is doing and get some experience for yourself. Not having all those babies cashing your child support checks to come to strip clubs and getting an education and stop chasing around the wrong man abusing and cheating on your dumb ass. Learn to get your lives together and have a kick ass group like mine, that did our time with stupid ass men we kicked to the curb years ago so we can look like this and have fun." The Lira says before she leaves them "One day you all are going to get my age and better to have a group to have your back than back stab you about your man or anything else" she turns and closes the door on them standing there looking at each other and hail a cab to go home. Elise was at the table drunk but still thinking about that Credit card, she starts looking through all the purses there at their table trying to remember which one was Mama Betty's. All the while she was getting filmed by Margret who kept recording and didn't know she was catching Elise in the act. It was time to leave and Mama Betty and her friends had enough except Lira and Elise they were giving some of the strippers the numbers to the room at the hotel they were staying at wanting them to come.

In the vehicles Hutch was talking to Donna referring to something he couldn't imagine a man was doing to his mother, he had no idea she was having the time of her life with his aunts. Thinking how torturous a man was getting at them not knowing just the opposite on what he thought. Just thinking about them being slapped around held in a chair, not knowing they were slapping men asses while sitting in chairs. How the men are holding and shaking them around screaming at them to tell them what they know, and on the other hand not knowing they are being held up on the men's thighs as they ride them like horses while the stripper ask "More you want more?" Hutch says "I try not to think of the horrible thing they would be doing to any of them" as he drives along and Donna trying to make him not thinking about any of that.

Larry didn't know Cordell had those women come there to keep him distracted but that didn't last long because the party starts getting out of hand with all those people there. Things start getting broke and Larry goes to check it out hoping they didn't do too much damage and he calls for Cordell to help him.

Hutch was thinking so hard about his mother and decides to get his mind off thinks and check on Larry to let him know who far they are but every time he calls there was a busy signal, so he had the operator cut in the line with his authority because the bills in his name. When the operator did both of them get rude answer about how dare they cut in on this man's call he was about to get some punani lined up after the party. Hutch asked the man "What party?" The man says "I was invited by his good Correl or Condell something like that, so he had to bust in this room to get away from the noise they were making" Then asked Hutch was he coming over and he needs to bring food because they're hungry and don't forget some beer too. Hutch asked "How money people are there at his buddy's house" The man answered he lost count at 24, he goes to the door opening it up to hear this Crash and Boom! Saying "My friend don't mind, oops that sounded like it was expensive." Hutch asked him where was he at and he told him again in this big bedroom he had to break the door to get into because Conell told him to go anywhere that's quite just leave him be for a while. Janet still sleep but hearing how mad Hutch was starts dreaming because Hutch was getting a little loud asking the man question over the phone about his house and brother. Janet sitting behind Donna on the passenger side of the vehicle asked "Who's having a party at your house big bear?" Donna turns to her and says "My brother's at my house with a bunch of people and they are tearing the place up from what it sounds like" Janet went "ah Larry sounded so sweet" From the grunting and growling they could tell Hutch was really upset but when he turns his head backward without turning his body with his eyes fire red and fangs grew out his mouth to tell Janet "It's my older brother Cordell who's got people there!" Her eyes got wide and brows went up at the sight of him doing that, she woke up gasping it was all just a dream. Erikaa too starts dreaming about their trip and in it she sees how Hutch was getting mad hearing the anger in his voice asking "Was Hutch alright he sounds very mad at someone." She saw him turning his head a full 180 degree while still driving with eyes on fire and big teeth talking to all of them one by one never turning his head back the other way saying "When I get hold of my brother who tore up my house, they need to stay out the way" Erikaa's eyes got wide and jaw dropped as she climbs over the back seat being scared of what she saw, then looks over to see Janet back there already holding her finger up like a cross at Hutch. They look towards Donna to tell her to come back with them but she's not there only an empty seat, then her head upside down lowers from outside the window asking "Hutch you alright baby" He looks over where Donna was and see she's on the roof of the vehicle and told her to "Get your butt back in there before they get pulled over turning his head back to Erikaa saying "Right!" Then she woke breathing hard from that bad dream she just had. Janet asked "You alright?" Looking around seeing things are normal in the vehicle. Hutch apologizes for sounding so scary to them explaining he really worked hard all his life for that house and never had things break at a party he threw. Then calmly tells the man on the phone if he's where Hutch thinks he is to look around on the dresser. The man asked "What for?" Hutch in a mild voice says to the man "If you look at the picture on the dresser they are of a big man holding a refrigerator over his head and another one of him breaking a cinder block and another one of the his breaking a car windshield pulling out a man through it and the last on of a man pushing over this small car with such an angry look on his face" Donna says "I thought the hulk was white baby." He smiles at her and says "Long story but true my niece took that one." She slides over closer to the door thinking "better looks for a soft place to jump out in case he starts to go green." The man says "Wow that's big dude in all these pictures doing all that. Candell really knows how to pick his friends huh?" Hutch says "There should be one big picture with the big dude standing outside the bedroom you're in and outside the house and in the kitchen and by the pool" He explains to the man that's the owner and he's about twenty minutes from the house and when he gets there, he's going to break any and every one there into pieces and then eat those pieces. The man thought Hutch was Joking till he says "Go ask your buddy CORDELL that's his name, who's house you are really at and that his brother Hutch had to turn around he's about 20 minutes from his house watch what happens next when you do ok" The man told Hutch to hold on and goes to find Cordell. He was in one of the other bedroom when the man knocks on the door asking Cordell "Who's house is this?" At first Cordell shouts back to the door "Mine why?" The man says "I thought So! Because some asshole I'm going to really cuss out good says he's your brother Hutch and he had to turn around, so he's about twenty minutes from the house but to ask you who's house this was!" There was a loud thump coming from that room, Cordell had a woman on him and he threw her off him like she was a rag doll. Hitting the floor as he raced to the door opening it up and looking for the man seeing no one in the hallway only seeing the bedroom to his brother's door broke open. Gasping he flies to the room where the man was about to get back on the phone, he tackles him to the ground, putting is hand on the man's mouth hanging up the phone softly hearing Hutch saying "hello." The man wants to know what was that all about but the phone rings again and Cordell turns his head looking at it afraid of it. Seeing the man was going to answer it, he drops kicks the man stopping him from answering it. Saying "This is my brother's house" With a shock look on his face the man asked "The one in those pictures?" He threw Cordell off him across the bedroom like he was nothing and runs out of the room screaming. "EVERYONE RUN FOR YOUR LIVES! THE REAL OWNER IS COMING HOME AND HE'S PISSED WANTING HEADS LIKE THE I.R.S AND GOING TO F&$K YOU UP LIKE A HUGE CONVICT THAT JUST GOT RELEASD LOOKING AT THE YOUNG MAN WITH HIS PANTS DOWN AROUND HIS ASS OR THE PIMP YOU BITCHES OWE MONEY TOO! HE'S A LINEBACKER A GIANT FAN AND YOU'RE THE QB FOR THE REDSKIN THIGHESMEN HE'S

GONNA BREAK YOUR SHIT. HE'S BIGGER AND MEANER LOOKING THAN TERRI CREW IN FRIDAYS 2 PLUS HE'S 2O MINTUES AWAY! At first they didn't pay any attention to him till someone looked up and saw the pictures of Hutch on the walls when he did play football at the defensive end position. How it showed him tackling some players and one he clothes lined hard flipping him around then holding his helmet in his hands. There was stampede of people trying to get out of the house stepping on each other and jumping out of windows, which made Larry come to see what was going on and Cordell told him Hutch will be there in about 20 minutes their dead men walking. The phone rang again and Cordell says let it go to voice mail and hear what he's got to say first before they answer it. Larry looks around at the place and seed how his house is tore up and in a very big mess. Mad that let Cordell talk him into this party but then tells Cordell to be quite as they hear this faint squeaking sound coming from somewhere. They walk around down stairs thinking it's coming from down there standing still listening real good. Larry asked "What is that noise, where's it coming from?" They follow the noise "Reek, reek, reek, creek" upstairs to the back bedroom where they find the source. Opening the door seeing this very thin man behind a HUGE woman and both of them are lying on their sides naked. It looks like the man is attempting to have sex from behind with the very large woman on the bed that squeaks from their movement. Seeing that Larry say "Ah that's not right! Does she even know he's back there?" Cordell answers "She got to know he's back there they're both naked in bed right! Just hope she don't roll over or otherwise he's going to be stuck in her ass cheeks, they'll have to call rescue for that and I'm not going to get that metal picture out my head for a while." They walk through the whole house to see how much damage is really done to the place and how what they need to replace or fix back. Then the phone rings again its Hutch saying on the answering machine "I'm not really on my way there but if those people are not out of my house and things are not the way I left them. There is no place on this planet Cordell or Larry can hide I won't BOMB to get to your ASS!" knowing there's more important matters to get to down where their mother is but he will return and get to killing when he gets back if his place has one thing wrong with it and hangs up the phone. They stand there looking at the how those people went through his frig and cooked leaving dishes all over the place with some broke, garbage everywhere cups, beer bottles, can, broke glasses, plates of half eaten food all on the floor. Cordell says "I'm going home and sleep on and idea about where to hide from Hutch" Larry looks at Cordell "Walk one more step toward that door, it'll be an ass whipping you never thought come from me." Cordell wants to know what they're going to do because Hutch s going to kill them no matter what, Larry suggest they first can clean up this mess and next time he's not listening to Cordell. All that night they clean up and every now and then Cordell would shout at the people up stairs "Yall better hurry up" because that squeaking was driving him crazy.

The next day in the hotel Elise is waking up seeing four men and two women laid out on the bed and floor naked as her eyes adjust to the sun light coming through the window. Her head is throbbing trying to remember where she was and what happened for her to get there and why she feels so full when she moves. Standing up and walking to the bathroom having to use it but when she gets there about to sit on the toilet feeling her stomach full and a strange feeling of something in her butt. She reaches and feels what is between her butt cheeks up her ass and a fat eleven inch dildo. Her eyes got wide looking at it when she pulled it out and wondering this is what making her feel so full and sore. Throwing that dildo back into the bedroom where she came from popping one of the strippers in the head with it as he laid on the floor sleep.

Hutch is still driving while the girls are sleep, he looks in his rear view mirror and sees the vehicle behind him as Mack now driving his turn at the wheel speed up alongside Hutch showing he's hungry and needs gas. Shaking his head he understands they speed on to the nearest gas station where they can fill up and get some breakfast.

Larry worked through the rest of the night still sweeping up as Cordell lays on the bags of garbage snoring, most of the work Larry done as Cordell maybe fill one bag of garbage making Larry so mad he goes and get a bucket of ice cold water and stand there looking at his oldest brother. Splash! The water comes down on Cordell soaking him and waking him up, seeing his brother fighting with the bags mad about being soaked as Larry done most of the work cleaning up. Now fully woke and wet he looks at Larry asking "Why you threw water on me like that?" Larry told him he put all the broken pieces of furniture in a pile so they could see what they have to fix, he tried to get it together but it doesn't look right. Cordell told Larry with all the stores open on that Friday how was they going to replace the things and where are they going to get the money from unless they call their mother. Larry told Cordell their mother gave him money and it should cover what they need to get to make things right. First Cordell smiles at him because the thought of replacing everything and having Larry pay for it was a good thing to him. Then it hits him and he asked "How come she didn't give me any money?" Larry answered "She didn't want to give you money because look what you married! You would only splurge on women with black wet noses and run on all fours not at the OTB either." Walking over to his brother giving him a serious look and says "Mama always wonder if drinking got you what you got now, shouldn't you give up drink period?" When he couldn't answer that question Larry says "Never mind bruh here have a beer." Cordell takes the beer and sips it then tell him since he got the cash all they have to do is look at some of the pictures Hutch got of his house and they could tell what is missing and replace it. Plus he knows where Hutch gets his food from because he took him along a few time to buy stuff for himself and his house so they kids would have the same things when they come over to his house. They get the photo album and go through it picking out all the pictures they need of the broken things and set out to the mall.

Back on the road after breakfast Janet is next to Hutch as they drive down the interstate and he was telling all of them how he grew up in this small house with his brothers. How the arrear was like one big family where if any one of the boys did something wrong they would get their butts whip and had to go tell their parents why Mr. or Miss whipped their behind only to get another whipping for doing it in the first place. He explains to them why he has so many he calls them brothers and they are to him because he not only grew up with them, ate at their houses got beat just the same by their parent and even given money, took to movies, had picnic's with them, slept over their houses. Like a normal big very big family they even fought one another only to realize they are family. No one could ever threaten or doing something to anyone of them even when they were mad at each other. After a fight they still would come together as a family strong unit never holding a grudge or plot anyone demise. Now they're children are cousin in that way, every GDM4L calls them their nephews or nieces and would die for any of them like their own kids. Knowing their brothers would take care of his family when he's not there. All the girls have tears in their eyes hearing what Hutch has to say, but in the other vehicle Tyrone, Byron, Ron, and Doug ride behind him. Hutch is being cussed out by Tyrone because he had to ride in the same vehicle with Byron and don't know most of the huge words or explanations he's using as he talks to the others about their finances. Trying to say how they need to improve on them by making the right investment since he became a stock broker. Mack, 2Soon, Steel and Dougie are laughing at how Tyrone looks pissed. Mack is betting that Tyrone is tired of hearing Byron talk about money and investment and by the way he keeps trying to get their attention when he rides next to them, but Mack keeps the tinted window up so he can't see them laughing at him knowing he wants to get out of that vehicle so badly. Dave driving with La-Machine, LiL-Rob and Jazz get a call from Dougie and he tells them what's going on with Tyrone and they laugh pulling next to the vehicle and watch as Tyrone tries to get their attention. Jazz calls the vehicle Derrick is driving with Goodie, Herb and D-train and they do the same as the others did getting a good laugh from it. Tyrone looked at Ron and Doug wondering why they weren't saying anything about why keeps going on about his investment that don't make sense to him. Then he looks back and sees the reason why, because they have in their ears plugins listening to music. Every time he would say something to them they just smiled and nodded and look back out the window bobbin their heads to the music. Tyrone thought to himself why he didn't think of that and the next time they stop he's getting a set too.

In the hotel room where Elise had showered and got dressed for the day she calls to find out where Mama Betty and her friends are, only to learn they are having breakfast and about to go walking around Manhattan without Lira. It seems she had even more to drink than Elise did. Rushing down to breakfast to catch up with Mama Betty and her friends Elise stops at the front desk and tells them about the people in her room, she wants them out by the time she gets back with her group giving him the room number then going to the breakfast room where Mama Betty and her friends are. Seeing the women all dressed nice and looking refreshed wondering how they did that. Hearing them talking about the hotels spa treatment early that morning they all had and wondered if she was going to make it down to join them, after seeing all those people she went up to her room with figuring Elise was busy. Elise ate her food fast because she was hungry and she wanted to walk with them while planning how to get that card from Mama Betty before they had to leave from there. Making sure they all had their camera's they set out to take some pictures and see some sights, since it was Friday in morning.

Elise warns them about the city being really busy everyone going to or coming from work. Everywhere they went Elise watched Mama Betty pay for things with that Credit card. She would think to herself how she's going to get it from her somehow. Lira was waking up and took another drink of their shine to mellow her out. She knew it would keep her tipsy till she had something to eat so she calls room service placing an order for something. Margret thought it would be funny for Lira to see herself from that night at the male strip club and left her camcorder with a note for Lira to look at herself on it. The food came and she asked the bell hop to help her hook the camcorder up the TV, but as he was trying to hook it to the TV he kept looking at Lira. She was looking really good in her long flowing house coat and short night gown as she walks around the room, but noticed the young man paying more attention to her body than what he was doing. She stood right in front of him and opened her house coat giving him a good look at her body. She asked "Be honest answering my question or I'll kick you out of the room" The young man shook his head "OK" and she asked him "Do I look good for a woman in my late 70's" he said "Hell yeah wow!" Then she said "Nice young good looking man like you has to have a girlfriend right? Now be honest" He answers "Yes" She laughs then said "Want to keep her? Then you don't want to mess with this (me). Because I'll have you sucking your thumb cured up like a baby ready to give me everything you got in this world and with what I know and how to do it to you puppy. So can you just fix the thing to the TV and leave you already got a tip" He watches her close her house coat up and fold her arms up standing there looking at him. He quickly fixes the TV to the camcorder for her and leaves the room. Watching what they did that night she laughs at some of the things her and her friend with Mama Betty was doing. Margret recorded it but then she noticed where Margret thought she had stopped recording but caught Elise at the tables going through everyone bag like she was looking for something. When she got to Betty's purse she didn't look at the others and went through her wallet looking at every card she had in it but didn't take anything from it. Lira though it was strange because no one didn't catch her doing it but why was Elise examining every one of the Credit cards in Mama Bettys purse like that and what could she be looking for in it.

Early in the afternoon they all wanted to go back to the hotel and drop off their bags and maybe have quick nap for some of them, Mama Betty wouldn't mind enjoying that spa again. They decide to walk back to the hotel instead of getting a cab and when they got there Mama Betty checks on Lira because she was the only one that stayed behind. Getting her to open the door because she sounded like she was really tipsy answering the door when Mama Betty knocked on it. Lira had a few more drinks while watching the camcorder but she didn't get drunk. Lira was mad because she couldn't figure out what Elise was looking for in Betty's purse. Then there was a knock on the door again, it was Elise asking to talk to Mama Betty. Asking her could it wait because she's in the middle of something with Lira and would get back to her about it, Lira slurs "let the lying little skinny ass bitch in and she's beat it out of her because she up to something that's making me mad!" Elise couldn't make out what was being said asking "Is everything alright?" then putting her head to the door. Lira looks at the door and takes a run at it kicking the door right where Elise has her head leaning against the door on the other side BOOM! The door was hit and the force knocks Elise across the hall into the wall ending up on the floor. Mama Betty looks at Lira asking "What the hell was all that for?" Outside the door Elise was seen going flying into the wall and then pick herself up off the floor holding her head as Margret and Ruby was walking to check on Lira too and seen what happened to Elise. Helping her up asking "You alright" and sees how embarrassed she is as Margret says "When eves dropping on someone's door especially Lira's make sure you're not the one getting off the floor with a speed knot ok shuga" Elise hold her head and leaves before they could go in the room. They walk in telling what they just seen outside of the door. Lira looks at Mama Betty saying "That's why I did, good for her!" Margret tries to hold back laughing as Ruby describes how Elise went flying across the hall into the wall, reminding them how they use to bang on the door when their kids calls themselves trying do that stuff. Mama Betty snaps her finger being reminded of another reason why they came up there to see Hutch in the first place. At the same time Mama Betty was thinking about getting her friends to go with her over to Hutch's house.

Cordell and Larry are at the mall looking at furniture to see what they can find to put back in Hutch's house. Going into one store not finding one piece they could match with any of the photos, walking out Cordell runs into Cheryl and her friends at the mall. She wants to know why her father is there at the mall because he never comes there and does it have anything to with Uncle Hutch house. He asked "Why would you ask about your uncle's house?" She answers "Ma sent me there to ask you for the money to come to the mall and the door was unlocked, so I went in and saw what the place looked like." Cordell looks at Larry as she said "You must've had a party and things got broke and now you're here trying to find the pieces that you broke so you could replace it right!" Larry told her she was smart but how did she know about it at all. She told her uncle Larry "A couple of my older friends were there at the party, they couldn't stop talking about if my uncle Hutch was the type to hunt people down. Because of the things that got broke at his house from the party." Larry wants to know if she could help them find the things to replace so he wouldn't get into trouble with her uncle Hutch. Cheryl told her uncle Larry she would help this time, but if he's going to hang out with her father the next time he's in trouble he's on his own plus he gave her that envelope of cash when he got there. Cordell asked "What envelope of cash and how come every one gets money but me?" She looks at her father and took the pictures out of his hand and told her father it's going to cost him. Larry was quick to say he would pay just as long as they can get the stuff in there before he gets back. Cheryl huddles up with her friends and then came back to her father and Uncle Larry, giving her price for the work they're about to do for them. She told him 3200 hundred dollars and that's not including lunch for today. Cordell looks at her repeating it loudly $3200 dollars is she out of her mind where are they going to get that kind of money from its better if they find the stuff themselves at those prices. Cheryl says "Ok but she likes a having walking talking father and not a wheel chair bound man that dribbles and laughs uncontrollably from getting punched in the head by his brother or an Uncle that can walk instead of using a motorized chair from getting his back broke by a man they damaged and smashed thing in his house!" Larry is counting out the exact amount and hands it to her saying "Don't worry he's going to pay me back one way or another!" Cheryl thanked her Uncle and went back in the huddle with her friends handing out pictures of what they had to get, a few seconds later they break the huddle on their phones talking very seriously demanding to get what's in the picture their sending a picture of to get what they need for Larry. Cordell and Larry stand there looking at these young woman like power brokers at a business meeting talking and haggling over what they need and how fast is it going to be delivered, threatening they didn't want any problem with the merchandise either. Making sure they got everything and Cheryl gave them all her Uncle Hutch's address, she walks over to her father and Uncle and told them everything would be delivered that Monday 7:15 am and no later and it's C.O.D.

He agreed to be there and ready for them to deliver things saying it would give them more time to clean up every little thing at his house. They went back into that huddle and came out for the final time and told her Uncle Larry it's done like she said, but she'll be there with her friends that morning since there's no school that day. Cheryl turns walks back to her friends and they all hi-five and walk away talking about what they need to get from the mall. Larry says "Wow did you see that?" Cordell says "Yeah bruh that's the future." They're smarter and connected better than any mob or any legal Organization and could infiltrate way better than all spies of any corporation, group or Community could think of. While looking good doing it to and getting what they want at the same time. That's a network that has any Government running in second place to them, wondering how they got beat by them of all ages. If they can only get rid of the stupid one that keep having babies and chasing after the wrong man giving them such a bad name for their network. The truth of it all, you don't ever want to cross that network. If they really got together and get rid of those stupid females that will, when the smart one won't! Larry asked him "What is the name of the network you are talking about?" Cordell looks at him with serious expression (And turns to YOU the READER also) saying "WOMEN! If they all really got together men are in serious trouble, well the full of shit cheating ass men like me any ways!" Then telling his brother to come on they got go back to the house but first they have to pick up some beer and talk about that envelope of cash he gave his daughter. They make it back to the house and the phone rings. It's their mother she told them she's coming over with his aunt to visit him so they can see how much he's grown up. Cordell goes she thinks she's talking to Hutch and don't know he left to go down there, didn't he call her to let her know he was coming down there. Larry didn't know what to say but they have to get all that garbage out of the house before she gets there. Then they won't have to worry about Hutch because she going to kill them both and remember she's got help too. They work fast getting the bags of garbage out of the house and sweep up then mop, while the floor dries they hurry to the supermarket with the list of things they have to pick up and replace in the Frig.

Mama Betty is telling her friends they're going to Hutch's house for dinner and she went to Elise room to see if she wants to come over there but find her in the room with a bag of ice to her head lying down in the bed. Going back to Lira's room laughing how she gave that girl a concussion kicking the door like that, poor child lying in bed with a bag of ice on her head. Lira says "Bet the next time she thinks about leaning her head on a door eves dropping on someone's conversation being nosey she'll think twice" Mama Betty said "She'll let her lay there and hope that swelling knot on her head goes down by the time they get back from Hutch's house."

Hutch is turning the corner of the street where his mother's house is. Pulling into the drive way looking at this strange house that looks like his mother's place, he don't remember it being so big or having a pool plus deck on the side as everyone says the house looks so nice and big for all of them to stay there. Hutch takes out his key and tries the door lock, it opens the door letting everyone coming behind him as he calls out his mother's name but get no answer. Telling everyone to be on guard for anything they might see or come across in the house. To him this doesn't look like his mother's house that he remembers some things has changed as he walks through the place. Donna shows Hutch the picture of his mother on the mantelpiece and on the shelf all over the place saying "If this is not your mother's house they took her pictures and putting them all over the place."

Hutch told them all to find a room and get settled while he goes to the neighbor's house to find out if they know where his mother is or has there been a bunch of men asking for her looking for him. Janet, Mack and Jazz went with him to walk around and talk to some of the people there to see if they saw his mother. Walking from the house he takes the short cut he remembers to Mr. Allen store which has him come out on the street where all shopping store are. Looking around and seeing how most of the shops had gone through a lot of upgrade remodeling with new front to every building on both side of the street. Passing the dress shop where Ms. Evelyn and Ms. Sandy work, and Ms. Evelyn came out to greet him when she saw him. Remembering what he looks like from the pictures his mother gave everyone, she talks to about him. He asked her about his mother and has she seen her anywhere, because he called and there was no answer at the house. She asked him to come in the shop where she could make some calls to find out if anyone else seen her. He introduces Janet, Jazz and Mack to her and Ms. Sandy in their shop. They walk in the shop and Hutch makes a comment about how the dress shop looks. Ms. Sandy told him "Your mother gave her and most of all the store owners a big loan to help with their businesses so they could do the remodeling on their places. In return she they gave her part ownership in their businesses that way they wouldn't have to pay her back. Ms. Evelyn came from the back after a few minutes and told him "Your mother is up in New York looking for you" She asked him "Doesn't your mother have a cell phone?" He thought about it and told her "No! But he's sure one of his aunt do." Thanking her and leaving the shop wanting to look around some more before going back to her house because he invited his brotherhood to come there with him. He walks around the town looking at all the places he remembers when he was a kid. How they now look new thanks to the remodeling they've had done to them. By the time he got back home to his mother's house it was night time. Coming in the house he saw some of the GDM4L up watching TV and the others was still laying down relaxing. Hutch was sitting down when someone knocks on the door and he opens the door to see one of his mother's neighbors had come over and she has a dish in her hands. She remembers Hutch when he was a little boy and says "Wow you really grew up huh, little Hutchy." Everyone stopped what they were doing when the woman said that to him. All he could do was close his eyes and get ready for the jokes to come about the name she just called him, she told him if they were going to grill let her make a call first and then she'll grill for him. Making a couple of quick calls then she head out to see the grill and get it already, then coming back to the kitchen getting what she needs and starts cooking for them knowing other are coming there too. A short time she has the place smelling so good they can't wait to start eating, but they need more beer and juice plus water. Again there was knock on the door and another woman with a younger lady was at the door with dishes of food in their hands and gets invited in but as he starts the close the door two more women came up with younger women and dishes. Hutch told them to go in to the kitchen and told the guys he was going to drive to the store to get more beer and ice and things. Janet and Erikaa went with him to help and get other things he might not think about too. When they got back the house was full of women and food, he walks over to Donna asking "Where'd all these older and younger women came from?" She explained one of the young women there told Donna she came with her aunt because you were here and word got around the community that Mama Betty's son is here with his brotherhood and he's still not married. Donna says "Guess they didn't say anything about us being with you." Hutch says "Baby I didn't know" She laughs "It's Ok, I don't blame them, you are a catch" Janet says "Yeah and now they know he's got it like that from what his mother did with his Credit card for the whole community and local town shops, who wouldn't try to get you if they heard you are not married yet!" Hutch told them all "I am married! To all of you, the others just don't it yet" and he held up the ring they had got for him. They held up theirs smiling and kissed him for reminding how he thinks about them. Getting the other GDM4L to help with the beer and things to bring in the house, then seeing to it they all had a good time while down there in all that company. Hutch was reminded by every older woman there how they knew him as a polite little boy with no girlfriends and showed him their daughters or young nieces saying 'Here's Mama Betty's boy Hutch." Making sure they got their younger family member a get a chance to talk to him. Steel came over to Hutch and told him "There are more young women in here with the tightest things on he could see what kind of coin they have in their shorts or tight pants pockets. Plus there's more boobs showing here than the World Most Dumbest Criminals Show. Oh wait I take that back just as many, I've seen their show." Hutch was sitting down and lots of the young women came over to him offering him a plate of food. Donna and Erikaa would tell them they'll get food for him, Janet would come over with a drink and had that covered. Hutch would introduce the young woman to the nearest GDM4L telling her this is his brother and have them talking. The older women there watched as Donna, Janet and Erikaa would block any of their female from talking to Hutch. To get Donna, Erikaa and Janet away from Hutch they told their younger women what to do and it should work. It began by one young woman standing near Donna with a big plate of food talking to her about the town. She dropped her fork asking Donna to hold her plate as she bent over to get it, coming up real fast knocking the plate back on Donna. Telling Donna she sorry for being so clumsy and Donna told her it was an accident and she would go upstairs to get changed. That gave the others a way to get rid of Janet now by spilling BBQ sauce on her from shaking the bottle thinking it was closed. Last was Erikaa who got it the worse with potatoes salad and punch spilled on her accidently, when one woman slips on some imaginary thing on the floor tossing her food backward on Erikaa. Another young woman tripped forward by someone spilling her cup of punch on Erikaa too. With them out the way some of the women there brought out the shine spiking the punch good and playing dance music. The party really starts to get going as everyone there was drinking a lot of punch and eating. Hutch went upstairs to check on his ladies and they were talking about how all three of them ended upstairs with food on them and nobody else seems to get stuff spilled on any of them. Hutch had big picture of the punch and ice with him and left it up there for them to drink and come back down to join the party saying he misses them. They start drinking the punch not knowing it was really spiked good getting toasted because it was so smooth and strong plus good tasting. They also talked about how those women were dressed down there trying to get their hands on Hutch. Erikaa said "They really prepared themselves before they came over Janet told her to go take her shower and use that vanilla scent soap Hutch likes so much then told her she'll join her. Donna said "Wait for me don't waste the soap." (WOW IMAGINE THAT SHOWER SCENE! HUH) they wash and clean each other off and help wash the other ones hairs (YOU PERVERTS!) and then Janet suggest they fight body with bodies. Making another comment about how good tasting that punch is while they are drinking it up. She lays out their clothes and picking out some clothes that makes them look very hot not slutty and they do their hair. Erikaa had on a short mini thigh fitting dress showing off all her curves with open strapped heel shoes looking straight out of magazine. Donna had on a two piece outfit short skirt tight top flowing loose bottom flowing out by her stomach with big heel open toe calf high strap shoes that made her also look like she stepped out of glamour magazine. Janet's one piece black tight thigh high dress and quarter way plunging neck line with shiny calf high cow neck black boots and flowing see through cotton top had her looking like classy rock star sex goddess. They finished that picture of punch and looking so hot everything just right from their cleavage, hair to lipstick nail polish and shoes and boots. They stand at the top of the stairs where no one could see them at first. Two young women were talking to Hutch finding out what he did for a living and how come he's not married. As he told them he's married and his brides are upstairs and they should be coming down. As if on Cue they come walking down the stairs to the song by Beyoncé "I'm a DIVA!" Everyone stopped what they were doing to watch them and all the GDM4L go in a low voices "DAMN! They didn't know they could look like that" Hutch sits there as the women he was talking to walk away from him staring at Donna, Erikaa and Janet as they walk right up to Hutch and kiss him sitting on either side as Janet sits in the middle of the chair between his legs. There is this low "Ah shit" said by every young woman in the place knowing they'll never get next to him now. Donna, Erikaa and Janet sat next to Hutch and he pays attention only to them. The young women look at all the other GDM4L deciding which one they're going after since they can't get Hutch. The party was going well and Mack wanted to show Steel this woman that looked like the woman he had in the bathroom at the club that night but he couldn't find him. He goes around asking everybody had any one saw Steel? So he check the bedroom thinking he could be up there but there was no sign of him, till one young woman said "I seen him with this big woman wearing a yellow, blue and white outfit on" Explaining there was another woman with the same outfit on but she was younger looking. Mack gets Hutch and 2Soon and Derrick because he's concerned about Steel and now everyone starts looking for Steel. Mack asked Hutch and 2Soon to come with him to talk to this young woman that seen Steel last. They find the young woman with the same outfit on as the bigger one outside counting money which didn't make any sense to them, why would anyone bring money to this party. Hutch walks up behind her and taps her on her shoulder, she jumps and says "OOOH Marveece, you scared me shuga" Hutch looks at 2Soon and Derrick and Mack then back at her asking her "What did you say? And say that again?" The young woman said "you scared me shuga" Mack says "That's not what you said at first, so what was that first part again?" She replies "baby you scared me is what I said" Derrick went "What happened to that oooh part you did?" The young woman didn't say anything else but put her money away and stood there looking at them. Mack went back in the house to alert the others Marveece is there and Steel is missing. Derrick and 2Soon looked at each other wanting to know how they were going to get this young woman to talk because they don't put their hands on females, Hutch gets an idea and told them not to let her get away and goes back in the house. The young woman told Derrick and 2Soon they might as well get out of her way because she don't know and won't say anything to them. If they put their hands on her she got a lot of brothers and cousin that would be there with their friend and deal with them so fast. They both start smiling and laughing at the young lady. She wants to know what was funny till a hand grabs her earlobe followed by a hand slap to the face spinning her around a voice says "Oh you going to tell or so help me!" The young woman turns to see her aunt and family members standing there with big wooden spoons and forks in their hands with mean serious looks on their faces like they want to jump her now. She turns to walk away but then starts backing up as this heavy set woman walks towards her with a big long switch making a sound that terrorized people who grew up down south know they're going to get it now! Hearing the switch go back and forth a couple time as the young woman says "MAMA please I'll tell what you want!" Her mother looks mad walking over to her asking "Where's his friend and child you better say who took him NOW!" The young woman starts explaining quick about everything, how Marveece came down there to visit his aunty because she was feeling down about a man in New York. She wanted to get her hands on him but he kept getting away from her so she decides to come see her aunty Doris because she always knows how to cheer Marveece up. When they heard about the party Mama Betty son was having at her house Doris decides to come and bring Marveece, they got to the party and found out that this same guy named "Steel" was here so he left back out and ran into her coming there in that outfit and said he's got the same one too. She talked to her about making some money if she did what she told her to do. She came back to the party dressed like her, so she gave the money to have him follow her to the back while giving him some of the good jar shine and she would take it from there once he was nice and smashed. Hutch thanked the young woman's mother and aunt too, Hutch said "They couldn't get far if she took him through the wooded arrear." Her aunty Doris lives a couple of miles away from there and his vehicle is still there pointing it out to Hutch. One of the women there said they would take some of them to Doris house and wait for him to show up. Hutch looked at the young woman up and down then saw her shoes asking her "Did Marveece have on the same heels like yours" she shook her head "Yes"

Hutch laughed because he knows a woman couldn't get far in the woods in those shoes and told 2Soon, Mack, Derrick and Herb to come with him. For LiL-Rob, Goodie, Dave and La-Machine with Jazz take two vehicle and let the woman show where Ms. Doris lives in case they don't catch up to them and Steel is now "Hot Rod!" They rush into go into the woods where the path starts and run to catch up with Marveece who is carrying Steel on her shoulder. They're just over a hundred yards from the house because the shoes in those woods were not made for each other, stepping on things hurting her feet as she carries Steel tied up on her shoulder. Now he's saying "I've got to pee!" Marveece sets him down and told him to "Hurry up, if they're going to make it to her aunty house" Steel so drunk says "I can't go with my hands tied up like this even though it's fun so you have to hold my hose while I put out the fire" Marveece smiled at him and went "OOOOH Marveece! I get to hold your Steel rod in my hands. OOOH Mar-veece" Just as he walks towards Steel about to unzip his pants he heard Hutch says "There! I can see the yellow over there through the trees spread out!" Marveece looks to see who is coming but all she could see is a figure moving thought the woods. She puts steel back on her shoulder and tries to get away but can't go that fast because the shoes she's wearing hurting her feet in those woods. Seeing a clearing a head doing her best to make it there and get out of the woods Marveece heads toward it and comes out on someone's lawn and now could move faster, but it's too late Hutch tackles them a few feet out of the woods. Steel falls away from Marveece and Hutch as they fell to the grass. Marveece gets up tussling with Hutch as they fight on someone lawn by their house. Marveece throws Hutch over the parked car and turns only to get tackled by 2Soon and LiL-Rob. Hutch gets up saying to himself "Damn she's strong oh that's right it's a he!" Marveece flips 2Soon on top of LiL-Rob but gets tackled from behind by Hutch this time holding his arms behind him and yells for Mack to get Steel untied before he gets loose. Marveece yells "Help I'm being rob by these men could someone help a lady getting rob or raped!" 2Soon and LiL-Rob look at him and Hutch on the ground as Hutch said "Yeah but you're no lady Man!" Four men come out of nowhere and one says "Hey leave that woman alone and let her go!" LiL-Rob looks around and says "What woman where?" Two men charge him and the other two heads towards 2Soon and he tells them "They got it wrong, if you turn on the light and get a good look at this thing." The one man in front of 2Soon says "I don't need light to see four men jumping one big woman and her have her man tied up."

LiL-Rob says "Trust me man, you need the light!" Marveece says "Don't listen to them. Please help us they don't want us to get married and plan on taking my man away!" Hearing that makes them want to help even more as they charging 2Soon and the other two go after LiL-Rob. Mack looks towards 2Soon first "Fam you good or do you need a hand?" It didn't take but a quick couple of second and 2Soon had the two men on the ground and LiL-Rob told Mack "Stay there fam" as he blocks the two guys punches and gut checks them having them stop holding their stomachs. Marveece thought he was going to break Hutch's hold but Hutch held him as Mack freed Steel. Who ever lived in the house cut on the light to see who was outside in front of their house making that noise, LiL-Rob walks over to Marveece being held by Hutch and pulls off his wig and threw it at one of the guys he gut checked. Going now you believe us and if you don't then you can be the one that marries that (pointing at Marveece).

They get a good look at Marveece and one man says "HOLY SHIT!" The other men just stare at Marveece with their jaw dropped. The owner of the house came out asking "What's going on out here?" One of the men knew the owner of the house saying "It's me MR Goreman. Tommy Wallace we were just horse playing and didn't realizes we made that much noise sorry to wake you we'll be going now" MR Goreman says "OK Tommy but stop your friend from ride of that ugly horse with the racing colors on and put it back in the barn because that nag look more like a mule than horse." They all looked at Marveece on his hands and knees when the man said that to Tommy. Marveece says "Why everybody looking at me. I don't have on racing stripes!" All of a sudden Marveece gets popped in the head with two apples and a voice says "Better feed it before you put it back in the barn this will help!" Tommy and his guys apologizes to Hutch and the others saying "They didn't know and was only trying to do the right thing. That's why he told MR Goreman that so they don't get in trouble with him for being on his grass because he don't like most people on his grass" Hutch except the apology wanting to know where was they were heading at this time of night and they told him there was big party at Mama Betty's and wanted to see if they could get in because they heard it was mostly female that was invited. Hutch told Mack to call the others to let them know they have Steel back, and told Tommy they can come because Mama Betty is his mother. Tommy asked "What's your name dude?" Hutch told him and they all couldn't stop apologizing to 2Soon and LiL-Rob, and Hutch enough as they walked back to the house. Hutch comes back with four new friends as the others look wanting to know how he does that when they went to go help Steel from becoming rusted iron rotor rooter man, Hutch comes back with four more men Mack said "Only Hutch this can happen to only Hutch".

Back at the lawn Marveece getting up after the men left with Steel and he was walking the long way back to get his vehicle from Mama Betty' house, a man in a truck saw Marveece from the back and thought to himself "Wow that woman got a phat ass, what she doing out here at this time of night?" He pulls up next to Marveece and says "Hey pretty lady where are you going and why that asshole let you walk at this time of night!" Marveece says "Going to get my whip from a house not too far from here." The man offers a ride and Marveece except and got in wondering why the interior light don't come on. The man explains only the finest of things gets in his ride light or dark so he don't need to see beauty just feel it if they want. He drives Marveece right to the front of Mama Betty's drive way and Marveece thanked the man for the ride but the man says "If you really wants to thank me you would give me a nice kiss on the cheek that would be worth it." Marveece says "What harm could it do." She opens the passenger side door of the pickup truck and turns to give the man a kiss on the cheek thanking him for the ride, but someone leaving the house drove right pass them and the light from the car shines in the pickup truck. The man gets a good look at Marveece when the light went by and he did a double take at Marveece, backing up falling out the driver side window and pops back up with a shot gun in his hands saying "What the hell did you do with that woman and get out of my truck?" Marveece says "What about that kiss?" The cocking of the shot gun as the man says "I don't care if you can change back into to a woman, you're not kissing me, now get out of my truck. Going around fooling people into thinking you're a pretty woman, when you need to be walking around with one of those daytime lights so you don't change back into what you are now." Marveece gets out and goes for his vehicle watching the man peel away in his truck.

Donna walks over to Hutch feeling frisky from the punch and told him something in his ear that had his eyes get wide and then she kissed him before going back upstairs. Erikaa came after she did and kisses Hutch hugs him and said something in his ear that made him shake his head "Yes" as his eyes got wide hearing what she said to him and then she too went upstairs.

Hutch went to get something to eat and sit down for a minute but Janet took his plate from him and sat backwards in his lap and kisses him then sucks on his neck and told him "Whatever they said to have you look that way when they said it, I'm going to be in on all of it too doing the same if not more to you" without any one seeing she reaches in back of her down and feels what she needed to feel then says " Umm good keep it that way!" Giving him plate and walking upstairs like Donna and Erikaa and being watched by Hutch and some of the others knowing what was going to happen when he gets up there. The party starts to wind down and everyone had either paired up or went out. Hutch went into the kitchen and found the older women had left but not before wrapping the food up making sure the kitchen was cleaned and most of the food was put away. Dougie came up to him followed by these two fine looking women and told him if he wants to go upstairs and handle his business he would make sure things is alright down there before those two woman take him back to one of their places. Hutch told Dougie to go ahead with them there isn't much to clean up. Beside Tyrone looks like he wants to talk to him and they both know how long winded he is, might be afternoon before he shuts up. Hutch showed Dougie who Tyrone was talking with earlier, Doug plus Tommy and his four friends. Dougie looked at Hutch and said 'I'm good with that, Peace!" He quickly leaves out and Hutch didn't stay to find out what that group was talking about and he goes upstairs to his bedroom and sees the lights out as he opens his bedroom door and goes in feeling his way to the lamp about to turn it on saying "Ok yall I'm here and I'm still the way you felt it Janet." Not hearing anyone say anything he calls their names softy "Donna? Erikaa?! Janet?!" then he heard what sounded like a snort and then another snort followed by all of them talking softly in their sleep. Turning on the lights he sees them stretched out on the bed and knew it was that punch that got to them, they were snoring like lumber jack after a hard day work. He went to kiss Donna on her forehead good night but get grabbed by her still asleep as she says "Now bitch take that!" Swinging four time fast connecting to Hutch's face making him back up but his movement back hits Erikaa arm hanging off the bed, she stops snoring grabbing on him and said "Jump my friend you Bitch!" She elbows and punches Hutch twice on both sides of his face. There was no snoring from Janet but reaction from their movement as she grabs him with her eyes still closed and hits him in the nuts making him double over.

She said "YO Elise-a bitch! I might be the youngest of the three of us but I kick ass good for my age BI-OTCH!" She punches Hutch in the face twice real fast and then in the head finishing with kicks on that same side of his face making him fall back hitting his head on the dresser knocking him out. He lies there slumped over by the bed as all three females go back to snoring and then smile at what they done in their sleep getting it off their minds.

Back up in New York Cordell and Larry was coming back from the supermarket and price ware house with most all the food that was in Hutch's kitchen and freezer, at his house they were unloading it when this van pulls and Mama Betty and her friends gets out while they were carrying the last of the boxes and bags in the house. Larry wants to know what are they doing up here in New York, aren't they supposed to be down at her house with Hutch? She told him "They came to see Hutch but from all the boxes and bags he's carrying in the house it looks like he's going to have another one of his big party's" Then she thought about it and asking Larry "Was the party going to be for you because you're here now and he knows you graduated from Law school?" Cordell came out the house and saw his mother talking to Larry and tried to go back in the house but she calls him over and asked him the same question. Cordell starts to stutter and she knew something was wrong and told her friends to bring them two in the house. Larry drops his head and gets his ear pulled by Ms. Mildred but it was worse for Cordell he got both ears pulled from both sides by Ruby and Lira. Mable had his shirt collar and Enid and Eddy had his belt from both sides. They walk him in the house and right into the kitchen where Mama Betty is looking at the empty shelves and refrigerator asking them "Did you two have a party here already? where's Hutch?" She looks at Cordell but he doesn't say anything just shrugs his shoulders and then she looks at Larry. He tells her everything she wants to know, even about the missing furniture. Cordell adds "They will have everything back by the time he gets back up here." Mama Betty said "They better check the whole house just in case there are people hiding in here" She told Larry and Cordell to finish and put up the food before the things frozen thaws out and spoils. She walks with her friends through the big house showing them all what he's done with the place he got still paying on it. She shows them his bedroom and how he built a walk in closet with the space he had, they were looking at his things in there and came across his work boots. Lira saw how big those boots were and then found his work gloves, she starts making a comment he's not little any more from the sizes of those boots. She asked "How big did he get?" Looking at those things and held it up with her hands making it seem like a giants boot but then something else caught her eye showing the others in that closet while in there. Mama Betty was walking in the rest of the house talking about she got the ideas from Hutch to do her bathroom with the shower like his, one that has showerheads coming from all five sides with the big thick glass sliding door and Jacuzzi tub right behind it, plus the 2 toilets in its own room. They all get a good laugh at what she showed them correcting her saying "One is called a Bade!" She said "Nope it's a spare! They know how a man can smell up the whole bathroom leaving a woman crying and choking gaging for air hoping it don't explode from the light being on if she had to come in after him. Now that he's got three women in his life they're going to need it too!" They look at her and Ruby says "3! When did this happen?" Explaining she forgot to mention it since her last trip up here and that skinny thing at the hotel is an ex-girlfriend, because as they can see she's turned out to be something he's not going to marry and bring into this family (they all shake their heads agree).

Lira wanted to know more about these three women and how she feels about them having Mama Betty and the others come back into his bedroom, showing them this big box of Magnum condoms he has by his boots on the closet floor. Lira said "No wonder he needs three women, didn't you tell us he wasn't with one for a couple decades and you were worried about him turning to the other team" Mama Betty clears her throat and told them all just because he's late bloomer she's not mad at that, she likes the three he's with and got to meet them they're going places in life. Explaining about Janet in school now to be a nurse and Erikaa is into corporate law with Donna as an accounting. He could get hurt and fixed plus sue and have some one count the money too, unlike his brothers couch monster that does nothing but leave foot chips and smokes then drinks up all the liquor someone brings to the house. Now THAT ONE should have worn 4 condoms making all those kids, not that I'm complaining. Girls you know like I do cheating ass men are weak and all they do is make girls 9 out of 10 times." Ruby said "My husband cheated on me and look at all the girls he made." Then Sheryl-Ann agreed "her husband cheated too and he had nothing but girls." Phyllis joined in and told about her cheating ass man and he had nothing but girls. Mama Betty stopped them from going on about their cheating men saying "Hutch is going to have nothing but boys big like he is and wouldn't cheat because he won't have time to with the three of them on his hands and their ok with it." Thinking about it she had them follow her back down stairs but grabbed a few of those condoms first and went right up to Cordell handing him the condoms saying "Here I don't know if you can fit them or not but if you can't use them as hip waiters before the next time you want to do anything with that thing on the couch." Then she looks at Larry and said "I know you better be carrying some now let me see them!" Larry looked embarrassed about it and pulls out the ones he's got in his pockets and she looks at them, then took a couple from Cordell saying "I know you're not as big as Hutch but grow into to them. Mama didn't raise no chumps!" Larry holds them up looking at them about to say something when she told him "Yep got them from Hutch's bedroom and he wears them too!" They help Larry and Cordell put away the food and things, then had a drink and cooked something to eat before they left to go back to the hotel. Mama Betty said before she left the house, "They better put back all the furniture and other things before Hutch gets back." Reminding them when he wants to he could put them somewhere that no one could smell them for years. Not that she condones things like that but she'll understand plus she's not getting in the way of him Hulk uh Hutch when he gets mad, she's seen him angry. Larry and Cordell kiss their mother and aunts bye watching the van pull away and first thing Cordell wants to do is have another small party since the house is clear saying "Things can't get broke now that things are broken." Larry turns slowly and had this look on his face as he watched Cordell go over to the phone. Cordell woke up in this dark place but felt he couldn't move and wondering why his head is still hurting and tries to call out for Larry but finds his mouth had been gagged as he struggles in the dark. Larry is watching TV eating his plate and could hear Cordell struggling in the closet he put him in after knocking his ass out. Looking at it for a moment then continues to watching his program and eating his food thinking he'll let him out after he's had a good night sleep.

The next day in Mama Betty's house Hutch is waking up still in that same positions by the bed, he stirs hearing laughing coming from down stairs and gets up cracking his back and going to take a shower before going down stairs. In the shower he was feeling his face thinking he slept wrong on it against the dresser draw like that, clean and dressed he walks into the kitchen from the back stairs and everyone in there stops and looks at him. Mack said "Damn Hutch I didn't see she-bruh connect one time on you. What happened" Hutch asked "What are you talking about?" Mack took him over to the counter where the toaster was, showing him his reflection then walks him into the living room where all the GDM are and they all said together "Damn! Whoa! What the Feezey!" Laughing about the condition of his face after they all seen his black eye, fat lip and swollen cheek. He explained that didn't happen when he was trying to save Steel from She-man. It happened when he went upstairs to kiss his ladies good night. They walk in from outside and looked at Hutch's face and wondered what happened to him now and which one of them hit their brother like that. 2Soon explains it was the three ferocious one's in the group, they wanted to have fun with him. Now he wants them to go give them others a piece of their minds. The ladies agreed! Mad that three of them could hurt him like that and they know he wouldn't hit back. Angry about Hutch and wants to know which three did that to him, 2Soon walks them right over to closet with the mirror on the back of the door and told them they're in there hiding because they know you are going to get on their case. Janet was very furious and wants to get at them opening the door seeing coats at first and not looking at the mirror. Then looks in the closet and sees no one there saying "It's not funny where are they?" The guy had a good laugh as Douige came over and had them all stand close together and showed them their reflection saying "Go ahead, get them." Hutch explained what they did in detail to him and what they were saying while doing it which made all the guys laugh even harder because they were asleep when they did that. Their faces are red embarrassed that they did that in their sleep as Hutch said "No more country punch for you three unless I puts out a hit on someone but first make sure you're full of punch that way you won't have mercy and recall what damage you did to them" They all had a good laugh and then wondered where was Steel and went to check if he was still where Hutch left him, and they all burst out laughing seeing him with that chain on his leg with a big lock on it in the library. Hutch had put him in there and had a chain wrapped around the desk a few times and one on his leg with this big lock, when they came in there he was still sleep and they let him sleep backing out the room. Hutch had all of them gather around him in the living room so he could talk about why he's giving them back their Credit cards now, looking at them putting out the question "What if they came into a lot of money, what would do with it and who would they tell?" Hearing all kinds of crazy ideas from getting big mansions to having wild parties to getting cars that talk and sparkle with chrome and wood panel interiors to the latest clothes and gadgets even making it rain in the strip club popping bottles of Chris. Hutch looks at the girls after hearing those answers as to say to them see why he couldn't tell them about what he's got, so he explains he won some money and wanted to share it with them. Adding he Just don't want it wasted for any stupid reasons on junk, to think of their families first remember F.F.C.F (Family Friends Come First) remembering the family not here. Mack, along with the rest of the GDM4L told Hutch he didn't have to say or do anything like that for them. They couldn't understand, why he done it in the first place. He explained something aren't meant to keep to oneself and with brothers like them we're in it for 4 Life remember no matter what happens family going to fight, but they always stick together good and bad. Tyron wanted to know how much is on the card because he got some personal things to settle and everyone threw their empty beer cans and cups at him for saying that. Hutch looked at the girls and put their cards down along with the others he got made for them as a surprise. Everyone took their cards as Tyrone said "Twenty grand would be nice for everyone if you could afford it" Hutch let that thought he put in their heads ride with them knowing he put way more than that in their account.

The girls knew he did with that big silent smile he gave as they all took their cards off the table. Donna walks over and gave him a big smacking kiss followed by Erikaa and Janet as she said "See that's why we all keep falling for your big hearted behind." Donna says "How many people really would do that for their family?" Erikaa says" Didn't we tell you we're not here for your money, but you keep doing things like that you know no bodies ever going to want to leave you especially us" They all hug and kiss Hutch. Tyrone nudges Jazz "Wonder how much they got?" Jazz pops him upside his head "What do you think stupid! They're his ladies you going to do to him what they do?" All the GDM4L and even the girls and Hutch heard Jazz say that to Tyrone and looks at him for a moment, guessing what the question he must have been asked. Byron said "Guessing from the reaction of everyone here including myself the question must have been from Tyrone how much did the girls get from Hutch." Jazz the first one to burst out laughing followed by everyone except Tyrone who told Byron "Smart ass!"

Up in New York Mama Betty and her friends were in the spa getting massages when Elise came down showing she didn't have a knot on her head any more. Mama Betty wanted her to have a massage before they went out to see the sights of the city and let her know they would be a while but she could join them if she liked. Elise got a quick idea and declined the invitation and went back up to her room where she calls the front desk, giving a story that she's with Mama Betty group and left her key card in her room and needs to get in there to get it. The front desk told her they would send someone right up and asked her room number so they could let her in. She gave Mama Betty's room number and said she'll be waiting there for them and hung up her phone and ran down to Mama Betty's room. Lira was the only one not with the group because she wanted to sleep a little late. She got up and went to Mama Betty's room thinking about what they were going to do that day. Her room was around the corner from

Mama Betty's, on her way there to ask her what was they doing for today. She heard this female's voice that sound familiar saying to the man "Could you hurry up and get her in the room." He was pressing the wrong numbers on the doors lock as she stood right behind him, then getting it open and letting her in. They didn't see Lira pull back not turning the corner instead peeking around it at them because she knew that was Mama Betty's room. Wondering why would Elise want to get into her room and for what she thought. Standing on the corner and watch as the man lets her in the room and when he walks her way leaving Elise in the room, she stops him around the corner asking "Why did you let that woman in that room." He explained she called down and left her card key in the room and wanted to get her medication before something happened to her. The hotel would be responsible for her not getting it so he let her in to get her medicine asking "Was there a problem?" Lira said "No problem." Letting the man get back to work, she walks down to the door and could hear Elise rumbling through thing in the room like she was in a hurry looking for something. Lira tries thinking what is it she was looking for in there but now and as things got quite. Lira goes back to the corner and waits to see when she came out of the room with anything in her hands. Elise opens the door and looks to see if anyone was out in the hallway then came out of the room talking to her just a bit too loudly saying "Shit I looked everywhere for that Credit card she must have it on her" getting on the elevator still cussing to herself. Lira went to her room thinking where could Mama Betty be if Elise went in the room, thinking she couldn't be sleep in there because Mama Betty's not a hard sleeper and would have woke to kick her ass coming in her room. She goes back to her room and calls to find out from the front desk where they are and get told she's in the massage parlor with the rest of the group.

Getting dressed and going down to talk with her but didn't want to spoil the trip up there with that kind of news, so she sees them and asked Mama Betty for her key card knowing she would give it to her without asking what for. Taking the key card and going back up the room to see it was ransacked. Thinking Mama Betty would be so upset to see her room like that so Lira fixed it back, putting all her clothes up but was getting mad while doing it. Wondering what could Elise possibly be looking for to do all that to Mama Betty's room and clothes, by the time she finished cleaning her room putting back her clothes in the suit cases with the new things she bought the phone rings. Its Mama Betty making sure that Lira was in the room because she was on her way up to it. Lira said "I'll wait here till you come." She got there and Lira asked "Do you noticed Elise acting funny in any kind of way." Mama Betty didn't notice but then didn't pay it any mind thinking she was just off because Hutch didn't want her anymore, and Mama Betty knew it but was doing this just to let her down easy. Thinking to herself that's why Mama Betty let her come with them and was being nice to her. Hutch has dumped her for the three women he's got now, but that still didn't answer a question. Why was Elise looking for something in Mama Betty's room and what is it. There was knock on the door and Elise said "it" me" as Mama Betty opens the door and Elise says "It's shame the maids would go through her stuff like that." Mama Betty asked "Like what Pressing her clothes and leaving her an outfit out so she didn't have to iron nothing, hell they can come home with her and do that down there at her house since they do things like this." Elise is quite trying to figure out what happened to the room and who fixed thing up in there after she left. Lira watched her look surprised that the room wasn't the way she left it and said "The maids did the same thing to my room and my clothes, but they didn't iron them maybe they were in a rush to get to another room." Mama Betty starts getting dressed and takes off her bra and the credit card had stuck to her skin. Elise perked up and watched the card closely as Mama Betty took off her bra showing the card there. Lira looked at Elise and saw how she was looking at Mama Betty wondering what she looking at, Mama Betty take the card and put it down on the bed and walks to the bathroom. Lira wanted to know where they would be going but then said she wasn't feeling right and might sit this one out, then she gets up and sit on the bed not realizing she sat on the credit card as Elise face changed but then trying not to show she was looking at the credit card on the bed under Lira now. Elise said "I'm going to get dressed" and left the room but kept looking at Lira's butt on the bed. Lira watched her leave the room and got up looking at the bed trying to see what she was looking at. Mama Betty came out of the bathroom and told Lira all she has to do now is pick up that Credit card so they can leave and hit the city. Looking at Lira as she sat on the bed Mama Betty didn't see the Credit card there not thinking Lira was sitting on it and starts wondering where she put it. Lira sees the panic on her face asking "Where did you have it last and calm down we'll find it in here. It couldn't have got up and walk out." When Lira got up to help look for it, Mama Betty saw it was under Lira's behind and said "Girl I should have known it would be there because your ass attracts more money and men then I can count" Lira wiggles it at Mama Betty and told her "If you loses that stomach and tighten those thighs, I would have just as big of an ass like you." Mama Betty laughed and asked "Sure you didn't want to come with them, because it's going to be lonely here in the hotel by yourself." Lira looked at Mama Betty "Who said I was going to be alone, you don't know me by now remember chocolate power!" Mama Betty laughs with her and said "Girl please don't turn that man out, what if he got a woman!" Lira just said "She can come too, might learn how to keep him with what I can show her ass and do to it at the same time." The other came to the room and Margret asked Lira "Since you were staying here could you get the picture they were having developed for her and calls the front desk to have them delivered to your room for me baby girl!" Telling her she could look through them and pick her favorite if she sees any one she likes because everything she had them make doubles of it.

Hutch was eating his breakfast being tended to by Janet, Donna and Erikaa feeling bad about what they did to his face that night. After breakfast he tries calling up to his house again and this time he gets Larry on the phone. Larry told him their mother was there and she was with his aunts having a woman's weekend time. Hutch asked "Did they say where they were staying?" Larry forgot to ask but said "They were in good hands from a not so old friend of his who knew the city and was showing her around with the rest of them, Mama said her name was Elisa or something like that." Hutch knew who he was trying to say from the sound he was trying to pronounce and asked did it sound like "Elise" right! Larry said "Yeah, She wasn't with Ma and her friends when they came there but stayed at the hotel waiting for them to get back there." Hutch told Larry if she calls back there to get the info from her and call him right away but then asked "Where's Cordell?" because the back ground sounds a little to quite for him to be with Larry. Explaining to Hutch he was right about not listening to Cordell but not giving him every detail on why he was right about their brother. Hutch didn't pay attention to what Larry was going on about since he mentioned Elise was around their mother. Hutch was thinking she was going to try and get the Credit card from her. He told Larry he got to cut their moment short but happy he's dealing with it up there, adding "If she calls him there just tell her I'm on his way if anything happens." They hang up and Larry walks to the closet and opens it up looking at Cordell who is staring at him saying something he couldn't make out because of the gag in his mouth. Larry drags him out of the closet and untied his hands and told him "It was for your own good" Cordell was mad that he was tied up like that and put in the closet, then asked "Didn't any one call to see if he was there or not?" Larry answered him "The twins and Cheryl came by and took a few pictures when I showed them where you were. They said let you stay there at least they know where you are." Telling Cordell he really forgot about him from it being so quite in the house, nobody wants to go out and chase women at the strip club or talk about how his beast gets on his nerves wishing he never should have drank that stuff in the first place. Larry asked him "What was it that you were drinking, that made hood rat thing look like a Nia Long or Janet Jackson, or Toni Braxton, Tamia, Mary J. Blige, Whitney Houston, Keri Washington, Sanya Lathan, Aaliyah, Gladys knight, Patti Labelle, Queen Latifah, Left eye, T-Boz, Karin Stephens (super head), Heather Headley, Mariah C, Alicia Keyz, Thelma (Bernadette Stains), Foxy Brown- Pam Geir or The Bratt or SWV!" Cordell scratches his head after saying "No" to everyone woman Larry referenced. He couldn't remember what he was drink but said "Even if I did she didn't look like any of the names you mentioned after I got drunk." Larry said "When you do please let me know what drink it was, so that way I can bring it to the science world and brewers. They can market it for woman around the world. Solving a big problem of men who could have any female star they see after drinking it". Then he talks to him about what Hutch said about their mother and wants to know when she calls so they can give him the information he wants from her.

While they were out site seeing and getting things to bring back to their family and friends Elise would watch Mama Betty again paying for everything with that credit card, staying close to her waiting to get her chance to get that Credit card from her.

Elise gets an idea to get her in the movies and there in the darkness of the theater she could try for it, asking Mama Betty and the rest of her friends if they should watch a movie. They all agreed and wondered which movie should they see, Elise picked a movie she already seen but didn't tell them and made her suggestion about it to them. Making it sound good to them, they agreed just to get her to be quite about it. Mama Betty paid for the tickets to get in the theater and Elise watch her put the card back in her bar. When they were walking to get their seats, Elise pushed passed Margret and Mildred and Sheila just to get next to Mama Betty following close to see where she was sitting. When the movie starts she put on such an act on how scary she thinks the movie is going to be, during the movie at certain part of it she was grabbing on Mama Betty's arm burying her face in her shoulder but really feeling on her to see where that card was. Acting so sacred at part of the movie she would pull on Mama Betty's arm and put her face near her cleavage then use her lips to move the card once she felt it, when a good scary part came on she reached across her and felt her chest almost grabbing the card. Mama Betty looked at Elise and told her she better calm down with all that grabbing even if the movie is scary no body gropes her like that, not even her boyfriend but if she do that again she'll knock her ass out quick and won't apologize for it either. Elise told her she was sorry and would compose herself about that but really looked at how much she had that card exposed. She just couldn't reach any more for it with her hands so when another scary part came up she buried her face in Mama Betty's chest, using her tongue and lips trying to get a grip on that car but it didn't work. Telling Mama Betty she was sorry and would clean it up but Mama Betty had enough telling her "Don't touch me." Elise tried to wipe the wetness away she left. Mama Betty slaps her hands and starts wiping away the wetness Elise left on her chest thinking she don't go for that woman burring her head in her like that, then thought about how she and Lira was kissing each other and carrying on stage at the male strip club with men and women. Looking at Sheila and knew she would knock her ass out quick if she licked on her like that so she asked Sheila to switch seat with her as Elise asked "where are you going?" Mama Betty said "Just curing you of being scared, if you grab on Sheila and try to bury your face in her chest, she'll beat the hell out of you real fast because she really don't play that Lira stuff" Sheila looks at Elise with a mean look and said "Lets finish watching the movie alright!" Elise looked at how much the card was right there ready to fall out with just a tip and then saw Mildred said "Betty!" Girl you about to lose that card out your chest you better put it back in case it fall out in here you would never find before someone else would and it be gone for good" Elise got even madder because there went her chance to get that Credit card from her, she sat there with them watching the movie plotting on how she was going to get another chance at getting that Credit card from her. Back at the hotel Lira was sitting there watching TV and the phone rang it's the front desk is telling her they are sending the pictures up. Since her date didn't show up yet she took the pictures and looks through them, she see her and the rest of them having a ball. Then she sees one of Elise looking through a purse and holding up something looking at it hard. Then she see another picture of Elise now with Mama Betty's wallet and pulling out what looks like a Credit card and looking at it, then she goes back to the video and sees how she's going through it again pulling out another card looking at it. Everything plays in her head a like a movie from starts to finish on how she acted and the way she would stare at Mama Betty and her reaction to something, when she was looking at her but on the bed and how it was the Credit card she was looking at. Now wonders if it's the Credit card Hutch gave his mother. A knock on the door and there stood Chocolate power flexing his muscle, Lira told him come in and sit down and listen.

Telling him look this is not how she want things because she knows he got a woman and he should be good to her, then she sat down at the table and wrote something down on the stationary there. He watches as she writes and writes and then told him to go home and give this to her with her number on it and have her call, don't worry she won't say anything that would get him in trouble. Explaining when she done talking to his woman, she would do to him what Lira did even better because she's younger and more flexible. His eye got wide at what Lira told him and she takes his picture and even told him to drop his pants just for old time sake and she snaps a couple saying "It's for my personal album!" She walk him to the door putting him out with a good slap to his ass, closing the door not giving him a chance to say any good byes. He walks away looking at the letter about to open it then heard "Hey don't open that letter like I told you" He shook his head and got on the elevator.

Hutch was telling the girls they need to get back up to New York because Elise was with his mother and he bets she wants to get his Credit card from her. Janet also wanted to get another chance at Elise for what she did to them and for Donna even if she doesn't want to but needs to. He told them they'll leave soon as the rest of the GDM4L gets back from visiting some of the new friends they made while down there. Donna reminds him if he waits till the GDM4L to come back they might be too late for getting back to New York and stopping Elise-the-bitch from ripping off the Credit card from your mother. Hutch looks at her then speed dial calling all the numbers telling them they need to get back there so he can get back to Ma she might need him it's important. A short time later every GDM4L that went out was pulling up in a vehicle driven by a female or two. Getting out of the vehicles with the biggest smiles on their faces and some had shopping bags to be loaded up in the vehicles. Hutch was outside the house with the girls when they all start coming there and says to them "Think they know about their cards by now?" Tyrone gets out this four wheel vehicle with two females carrying his bags, then gave him the biggest kiss bye and said "Remember call when he gets back there" Janet laughs and hugs Hutch going "Oh yeah I think they know about the cards by now!" Byron was the last one to pull up in this convertible with four females in it and another suburban behind them with a couple more with bags for him, as everyone looked at him kiss all six females bye. They stand there looking good and sexy in their business suits that fits just right on their bodies and Byron says to them "Look sharp! Think sharp!" and they all together said "Be smart!" Putting on their shades and getting back in the vehicle and drive away. Hutch with everyone looked at Byron walking to the house in his suit saying "Give me a minute I'll be ready" They all look at Hutch and he couldn't say anything throwing up his hand trying to find a word to say. Erikaa laughs again "Guess they really do know about the cards they got huh?" Hutch still trying to find a word to say stumbling over his words, Janet just pulls him by his shirt back inside "Come on baby let get our stuff ready too." Everyone got their stuff and was in the vehicles ready to go and in each vehicle there was plenty to talk about what happened down there, from Steel being kidnapped to the party and the women they met till now learning about how they are set for life with cash. On the way up Hutch decides to call Larry letting him know he's on his way up there and see if their mother had called him, talking to Larry he asked him "Did ma tell you about the money she got from me." He answers nope but all she said was not to tell Cordell anything about you having money to retire for life. Hutch was about to warn Larry that Elise his ex- almost girlfriend he started talk too is now with her and how he knows she wants to get his credit card from their mother but then thought he better not say. Cordell picks up the phone coming in on the tail end of the conversation, listening and heard about money so he got mad saying "How come she would want to keep me from getting money too since she gave Larry money and if your ex chick thinks she's going to get money from Ma, she could give me that money so I'm going to warn her" Hutch shouts at Cordell "Stay away from their mother right now and let me handle it" not hearing anything he says "Larry stop." Dropping the cell and trying to reach for it but can't, Donna sitting next to him saw him reaching for the cell he dropped on the floor. She reaches over to help him get it but while down there her hair gets caught in the key ring on the set of keys in ignition. Janet sitting behind Hutch told him to lean back so she can come over top of him to help get Donna get unstuck, but the vehicle hits an bump that makes Janet slide more down under the steering wheel and now her head gets caught between his legs and the steering wheel. Now Hutch is asking Erikaa "Hold Janet's legs to keep her from sinking any further down under the steering wheel" Now she's behind Janet who's in a sixty nine position with Hutch's head between her legs trying to look over her butt in his face as he steers the vehicle. A grey hound bus on the same road heading the same way pulling up next to them to pass but the driver happens to look over at the vehicle and stares at what he sees. While passing he said Loud "Wow that's eating on the go" that made him slow and take a good look at them and smile, leaning more over to get a better look not realizing the passenger behind him are looking at him leaning hard making the bus swerve looking at something on the right side of the bus. The passenger closest to the front looked at him and then turned to look over to see what it was he was looking at, in the vehicle a man's head between woman's legs bobbing as another woman in the back him were holding the woman's legs. Janet wearing a short skirt made matters look more of what it looks like than what it really is, as Hutch's head kept bobbing up and down as her legs just shook. Passengers on the right side of the bus were taking picture and some were coving the eyes of the kids that were trying to see what the older were talking about. Some passengers was saying "That's a good way to eat on the go" agreeing with the driver but one women said "It keep things interesting and thrilling too" Some Japanese people was saying "Huh who said black people don't know how to multi task and in a bigger way with more than one." Then took the pictures of what they were seeing, even people on the other side of the bus stood up to see what the other side was talking about as the driver passes by slowly giving everyone a good look then drives on. 2Soon driving behind Hutch's vehicle starts noticing more and more vehicle pulling next to Hutch's and either gave thumbs up or blew their horns and gave a thumbs up then pull away fast. Goodie driving behind 2Soon saw the same thing and got curious too moving up to see. When 2Soon pulls next to Hutch's vehicle his jaw drops and he laughs "Get it when you can get it huh!" Dougie behind him shouts "Yeah man that's what I'm talking bout!" Tyrone next to Dougie saw Hutch and said "Man why he always got to try and one up everybody!" Goodie driving pulls up next to Hutch's vehicle on the driver side and shouts "Hot damn!"

That makes Mack looks taking pictures of it saying "When we want fish we use a drive thru, but he just drives and gets it Damn!" They call the others to come up and take a look at what Hutch is doing and some trying calling but can't get an answer and they see why. Dave saw them asking "Didn't we all have breakfast before we left?" La-Machine saw them answering Dave "Maybe he's on a new kind of diet!?" Dave just looks at La-Machine for a moment and the whole vehicle busted out laughing having their own answers in their mind to what La-Machine said. Erikaa manages to pull Janet back up with Hutch's assistants and then he manages to get Donna's hair loose from the keys in the ignition, they all look at the vehicles around them was still blowing their horns at them and giving thumbs up. Donna gave Hutch the cell phone so he could continue his call with his brother.

He just told Larry to stop Cordell from talking with their mother or Elise because he could make things worse. Do whatever it take to stop him from calling or going over to see either of them alright. Larry said "I will" but want to know what the concern about him talking to either of them. Hutch told him he'll explain it when he gets there but for right now he don't need Cordell messing things up and making it worse for their mother and her friends because he feels hurt about not getting any money.

Hutch finished his call with Larry and then saw he had messages on his phone, answering them to finding the text pictures all the GDM4L sent of himself and the girls while he was driving trying to get his cell off the floor. Laughing showing the girls what they sent him as Donna and Janet blushes, Erikaa laughs at all of them. Well into the night the other GDM4L are getting tired from the activity they did earlier and wants to pull over because some of them are not drivers like Hutch, La-machine, Jazz, Steel, Goodie and Mack. Those 5 are either driving professionally now for a company or used too, and still know what it's like to do drive long periods of times on the road. Hutch pulls in at this motel and they all get rooms and rest up.

Back in New York Mama Betty and her friends plus Elise are out having Dinner and walking around the city taking pictures of the places they want to remember and show their gran kids. Elise still plots to take that Credit card from Mama Betty and knows her time is running out before they get ready to leave and go back down south.

Larry is asking Cordell "How can you be mad about Hutch's money because that's your brother and Hutch works hard for it so where does you get off being mad at our mother, it's not her money but his. Reminding Cordell of all the damage his friends did to Hutch's house and furniture making him think. Is he really going to risk making his brother even madder after he almost ruined the house his brother worked hard all his life for, damaging and breaking some furniture plus drank and ate all the food in the place. Making Cordell think about messing something up he's doing with his mother because your ego about not getting any of his cash, a brother that could snap you spine, neck and legs like a twig when pissed off. Cordell thought about it and said to Larry "Since you put it like that, I could wait to talk to Hutch after he forgets about the damage we did to his place" Larry looked at Cordell wanting to know what's this French speaking Africa American bull shit your saying with the WE stuff. Cordell says "Never mind" and wants to know what Larry is cooking for dinner. He looks at Cordell asking "Don't you have a wife at home that cooks for you?" Cordell says "What about take out if they order some Chinese food" and then goes to get another beer from the Frig waiting to see what Larry would go for.

Lira sitting in the room looking at the pictures on the bed and having a drink, getting mad at what she comes to conclude about Elise. How it occurs to Lira when Mama Betty told her about the first time she came up here and her son Hutch had to get rid of that crazy skinny heffer. Now Lira realizes why she sucked up to Mama Betty and wanted to show them all around the city but stays close to her, she's only with them to get Hutch's Credit card from Mama Betty. Thinking she want to get even with Hutch for dumping her ass to be with those three new women Mama Betty told Lira about. The more she drank the madder Lira would get, seeing how she was going in the purses at the strips club. Feeling she was drinking a little too much Lira orders some food, waiting for the food she watches TV wondering what time they would get back.

The food came and she ate while thinking what to say to Mama Betty when she gets there but Lira falls asleep. By the time Mama Betty and the rest get back from going out on the city she check on Lira who is sleep so Mama Betty let her sleep.

In the motel just off the interstate Hutch is waking at first light he does what he always do turn on the news to see the weather for the day, then he wakes the girls and when they're moving around since he was always showered and dressed he goes to wake the others. He pounds on their doors to wake them all up so he could get moving, some fall out of bed forgetting they're at a motel because of having good memories about the women they meet on this road trip. Others get up with mean looks as they open the curtain and see Hutch standing at the window saying "Let's go" then getting the finger from them and curtain closed in his face. Back on the road after they checked out and Hutch got cussed out by some of the GDM4L that wasn't ready to get up and went back to sleep in the vehicles. He was down to less than a quarter of a tank of gas and they pull into this mini market gas station to get something to eat and fill up the vehicles. All those driving filled up the vehicles while the other went inside to get something to eat. Hutch made sure his vehicle was going to be the last to fill up as he pulled to the side after starting the pump using his Credit card and filled everyone's vehicle up then telling them to park and go inside to get something to eat. Walking inside first was Janet, Erikaa and Donna, followed by the rest of the GDM4L that wasn't driving. The clerk behind the register was smiling at the girls when they came in but then saw these big black men right behind them. The girls were talking how it feels like they were kidnapped hostages the way he is ordering them to move so fast at things. The clerk a high strung nervous type of man with a very wild imagination and overly zealous reaction to everything quick to draw his on conclusion that was robbed twice by black saw all these men walking in right behind the girls. He heard 2Soon tell the girls "You know he's going to kill ya if you don't hurry up right and you can't run because we have the whole place covered" The clerk took that out of context listening and being nosey thinking the girls were kidnapped and wanted to give him a sign that's happening to them, he knew they had to play it cool not to give themselves away talking to him in code. There were other people in the Mini-Mart gas station an old woman trying to get some tea from the top shelf and Doug told "Here ma'am let me get that" and she thanked him "You're a nice tall man" he told her not a problem if she needs anything else just let him know and he'll get it for her. Mack came over to him asking "What's up?" Doug reply "Getting something for the old woman" then Mack said "We better hurry up before he comes in here and kills everyone because they wasn't grabbing what they needed" The clerk heard him say that thinking he was going to take the purse from you old lady and when Mack walked over to Doug. The clerk trying to keep his eye on everyone thought he heard Mack say "They were going to hurry up and grab everything they need and kill everyone in there." The other clerk was ringing up all the food and thing everyone else was getting, because the first clerk was too busy following and trying to listen to what they all were talking about instead of doing his job at the register. There was this little boy playing an arcade machine there and this old man with bad hearing with a hearing aid doing his shopping there, plus a few more people doing some shopping to get things. Mack and 2Soon starts teasing Steel when they saw the bottle of pipe cleaner making jokes on Steel, on how he was going to clean some other pipes if they didn't get to him in time. Mack said "He'd be a softer metal like Aluminum" They kept teasing he wouldn't be known as Steel any more but a softer material following Mack's lead coming up with other names of bendable metal like tin, lead, tungsten, sheet metal. The biggest laugh they got was from Byron who said "The most fitting metal for his situation would be copper its rusted color and bendable!" They all looked at each other for quick second and burst out laughing, the high strung clerk heard them laughing and wondering what was they going to do now. Everything they needed the others got and paid for taking the stuff and loaded in the vehicles. Hutch was standing by the vehicle 2Soon was driving when this mechanic came over to him wanting to know was he the driver of that vehicle? Hutch answered "No" then he showed Hutch were it had a leak from underneath and told him he could fix it for 150$. Hutch told him no thanks but he got it because he knows about vehicles too and looked at the fluid and knew it was radiator fluid. Looking at the mechanic and heading inside the store where Mack and 2Soon and Steel were still in there getting a few more snacks for the ride. Hutch walks with a mad look on his face as Mack says "Uh Oh someone made eldest mad and they're going to get it now!" 2Soon wants to know what's up with Hutch and he told 2Soon "That mechanic out there tried to get over on me, so he's going blow up his spot and show him" Taking a bottle of stop leak going to the other clerk paying for it. Before he walks out the store he turns and says aloud "They better hurry up and take everything they'll need because things here are a steal compared to other places." Mack agreed and starts getting some of the penny candy they don't even sell up in the city no more. 2Soon starts back with the jokes about Steel when he gets mad at them and shouts "HOLD UP MAN! You both are going stop getting on me about She-Ra!" The clerk raise his eye brows and thought this is it their being robbed and went into action, first he takes the money out the cash register and puts it in a paper bag. Then walks over to the old man doing some shopping and told him their being robbed he'll need his wallet so they all don't get hurt. The old man asked "Who's robbing them" trying not to tell him too loud but give him head nods and signals seeing he didn't get, the clerk punched him in the gut hard and threw him to the floor taking his wallet leaving him there in pain, saying "I don't want anyone hurt on my watch." The clerk goes over to this woman and told her "Those men are robbing the place?" Then asking for her purse, she told him "no" so she drops kick her into the card broad potato chip stand. Then gives her the flying elbow knocking the wind out of her then taking her purse going in taking the cash out of it saying "I don't want anyone hurt because I've been robbed before and they can get very nasty with them." He runs and slides along the floor and flipping the little boy playing the arcade machine and taking all his change holding him upside down emptying his pockets then quickly tying him up with duct tape and gagging him saying "Be quite we all have to give to survive." Then going over to the old man with a walker helping him move quick into the storage closet telling him they're being robbed by some black men so taking his wallet and punching him out closing the door saying "It's better than getting beat to death by them". Going over to a few people that wants to know what's going on, he tells them "Their being robbed" the clerk leads them into walk in cooler saying "You'll be in there but I needs your wallets and cash so no one gets hurt when those men starts asking where's the people" One of the people in there didn't want to give up their cash, Saying "I have no time for this." Moving fast the clerk grabs and starts punching out the people in the cooler, kneeing a man in the gut then doing a judo flip on the other man and taking his wallet getting all the cash out, the GDM4L doesn't see him in the cooler doing this as they walk by it and even Mack takes a soda from the Frig. A woman in the cooler turns to run out but the clerk came up behind her fast and bull dogged her to the ground taking her purse as she laid there out cold, then going to everyone in the mini-mart and taking all their cash after beating them up in some kind of way explaining he's not going to let them get hurt by those evil men robbing the place and doesn't want anyone killed in there on his watch. Outside an old truck on the interstate went by and back fired a couple times and the clerk shouts to them "See they killed they mechanic because he didn't give them what they wanted" The other clerk was coming out from the back and the high strung clerk saw him and took a running start, diving on him knocking the wind out of him as he took his wallet and cash out of it them putting it in the bag with the others. All the while Mack, Steel and 2Soon was watching him go crazy in the Mini-Mart laughing at what he was doing thinking it was some kind of joke. Hutch came back in and told them to "Hurry or their dead" They looked at each other and 2Soon wanted to pay for the things they had but the clerk told him "Take it and anything they want just leave them alive please!" Mack looked at the clerk saying "This guy is missing something up there." Putting down 20 dollars telling him to keep the rest and pay for his medication they walk out of the mini-mart. Hutch was waiting and Dougie was riding with him and the girls so he could talk with Hutch. Mack, Steel and 2Soon got in their ride and pulled off, Hutch was the last one pulling off when the clerk came running out to them with this bag saying "Here they forgot this one and don't want them to come back there mad because they forgot it." He hands it to Janet sitting by the window trying on her pink hand cuffs playing with them as she took the bag from the clerk. He looked at her one wrist in the hand cuffs and thought those poor girls they are going to be killed by all those men and he ran back inside to call the police. Looking at all the people in the Mini-Mart lying on the floor hurt and the little boy taped up telling them all he knows but it was for them to be alive. Turning his back to them as he calls the police talking to them telling them they just got robbed and he gets hit with a couple of fruit cups in the head while on the phone. He told the police to get there as fast as they can because the people there didn't like being robbed and they'll need medical assistants.

Janet took the bag wondered who could have left it in the store, Hutch told her to put it in the back and they'll give it to one of them the next time they stop, then saying "It's either's 2Soon's, Mack's or Steels food so put it where it doesn't spill on something." Donna was wondering what was all that he was saying "He don't want them to come back mad about?" Erikaa said "Every go to mickey Dee's and they forgot your fries maybe it's like that" That saying made sense to them all because that has happen before too all of them as they laughed about that.

Back at the Mini-Mart the police was taking statements about what the guys looked like from the neurotic clerk and every time one of the people there was about to say something the clerk came over telling his version while they were getting treated for their injuries. He would cut in saying "What I did was save their lives" and continue talking putting on the oxygen mask for the person injured and help strap them to the gurney explaining "They're in shock and need air." Asking the EMT was those needs morphine for their pain? When the EMT said "Yes" the clerk distracted the attendant asking for some more ice packs from inside the ambulance and took the whole bottle of morphine plus empty needles and loading up some of them. The EMT looks at the clerk about to say ask him "What are you doing?" When he cuts him off "I've had over six years medical training and examinations in the major city Hospital and know how to ad mister the right amount of CC of morphine to a patient" Old man with the walker was about to tell who did this to him raising his hand about to point at the clerk. The clerk saw him pointing at him and walks over to the attendant taking care of old man with the walker and pops him with a needle.

Then says "Yes! I was there and it was brutal on you, they could have killed this old man with one blow that's how big those monsters were!" Old man with the walker rolls his eyes up in his head after hearing that bullshit story but the needle he just got makes him woozy and he fall back on the gurney the clerk puts on the oxygen mask "Sleep old timer you suffered enough" another old man was saying "He beat the carp out of everyone there" The clerk shouted "One of them jumped on him like this" coming over there but stopping short of touching the old man but injecting him with a needle without no one seeing him do it, telling the old man to breath with nothing coming out. Watching old man starts to choke then taking his foot off the hose watching him gasp for air. Telling everyone sorry he didn't mean to have him live through that experience again because he knows it must have been horrible for him so please get this man to a hospital immediately. The cop still taking statements from everyone and they asked the little boy what he remembered about them. He told them he didn't see which one but they held him upside down and shook his change out of his pockets. All the attention went to the clerk because everyone except the boy couldn't talk fainting from their experience whenever the clerk came over to them to help telling the story of the robbery, not one officer there noticed the clerk injecting the older people there that could show he did that to them. They asked him "What kind of vehicles they were driving and about the girls they had kidnapped" The clerk told how they had to be high on that "Reefer stuff" because soon as they came in there the girls said they had the munchies and something about those guy had Steel and was packing it or he was packing. Explaining "I took what they were saying as if they had guns on them because nobody talks about packing Steel like that!" The police listen to the clerk tell them he's been robbed before and he didn't want what happened to him to happen to any of his costumers in the store, so he didn't put up a fight or nothing just gave them what they wanted so they could leave them in peace. The police told him he was a hero and the woman he dropped kicked into the potato ship stand smacked him with her purse as she went by on the gurney and they loaded her up in the ambulance. The head chief wanted to know if they had a security system in the Mini-Mart and the clerk told them they took the tape too because they were smart thieves and didn't want to be filmed, but he knows what they look like the cowards and wouldn't miss them in a line up if they wanted him to be there. The chief told him he'll get his chance because they couldn't have gone far in those, stopping and asking the clerk "What kind of vehicles they were driving again?" The clerk puffs up his chest and said "They had them SUV's with the chrome wheel and all black even the window and spoke Spanish because they answered this one guy going C-man and the girls they called Ma short for that Mama cita" The chief told the clerk be ready when they call on him because he's a hero in his book, taking on such scum and making sure all the people in there was safe. There should be more citizens like him not here in his county but somewhere with your odd acting self-getting that big ass bump in the process of protecting people. Saluting him saying "I'm proud to be an American and told myself when this moment came I wouldn't cry, so could I get a hug and pat on the back right now because I'm feeling very emotional" Tearing up and looking at the chief who's eye brows went up behind those shades, then he turned to his sergeant and said "Sergeant hug and pat that man on the back, that's on order" The sergeant held his arm open and turns his head as the clerk ran over to hug him then crying like emotional person releasing their pressure. The chief standing next to them said "You go ahead cry man let it out, you deserve it and lots of mental help too. Left up to me I'd shock a whack job ass like you, make a man out of you. Sergeant more patting let him get it out fully!" The chief said "When he's done crying like a bitch! Get some more statement for other people there I'm going after hose punks"

They watch the chief pull off and get on the radio calling in the description of the vehicles the clerk gave him. The other officers there went to get statements from the people that didn't need to go to the hospital asking what was took from them and their side of the story. the people asked didn't they have a good look at them from the video tape and the cops told them the clerk didn't have it because they crooks took it. The people knew the clerk did all the damage and looked at him to replace their money and things and starts to tell the cops about his real actions. He said to everyone there the store will cover anything they need so get whatever they were going to get before they were robbed. Knowing that would keep them quiet about him, one lady asked "Are you on some type of medication?" And are you still on it to have a job like this because they need to know you're not taking the right amount of dosage and needs to up it something seriously. One man asked "Who hired you for this job and who are you related too working here." The clerk answered is cousin owns the store and he's the manager. Another old woman asked "Is there any more in your family like you and what do they do for a living so I don't make the mistake of calling them for any important repairs like plumbing work, carpentry, masonry or electrical even gas pipes work" then asking what's his name so she know for sure. He was about to say his name and noticed everyone there had a piece of paper and pen ready to write down his name as he said Pudamsytic Fargus Ryaumdukey. The man asked what country and state is that from? The clerk looks at them and says PITTSBURGH P.A King of Prussia. Everyone looked at him and shook their heads.

Four hours down the road Hutch is telling Donna they should have been out of there because the more time they waste on the road the more time Elise-a-bitch would have to try and get that card from his mother, and he's hoping she hasn't contacted Markola and they both are going after her. Dougie tries to calm Hutch's thought with help from the girls, he asked Janet "Pass me a sandwich from the bag in the back" telling her it's in one of those paper bags they put back there. She turns and looks at all the bags there and went into the small one first, it had candy and gum in it with some lip gloss. She thought it had to be either Donna's or Erikaa's, then looking in the other small bag and saw all this cash and jewelry with some wallets and a lot of change in it. Putting it a side and then going into another one and finding the turkey and cheese sandwiches handing it up to Dougie. Then sitting there for moment thinking about what she just seen in the bag and goes to look in it again, seeing all that cash and jewelry she taps Donna and shows her what's in the bag making her "gasp" at what she sees. Erikaa looked at Donna and asked "What's wrong" she leans over to show her what's in the bag and she lets out "Holy Shit!" Donna quickly covered her mouth and looked at Hutch's eyes looking at them in the rearview mirror asking "Is everything alright, you look worried?" She looks back at him and shows her smiling eyes at him "No baby things alright!" He looks over at Janet who is looking at Donna with her eye brows all scrunched, but then raises them up when she saw him looking at her and she show smiling eyes at him too. He looks at Erikaa and she shows smiling eyes at him that makes him say "Come now, you three don't have to hide anything from me. I can take whatever you have to say and not get mad at all" Janet told Hutch "The bag the clerk from the Mini-Mart came running out with, saying we forgot this one. Its filled with cash and wallets and jewelry and one small purses" Hutch thought that's not so bad maybe one of them forgot their money and jewelry in the Mini-Mart. Dougie took a look at the bag of money and stuff and told Hutch "It looks like we just robbed the place and everyone in there from what's in the bag." The front vehicle of 5 SUV's traveling on the interstate pulls over having the others follow him and stop on the side of the road. Hutch is trying to figure out why would the cashier of the Mini-Mart come out and give them a bag of cash like that. Steel, Derrick, 2Soon and Mack came up to Hutch's vehicle wanting to know what's wrong for them to be pulled over like this on the road. Hutch explained the bag of money they just found and it hits Mack and Steel that's what the clerk was doing with all that jumping around in the store jacking people up like he was crazy. Hutch asked "Tell me everything about what went on in that Mini-Mart" hearing everything they had to say, he told them that stupid idiot thought they were robbing the place. That's why he came running out with this and shows them the bag of cash and jewelry with the wallets in it. Mack said "Man if we're get caught with that down here, where they still hang a brother don't they?" 2Soon said "Nah man that's west like Iowa, Utah, Wisconsin or Nebraska" Steel said "They only hang ya in Nebraska if you lose the NBA finals, glad I'm not a on the Thunders team right now!" Hutch ask "What about L.A?" joking but 2soon said "Nope your wrong bruh, out there they make you go out with a white woman then divorce her so they can take half your loot and charge you with child support nonpayment putting you on jail or unless you're a boxer like May weather and bitch out talking about your dehydration is kicking in and you need to be home to train." Mack asked "What are they going to do about the bag of money?" Hutch wanted to pull off at another rest arrear and think about what they were going to do about the bag before they went any further and got pulled over by the police with it. At this rest arrear they all went to the bathroom or stretched their legs and talked about what happened at the Mini-Mart going in the bathroom. Steel came out the men's room heading back to the vehicles the girls saw him and walked along. This big guy saw Donna walking along with Steel thinking he could talk to her and scare Steel away because of his sizes and blocks their way to the vehicles saying "Damn shorty you need a real man to be walking with not some skinny man that look like he couldn't handle you." Steel looked at the man and Donna told Steel to ignore him and Erikaa came over to them agreeing they should just go back to the vehicles. The rude man went "Wow you have two of them, how did you manage something like that, doing their hair and nails" Steel just looks at the man and shook his head about to say something when Janet came up to Steel and went "Come on don't let jerks like that get to you Sweety!" The rude man saw how hot Janet was looking and thought he could just take her away from that skinny guy and he wouldn't do anything. He says "Oh shit he got now two but three of them, wow they must be desperate for a real man!" Janet start walking when the man grabs her by the arm and says "What's your rush honey you don't have to be so bitchy to me, I'm all the real man you need!" She jerks her arm from him and told him she's got a man and he's not going to like you putting your hands on her. Hutch walks towards them and the man says "I know you need more than what he's got!" He looks at Steel adding "That tooth pick don't have enough meat on him to make a sandwich, you need a real playa!" Janet smiled at him and says "like a football player huh! A real lines men right well I got a big defensive end" Hutch walks right to them "Hey baby everything alright" Then curious about the man grabbing on his lady and he wants to know why and what did she do? He looks at Hutch who's just a bit taller and leaner in size but had more muscle mass than him as he steps back from Janet as Hutch stood by her, now faced with a man with more muscle and serious look on his face asking "Say my man you still didn't answer my question about why you had to grab on my lady like that?" He looks at Hutch and told him he thought she was with the little guy and was having a bit of fun with them. Also don't think that he's scared or nothing because he's not taking a step towards Hutch to save face now that he seen his friends standing close to them. Hutch smiled at him down playing the threat challenge and took a step toward the man in response adding

"Why give a guy like you any reason to be afraid of me." The man's friends came up from the side of them asking "Was there anything they could help their friend with" and Hutch looked at all three of them and laughed "Yes you can maybe you three can help him find an answer to why he was grabbing on my lady's arm like he is stupid!" Two of the three guys now standing to the side of Hutch are much shorter and lighter than the man Hutch looks at, the third one is a stocky but Hutch never takes his eyes off the man in front of him. Mack saw Hutch along with Dougie, Derrick, Goodie, 2Soon and herb walking over to all of them saying to Hutch "Yo fam you got a meeting you didn't tell us about or something?" Now the four men look at the numbers they face as the rude man says "Wow you got number huh? Well we got numbers too" He whistles and six men plus two women get out of their SUV's and come running over to them ready to help out from what they know is going to be a throw down. Steel stood next to the girls and saw Hutch hand signal for them to back away and Steel told the girls to move back. La-Machine, Jazz, Tyrone, LiL-Rob, Dave, D-train, C-man, Troy-H, with Doug and Drea all sat by the benches and tables not getting into it because they knew those eight could handle the group before them. The rude man wants to know now that he's got numbers too, does Hutch want to know the answer to his question. Hutch gave a big smile at the man "Hell Yeah I still want to know why" and the man goes to punch Hutch but gets knocked back out then saying "See stupid moves like that he'll want to know why it got him knocked out!" The rude man's friend charges Hutch getting flipped over his hip as his friend went to jump in on their fight. Mack grabbed one guy from jumping on Hutch's back and start fighting with him while another man goes to kick Hutch while he's tussling with the man on the ground but Goodie drop kicks that guy and jumps on him. One man picks up a garbage can and charges at Hutch but he gets blindsided by 2Soon. The friend of the man that got blindsided gets stopped by Derrick and they start fighting. Another man attempts get involved by hitting Derrick with a stick from behind Dougie clotheslines the man as he starts to run pass him with the stick, but didn't pay any attention to Dougie as he stood there. The two heavy set women one with short hair and the other with long hair blocked Steel and the girls way saying "If they had just been nice to their guy none of this would have happened" Janet smartly says "What your guys getting their asses kicked for being stupid and grabbing a woman's arm like that" The two heavy set female look at each other guessing which one was going to go after Janet. The short haired woman went after Janet from the comment she made and the longer haired one was surprised at how good a boxer Donna was, as she gets in punches like a good fighter connecting and not getting hit back. The short haired woman saw what Donna was doing to her friend and told Janet "That's not going to happen to me" Janet said "I don't box bitch, it's too hard on my nails" She round house kicks the short haired woman knocking her off her feet saying "Now! I do things like that!" The short haired woman got up and shouted "YOU BITCH! You knocked my tooth loose" She charges at Janet who side steps her charge and watches as she falls to the ground then gets up and comes at her again. Janet sidekicks connects to her face and head on the short haired woman but she caught one of Janet's attempt to kick her holding that foot saying "now what BITCH!" Janet didn't give her time to decide what she was going to do holding her foot, so Janet quickly backflips kicking the woman as she went around watching a tooth come flying out of her mouth and she lands backwards on the ground out cold from it. All the other fighting going on ends with a finishing moves or punches as Hutch fighting with the rude man now woke from being knocked out for a while, gives him a spear move from wrestling followed by the people's elbow knocking the wind out of him stopping their fight. 2Soon saw Hutch finish his guy and yells "Yo fam" as he punches the guy he's fighting with having him dazes and grab held of the man up by his legs as Hutch ran and jumped up grabbing the man by the head to give him a 3-D threw a table and 2Soon went "TESTIFY!" Dougie's fight with the man ended by him giving a series of good punches followed by a rock bottom slamming him in the grass knocking him out. Mack didn't want to be left out so he gave his guy a stone cold stunner followed by a clothes line from hell. Derrick grabs the guy's head and bull dogs him to the grass dazing him and with 2Soon and Hutch's help they lifted Derrick up so he could give the flying elbow to the guy knocking the wind out him ending the fight. This big dude Herb was having just a bit of trouble gets hit from 2Soon who punched the man then Mack drop kicks him and Hutch spears him to the ground, giving Herb an opportunity to do the frog splash on the big man knocking him out. They rest of the GDM4L starting making ewe and Ah's sounds when they saw Donna give the woman she was fighting with a suplex and leg drop. When the woman got up again Donna did the rock bottom slamming her in the grass on her back followed by the electrifying move with the people's elbow and Dave ran over there to give the 1, 2, 3 on her lying there. While all the fighting was going on Erikaa had slipped away and went over to the vehicles for a while and came back before the fighting ended and everyone were heading to the vehicles. People watching starts calling the police and reporting the fight which made Hutch tell the other they need to get out of there because now is not the time to have to explain this or that other thing they have to deal with. The rude man and his now all beat up hurting crew watch Hutch get into his vehicle and leave laughing and joking about what they did to those guys. Hutch leads four SUV's behind his back to the interstate and he remembers what they stopped there for in the first place, thinking they better hide that bag in case they get pulled over and asked questions about the fighting that went on at the rest arrear. Janet looks in the back for it and can't find it so Donna and her look in the back together. Erikaa tries to say something about the bag but they aren't listening to her because they all were talking at the same time not listening to one another except wanting to find the bag of cash that's missing in the vehicle somewhere. Janet and Donna climb in the back and starts going moving bags around and Hutch kept asking "Did you find it" then told Dougie to climb back there with them and see if he could help. Erikaa Shouts "WOULD YOU ALL STOP AND LISTEN TO ME" Now that she got their attention, she told them she took the bag while they were fighting with those people. She went into their vehicle because they didn't lock their doors, putting money and jewelry in their jacket and coats knowing if they get pulled over they would have a lot of explaining to do. Janet told her "I could kiss you for that" and Donna seconded asking "Whatever gave you the idea to do that?" She explains it would be better if they had to deal with the police then them. Hutch is trying to get back to his mother hopefully to stop that bitch from stealing her Credit card and giving it to Markola. They went back to talking about the fight as three SUV's speeding up the interstate like they were the police comes up behind the convoy of GDM4L. When they got up to the second vehicle in the GDM4L convoy, Mack was driving the vehicle behind Hutch's and saw the black SUV with tinted windows ride alongside them for a minute then the windows starts to come down. They were approaching a tanker tractor trailer in front of them so the other SUV's went to the left of the tanker and Hutch's convoy stayed to the right of it. Passing the tankers Mack still noticed the windows were down on the black SUV but he couldn't see inside from it being dark. Then he saw a barrel of a shot gun being stuck out at him. Hitting his brakes in time just as they fired missing his vehicle, but making the rest of the vehicles pull off the road behind him. 2Soon starts looking for the two way radio to call Hutch and let him know they were just fired at by the last of three SUV's coming up behind him. Inside Hutch's vehicle Dougie asked "What vehicle is back firing like that" because he heard it so loud.

Hutch looks in the rear view mirror and saw the others slowing down but then the blast of the shot gun shattering the back window let him know it wasn't a back firing engine. Hitting the gas and pulling away from the three black SUV's that are chasing him. 2Soon finds the 2way and calls Hutch to see if they're alright and what can they do to help. Hutch yells for the girls to "Stay down" and gets on the 2way and told him it's the guy they were fighting with. He could see the one he beat up leaning out of the passenger window trying to take aim at him, then asking 2Soon "Did he get anyone back there before he came up to started shooting me!" 2Soon's answers "Nope seems they want you because all three vehicle are right behind you fam" Hutch looked at the vehicles good behind him in the side and rear view mirror and knew from the way they had them tricked out they couldn't follow him on off the road surface. Telling 2Soon there's a state troopers barracks ahead on the interstate and he know this part of the interstate where the roads leads out to so he's going to have them follow him since they want to shoot at him. Telling 2Soon lead the others to the state trooper barracks there's signs that show where they are and let them know we're coming with company. Hutch gets off the interstate followed by the three vehicles and they are really shooting at him now because there's no other vehicles around as he leads them on the off road surface. With his regular tires on the expedition he's able to take the bumps and dips the dirt road has pulling away from the other vehicle while kicking up such dust in back of him. The rude man shoots his automatic weapon wildly hoping to hit Hutch's vehicle or make him slow down but going in and out of the tree line didn't make it any better for them trying to shoot and hit the vehicle only the tree which got in the way. When Hutch got a big lead on the vehicles he would stop and wait for them to have him in sight again making them even madder like he's playing with them in the trees on the dirt road. They would lose sight of the vehicle and coming around a bend some yards away he would be waiting there then take off kicking up dust and dirt. Frustrating them to the point they wanted him so bad they would shoot ahead of him hoping he would drive into the bullets. They would hit a tree or miss and Hutch knew where he was from the marker signs, he gets on the service road way ahead of them and drove like a mad man to get to the one section where the last dirt road part was before the State Troopers barracks were. The vehicles chasing Hutch saw where there was a service road ahead and came out on the straight away only to see there was no sign of the vehicle they were chasing but as they drove a bit way down the road they saw Hutch standing outside his vehicle waving at them making them even more madder at him. Mad he would even do that they speed up to catch him getting reloading and cussing about how they want his head. Hutch stand there all calm looking at them racing towards him and he peels a banana eating it looking at them. The rude man is furious he would stand there eating taunting them like that and takes aim at Hutch and shoots, even though he's too far to get a good aim and with the wind rushing at him leaning out the window making it hard to see clear and aim well. Hutch walks the peel too the garbage can across the road as an insult and gets back in his vehicle when they were close enough and hitting the gas kicking up dust and dirt, they starts shooting now they're close enough but they slow when they have to turn off road again. One vehicle hits on the side smashing their window on the tree not slowing to make the turn in time because of the dust they slid in. Hutch could hear the gun fire and calls 2Soon and lets them know where he's going to be coming out so have the troopers ready. Hutch lead them around for a little bit giving the trooper time to get the local sheriff and police to get there and when he came out he manages to kick up enough dust making a big cloud. When the vehicles chasing him came out from the dirt road and saw him standing outside his vehicle they all hurried and got out.

Looking at Hutch so calm again they stood like a firing squad a told him pray because they're going to send him to hell riddled with bullets. Hutch laughed "If you fire one shot it would be your last" calmly pointing to the right of them as the wind blew away the dust to show them a whole squad of troopers, police, and sheriff on their sides cocking their weapons at pointing at all of them. The loud speaker had a thunderous voice "DROP YOUR WEAPONS YOU HAVE THREE SECONDS OR WE OPEN FIRE!" They look at the guns pointed at them and drop their weapons and put their hands on their heads cussing up a storm at Hutch. Coming from around the side of the vehicle was Dougie and the girls glad that they didn't shoot. The troopers and police arrest the rude guy and his crew taking them into custody by putting them all in cuffs, then gets a radio call that this chief is coming there with his witness so keep them there till he arrives. The police and sheriffs take statement from Hutch, Dougie and the girls on what happened and what they did till the chief got there.

Back up in New York Mama Betty is talking with Lira and she telling her what she discovered about Elise, how she's after that Credit card Hutch gave her to hold. Mama Betty wanted to be sure of what Lira was saying before she confronted Elise and beat her half to death, even though she knew that Lira would never persuade her against anyone unless she felt they were up to no good. Wanting to test it herself Mama Betty took the Credit card out to look at it but then saw on the bed the strip club card that looks so much like it, she took out two envelope from the draw and put Hutch's credit card in one and the strip club card in the other. Lira agreed with Mama Betty if she takes the envelope get rid of her right then and there because now you'll know that she wants his Credit card and might do anything getting desperate enough, they are leaving soon and she might want it that badly. Mama Betty asked Lira to give a few moments with Elise but stay by her phone and she'll call her when Elise leaves her room. Lira left the room to give Mama Betty a chance to see what Elise would do about taking the card from her. Mama Betty takes the Credit card and puts it in her bra like usual and calls Elise to say she want to take to her about something. Elise hung up the phone and ran down to Mama Bettys room so fast her hair looked as if it was blown in the wind, knocking hard and fast on the door so Mama Betty won't change her mind about seeing her. Elise has on a big smile when Mama Betty opens her door asking "Was you just blow drying your hair" Elise laughs and told her there is a strong wind coming from the stair case when she came down but then quickly wants to know why she called her down to the room. Mama Betty takes the Credit card of her bra and puts it in an envelope and lays it in the night stand draw, she told Elise she was thinking about one last dinner since she was leaving tomorrow and wants to know where they should go. Grabbing her stomach telling her to hold that thought she goes in the bathroom, that's when Elise knew she either take it now or lose her chance never again to get that card. She quickly and quietly opens the draw and takes the card out. Mama Betty says to her while in the bathroom she needs to go back to her room and think on it and later she'll call her to let her know what they want to eat, Elise agreed and was out of the room so fast heading to her room with the biggest smile on her face knowing she got the card. Mama Betty came out of the bathroom and calls Lira to her room, they look in the draw and saw the envelope and opened it to see it was empty then taking out the other envelope Mama Betty says "She can't wait to see the look on her face when she goes to use that card" opening the other envelope looking at the stripers club card Mama Betty fell back and felt sick saying "OH My GOD! I gave her the right Credit card!" sitting on the bed from making such a mistake. Lira took that card and told her wait there and shot out the room running up to get to Elise's room before she left the hotel for good. Lira was at Elise's door and composes herself before she knocked on the door waiting for Elise to answer it. Elise was packing her bags when she heard the knocking thinking its Mama Betty but then again saying to herself she couldn't have gotten up there that fast, she goes to open the door but didn't want whoever it was to see that she was packing. Telling them just a minute Elise throws her suitcase in the closet and goes for the door, to her surprise its Lira standing there with a smile on her face asking "Can I come in?" When Lira walks in the room she starts looking for the card and spots it on the night stand by the phone. Elise was in such a hurry to leave she put the card down by the phone thinking after she packed ready to leave she would know where it is. Lira told Elise she knows this is their last night together and likes the way she helped out Mama Betty with them, but then wants to know what kind of cologne she was wearing because it smelled so good. Elise wanted to get rid of her fast in case Mama Betty found out that her card was missing, she went into the bathroom and came out with the whole bottle and gave it to Lira saying "Here think of it as a going away present." Lira went into the bathroom to try some on and Elise saw that she didn't put up that card and went over to the night stand grabbing the card up and putting in her bra real quick. Lira came out the bathroom and thanked her for the gift. Elsie said "I'm a little tired and Mama Betty was going to call me for the dinner plans, so I want to rest up before we got together." Lira looked at her for a moment then broke into the biggest smile saying "I understand so I'll see her later?" Elise went "Sure I'll be around" and closes the door behind Lira and went right into the closet to finish packing by throwing everything in the suit case and call for a cab.

Lira came back to Mama Betty room and saw how upset she was then saying "I'm going to beat her ass and get back my sons Credit card from that thieving bitch!" Lira told her to "Sit down and calm yourself" she was apologizing to Lira saying "I'll never disagree with your gut feeling about anyone ever again." Lira laughs at her friend asking "We've been friends so long people would call us sister for all the things they've been through together, not just her but all of them and to think she would let some trash like that upset my dearest friend." Lira got a chair so she could face Mama Betty when she sat in front of her and took her hands looking at how worried her friend/sister was and held them together and told her "Your my sister Betty I'm not going to let nothing ever hurt you or the family." Mama Betty open her hands and see the Credit card in it and tears in Lira eyes as she tries to hold them back with a smile on her face knowing she didn't have to let her friend down. Mama Betty grabs and holds Lira in that hug not holding back her tears as they rock back and forth and she says "Thank you, thank you thank you thank you JESUS thank you" Margret and Mildred are the first one in the room seeing them that way and wants to know what's going on here Lira says "pull up a chair and I'll tell you."

Elise had called the front desk and wanted to know is her cab down stairs the man at the front desk said "Ma'am there are cabs always at the front door just come down and get into one" she hangs up on him and to make sure she's not seen, she took the service elevator down and came through the back to the front getting in a cab quick giving him the address of the building next to hers just in case. Laughing like she just got away with the crime century looking back at the hotel then closing her eyes smiling as the cab drove away from the hotel.

Hutch is standing there with the girls as the chief pulls up and gets out asking one troopers there to fill him in on what happened. He walks over to Hutch asking "Is this your vehicle son, looking like it came back from Bei Ruit!"

He wants to know why they shot up the vehicle like that, Hutch explains they were at this rest arrear and the one guy seated in the back looking at them now grabs his girlfriend by the arm because she didn't want to talk to him nor go with him. Telling the chief he confronts the man and his friends tried to back him up so his brother came to his aide and that's when the big fight started, the chief looks at Hutch and cuts him off saying "I can tell who won by the way they were shooting at you and have those bruise on their faces" Hutch continues letting him know they just left after whipping their asses and down the high way they pull next to his brother Mack rental vehicle and almost shot it but came up to them and starts shooting. The chief asked Hutch "Where are you heading at the time of the shooting. Hutch answers "We were going back to New York to get his mother she might be in trouble and would like to get on my way if you didn't mind. I gave all the statements to the other officers." That's when the chief said "Got a report of a robbery of a Mini-Mart and the robbers were driving a SUV's, seeing how all of you have SUVs. I need to know which one I could let go and which one is going to jail." He walks over to his car and leans over talking to someone in it, then backs away and has the passenger come out. It's the clerk stepping out of the sheriff's car with shades on like the sheriff walking like him too. The Sheriff leaning on his car with that sneer accented by the tooth pick in the corner of his mouth as the clerk comes around and walks over to him not saying a word to him, but pointing for him to go over to the patrol cars that have the rude guy and his crew sitting in the back. Hutch looked at the clerk wondering what's wrong with this guy. Mack came over to by Hutch to let him know that's the one going crazy in the store attacking people and they thought it was a joke or some kind of prank, they didn't know he was thinking we came in there to rob the place. Mack adds "We paid for everything we needed." Hutch watched the clerk walk over to the police car and knock on the window telling the man to "Hold your ugly mug kisser up to the window so I can get a good look at this face only a mother who's ugly too can love!" When the man didn't show his face the clerk just shook his head and said "Yep! Guilt does that to a man!" Walking to the next car even bolder doing the same thing and got the same reaction from that man too. As they watched the clerk walking to other cars Hutch said "Can anyone remember while in the Mini-Mart with this fool did he get a good look at you or was he too busy going stupid, because I thinks that fool didn't see anyone good but just in case." 2Soon, Mack and Steel said "They were in the store but that nut ass was too busy jumping on people in there and didn't see them up close" then Hutch turns to Janet asking "Did he get a good look at your face when he handed that bag of money to you?" She had to think hard because it was so fast and told Hutch she wasn't sure, so he told her if that nut remembers his name he'll be impressed. Then had Erikaa stand by Steel and Mack and Donna by 2Soon and Dougie. They all wanted to know why the ladies must split up like that, Hutch said "It's kind of hard to remember the guys but three ladies are not that hard to forget!" They agreed and did what he said, as the clerk walks back to the chief and talks with him for a moment, then came over to Hutch and the GDM4L looking at them like a drill sergeant giving his men the once over. The clerk walks pass everyone and looking them up and down except Hutch where he stops right in front of him and looks up at him hard saying "You eye balling me boiy?" Lifting his shade and looking at Hutch with one eye. Hutch was about to say something smart Janet knew it grabbing his butt hard to remind him making Hutch snap straight up and lets out "Sir no sir" The clerk shook his head a little and turns to the sheriff saying 'I like him." Then walking back down the line of GDM4L, seeing them all at attention for him going along with what Hutch did. The clerk says "Sheriff! Did you search the vehicle for the bag of money because it's hard to tell with this bunch of pukes in front of me" Standing right in front of 2Soon looking him in the face when he said that and turns his back to him. 2Soon was about to slap him in the back of his head but Donna grabs his arm stopping him. The clerk walks away from 2Soon and Hutch told Janet "See I would have slapped him" and she said "that's why I grabbed your ASS!" The troopers and police search the vehicle and came out of the rude guy's vehicle with the bag of cash and found some jewelry in the clothes, taking a big sigh of relief was Hutch, Janet, Dougie and Donna knowing what Erikaa did with the bag at the rest stop putting it in their vehicle. The clerk told the sheriff he needs to see them face to face so get them out of the cars and the troopers got them all out so they clerk could see them up close standing next to a trooper or policemen. The clerk walks like a sergeant and again but stopping at each taking his shades off and saying "You eye balling me boiy!" The rude man answers "Go F-- yourself man! That bag's not mine." Backing away from him because he is a bigger man than the clerk in hand cuffs but he didn't want to get hurt by him and heading to the next man that gave him the same answer. The rude man and all the men gave the same answer but when he gets to the ladies he was about to say something when one of the Troopers shouts "Hey sheriff!" He comes over to him and they talk for a moment. The Trooper found bundles of weed and cocaine in panels of the vehicle. Clerks looks at the rude man "You're going away for long time there son, confess!" The sheriff gave the signal to put them back in the car and told Hutch they can go and if they need him they can find him with the information right? Hutch shook his head "Yes" and turns to leave but that clerk walks over to the Sheriff and said something to him, the sheriff looks at the clerk and then Hutch snapping his strap off his gun.

Hutch starts up the expedition about to put it in drive and the sheriff says "Hold it man turn off the engine and get out the vehicle now!" Seeing the sheriff with his hand on his gun Hutch turns off the engine and gets out the vehicle and stands there. The sheriff said "Everyone in that vehicle get out now and come stand next to the driver." Hutch thinking to himself he shouldn't have let all three girls get back in the same vehicle that was a dead giveaway. The sheriff walk over to Hutch and looks at him and turns back to the clerk standing over by his car shaking his head pointing at him. The sheriff told Hutch to come with him and they both walk over to his car by the clerk, the girls and Dougie wonder what's going on and did Hutch do something. The clerk gave Hutch a good look at and shook his head again yes, the sheriff told Hutch to go back over to Dougie and the girls. The sheriff came back over explaining he had to make sure the identification was correct about him pointing at Hutch. Donna asked "What did he do?" The sheriff answers "Thought you could fool me but thanks to my eye witness you're going to give me what I want" He take his pen and piece of paper and says "When you sign your autograph could you make it out to, Sergeant Royce Ernie Claremont" Explaining to Hutch that him and his wife went to the 70's Jam he had in the Caribbean Islands with Earth Wind and Fire and Stephen Mills and the Gap Band telling him they rock those jams and waiting for him to do another one. Plus after the concert he really knocked her boots and dug her back out feeling good after all that good baby making music. Hutch looked at him asking "Is all that is your name" thanks for the coming there now let me limbered up before I have to write a novel which is your name. Donna Looked at Hutch asking "What are you doing? Smiling at Hutch as he told her "If the man wants my autograph I'll give him one just to get out of here," Then she asks "Fool what name you're going to put there when he looks at the autograph." Donna walks over the chief figuring if she talks to him then he would say why he wants Hutch's autograph. She says "Chief now you're not going to be bragging about you got him to sign one for you" The Chief looks at her and says "I know you work with him every day and it might not seem much to you to be working for such a star but I need this one." Dougie looks at what Hutch is doing then wondering why Hutch is signing an autograph to the chief. The chief comes over and asked Dougie "Who are you" and Hutch said that's my brother. The Chief looked at Dougie and said "I didn't remember Sinbad having any brothers?" Donna, Janet, an Erikaa looked at Hutch and then took another good looked at him as Dougie said "We're not blood brothers but I'm his manager like his brother" Clerk shouts "I knew when I saw him standing there who you was!" Then asked for an autograph too and told Hutch "I'm celebrity like you, I'm a hero saving all those people at the Mini-Mart and I should be giving you my autograph too." Looking at Donna, Janet and Erikaa asking "Are they your groupies because stars always travel with groupies" Feeling his pockets for a piece of paper so Hutch could sign it for him. Dougie leans to say to Hutch "I told you that Sinbad thing was going to save your ass one day so stop denying you look like him and just except it." Hutch told the clerk the ladies are his personal assistants Donna, and account Erikaa, and makeup artist Janet" The clerk said "Wow Sinbad and his entourage but one would think you get a better looking assistant then the one you have. That heffer looks like the milking is over and needs to be butcher for the meat look at those thighs and butt" Donna went to go after the clerk but Erikaa and Janet grabs her and hold her mouth from cussing him out. He looks at Erikaa saying "Accountant huh, better watch your money around that crack head. Next thing you know you'll be broke wondering where all you money went from the looks of her is she still using" Hutch drops the pen and the clerk bent down to pick it up just as a can of soda hits Hutch in the chest. He looking at her as Janet and Dougie are holding her back from going over there. He saw her jumping around and said "How you know she isn't high right now acting like that in public" The clerk looks at Janet and says "It must be nice to have a good looking makeup artist with you huh, too bad that one looks like her hand shake from drinking when she puts on makeup maybe she needs rolling pins and painter brushes and don't know how to stay in the line either" Hutch was blocking the kicks about to hit the side of his head as he looks at the clerk saying "The dragon flies here needs swatting" every time he turns to see what Hutch was swatting at, Hutch kept his attention on him and not to the side where he could have gotten kicked by Janet. Dougie grabs her and puts her in the vehicle with the others and told Hutch to come on before they get in trouble, he signs the clerks paper and goes to get in to leave when another Trooper came over to Hutch with a piece of paper. The clerk walks back over to the car with the rude man sitting in back of it and looks at him as he sneers at the clerk. Telling him "If only you didn't want to be a smuggler I wouldn't have to bust you like that, you must get a good job like me serving the people not getting them high. Just say no to dope OK" The man growls loud at the clerk making him run back over to the sheriff as Hutch is taking a lot of picture with the Troopers and police as this big tour bus goes by and sees all the policemen taking picture with this one man in the middle posing with them.

Inside the bus is the real Sinbad looking out seeing the law enforcement taking picture wondering what's going on there, his manager says "Maybe a local fish man had a good catch, now let's go over your schedule for the next week!" The bus drive on and Hutch gets back in his vehicle and leave to find a repair shop that would replace the glass in the back on the same day, but the Trooper told him they have their own repair shop that would do it so go check into the motel down the road and they'll call him when it finished if he gives them a few more picture and autographs. Hutch told everyone their checking into the motel till the vehicle back window is fixed. It was later but the Troopers repair shop got it done and Hutch was on his way again.

Thinking about making it this time without stopping or have anything go wrong, they got hungry and stopped to eat at this big truck and travel restaurant and fuel up while they're there. The GDM4L walks in the place wearing their black shiny jackets looking like huge body guards to the girls as they walk in after the guys and they all went to find a seat in the diner.

Taking tables that surrounds the girls having everyone in the place think their some stars or singing group, when the rest of the GDM4L came in and saw where they were seated they joined them. Hutch was the last one in and came to the girls table and told them he'll be back as he went looking for the rest room. Hutch had to use the bathroom going in opening the door the smell was over powering because the exhaust fan wasn't working in there and that odor was stuck in there, the only urinal open was all the way at the end of the men's room. He had to go bad and held his nose and went in there pass all the men making some serious gas as they used the toilets. Hutch looked back at the front and could swear he sees this green mist floating about over the stall. Trying to urinate fast as he could so he can get out of there listening to all that rapid fire going on, he cut short his task and heads toward the front holding his nose hoping to get some clear air. Making to the door without passing out he opens it and this old man stood right there with a lit cigar in his mouth. Hutch's eye got wide as the flames went around his head like Ghost rider and the back draft sucked them both back in the men's room. The flames looked as if it had a life of its own going up the wall on the ceiling reaching down to every stall in the place growing bigger, at the front of the men's room the door buckled and blew out throwing Hutch and the old man with the cigar out of the men's room. Both Hutch and the old man laid there on the floor as people came over to see what happened, some of the GDM4L went out to their vehicles for their wallets and saw this big blue flame shoot up from the building like a rocket launching, they ran in to see Hutch and the old man surrounded by people asking "What happened?" Hutch looks at the old man who still had his cigar in his mouth and gets up to walk over to him, seeing his head still smoking because his hair is singed. Hutch stands over him looking at the old man then taking the cigar out his mouth shouting "THAT'S WHY THEY BANNED SMOKING IN PLACES YOU MORON!" Turning to walk back over to the girls and GDM4L looking at him with his head and clothes smoking as well. Mack starts laughing and says "Whatever any of those guys inside the men's room had to eat here, I'm canceling my order if that's what happens when it comes out the other end" Hutch looks at them and asked was the vehicle all fueled up so they can leave before anything else could happen to him.

Morning at Hutch's house and Cordell and Larry are woke up by Cheryl and her friends at the front door banging on it because the delivery men are about to come there and bring the stuff they ordered so they can put back the stuff they broke at the party. Truck after truck pulls up and has the piece they need to put back in Hutch's house and Larry is paying the C.O.D cost to the delivery man plus tipping them for being so early and on time. This van pulls up and Mama Betty and her friend get out. They see all these delivery trucks lined up making deliveries there and head inside to see Cheryl and her friends with their boyfriends helping move things about the house. She wants to know what these young people are doing in Hutch's house. Cordell saw her asking Cheryl question and he slips upstairs so he didn't have to face her. Cheryl had picture in her hands giving them out to her girlfriends and their boyfriends to show where everything went. Larry explains what happened to his mother and he didn't mean to break things up in Hutch's house but they did replace everything broke.

Mama Betty told him she didn't buy that they were having things cleaned for him bull crap, so she told her friend "Girls these people are going to be hungry when they're finished so let hit the kitchen and have Cordell fire up the grill see if he can do that right without breaking that" They all work hard putting everything back and Bernise came there in a cab with the rest of the kids. Larry paid for the cab she took over there and told Cordell he'll pay him back for that but go do what their mother wanted him to do. Bernise saw the big clean couch and plops down on it and puts her feet up on it and starts to order her kids to bring her food. Larry's new girlfriend came there and every one stops to look at her as he introduces her to everyone especially his mother. Cordell asked Larry "When did you find time to meet her" as he looks at her like a piece of meat. Larry smile and told his brother you're not the only one that goes out and sees thing making new friends at new places. Telling him to close his mouth and turn around because on the couch there's something he's got to deal with remember that thing pointing to Bernise. Cordell closes his mouth turns slowly and see Bernise there with her arms folded, remembering he better take care of the fire out back and runs out there. Larry walks over to Bernise and asked "Why don't you help" She told him "Do you live here? Do you pay bills here? Is your name on the ownership of this house, so why should I help?" Larry looks at everyone there and doing something and yells at Bernise in a Jamaican accent "YO LAZY MUMP PAY! LIFT YOUR BACK SIDE OFF ME BRUDDA COUCH! AND TEK CON TROLL OF DEES WE PICKNEE, FOR MEH PELT SO BLOWS TO THE BACK OF YUR HEAD NOW GAL!" Mama Betty looked at Larry then his new girlfriend and said to her "Damn! You putting it on him like that making a man speak a whole other language" Larry walks over to his girlfriend and give her a kiss then looks back at Bernise tilting his head as to say "Well get moving" She looks at Larry and moved to the love and yells for her little ones to stop running around the house. Larry girlfriend was impressed and so was his mother and niece Cheryl. They get everything back in place and Jordell saw Hutch coming and yells to everyone "Uncle Hutch is here" This convoy of vehicle pulls up in the driveway and he goes in the house to see all these people waving hello and then he sees his mother and her friends coming out of the kitchen. He looks the place and walks around looking at everything as no one there said a word, then he looks at everyone saying "You think I'm stupid huh, I know there's something here different" and walk over to Bernise and says

"This here! How did yall get her fat ass off the couch and not have foot chips on it" Everyone points to Larry and everyone laughed again Mama Betty wants to know is he alright because he look like he's been in a fire and he tells her it's a long story, Larry came over to him and asked "What happened to my vehicle" Hutch again just says "That's even a longer story see why I don't go on any vacations their too dangerous and too much trouble" Hutch took his mother to the side and asked about Elise and the Credit card. She told him "It's safe and so is its secret thanks to Lira and that's a long story of hers." Everyone was in the house and Mama Betty told them about Elise how she didn't know this tramp was trying to get her Credit card (winking at Hutch) and did things she wouldn't think a woman would do and she told everything not leaving out any details with Lira help. Janet wanted to know where she was now and wonders does she know what Lira did? Mama Betty says "I would like to be there when she goes to pay for anything with that strips club card and wonders what she's going to buy with it".

That same Morning Elise is having breakfast and on the phone with the cruise line making arrangements for a three week Cruise to the Islands. She took what she thinks is Hutch's Credit card not looking at it good and put it in an envelope and puts that in her purse.

Getting dressed with some of the things Mama Betty bought for her and packing a nice big suit case she calls a cab to take her to the Cruise Liner docking port, there she looks at all the people in that long line to get their tickets as she walks up to the counter. Markola was there to get away for a while but was thinking about where to go when he sees Elise walk by him and he follows her. She gets to the counter and tells the woman there she's got a reservation for a Saying it loudly for everyone to hear "A Platinum Premium Three week full package" The woman looks at her then goes "I think the people outside getting their bags did hear you too or do need the microphone to say it again" asking for her name? Elise told her name and the woman says "How would you like to pay for that or do you want everyone not to know" Elise gets in her arrogant mood and goes in her purse and take out the envelope and slams down what looks like a Credit card on the counter in front of the woman. The woman picks up the card looking at it and starts laughing trying to figure out why she's paying for a Platinum premium three week package with this. Falling out laughing at Elise she wants to know "What's so dam funny" to them. The woman says "I been there too and trust me, I know chocolate power got turned out by some old woman. Now he's chocolate milk, so if they turned you out like that thinking there shit is gold and could pay for anything. Then Honey you need to stop going to places like that or they'll having you outside looking for it in the daytime with a flash light because you need dick in your life badly" Elise grabs up the card looking at it, then screams "YOU FUCKING OLD BITCHES NOT AGAIN! HUTCH I HATE YOUR ASS AND NOW YOUR MOTHER TOO!" A shoe pops her upside her head "Move aside woman!" Looking to see who threw the shoe as this stack of cash Markola puts in front on the counter and says "Where ever she's going book me a second ticket too" Elise looks at Markola and asked "Why did he do that for" He picks up that strip club card and shook his head laughing and says "Call it an investment for when they get back after planning on how to get even with that mook your ex-boyfriend and get the card." Elise shook her head agreeing and they took their tickets and went to get on the ship to talk about how much they both loath him and the girls and want to get that card.

At Hutch's house alone with his mother and says "I saw what you did to your house and the other place around the neighborhood" She asked him "Are you he mad at me" and he told her "Nope! It did the place and everyone down there a lot of good. She brings out the card and hands it to him. He told her he sees she could handle herself with it so he wants her to hold on to it for a while and promises not to let anyone know what it is and not to use it unless it's necessary. She promises and asked him "What about you son are you alright" He smiled saying "With the girls now here things are going to be good, so let get back to the food I'm hungry" They walk back down stairs where 2Soon and Mack are telling everyone about the clerk and how he talked about the girls. Mama Betty walks over to Bernise in the love seat and told her since she didn't help with the moving of things or cooking that she was going to wash the dishes. Bernise say "ok" and then mumbled "I'll get the kids to do that shit because she is not washing shit!" Mama Betty and all her friends came back out and stood in front of Bernise as Mama Betty said "I heard that and I got enough here to whoop ass for days if we all take a turn!" Hutch was out back looking in the house at all the people there and the girls come out asking him "You alright?" He looks at them and says "Thing are going to change for us and it's going to be a hell of a ride now with this card, so I want to know what should I do with it?" Janet says "Whatever you want to do we'll be right by your side if you want" They all shook their heads agreeing he should think about owning his own business, now that you can retire from driving.

Hutch thought about it saying "There's plenty of time for deciding" taking them back in the house to enjoy the party that's going on and get his drink on with family and friends.

(See what happens to Hutch and his Ladies in the J.C 2 & J.C 3 and what they did with the cards)

Look for future books like: Transfer Project/ and Para Transit Wild Access Ride/ Shadow Soul Stealers/

P.H.A.T.T—L.E.P.P.S.S/ and others

THE END

WRITTEN BY

GRAND DRUNKEN MASTER 4 LIFE

MAURICE HUTCH MADDNESS WHITE.

www.ingramcontent.com/pod-product-compliance
Lightning Source LLC
LaVergne TN
LVHW020354250125
802081LV00001B/33
* 9 7 8 1 6 4 9 3 4 1 7 7 8 *